THE SWORD
TO UNITE

Peter J. Hopkins

DIGITAL FICTION

PUBLISHING CORP

Copyright © 2017 Peter Hopkins
Published 2017 Digital Fiction Publishing Corp.
All rights reserved. 2nd Edition
ISBN-13 (paperback): 978-1-988863-44-3
ISBN-13 (e-book): 978-1-988863-45-0

DEDICATION

For Kenny.

Act I
The Lord of Orford

Chapter 1
The Dawn at Orford

The sun began its journey across the sky, overlooking the small village of Orford, its burning brilliance shown bright as a radiant herald of the new day. Its light danced across the lush alder trees of the nearby forest, the lake glimmered as if it had been transmuted into gold, and the chirps of the songbirds appeared amplified by the star's warmth. The villagers rested peacefully, the warm wind blowing through their open windows, with only a handful of farmhands tilling the fields and pitching tents. There was nothing architecturally significant save the remainders of an ancient elven statue resting on the edge of the village towards the road. Its visage and inscription had long since been ebbed away from weather and time, with only its sentinel watch over the village remaining.

At the basin of this guardian, the other protector of the village rested. Cedric, the lord of the village, sat with his arms wrapped around his legs, at his hip, his father's blade rested at his side, Bayeux, it had seen many wars, but none with its current master. At his side, the metal holder for a candle, the wax had now melted down to a puddle. Many glass bottles were sprinkled across the grass, their contents, consumed in the night.

Cedric sat on a restless watch, staring at the road ahead of him, unsure of what lay beyond it. As the sun continued its great race across the sky, Cedric spotted a cart coming out of the forest. At the driver's seat was Eadwine, the wood elf. His face pointed and sharp, just like his ears, steadily he guided the mule along the road, humming a tune of his kin.

As Eadwine approached the village he spotted Cedric, calling to him he said, "Defending the village from foul bands of rabbits and birds Cedric? I'm sure they'll be a formidable villain."

Eadwine paused before answering, "Well…in a way, you see I was continuing my usual path through the woods, leaving my cart on the edge of the road. It was an ordinary night, I set my snares and waited for some buck or doe to cross my path…and that's when I saw the Guardian."

Cedric sat unconvinced, and his eyes were filled with doubt, "Really?"

Eadwine quickly responded, somewhat in disbelief his friend would question him, "Yes! I was crossing a small brook when I saw a trail of blood, deer blood. I thought it would be injured, so I followed until I realized there was more than blood on the trail, a bit of liver rested on a rock. When I looked up, I saw it through the bushes, its eyes were just staring at me, and it was as if they were glowing from the light of the moon. I ran as fast as my feet could carry me, and made sure to avoid that brook for the rest of the night."

Cedric listened patiently, and he leaned in, deeply engrossed in the story, "Well I suppose it is possible, at least it was occupied with a deer. Come on, let's head back to the village together."

The pair rode the cart the rest of the distance to the village, which had now fully awoken. The sounds of the craftsmen and shop owners overtook the streets, in a chaotic but rhythmic fashion. The smell of fresh baked goods filled the air with sweet delight. All in preparation for the festival of Marsancius, marking the first day of the summer season. Marsancius had saved the city of Wulfstan, many years ago during the great Summerspot plague which gripped the city. The alchemist had long studied the effects of the disease when he discovered a strain of the toxin practically harmless that caused immunity from the illness in its entirety. Now the cruel memories of summerspot remain in the back of the commoners' minds, and the festival serves both to honor the alchemist, and to signify the happy days of summer to come.

The village was composed of narrow streets, lined with wattle and daub houses, each thatched roof bellowing the smoke of cozy fireplaces. The doorways of many homes had gold paint designs of flowers and family inscriptions. The true pride of the village was the townhouses abundance of glass windows, the envy of every village and hamlet near and far.

Along the outer railing of some of the more affluent houses, banners of brilliant pattern and color were proudly waved, each a tapestry of history for the families. Cedric had long since placed his own banner inside his home, now destined to grow dust and spider webs. Cedric's family, the house Thorne, on their tapestry a weaving of legend dating back to his great-grandfather, Edric the Marksman. At the top of the fabric, a depiction of Edric's battle with the great cyclops Rolf, the only of his kind to possess cunning in his skills. In the weaving, Edric is shown slaying the beast with a single arrow to the eye, while at the same time rescuing a daughter of the king of the time, Orfric, who granted Cedric's family his current estate as a reward.

Cedric and Eadwine passed by the brewery, where the brewmaster, Hamund, was perfecting his art as an alchemist is to transmuting grain into gold. The honeyed mead wafted through the air as if it were a thick rolling fog. It was his special reserve, only made for the summer festival, leaving all who drink it dissatisfied by all other alcohols. "Sirs, if you would indulge me, would you like the first test?" Hamund cried out to two. Like eager children awaiting sweets, the two hopped off the cart and rushed into the small stone brewery with lightning speed. Grabbing the two flagons, they drank the heartiest mead ever conceived, its contents more akin to molasses than alcohol. They drank until the cups were emptied in their entirety, leaving not a single drop unsipped. Hamund all the while stood smiling over a large vat, adding in spices and other ingredients. Originally hailing from the north, all the way to Canterbrick, he had brought his trade south when the cold began to bite worse than his aging bones could take and now lived as a beloved member of Orford. Eadwine leaped over the counter of the store, leaving gold in exchange for another bottle, "for the road," the elf explained, and the two left giving Hamund their most sincere gratitude.

When the pair arrived at Eadwine's cabin the two parted ways, "Eadwine, don't forget about the tavern after the festival begins, Alfnod might even be able to make it." Eadwine responded, "Humph, I would not doubt he'll arrive late, trying to convince some poet to write down his epic tales." Cedric wandered the streets, remembering his old friends, thinking of all the stories they would have to tell of the world outside the Kingdom of Lorine, what wonders were just waiting to be discovered in the distant snowy peaks of Belfas, or perhaps the ancient land of Essaroth. These tales were sure to impress the youth of the village, probably would give them the thought to go out on some heroic journey rather than till the land. But Cedric recalled his thoughts to the tales of the merchants passing through the village, and what strange occurrences had overtaken the outside world.

The village had only a handful of regular outside traders, often bringing in common goods from Wulfstan, the capital of Lorine. Cedric remembered the time the village had a merchant all the way from the Tanaric Kingdom, the spice capital of the world, who told tales of such distant and strange wonders that the whole village was abuzz. Now it seemed, trade had all but diminished, with the few remaining merchants now only bringing word of bandits overtaking roads once thought safe. On more than one occasion, tales were exchanged in the inn by terrified traders from up north, of a man in a golden mask, preying on the strong and weak who stray too far from the road. Cedric did not know whether to believe in these stories, which were relayed like the tales of ancient monsters meant to scare children. All Cedric knew was that if every road in the north were overtaken by the demon lord Baphomant himself, Orford would be unaffected.

It was truly a gray age of time, where all Yennen appeared slowed and saddened, though never to the brink of collapse, merely teetering on edge. Yennen, the largest of the continents of the world, where icy tundra, rolling fields, and expansive sand all laid together. The ages of great kings seemed so distant, now told as myth more than history. Lorine was a little version of Yennen, stalled, awaiting a burst of new life to break it from its cumbersome and rusted chains. Northmen had long awaited this revival, since the time of their first real king, Adalgott, who some say ruled for one hundred full years.

Undoubtedly, Alfnod would share some news of the rest of the continent, Cedric thought. He would bring tales of bravery and adventure, of life beyond the smallness of Orford and Lorine. Cedric arrived at the end of the marketplace and now headed up a small hill, towards his lordly manor.

Along this hill, a massive man rested on a stool outside a humble cottage nestled like a bird's nest by the trees. His hair was very short and black on the sides of his head, a militaristic style, and it had begun to grey. His name was Beorn, the village lumberjack. He sat with a pipe in hand, resting next to a pile of freshly cut wood for the festival that would require much fuel for light. The top of his head was cleanly shaven, which shined from the light of the morning sun, and his beard was long and black, with many knots which stretched to his abdomen. He waved at his lord but did not speak.

"Good morning Beorn!" Cedric shouted out to Beorn's dismay, as the brute of a man leaped from his seat and shushed at his lord. "Hilde and the lad are still asleep inside. I am sorry I should have said something." Beorn spoke in a quick tongue, with much worry behind every word.

"No apologies Beorn, I was at fault." The lumberjack offered his lord his spare pipe, and the two sat on the grassy knoll overlooking the village. Beorn had built many of the wooden homes that dotted the outskirts of the town, including Eadwine's. He was shrewish in nature, refusing any payment in coin, preferring the offerings of baked goods and hunted meats that villagers offered on his doorstep. "Shall we see you at the festival Beorn? I know the little ones would enjoy it, see the man with the strength to lift ten of them at once?" Cedric joked as the pair overlooked the peasants who were hard at work setting up tents and tables.

"I don't know, I might stay at home, but I'll encourage Hilde and the lad to go," Beorn murmured.

Cedric made a humorously sad face and prodded at the shy giant. "Oh, you're not fun at all, half those people down there owe the roof over their head to you, and you're too stubborn to say hello."

Beorn shrugged and looked back towards his cabin, his family still resting unstirred. "I live my life satisfied and happy, and I prefer to keep it that was Cedric. I'll tell you what my lord, I will try to my fullest to make it."

Cedric hopped up and spoke, "I'm sure it will be absolute torture Beorn, interacting with the rest of the village." Cedric walked away moaning like a tortured prisoner of war, as Beorn sat quietly, almost unaffected save a slight redness in his face as he returned to his pipe.

At last Cedric reached the top of the hill, from where one could gaze at the whole of the noble's land. The house was of the same material as the village, mixed in with a stone foundation, imported from nearby quarries in Lahyrst. Adoring either side of the walls were majestic stained-glass windows, upon which many great legends were presented. There was a stark contrast with the rustic beauty of the outside to that of the interior. As Cedric swung open the door, the incoming sunlight danced off storms of dust swept up from the rush of fresh air. Bottles clanged and rolled along the floor. The whole house was dark, not a single candle was lit, nor was there a servant in sight, Cedric dismissed them back to the fields long ago. Cedric dropped his sword and sheath on the entryway table, lit a lantern, and retreated to the cellar.

Many fine Elven wines had been collected by his grandfather, Derwyn, The Elf Friend, in his adventures through the Golden Court and Geladhithil, where the wine appears as common as water. Another staple of Cedric's cellar was the Dweoran ales and ornate mugs his father, Albert, received for his service in the War of the Green Mountains, where he and his companions defended a hamlet of Dweoran shepherds from constant raids.

The Dweoran were a stout, bearded, and fickle folk, dwelling in caves and mountains, keeping to themselves in most matters. They acted as master craftsmen and shrewd traders to the outside world, bringing trinkets and baubles valued like precious stones. These raiders came from the far south, where grass fields turned and dried to never-ending seas of sand, and where the men ride horses with strangely humped backs. The Dweor were too poor to pay in gold, so they gave their ale and stone carved mugs as a sentimental compensation. Now it appeared Cedric was left to drink away his ancestors' legacies. The noble son could not help to think this as he shut the cellar door, with two bottles of aged Sironde brandy under his arm.

There came a knocking at the door, its tone familiar to Cedric. The young lord opened the door, revealing a round-faced youth, with eyes bright with eagerness. His figure too, was plump in nature, though in no way fat. His hair was wispy and golden as the rays of the sun. It was Galdwin, the squire in training, and Cedric had forgotten his lessons were due for this hour. The boy, not yet old enough to grow a beard, bowed with admiration at his lord.

"My lord, apologies I forgot our lessons for today." He spoke in a nervous voice.

Cedric waved off Galdwin's attempts to apologize. "No trouble at all Galdwin," he said as he downed more of the wine in his bottle. "Come, to the field then."

In the back of the manor, a basic training ground had been set up, complete with hay men and archery targets in shapes ranging from bears to the size of a hummingbird. Cedric took his place on a pile of hay, where he sat and drank while Galdwin sharpened his blade on a whetstone.

"What did we leave off on last time Galdwin?" Cedric said as he rubbed his temple.

"Footwork sir," Galdwin responded eagerly.

"Right…well have at the hay man, let me see your form," the lord said as he motioned to the target with a wooden bucket for a helmet.

Galdwin approached and took his position in front of the practice target. He had good foot form for one so early in practice. It was when he swung that his inexperience showed itself. He hacked at the haystack with violent two-handed swings, throwing his feet off balance and exhausting himself.

"No!" Cedric suddenly burst out, causing Galdwin to jump a foot in the air. Cedric calmed himself and took a gentle and wise tone. "We do not slash and carve at our foes like some piece of pork on a dinner table."

Galdwin interrupted, with a somewhat harsh tone. "But he'll be dead in one swing that way, why not get it done with before he can take a strike at me?"

Cedric got up from his seat of hay and approached Galdwin. When he came to meet his squire's side he spoke,

"Well if it's so easy for you to cut down a sack of hay, why not try on me?"

Galdwin was confused by this. "My lord?"

"Come on." Cedric motioned his hands to himself. "Take a swing at me."

Galdwin tried to laugh off the command, producing an awkward smile. "My lord I can't."

"What, had too many of the old lady's sweet cakes today? I swear Galdwin you look more like a circle every day..." Galdwin's face turned red hot, and in a fit of rage, he lifted his practice sword above his head and swung down at his lord.

Cedric effortlessly stepped to the side, his feet gliding with the speed of a bird in flight. Cedric did not even look at Galdwin as the squire took his next swing, and again Cedric dodged the blade with ease. Cedric saw that Galdwin was no longer focused on his footing, and kicked the squire's feet out from under him. Cedric drew his blade and placed it at Galdwin's neck, as he lay there in a mess on the ground, with his hands at his head in surrender and the look of panic in his eyes.

"When you can hit me, then I'll let you swing two-handed like some deranged oaf." Cedric sheathed his sword and gave his hand to help Galdwin to his feet. "Get yourself to the stables to feed the horses, and polish every saddle there for good measure." Galdwin sighed in protest but nonetheless trotted off to the stables.

Cedric retired to his study, a smaller room of the home, it contained a wide variety of books and stylish furniture. He sat stoking the stone fireplace in front of him, all the while enjoying the Sironde. His exterior appeared calm, but his mind was in discord, attacked by indecision. All his life he had lived in peace, no great journey, no epic poem to be told. A life of peace in his village was all anyone could ever desire, and yet he had a yearning, a deep and almost unspoken longing for a life beyond comfort, beyond pleasure, a life where not everything wanted was a guarantee. Cedric was violently awoken from his daydream when a shriek was heard in the marketplace.

Chapter 2
The Guardian of the Woods

"The Guardian! The Guardian has Alfred!" The villagers huddled around the boy, covered in mud, with his left arm bleeding profusely. Cedric immediately rushed to his side, putting pressure on the wound with a nearby rag.

"What were you two doing in the forest Edmund? You've been told time and time again never to go in there by yourselves," Cedric's voice was a mixture of dread and respite. The boy continued sobbing about how he and his brother had been looking for berries in the forest, with their goat Bessie, when the Guardian suddenly attacked them.

Cedric waited for the boy to finish his story before responding, "Listen to me Edmund, you are never to enter that forest again, understand?" The boy nodded, tears rolling down his face. The boy quickly returned to his father, Sigmund, the herbalist of the village and the most advanced in years of the village elders. As the old man attempted to grab his axe to find his other boy, he seized at his chest; his body winced from the slightest exertion.

"Alright…" Cedric said as he turned to Eadwine and the men of the village, "we have to get Alfred." The townsfolk stood petrified, none who dared hunt the Guardian ever returned alive, let alone was enough of a body left to identify the poor souls. Even Eadwine, who knew the forest as if it was his home stood in fear. Cedric could feel his heart beating as if it were to break from his chest at any moment, he too was afraid. Cedric's fear was somewhat tamed when he saw Beorn step forward.

Advanced in age compared to the youthful Eadwine and Cedric, he had seen the world one over in his youth as a warrior but now was content in his rural lifestyle. Beorn spoke bluntly, "Well, no other way around it," swinging his axe to his shoulder, "let's get on with it." The giant of a man shrugged his whole body and stood fidgeting his feet, unsure of what the others would do. One by one, the other men of the village began gathering their weapons, some wielding clubs, and axes, others resorting to rakes and wooden spades. To the side, Cedric spotted a young woman staring at him with a stern look. She did not budge nor speak as the wind blew through her hair. Cedric did nothing but grasp at his hilt, waiting for the men to be ready. Cedric gathered his army by the stone elf, and altogether afraid, they marched into the forest.

In dispersed groups, the men combed the forest for the missing child and his goat. In Cedric's group, Eadwine walked close to Beorn, practically using him as a shield. A youth of the village, Galdwin accompanied them, his shield and axe both weighed heavy on him, and he struggled to keep up, but never complained, knowing the severity of the situation. With every snapped branch or crushed leaf, there was a fear of the Guardian's cry being its response. The men grew terrified as they went further and further into the forest, the trees soon blocking out much of the sunlight. Eventually, the group stumbled across the brook Eadwine had discovered last night. The elf hunter was first over and paused at the bushes through which he had seen the Guardian. Fear drove his body to freeze and yet compelled his arms forward, slowly reaching through the bushes. The men too froze in their path, each one clutching their weapon, as Eadwine pulled back the leaves. Nothing.

Each man sighed a heavy breath of relief but soon realized this meant they needed to go deeper into the forest. Not far off the brook, they came upon the slain deer from last night, its insides had been picked clean, leaving only an empty carcass.

"We should just head back, that boy has to be long gone by now, I mean look at what it did to that buck," one of the village men spoke up, the rest of the group stopped and stared at him. He soon realized this and began awkwardly shifting his legs and wagged his mustache, "Well there's no use in us dying with him that's all him saying."

Cedric approached him, "what if that was one of your boys out there ey? Sigmund cannot help, so you must. If this is not a sufficient reason, then remember your oath." Cedric lifted his hand, showing his ring and the symbol of the kingdom. Beorn placed his hand on Cedric's shoulder as a sign of support while speaking no words. Eadwine was next to step forward, offended by this man's words of fear. "We may all be filled with fear amongst other things, but do not doubt my skills in the art of the forest, I have lived half my life here. You keep your mouth closed and your eyes open, you'll come out alright." The dissenter and the men with him quickly fell back into line, feeling ashamed of their cowardice while all the while being overcome with fear.

The youngest of them, Galdwin, walked nervously behind Cedric, leaping with every snap of a branch. He spoke with a hushed voice to his lord, "Cedric, what will we do when we find it? I've heard stories the Guardian can snap a man's arm in two with a single blow. That it always sees who's in the forest, but it will itself be seen, lest it wants to." Cedric turned and placed his hand on the shoulder of the youth, and raised Galdwin's sword arm high.

"Galdwin, remember this blade, it is your protector, if you believe in it, you shall not fall today. It's just like the tactics I've been teaching you, move softly and stay behind me." The youngster silently shook his head, his eyes seemed to relax, and his shoulders loosened as they continued their way through the greenery of the forest.

The group stalked and crept through the woods for near half an hour without the sound of a crackling branch nor the chirp of a songbird, and not even their boots seemed to make a noise. The whole of the forest was silent. Cedric felt the weight of all the men's fears on his shoulders. Perhaps the men were right, Cedric thought. If they came upon the Guardian and the boy were still alive, what could a sorry band of villagers and a landed noble do against such a powerful beast? They would inevitably fail or worse, perish as a meal for the creature. Cedric was at his breaking point, as were the men, he could sense it. Even Eadwine had begun to look back towards the path they came, hoping that Cedric would call off the search. But Beorn never doubted Cedric. It was a strange thing, Beorn could easily turn back now, no man would dare to challenge his decision, and yet he continued in utter silence.

At long last the men reached the top of a hill and rested beneath an enormous tree, their heavy breath bringing sound back to the world. They could see for miles across the land, the mountains and woodland stretching as far as the eye could see. In front of them, the hill rolled down into the forest, thick with leaves and needled pine. Cedric pulled out one of the Sironde, drinking as if it were the last drop he would have. "I'll go just ahead lads, see what is to be seen," said Eadwine, who appeared well rested and not at all winded. The men all sat resting, passing the Sironde around, each holding in their eyes a dark look, Galdwin sat on the side of a large collapsed branch, cleaning his blade. Not five minutes later Eadwine appeared like a rabbit running from a hound, bolting out of the wood and up the hill. All the men jumped up, weapons in hand, prepared for the Guardian to come rushing out after Eadwine. Out of breath, the elf panted, "I found its nest, the boy's alive, come quickly!" The men ran with vigor down the hill, their feet carrying them like they were weightless. Through a thick bundle of thorny bushes and trees they discovered a clearing in the wood, and in a crater, the Guardian had made its nest.

Within the crater lay an enclave that protected from the elements. Within it, bones and branches lined a large nest, and molted feathers and twigs made a cozy bed for the creature. The men stood behind the trees surrounding the crater, all grasping at their blades and praying to the gods. Cedric stared at the beast in total astonishment. This was no wretched wild animal with tufts of fur and broken teeth nor some cursed being, twisted by magic or some ancient god-like being. Before Cedric rested the most majestic animal, he had ever seen. Its feathers were of a dark red as the primary coat, and silky white graced its wing tips, with smaller black ones in a perfect pattern along them. Its beak was a near golden yellow, save for the goat blood. Its tail and feet, though covered in feathers, were that of a lion. Its eyes pierced the very soul of Cedric, without even making direct contact with the human. The Guardian was a Griffin. It lay in its nest, enjoying a snack of goat, using its two front claws to hold the body down as he tore off its head. It appeared as if it was playing with its food. The men's fixation with this creature was interrupted by the crying of a small child. All at once they caught sight of Alfred, sitting just inside of the nest, clutching at his broken leg all the while crying. The Griffin kept the boy under its wing, dragging the child back at each attempt of escape.

None of the men moved forward to help, what could they do, to confront the Griffin was a fool's strategy, nor could any man hope to sneak past the crafty devil. Galdwin both was in distress, overcome with the dilemma to act, Beorn knelt trying to understand his foe, and Eadwine looked around the brush behind the beast, hoping for a clear shot. Cedric felt numb, and suddenly he did not even feel that. His body moved of his accord, and yet he gave no order for it to move. All the men called "Cedric get back!" In hushed tones. Fear overtook the noble, and his heart fit to burst from his chest, as he walked into the crater.

The Griffin noticed this bold act, and gave a mighty cry, enough to shake the leaves from a tree, and yet Cedric advanced, not increasing or decreasing his speed. The Griffin hopped from his nest, and repeatedly dug its claws into the dirt, a sign it was ready to charge. Cedric stopped about twenty feet from the Griffin, the two stared in mental combat with each other, neither showing a sign of breaking.

Finally, the Griffin initiated the physical battle, charging forward with a large gust from his wings. But Cedric did not move, not even to reach for his blade. The Griffin stopped dead in its tracks, just inches from the man's face. It breathed hot breath on him, and yet Cedric continued to stare it down, never yielding to the king of beasts. The Griffin began to cry and buck, attempting to entice him to combat, and yet it failed. It started bowing his great and wide neck, all the while staring deep into Cedric's eyes. It was a recognition of nobility, from the lord of beasts to that of man. The pair saw each other and knew one another, it was an incredible sight for the party accompanying Cedric.

The Griffin let out one last mighty cry and retreated to its nest, Cedric's expression remained like that of the elf statue at Orford and proceeded to pick up Alfred and calmly walk back towards his allies. As soon as he reached the forest and was out of the griffin's sight, he nearly dropped the child and fell to the ground vomiting.

Chapter 3
The Festival and the Bird

The people of the village rejoiced that night, the festival of Marsancius finally began and to add to that, the boy Alfred had been safely returned. When the search party returned to the village it was near the dusking hour, the whole of the village came to greet them. Sigmund collapsed at the sight of his child, and thanked his lord nearly one thousand times, kissing his ring and offering any reward. "None is needed, my good man. It was something any man in the village would do for you." The others in the search party looked somewhat embarrassed by this comment. The last of the tents were pitched, and the summer festivities began.

The previous aromas of foods and drink now seemed tripled, and everywhere Cedric looked, a villager was eating, drinking, or dancing under the light of lanterns. Beorn sat sipping at an exceptionally large flagon of ale, next to him his wife Hilde rested her head on his shoulder and his lad, Godfrey, bounced on his knee. The young child did not have many features of his father. He was more of a slim build like that of his mother. His mother had hair as dark as a raven with frayed ends, and her face was thin and pale. She wore a green dress which revealed that she was with her second child.

Beorn smiled contently, his family was his pride and joy and was satisfied to sit rather than celebrate. His son was exhausted by this time and began to collapse in his father's arms as the war dog lifted him up and threw him across the soldier like a freshly caught boar. Both of the two laughed with glee as they continued their game and Beorn had a massive grin on his face.

Eadwine and Galdwin were an entirely different story. Both had drunk freely, causing any drop of alcohol to disappear as if they were an arid desert. The two were boasting to each fair maiden and villager willing to listen of their great taming of the beast. How without them, Cedric was surely doomed. Galdwin was truly sloshed, he sat on the ground, in a puddle of spilled wine, giggling with a wide grin. Eadwine on the other hand, leaped from table to table, a testament to his kin's agility, all the while spilling ale on those below. "Come now good people of Orford," Eadwine slurred, "a toast to our hero...Cedric!"

All those in the tents raised their mugs, their contents spilling out and glowing amongst the lantern light while Cedric stood quietly and gave a humble bow. Eadwine collapsed from the table onto the grass below all the while attempting to hold his mug straight.

The wood elf jumped up, with a look of determination, grabbing a lute nearby, he took a chair nearest Cedric and began to strum. All the people grew quiet, in hopes of hearing one of

Eadwine's ballads. The elf had a reputation of a bard in the village, though he had never trained, so the people often heard the tales and songs of the elvish culture. Their shrewd leaders, skilled warriors and beautiful princesses were the familiar stories for the people of Orford. "Gather around," proclaimed the drunk elf, "and I shall tell you all the tale of Gendore, the forest master'. All the children quickly rushed to the bard's feet, their eyes alight with excitement and all the men and women of the tents turned to face the storyteller. And so, strumming the strings of his lute, the elf began his tale,

"There once was an elf named Gendore the Beast Tamer, his legend known far and wide. Of his imprisonment in old Geladhithil for the crime of theft. Brought before the king he did beg and plead, for a chance to prove himself. He said, "dear lord, let me pass through the trial of Animeister." And so the king, moved by his plea, allowed this lowly thief to enter the den of the great lion. The whole of the land stood quiet, awaiting the assured fate of this fool. There was no sound of lions gnawing upon elven bone that day. Gendore was quick and tackled the lion, and he did force it to submit. After hours, the lion lay cowering in fear, of the lowly criminal who had now proven himself its master. And so, all the land rejoiced his name, and his charges promptly cleared. Now, all know the tale of the Beast Tamer Gendore and his battle with the lion."

All the children applauded with glee as Eadwine let out a mighty roar like the lion of the tale and all those seated were clapped and whistled. Cedric could only stand laughing, attempting to brush off the similarities of the two stories of the day, when again, on the opposite end of the tent, he spotted the young woman at the marketplace. The two exited the tent on opposite sides and met in a green meadow just nearby.

Her name was Aderyn, and her features lived up to her name. Her face was pointed and yet had an incredible smoothness to it. Her hair was a dark brown and her eyes as blue as the clear summer's sky. The two stood in the meadow for sometimes before speaking. Lifting his hand to her face, she broke the silence, "are you sure you're alright...you could have used me today. I could have helped." She spoke rather impatiently but with a caring nature.

Cedric looked down to her, "I know...I know, but you know you are not ready, not yet at least."

She responded, "If not now then when? We have been practicing for over a year now, and I am just as good as you."

Cedric stood back, jokingly he appeared stunned and offended, "my good lady, you insult my honor, and I demand satisfaction," with a sneering scoff like an upstart noble, he drew his blade, striking a dramatic pose.

Aderyn smiled and began looking around the meadow, until she came across, a sword, blunt and worn, it was hidden in the brush. She took a high stance, and the two began. As soon as the duel began, however, they immediately shifted to a serious tone. The pair seemed to dance around each other, the steel clanking with each parried blow, but seemed muffled, held back, as to avoid attention from the nearby party-goers.

Aderyn was far faster than her counterpart, but she was reckless. With each swing of her blade, she shifted her feet as if the blade dragged them. Cedric quickly took notice of this, and focused on defensive strikes, waiting for her to make a mistake. And that she did, with a great overhand swing, she knocked herself off balance, and Cedric quickly tripped her to the grass. Cedric gave her his arm for support, but she quickly pulled him down as well. They both sat laughing on the green field, looking at the shimmering light of the moon upon their village's lake.

Cedric broke their silence, "you've certainly improved, no doubt about that, but there's still much room for betterment. The real world doesn't consist of battles with dull blades."

Aderyn was quick to respond, "I've still got the faster swing, that's what matters, and what do you know of the real world? Lest you forget, you were forged in a cool fire like myself." Cedric sat there silent, what did he know of the real world? His training was the closest to combat he had come, and now it appeared as if this village would serve as his world his whole life. The two realized they should return to the festivities, the two stood, hide the practice blade, and headed back towards the light of the tents.

The couple danced the night away for hours to the tune of Eadwine's strumming and singing. The village was illuminated in rustic majesty, and all was right with the world as they ate, drank, and made merry under the moonlit sky.

Chapter 4
Alfnod and Edward's Adventures

When Cedric had returned to the main tent, the men who composed to rescue party were now huddled around a table, playing cards. Eadwine was first to spot their company's leader, and he stood to salute though somewhat askew from the ale. Cedric quickly caught on to the act, and like a military commander snapped into a leg kick march. "Good sergeant, your report of the men's morale!" Cedric barked like a vetted war dog.

"Downright miserable sir, the cards simply aren't doing it." "Well by the gods sir we'll need to see to it." All the sudden Galdwin, still sitting in his little puddle, leaped into action, "sir I've word there's a pub nearby ripe with supplies, ours for the taking," the youth managed to spout this out before falling back to the floor. Cedric assembled his men, "right lads, now all together for crown and country!" Pulling out his blade, he pointed it onward, and the men began their drunken walk, with Beorn supporting the flank, guiding any who fell from the path as he and Cedric were the only somewhat sober of their group.

They walked towards The Green Devil, the only inn in Orford and the only one for miles for that matter. Upon first glance, it appeared as a traditional tavern for Lorine, a simple back patio with stone walling with grass vines climbing around it. The main building itself was an intimate three-story affair of wooden beams and wattle and daub. Some of their company had now been lost to the call of angry wives and the desire for a comfy cot. Now left were Cedric, Beorn, Eadwine, Galdwin, and a small number of those who could hold their liquor. The tavern maiden, Gilda, quickly welcomed them in and offered them seats round the roaring and freshly stoked fireplace. The men recounted the day's events, quite pleased with themselves. Eadwine sat plucking a vine of grapes, Beorn sat carving a small log of wood, and now Galdwin was resting under a layer of warm blankets, at long last the festivities were drawing to a quiet close.

Suddenly there was a cantering of metaled horseshoes from outside the inn, through the window they spotted the sight of shadows moving through the moonlight and heard familiar laughter. The door swung open, allowing for a cool summer night's breeze to roll in. There in the doorway stood long awaited friends, Alfnod and Edward. Though the two had come from separate journeys, they connected just on the outskirts of the town and agreed to surprise their friends.

Edward was dressed in strange garb, his jacket of a light blue with golden frills, too thick for this season and his cap was of the eastern Cossacks which now appeared more like a nightcap. His beard was unkempt and his face tired but not worn from his long journey east.

Alfnod appeared as the same day he had left, wearing his signature long coat, with yellowed leather and metal beads embedded as armor. Upon both sides of his hip rested two blades, Alger and Brandr. Cedric was first to smile at their sight and first to leap to great them. Cedric pulled the two together and heartily hugged the two of them.

Cedric spoke, "We were not expecting you so late, come, come tell us of your journey, dearest Gilda, give these poor vagabonds something to eat."

Edward and Alfnod took their seats around the fire, and the exchange of tales began with Edward, "Well as you know I've been in Ritterland for some time now, discovering new trading, mostly in clothing and other baubles. This time, however, I decided to make the journey all the way to the eastern coast, to Dradania, and my way it worth it." All those still present at the inn leaned forward with anticipation as Edward reveal a small pouch from his traveling bag, pouring the contents on the nearby table, he amazed them all. There on the table lay various gems and precious stones, which appeared as if the stars themselves could not match in number or beauty. Edward smiled, "I got these off a merchant from The Burning Sea, and they say these types of gems line the ground like grass in our fields." Before them lay a valuable amount of diamonds, rubies, and sapphires, they would fetch a price fit for a king at the capital city, Wulfstan.

Distracted by their merchant friend's bag, Cedric pulled out more baubles and trinkets from Edward's journey. All manner of fine silks and household items were here, all of which could make a man rich at half their price. Cedric pulled out a book which appeared ancient, its gold lining across its cover had begun to fade, and it seemed the precious jewels that once aligned it, had been ripped clean.

When he opened it, the words made no sense to him. It was a dead language, spoken now only in the dark. Diagrams of strange rituals and beasts filled its pages, it was unsettling for Cedric, and he immediately shut it. "Where on earth did you get this book, Edward?" The merchant glanced over at the book, "Oh yes, I won that at an auction in some lesser noble house in Ritterland, Castle Verge if I'm correct. Isn't it a strange thing? They said they were excavating an old site of a citadel far in the Amach forest when they came across this book. Supposedly used for some kind ritual but it's all gibberish to me. I wasn't even going to bid on it until I saw some scoundrel looking chaps come in and start offering significant coin on it. So, I realized I could easily outbid them and sell it to some rich noble who has no idea what the book is, tell them it's a collector's item. You should have seen it," the merchant chuckled, "they turned red as a smithy's forge when I outbid them, came right up to me and offered all the gold they had, plus more when it was delivered. I scoffed them away, I know I've got something that some bloated rich man will pay a fortune's worth but not even bother to go get it himself."

The mood of the story quickly changed to suspicion, "they did not leave me alone for some time after that, all the way through Ritterland and the east of Lorine, I saw them tailing me, I remember I about near killed my horse losing them in the Glanfech forest." The whole of the inn had become tense at this news, but Edward was quick to break back into the normal conversation, "So," he said to change to topic, "What new tales from the village?" All the men smiled, and Eadwine brought out his lute, ready to tell the story of Cedric the Beastmaster.

As the night grew late and the candles had been worn down, the exchange of tales had stopped. "Well lads, I suppose we should all head home, plenty of time tomorrow for storytelling, Alfnod, shall you be staying with me then? The inn is fully booked." The elf was still sipping his wine by the fire, "that sounds alright to me, let's head out then." The pair parted ways with the rest of the group at the door of the inn, each returning to their home. Eadwine headed for his cabin, just on the edge of the woods. The noble and his friend reached the top of the hill and entered the estate grounds. Cedric and the elf entered the undercroft of the home, in hopes of finding some aged spirits. When they emerged, they lit candles in one of the houses many dining rooms, illuminating the wooden walls with red and yellow light. This house was different from most noble houses of the land as it had no great hall for feasting, rather an offshoot of smaller dining rooms, and the two had chosen the largest of these chambers. The two pulled their chairs close to the fire and drank. Along the floor, some bottles rested from previous nights. Cedric poured a cup into the fire, a gesture to Domovoi the god of the hearth and dreams. Cedric placed his glass in the hand of one of the statues carved from the fireplace stone, three on each side of the roaring fire.

Cedric spoke, "Come now Alfnod, tell me, how was it, the southern lands. Were they filled with foul monsters, were there damsels at every castle waiting to be rescued, poor innocent farmers to be protected by knavish rogues?"

Alfnod smiled and looked down, "It was quite the journey, I travel quite far," he paused and looked back at his friend, "but what about you, what's been going on in the village?"

Cedric seemed uninterested in the topic, "Crops grow, we

harvest, winters arrives, spring springs, and we sow again, same as it's always been."

Alfnod frowned, "Come now, there's more than that."

Cedric hesitated before speaking but realized how much he trusted his companion, "I…I've been training with Aderyn, primary the blade and bow, she's gotten superb at both."

Alfnod was pleased to hear this, "ha, she always did have a fire to her that girl, happy to know she's learning to forge with it."

Cedric next asked about an old mutual friend, "Alfnod you went down south, so tell me, any word of Lafayette?

Alfnod smiled at the name of their dear friend, "Oh yes, he's patrolling down towards that old fortress Arazor, some word of bandit activity or something of the sort, I met him along the road, he and his company are in good health."

Cedric smiled at the new that their friend was in good health. Alfnod's mood quickly turned, "Cedric, you know Edward left far after I began my journey," he leaned forward, his face now split by the light of the fire. "Well when Edward caught up with me outside the village, he told me about something that began happening about a year ago. He said you started drinking more than any man in the village and that you've been resting on the edge of that damned statue for months. You must tell me what ails you, my friend."

Cedric slowly reeled back in his chair, unsure how to explain. For so long he had stayed in his routine of drinking and resting at the foot of the statue, he could not understand how to start. Cedric began, "it began before you left actually, these visions I have. It started off as nothing but dreams, strange visions of a lake in the center of a forest clearing, with a massive glowing tree resting on an island in its middle. There was no problem with them, but that it happened every night, then it got much worse. After you had left, I began hearing voices in the dreams. They started as whispers, practically just the sound of the wind. But now, they are booming shouts, like thunders rolling off clouds."

Suddenly, the fire flickered, and the room darkened. Along the wall, the shadows grew taller than their counterparts, and eerie silence fouled the place. Cedric leaned closer, as though to keep his voice hidden from the shadows, "And just recently, I have seen that lake burn and the forest around it reduced to ash, all the while hearing screams that sound familiar, like the people of the village. All I can do is drink. It numbs the visions to mere blurs. Now even when I wake, I see the image of this burning tree, carved into the back of my mind and I cannot get away from it."

Cedric paused, he realized the look of horror on his friend's face. Cedric leaned forward and placed his hands on his listener's shoulders saying, "Alfnod, I think it is a warning of some kind, some cruel vision of what may be. And I am afraid."

Suddenly the windows burst open, bringing in a howling wind, which seemed to shake the whole foundation of the estate. The fire went out, and ashes spilled onto the floor and in the drinking cups.

Cedric closed the windows and relit the fire, while Alfnod poured fresh drinks. Alfnod summoned a smile, "Cedric, you've been drinking, but nevertheless, I believe you and that you've been having these visions. But is this your plan? Sit here and drink, standing watch exhausted and hungover? If you believe this is some warning, then prepare, time and fate wait for no man. Tomorrow morning we'll get the lads together, let them know you aren't drinking yourself half to death for the thrill of it, we'll find out the meaning of this cryptic nightmare."

The two finished their drinks and Alfnod guided his friend up the creaking steps towards the bedrooms. Alfnod reached the guest room first and bid his host a good rest, one with no burning visions. Cedric arrived in his room, candlestick in hand, and collapsed on the bed. Before he rested, he guided the light across his bookshelf, revealing not a row of dust and cobwebs like so many other rooms of the house, but of perfectly preserved tomes and books. Each book was meticulously kept and had been read by Cedric many times. His personal favorite, Knights of Chivalry, by Sir Galford of Cafold, was open on his desk and was open to the story of Richard of Burhungy who led the first group of explorers to the Southern Deserts. It was Cedric's favorite tale of adventure, one in which man could strike out on his accord and live life on his terms.

Chapter 5
The Burning

Cedric realized how late it was and finally blew out the final source of light in the house, plunging himself back into his dreams. It came again, the vision of the lake. All around him, a fire burned the grass and forest, and it felt as if it would consume his flesh at any moment. The lake burned like oil or Nacian fire, a tar so dense and flammable water cannot extinguish it. Between and amongst the tree which now appeared like burning kindling, dark figures of people were screaming in the flames. They were the whispers that became screams, and they called to Cedric, for him to save them.

Cedric turned his head back to the glowing tree, just as it began to snap and crack from the flame, its insides of pure light poured onto the ground like freshly gutted game. From the other side of the tree, a blade was plunged into this essence and turned it into blackened ash. The figure wielding this weapon emerged from his cover and revealed himself. At his feet, there were flaming boots, which turned the grass around them to ash. His cloak was of ash and metal, upon his head rested a crown of ten rotted fingers. His face could not be seen; there was a void of existence upon it. Only his eyes were visible, calm and yet full of hate, and they lightly glowed like embers of an extinguished fire.

Cedric awoke with a gasp, but there was no time for contemplation or breath, a blade was plunging at his face.

In the dark of night, a steel sword stabbed at Cedric, narrowly dodging the attack, Cedric rolled out of his bed as the steel ripped through the stuffing of the pillow. In Cedric's room stood a brute of a man, his face covered in dirt and his clothes ragged and muddy. Bayeux rested in the main hallway. There was no weapon for Cedric in this fight. The intruder tore his blade from its place and charged at the startled noble, who was left to grab a candlestick as defense.

The two grappled as Cedric heard muffled noises from the other room, Alfnod was no doubt dealing with a rude awakening as well. It appeared there would be no clear victor in this match until Cedric latched to the back of the man, and jabbed the candlestick through his right eye. This gave Cedric time to disarm the bandit and run him through with his own blade. With that business dealt with Cedric rushed into the hall to aid his friend.

When Cedric reached the hallway, he caught the sight of Alfnod's door being thrown to the ground as his assailant was pierced through the shoulders with Alger and Brandr, with Alfnod pushing them through. The two prepared their gear and finished off the second bandit, thinking the night's horrors were passed, only to hear screaming coming from Orford.

The two ran outside as Cedric strapped Bayeux to his side,

and witnessed the burning of Orford. The village was in such a blaze that the fire illuminated the two's figures. Cedric stopped in sheer terror, "Alfnod, those, those are the screams from my dream." Alfnod could do nothing but look at his companion, unable to think of a proper response he only said, "Come on! We've got to help!"

The two reached the main streets of the village in record time, many of the villagers huddled around the two, Beorn was leading a group of men, rounding up as many as they could. Beorn was glad to see the two still alive, "we need to get these people to safety, we'll barricade in the old temple, round up as many as you can!" In his hands, his axe found its home and Beorn was reinvigorated as the warrior he was. Cedric and Alfnod went from house to house, directing those inside to the temple.

Bandits tore across the market street directly at them, too many for a fair fight. Before their charge came to fruition, a fury of arrows was released by Eadwine, who shot and hit three bandits all while running to his friends. The three of them assembled more and more of the villagers at the stone temple, a perfect sanctuary from the fires that burned around them. Galdwin brought in the last group, and they began to barricade the doors.

"Where's Edward, is he still at the inn?" Cedric asked, spinning in a circle. None had seen him this night, and they began to fear the worst.

Beorn continued piling on wood and loose stones saying, "I'm sorry Cedric but we have to keep barricading, we can't risk the whole village." Beorn seemed saddened by his own words, the two were close friends, but the needs of the villagers had to come first.

Cedric looked out onto the street, the houses had begun to collapse from the flames, unsure of his plan, and Cedric turned to Beorn and said, "Give me five minutes." And like that Cedric had leaped over the half-constructed barricade and rushed towards the inn, taking the alleyways of houses not yet burned, to avoid being seen.

At last Cedric reached the central courtyard, the inn was just steps away. Suddenly, Cedric leaped back into the shadows of the alleyway. In front of him stood Edward, who now was walking through the courtyard, coughing up blood. Behind him, a pack of bandits laughed at the sight, as one atop a horse poured arrows into the merchant's back.

Finally, Edward collapsed on the stone square, arrows riddling his back. The horseman amongst the bandits dismounted and approached Edward's lifeless body. His features were truly disgusting, his hair long and dirty, his teeth rotten and along his face were tattoos of strange symbols. He smiled as he reached for the merchant's bag, ignoring all precious gems and other great valuables, he took the book Edward had bought at the auction. He grinned and wide and slimy grin as he stuffed the tome into his satchel, and with a whistle called his men to the square.

The other bandits, clad in rugged leathers and with faces equal in malice to their commander, gathered around the plaza. Their leader with a great cry revealed the treasure in his arms. His bandits cheered and snorted, as they wiped blood from their blades. The group set out, running towards the southern-most edge of the city. Cedric turned to return to his allies, to tell them the grief of Edward when he was intercepted by a falling beam of wood, which cracked upon his back. Collapsed in an alleyway, Cedric felt his doom was sure as he drifted into unconsciousness.

Again, Cedric was in the world of the lake, this time there was no great fire, only its aftermath. All around him, the fields had been transmuted to blackened ash, and there was no life in any that once did. Even the glowing tree had succumbed to this force and was withering in the wind, each gentle breeze removing more and more torched branches. The only thing that remained the same was the lake, and its blue water continued to reflect off the light of the moon. A voice, unlike the ones that appeared here before, spoke gently but with authority, "He cannot go on, we have failed."

This voice was matched by that of a woman's, "No, there is still hope."

Chapter 6
Charred Ash

Cedric was awoken by this voice in his dream and came to coughing. All around him there was ash, of the building or flesh he could not tell. The beam that had collapsed upon him had also saved him, shielding him from the burning fire around him. As he stood up, he surveyed the destruction around him. It appeared like the end of the world. Nothing of the townhouses remained but little stone fireplaces, still reaching towards the thatched roofs that had burned away.

Cedric's face was covered in soot and dirt, but he did not notice, he was left voiceless by the destruction of Orford. Suddenly his body jerked toward Edward's corpse, which was saved because he remained in the center of the village's stone square so the smoldering flame could not reach him. Cedric removed the arrows delicately and turned his deceased friend onto his back. Cedric wept as he saw the ghostlike visage of his friend, so filled with fear and shock as in his last moments. Next

Cedric reached for the contents of his bag, realizing not a single gem was missing, they had only come for that book.

Cedric walked towards the temple with Edward's body on his shoulders, the ashen remains of his villagers kicked up with every step and was lodged within his boots. Cedric stopped when he felt the crackle of something beneath his feet, it was the stained glass that once adorned the snug and safe homes of Orford, now burned to the point that no image could be seen.

Along the ruins of the brewery, Hamund's bones were all that remained of the poor brewmaster. The stone foundation of the once happy home was still intact, and Cedric dropped Edward at the door and went inside. All the barrels and distilleries were in ruins, except for one tiny bottle on the ground. Some of Hamund's special reserve, tasted by none in the village, it was meant to be a surprise on the second day of the festival. Stuffing it in his pocket, Cedric made a silent vow with Hamund, that it would only be drunk when he was avenged, to this vow, Cedric also made with Edward and the whole of the village. At last, with Edward in tow, Cedric made it to the temple where the remains of his village had come out to see the destruction. The village was in a flood of tears, many had lost those they loved in the confusion of the fire and now could only find them as charred corpses.

Beorn was running through each street with a look of pure terror on his face, in the panic, Beorn thought Godfrey was at his side the whole night, and only awoke to find he was nowhere to be found. Hilde was weeping at the temple steps, for she knew her son's fate was sealed the moment the final stone of the barricade was placed. Beorn returned only minutes later, a small little, charred body in his arms. He collapsed before he could even reach his wife, his grief overcame him.

His face turned purple, and his eyes seemed fit to burst as he wept for his son, slamming his head on the hard stone as he screamed. He held his child in his arms just like the previous night, only this time it was an event composed of pure devastation and sorrow.

Cedric became numb, the world around him seemed to slow as sound became an ambient static. Alfnod hurried to him, Cedric could see the elf mouthing his name, but could not hear him as it sounded only like a muffled sound.

Alfnod shook him violently, snapping him out of his daze and spoke, "Cedric we're going to kill those bastards, you hear me? We are going to gut every single one of them." The elf's eyes were a hot red, like the fires from the night before. Behind him, many the village's remaining men carried axes and the same burning fire for revenge.

Beorn joined them after he returned to the remains of his home, within his protected basement, he brought an axe, a noose with rope, and a strange mask. Amongst the remaining men was Galdwin carrying a pile blades and shields for his companions, he was ready for battle.

Cedric had the same fire in his heart as the men before him, but also had a cool head and spoke justly, "we will, but first we must see to the men who cannot fight and the women and child, we must lead them someplace safe." Cedric sat on a piece of carved stone to think and finally devised a plan, "we know they left the village heading south, my bet is that they're heading to Arazor like Alfnod said there was word of bandits near there, perhaps this is them. We send the rest of the village north towards Wulfstan, they'll be safe on the road and can get supplies and shelter from the king."

The villagers agreed this was a sound plan and so they

packed up what remained and began on their journey to Wulfstan. Before they left, however, Aderyn approached Cedric, she had the same fire in her eyes as the men.

She spoke bluntly and to the point, "Cedric I'm coming with you. Don't argue, if you think I'm not ready for the blade then I'll use the bow with Eadwine." She said as she motioned to her longbow slung across her back. "But either way, I'll have my revenge as well, we were both Edward's friends." Cedric looked to his men for approval, they all stood mystified by the woman's tenacity and boldness, and so Cedric took it as the opportunity to welcome her to their company.

Before the group set out on their quest for vengeance, Cedric returned to his family home, luckily untouched by the flames. He surveyed each room one last time, keeping every detail in his memory. In his chambers, he uncovered the ceremonial banner of his family and rolled it into a smooth lump in his bag. This would become the banner by which men lived and died, by which the fates would present the tale of Cedric of House Thorne. Under this banner, stories of brave heroes of the north were forged, and Cedric would do well to honor them.

The hunting party readied their horses in the stables, which were thankfully untouched by the carnage. They watched as the rest of the villagers headed out on the main road towards Wulfstan, their carts filled with family heirlooms and leftover food and drink from the festival clinked and wobbled along the cobblestone road. "It's two days' ride south to Arazor, and they have a lead, we'll need to head out soon," Cedric said as he overlooked the village one last time. He memorized each detail of the lake and forest surrounding it. It would be the last time his feet would find themselves on the landscape of Orford, before him, the road to the world now stretched and it was time to take the first step.

The company set out before dawn, taking small dirt paths through the wood towards Arazor, amongst them were Cedric's close friends along with a few other men of the village. Their number counted ten warriors good for fighting, going up against some fifteen who attacked the village and however many were at the old abandoned fortress.

None of them spoke along the winding paths, for none knew what to say. During their first day's journey, Cedric spied a strange figure moving through the forest, not like a man or elf's shape. It was only at the dusk of the day after they had cross through much forest and many rolling hills that Cedric realized it was the Guardian. It had followed the party throughout their ride, and Cedric only knew it was the Griffin by its sharp eyes peering through the shrubbery. When they stopped to rest, Cedric gazed deeply into its eyes, telling no one of its presence. The Griffin kept its distance, just far enough and well enough hidden that only Cedric could see it. Its eyes were filled with mourning for Orford and almost appeared as if it were crying.

Chapter 7
The Lighthouse of Evrand

They stopped and made camp on a hill overlooking the southern country of Lorine and the northernmost regions of the Golden Court, the last real kingdom of elves. Far into the southern sky, a faint light could be seen, not a star or the sun but of a burning fire. Galdwin broke the long silence that had huddled over their company, with a shy and muffled voice he spoke, "Eadwine, do you have any tales to tell, something to lift the spirits." Eadwine smiled and quickly thought of a tale to tell, looking towards the burning fire in the southern sky for reference.

"You all see that burning in the heavens? It is no star or illusion of the mind. It is the Lighthouse of Evrand, the tallest building in the world. Long ago, when the world was still young, darkness had swept over all of Glanfech and the lesser elven kingdoms. It was a sign of the deceiver himself, Crassus Baal, the demonic lord of tricks and deals. In this time, the gods were at war with the demons spawned from Kryn and there was no clear victor. Crassus Baal's greatest servant, Azrael was summoned to the earth and rode across the sky, leaving a trail of black cloud where he went. The stars and the sun could not pierce the thick cloud of shadow that had gripped the world. Within this cloud, our people became misguided and separated, and there was war between the elves. Many of the elves fell to the corruption of Crassus and became what we know was Tethraki, the cursed. The great elf king Rohiel came down from his lands in Glanfech and was pained by the sight of his people's civil war. So he cried out to his god Duwel, "Duwel, your people are in peril, they cry out to you, but their prayers cannot pierce the thick darkness that corrupts them. Give me the strength to unite them." Now the elf god Duwel knew of his people's suffering. This prayer did not go unanswered, as Duwel descended from his eternal throne and stood before the elf king and gave him a silver hammer and pick, telling the king, "You shall build the light of the world, and within it, my people shall survive and prosper." For the next century, Rohiel constructed a great lighthouse in Evrand. He had no plans drawn out or any form of aid, it was in his mind that the vision of the tower resided. When he had laid every stone, and carved every step, Duwel was pleased and from his throne sent a flame which was placed at the top of the lighthouse. This light burned out the shadow that had blinded the world and guided the elf people to Evrand, where they became united as a people and forged the First Empire of the world.

However, this did not end the battle with the demonic horde, for Crassus Baal summoned his servant Azrael once more and summoned forth his whole host of demons. The Lighthouse guarded the city of Evrand, and so Rohiel's people were safe and refused to leave the gaze of the eternal fire. Azrael knew of this, and so he commanded his legions northward, to the lands of men in what is now known as Lorine, Midland, and Belfas. One by one, the cities and fields of men burned. From the former ten kingdoms of men found there, Azrael forged a crown of their fingers, Degsedd, and with it proclaimed himself the true king of man. Even to this day, it is not known if this Azrael was once man, it has been lost to history, and he is now regarded as a lesser demon, a mere servant of his god. Godric, the lord of the hunt and wilderness, attempted to duel this foul creature but to no avail. The god was beaten back that day, his left eye plucked away, which is why he is depicted with an eyepatch. The hopes of the armies of man faded that day, save for in Belfas.

In Belfas, a great host of men gathered at their ancient citadel called Broken Fang, as it was carved into a mountain with a jagged peak where once a tower stood. At the helm of this resistance was Adalgott the Lawgiver, a lord from Canterbrick. His great flowing beard was woven with the silk of the gods, and in his hand, he held the horn of Godric, which rallied the men from faraway lands to his cause and at Broken Fang, the duel between the gods and demons reached its climax. Loden and his kin descended from their divine halls and met Crassus and the dark god Baphamont and their hordes on the battlefield alongside the men of Belfas. The battle was hard fought, but in the end, the gods and their men stood victorious, the demons were driven back to their realm. From this event, Adalgott was named the king and made Wulfstan his capital, united the former ten kingdoms under his banner and codified law with a great pillar of stone so that all would know his law.

It is a strange thing how stories that can seem so distant are so related, such as the tales of Adalgott and of the Lighthouse. The kings of Evrand after Rohiel were known as the torchbearers, and it was their sacred duty to guard and unite the elf people as the lighthouse did those many centuries ago. That light has never gone out, for so long it has burned and been seen across many nations. It is said that when the end of the elven people draws near, Duwel shall once again walk upon the earth and take back the flame of his people. He shall use it to guide his kind to his realm where the will live with him forever." Eadwine slunk under his cloak and went to sleep, pleased with his storytelling.

The company looked out onto the Lighthouse, burning brighter and brighter as the sun retreated across the sky. Cedric felt as though the heat of the structure was surrounding him, it was unlike the flames of his nightmares, this heat was calming and peaceful. The last of the company finally fell to sleep, a feat most impressive given the horrors of the past day. In the nearby forest, the Guardian slept as well, it was exhausted from the journey and had now ventured farther from its nest than ever before.

Cedric could not sleep; his mind was abuzz from Eadwine's story. Alfnod sat next to his friend to console him, "How are you holding up Cedric?" Alfnod asked.

Cedric simply shrugged and said, "I do not know, these dreams I've been having…I think I saw the destruction of the village before it happened. Or at least a warning that Orford would burn."

Alfnod rubbed his hands by the campfire and replied, "I think it was supposed to be a warning, perhaps a vision from your gods?"

Cedric responded, "I don't know, I don't know anything.

One day the village is safe and happy, festive indeed and in only a few moments it's all ripped away. In my dream the night Orford burned, I saw the outline of a man with a crown of ten fingers. Alfnod, you don't suppose it could be Azrael, like in the story?"

Alfnod received this news grimly, "if you really did, then I think this is much larger than some rogues attacking a village. They had a target. They wanted that book. It frightens me to think of what they or whoever will use it for. When we've dealt with them we can head to Wulfstan, I'm sure we can find answers there."

Cedric replied with a monotone voice, "If we even make it out of Arazor."

Chapter 8
Arazor

All along the forest surrounding the ancient fortress, there was thick underbrush and numerous trees. The land felt as if it were somehow older than the land they had already crossed through, there was a mystifying wonder to it. Along a creek, Eadwine discovered an unholy site. A deer carcass was strung up upon a tree, and its blood was used in some sort of strange ritual, no doubt some form of dark magic.

The whole of the company was palpably tense and afraid. Galdwin gripped his axe almost to snapping point, ready to strike at anything that moved. Beorn gave away no emotion with his facial expression, only beads of sweat were an indicator he was nervous. At the front of the group, Cedric was breathing heavy, expecting an ambush at any moment, constantly looking back to see if Aderyn was still safe. She was gripping an arrow in her hand, ready to draw upon the rogues inhabiting the fort.

After a half day of travel, the company of Cedric arrived at the fortress. Eadwine and Cedric went to scout the exterior and uncover how many foes they would face this day. Sentries were placed along each ruined tower of the fortress, making six in total, each of them wielding bows or crossbows. At the gate stood three of the larger bandits, who were the best equipped regarding weapons and armor of their outfit, sitting and eating by a fire.

"Look, Cedric, by the hall's main gate." Eadwine pointed out the leader of the bandits sporting his grin, but instead of the book in his hands, there was a large sack of golden coins, with two more huge sacks by his feet. This bounty had been given by the cloaked man standing next to him, it was a shade of dark red, with golden patterns on the sleeves.

The two men shook hands, and the hooded figure prepared his horse. At this mysterious figure's side were two bodyguards, completely unlike the bandits, they held themselves in a refined manner and wore full plated armor. Cedric would be glad to see them gone, as it would mean fewer thieves to deal with in the main assault. In the courtyard, there was a full dozen of bandits tending to menial tasks, they looked fat and lazy, apparently the main garrison never actually left the fortress.

The fort's main building was still standing, and Cedric nor Eadwine could see how many bandits were inside, but both agreed there were bound to be more somewhere in it. Slowly the scouting party retreated back along the tree line, the fortress had an open field facing its forward gate, with lush wooded landscape covering its back. There was no need for the original inhabitants to worry of this flank as the wall at the rear was built up the highest, meaning no army could effectively approach from the rear, they would be forced into combat on the field.

Cedric drew out an outline of the castle's exterior in the dirt back at camp, each of his companions eagerly awaiting his command.

Cedric knew the sentries had to be dealt with first if they were to approach from the front, they would certainly lose some of their force to the bolts and arrows of the bandits. "Before we can manage into Arazor, we'll need to deal with those placed upon the guard towers. I propose we flank from the rear, from the forest where they would not see us, we send two of our most nimble up the intact wall. From there they can deal with the sentries while we push through the castle gates. From the incline of the courtyard, we should have a few moments before those there can reach their allies as the gate, allowing us to divide them up."

None were surprised by Cedric's sudden leap into military commands, like any noble's son, he was trained at the military school of Wulfstan, where he studied the greatest generals in the world. These tactics he was using were most akin to Hacra the Elephant Rider, the commander of the Tanaric people, choosing a frontal assault combined with more efficient flanking maneuvers.

Eadwine and Aderyn stepped forward as volunteers to scale the wall. "If Eadwine and I can reach that wall, we'll be able to take out the sentries and provide you cover with our bows, it's the best strategy for keeping us all alive," Aderyn said confidently. So, the plan was devised and put into effect.

The assault party consisting of Cedric, Alfnod, Beorn, Galdwin and the other men of the village nervously waited at the edge of the forest for the signal. Cedric and the others spotted Eadwine reach the top first, then reach his hand for Aderyn, the elf was a testament to his kin's agility. The two hurried to their positions, taking cover behind rubble on opposite sides of the wall, as it stretched across the whole fort, including the main hall, and fired their first shots. Both direct hits against the first two sentries, both ripping through the skull as to avoid any unwanted sounds. The courtyard garrison had not been stirred, they were preoccupied with drink and a hog roasting on a spit. It would be too dangerous for the archers to continue their crafty work, as the next four sentries were all in each other's sights, it was now up to the main force of the party.

Cedric raised his fist and threw it down, giving the order to charge. They ran at full speed, with no intention of raising their shields as their archers were now making quick work of the remaining four sentries. They ran silently across the field, giving no sign that they were even there save the heavy breathing and beating footsteps. The three gate guards raised their shields as Cedric's group closed the gap between them, the bandits barely had time to scream.

Beorn was the first to reach the group, his body moving like a howling wind across a lonely hill. He raised his two hands axe and began carving up the shield of the largest bandit. It was an old combat style, Beorn would swing his axe with such speed and strength, aiming specifically for his foe's shield, that the bandit had not a single moment to counter. Beorn continued this for at least ten blows then quickly switched his swing halfway through, beginning at the legs, but moving to the skull. The bandit's shield was still hanging by his feet, it had moved to protect against the first swing, and the bandit fell to the ground, an axe ripped his head clean away. Cedric and Alfnod made quick work of the other two, their feeble leather and hide skin armor only gave the appearance of protection.

Next, the assault party went up the gate's stairs and into the courtyard where the fat and drunk highwaymen were already greeted by a volley of arrows, their numbers dwindling fast. The whole of Cedric's party took their share of revenge upon them and the party reunited at the steps of the central keep.

They went from room to room in the keep searching for this bandit group's leader until they came upon the door to the main feasting hall. Cedric and Alfnod opened the two large wooden and doors and were stopped silent by what they saw. At least fifty bandits were feasting in the hall, throwing food and drinking merrily. At the main table, their leader known by his people as Wedgrud was laughing as he counted piles of gold. All at once, every bandit turned to face their intruders, and a silence overtook the room.

"Run!" Cedric shouted, already pulling his party back into the hall. The bandits all gave chase, and the party of Cedric was separated. Cedric, Galdwin, and Alfnod took flight to the stairs, hoping the high ground would give some advantage, Beorn and Aderyn and a few others went back to the courtyard hoping to take them the bandits on one at a time as they pour through the keep. Some men of the village found themselves trapped in the dungeons of the castle, trapped like rats. They fought courageously and proved themselves brave on more than one occasion that day, but the group was too few and was overwhelmed by the onslaught of bandits.

Cedric and his two friends now snuck about the castle hoping to reunite with Beorn's group. They crept back downstairs, to find the main hall emptied of the army of bandits, returning to the feasting hall, they hoped to find their separated friends. From the back room, Wedgrud appeared, bringing with him five of his best men. The cruel man smiled with his rotted teeth and barked at his men to kill. Outnumbered, the three made their stand in a corner, taking strikes at precise times, all the while holding their shields high, save Alfnod as he did not carry one. One by one the bandits fell, Galdwin was hurt, an axe had taken a strike at his thigh, and it was now bleeding.

Wedgrud looked displeased, and his eye began to twitch but continued his wicked smile. He rushed at them, with two axes in his hands and began a whirlwind of fury. None of the three could land a blow, they were on a relentless defense against this madman. As they continued their spar, Galdwin's shield was broken, and Wedgrud's axe was struck into his chest.

Cedric and Alfnod were thrown into a blind rage as they watched the youngest of their party, barely able to grow a beard, collapse to the ground spewing blood from his mouth. Their swings were vicious and filled with hate, but they could not fell Wedgrud, they had played into his hand, and now he was toying with them. Next to be struck was Cedric, an axe made its way through his lower side, and he fell to the floor, not dead, but in severe pain. Galdwin lay bleeding as well, but he held to life with the entirety of his will.

Now it was down to Alfnod and Wedgrud, the two circled each other, both severely out of breath. Alfnod was first to swing, in an elegant elven style known as Daugwyn, or two winds, with each blade's strike coming in succession to the other. The dueling parties both received wounds from the other, and there was no clear superior. Alfnod was breathing heavy, a strike had grazed his ribs and it was beginning to bruise, his armored coat weighed heavy on him. Alfnod stepped back from his dueling partner and ripped the jacket off leaving only his shirt, hoping it would give him a quick burst of speed. Wedgrud politely waited, he wanted the elf to know he was the better duelist. The next blow on either side would surely be fatal, both men without a defense in armor or shield.

The two began again, this time Alfnod was imbued with the agility of Duwel's people and created an unstopping motion of bladed fury. Wedgrud was placed off balance, began to stumble, finally and fell to the floor.

Alfnod seemed ready to finish off his foe but paused, and lifted a spear and rammed it through the bandit's shoulder all the way through the table he had fallen over. Wedgrud continued to smile as Alfnod leaned closer to him and spoke, "I will not kill you, don't move," he said as he dug the spear deeper through Wedgrud's chest, "I have a friend for you to meet." The elf smiled and walked over to Cedric and ran out to the courtyard as they knew their friends needed help. The pair carried the wounded Galdwin to a nearby room and bound his wounds, they knew that he would live long without proper medical treatment for his injuries were deep and bleeding profusely.

The largest of the three separated groups was composed of about seven, with Beorn and Aderyn leading them. They were attempting a final stand in the courtyard as the gate was surrounded by bandits. They had felled many of the villains who gave them chase, but there were simply too many. Cedric and Alfnod were overwhelmed by the bandits nearest them when they reached the courtyard and could not help their friends. It seemed as if Edward would lie unavenged with them to show nothing but the death of more friends for it when suddenly a trumpet of Lorine was heard in the distance.

All the bandits froze in their steps as knighted horseman shattered through the bandits near the gate, the men in chainmail atop noble steeds filled the courtyard as they put each bandit to the sword. Along the sides of their horses, many banners of lesser noble houses waved proudly, symbols of lions and bulls were the most common among them. The only similarity between each knight was the shield, the image of a red painted falcon diving as if about to strike.

The bandits were made quick work by these heroic border protectors, and soon their leader dismounted to speak with Cedric. The knight's leader had long flowing brown hair, and he dripped of duty and honor. His chainmail was covered by a thick cloak of gilded flowers and three majestic lions in a column formation, at his hip was a short pilum, which served as his symbol of authority. His sight brought a sigh of relief from the villagers and a smile to Cedric and Alfnod.

It was none other than Lafayette de Sailes, Knight-Commander of Wulfstan. He was surprised and happy to see his friends this distance from home, and he embraced the pair standing by the keep. He spoke, "my dearest friends, what brings you all the way to Arazor, what news from Orford eh?"

Cedric mood was quickly changed to sorrow. "We were hunting down the bandits who killed Edward, they killed him and burned the village for a godsdamnn book."

Lafayette was deeply saddened by this news. "I am sorry for this tragedy, my men and I were hoping to catch these bandits off balance today...lucky we chose today to strike. Your party will find itself most welcome in our ranks, as we now head back to Wulfstan to give the king a full report of this incident." Cedric nodded silently, and the knight began to return to their camp, leaving Cedric's party to gather and burn their dead.

Alfnod returned alone to the feasting hall, where Wedgrud still sat with a spear through his side. "Nothing you do to me can break me you know, you came all this way for revenge, but you won't get it, ha." Wedgrud laughed as he coughed up blood.

Alfnod smiled with his arms cross, resting on the doorway he spoke. "I know, that's why the revenge isn't for me…it's for him."

Alfnod turned the corner and left as a massive man in a loose leather mask came into the hall with a noose and some feet of rope. Wedgrud's smile quickly vanished from his face, and he struggled to free himself as Beorn approached. It was his eyes that terrified Wedgrud, they gave the illusion that whoever under that mask was not human. Wedgrud screamed as the giant pulled him by his hair out of the courtyard and into the forest.

The rest of Cedric's group burned the bodies of Orford's people who died in the fighting, now only a few villagers remained amongst the living. They waited patiently as they heard Wedgrud's screamed become a muffled choking. And a few minutes later, Beorn marched out of the forest, noose, and mask in hand.

In the days when the neighboring kingdom of Ritter was in a terrible civil war, Beorn was called upon to serve in the army as a mercenary, a gift from the now deceased King Oswald. His lord was too young to command, so he was placed on patrol along the border, protecting the small hamlets of eastern Lorine. For weeks, he quietly kept the watch over a small village just along the Lahyrst riverbank.

One day, a group of severely wounded soldiers loyal to the king of Ritter passed through. The village offered them food and board, as it was their tradition for hospitality to all guests of the land. They were a friendly lot, though beaten badly they talked proudly of their cause, the protection of Ritter from the rebels who would seek to divide the land. Beorn made friends with the captain of the brigade, a man named Olaf, a plump war vet who had seen his shares of wars equal to that of meals.

The next day, as the soldiers rested and made plans to reunite with the main crown army, rebels under the command of Lord Aldus rode into the village, demanding the immediate handing over of the soldiers as prisoners. To do this would be a breach of the most sacred traditions and values of Ritter, and so the villagers refused. Lord Aldus drew his blade upon the village's elder, Virmund, and killed the wise old man. Next, his rebels executed the entire loyalist group, including Olaf. Beorn was only kept safe by the cleverness of a thin and pale woman, Hilde, who hid him in the floorboards of her hut. When the rebels had gone, Beorn personally burned the bodies of his former comrades and the village elder. Without saying a word to any who remained, he donned a flimsy mask, some lengths of rope and his axe, and set out after the company of Lord Aldus.

The rebels made merry at their victory of the crown that day, and their ale and food poured like water upon a river in their camp that night. Each was exhausted from the merriment and fell into a deep sleep. While they slept, Beorn took each of them at a time to the nearby trees and hung them. When the morning had come, the trees along the western border of Ritter became the stuff of nightmare. It was on this day that the rebel army was turned back from its attempted assault on the city of Ossen, their commander appeared like a pale ghost at the sight of tree upon tree along the road with the hanging corpses of his comrades. The rebels proclaimed that the loyalist had demons on their side, for only one such as them could commit such a deed.

Beorn returned to the village and lived with Hilde for many months before returning with her to Orford. He shall entreat those who ask about his past, though he never mentions it of his own accord.

Chapter 9
The Road to Wulfstan

Cedric rode alongside Lafayette and his Knight-Commander who introduced himself as Esmond. They traveled along the main road to Wulfstan which served as a pleasant change of scenery from the thick forests of the south. This road was built upon a rolling set of hills filled only by grass, with trees along the road serving as cooling shade rather than blockers of the sun.

The knights that accompanied them were very peculiar. Unlike most other knights, they were made up of lesser nobles and wealthy townsfolk, many of which had no claim to the chivalric code. They acted in complete accordance with their oath, appearing as if out of a fairy tale. Cedric was confused by this display and asked. "Master Esmond, what order do your knight owe their allegiance to? The bird on the shields has peaked my interest." "We are the order of the Red Gyrfalcon, a majestic creature she is. We have our castle not far north of here. Though we may not be as well landed or known as the other orders, we pride ourselves on our code of honor and bravery in combat." The old man laughed as he responded, clearly he had had to explain his order's existence on more than one occasion.

Eadwine poured water from a wet rag upon the head of Galdwin. His face grew paler with each passing hour. The healers amongst the knight's retinue had done all they could for the boy, and now his fate was known only by the gods. He laid limp upon the back of Eadwine's steed, not speaking for quite some time. When he did gather the strength for words, they came out as muffled grunts, almost as if the horses cantering was blowing the breath of life from his body.

The two parties came to rest along the edge of the road and built a giant bonfire. The knights and Lafayette drank and celebrated their victory over the bandits, while Cedric's party remained in a soberer state. Eadwine poured out his cup of wine. "To our fallen brothers." The elf said. The rest of the group from Orford followed suit. As Cedric remembered his dear friends now lost, he pulled out the Hamund's reserve, opened the top, and poured it out as an offering. The final drink of the late brewmaster would never be tasted by man, for no one deserved the alcohol fit for the table of the gods. After this was done, Aderyn and Eadwine went to watch over Galdwin, his condition had finally stabilized, and the bleeding had slowed, but there was still no telling if he would survive. He was fast asleep, his body appeared like a ghost from the loss of blood, but he was well fed before he entered his rest and it would undoubtedly aid in his recovery.

Alfnod and Cedric sat alone, the rest of their company was fast asleep from the exhausting events of the day. "Alfnod, that story Eadwine told of the Lighthouse, I think it is related to Orford's burning." Alfnod's curiosity was peaked, and he listened attentively. "I believe I saw Azrael in my dream, the one just before the raid on Orford. He was stabbing a tree. I know it was Azrael as he wore a crown of ten fingers. If I am correct in my thinking, Edward's stolen book is in some way related to this. The figure we saw leaving with the book was heading on the road towards Orford. If luck is on our side, his destination will match ours."

Cedric concluded his thoughts and Alfnod raised his voice in agreement. "Ay, there is no doubt in my mind these visions are some warning, with the help of King Oswine, we'll uncover their true meaning. But for now, we must rest, for if this is in some way related to that vile Azrael, we will need all our strength. I have a few ideas on that in fact, but they will only be put into action once we reach Wulfstan. I have a large complex of contacts throughout the southern lands from my adventures, many of whom owe me favors, but again we shall see," the elf said as he rolled onto his back preparing for sleep.

Cedric, at last, fell into a deep sleep, the day's troubles had ended but tomorrow would no doubt bring more turns down the path he took. Again Cedric was confronted by the image of the lake this time returned to its original shades of blue. Here he saw his friends and the villagers who had fallen in battle, each laying by the glowing tree, though their bodies were cold and dead they appeared peaceful. There was no sound of rustling tree or songbird. It was completely quiet. Next to Cedric, there was what seemed to be a white ram. It grazed without a care in the field. A slight sound came from the lake.

On the surface of the water, a small stream of bubbles was flowing. A withered, skeletal-like body emerged from the water, it was Azrael, and though he did not wear his crown, his flesh was the same as before. Suddenly, the whole of the lake turned to a red boil and was alight. Azrael no longer appeared as a rotting corpse but as a powerful warlord.

From all sides of the forest's clearing, hooded figures emerged wielding daggers and blades. They approached the ram and yet the wild animal gave no sign of fear or even a hint of the presence of its enemies. Suddenly the ram screamed as the servants of Azrael stabbed and pierced its white flesh. Cedric awoke sweating and panting from his dream, the cry of the animal was carved into his ears and continued for what seemed like an eternity. Cedric stood watch for the rest of the night, unable to sleep.

When the rest of the party had awoken, and made ready to travel, Cedric went over to wake Galdwin.

"Galdwin, come now just one more day of travel, and we'll have you in an apothecary good as new," Cedric said as he rubbed his friend's back and jostled him. But Galdwin did not move, his body was stiff and felt cold through the blanket. Cedric pulled at Galdwin's shoulder and recoiled in grief at what he saw.

Galdwin had passed in the night. His wounds proved stronger than his will to live and his face had been made pale and lifeless. Cedric collapsed to his knees and cried out in pain as his other companions came before him and wept alongside the noble. Beorn lifted Galdwin's body without saying a word, he simply hung his head lay and began gathering stones for a burial ceremony. Alfnod and Aderyn prepared a pile of dry grass and sticks and laid them beneath Galdwin's body. Cedric sat by his deceased friend, unable to muster the strength for any activity.

As the sun reach higher in the sky, the ceremony began. Eadwine began to strum his bardic lute and hummed a low pitched burial song. Galdwin's body had been placed in a stone furnace, with some stones left out as to let the air flow from the fire. Each knight in Lafayette's party held their heads low and their helmets in their hands.

Cedric took a torch and lit the wood resting beneath the deceased. His body burned and crackled from the heat of his stone tomb. By Alfnod's word, it appeared as if they could see his soul leaving and dancing with the smoke towards the sky. None left their spots until the last of their dear companion had become ash. As the final step in the ritual, Cedric took a handful of the still hot ash and sprinkled it in the wind, reuniting Galdwin with the earth that produced him.

Chapter 10
Wulfstan and the Ram

At the early afternoon of the day, the company finally reached their destination of Wulfstan. The largest city of the North, it was once an elvish city in the days of Rohiel when these lands were known as Glanfech. Practically built on top of the elvish ruins, the city of men was dominated by bold stone architecture, with townhouses of carved wood and elegant glass imported from Essaroth.

The walls were a stretch of heavy mortar and stone, with guard towers placed evenly across the whole of the structure. At each tower, a great banner flew in the wind, the banner of the Ram. The Ram was the household animal of King Oswine, and it had served the city as its guardian upon the wall for many generations.

Beyond the main walls of the city, the port and ship markets bolstered with activity, here a man could find all the goods of the world under one port. In the center of the great city, rested the palace, one of the few exposed buildings of elvish origin, as most had sunk far beneath the ground. The castle was built from a massive stone stretching from the ground to the sky, from which Adalgott carved the laws of man. Along the lower sections of this rock, the estates of the great houses rested snugly, each more majestic and magnanimous than the last. Alongside this walkway of nobility, lay the tomb of Francia, the patron of the vineyard and feasting, who planted the first vineyard in the north by order of the god Domovoi, who guards the hearth and home of all who pour out a portion of their drink as offering to the merry god. This tomb was a great mausoleum, where many other patrons of the gods laid their heads in final slumber. Along the stone front wall, great vines and wine presses were carved from the rock, illustrating the happy and dutiful life of Francia's followers at their various monasteries throughout the land. These monasteries were common as houses of refuge for any weary traveler in the north, where happy song and good food are made available for all who find them.

The port of Wulfstan was a bustling hub of activity. It was the last port in the north until the land of Belfas and served as a major resting place for any weary traveler or merchant. The merchant stalls and market tents were each a plethora of brilliant color, from bright red to royal purple. The docks held many merchant vessels from the far south, hoping to impress their northern kin with their sweet wine and luxury goods.

Along the market streets, the sounds of smithies at their workshops filled the air with rhythmic music. The smiths of Wulfstan, and of the whole north were coveted for their blades, both strong and beautiful, as each appeared as if fit for the side of a king.

Across the cove, stretched deep into the water, the citadel known as Stormwatch could be seen. A massive complex of docks and stone keeps, all connecting to a central tower, Manton's Watch, where the legendary admiral led the defense against the fire ships of Verid, a kingdom known for magic and naval prowess. This historic island now served as the headquarters of the Lorinian Navy, where all orders and movements were relayed. In the days of yore, when Lorine ruled over both Midland and Belfas, the navy would proudly sail up and down the coast, featuring to all the might of the Northern Kingdom. Now many of the ships had been scuttled, and the mariners' forces had been reduced to patrol ships and lightly equipped Birlinn, a style of long ship that acted as both transport and war vessel.

In the recent years of the declining kingdom, the Magi court of Lorine had moved their court and scribes to Manton's Watch, serving as a powerful conduit for magical forces. Now the grandmaster and his disciples study away at the books brought in from trade ships far from the south, uncovering lost knowledge of the material and the ethereal worlds.

Upon King's Street, the largest of the stone laid streets of Wulfstan, a grand spectacle of buildings from different ages rested. From a distance, the songs of the bards could be heard from the great drinking halls, where men came to listen to the tales of yore and drink in revelry with their companions. The biggest of these in the world had its home in Wulfstan, the Hall of Ygbirt, the greatest poet and composer of the Northern Kingdom. He once served as a soldier in Adalgott's army, in the time of his strife against Azrael. In this period, he crafted words like that of the elven smiths and their silver steel, each composition forged as beautiful as the shining light of the stars.

The many townhouses build in Adalgott's time remained intact, their glass windows reflecting the candles burning within. The taverns still proved spacious and warm, with songs of happy days caught by the ears of all which passed. It took a trained eye to uncover what ailed the city. It was in the strained and restless patrols of the guardsmen which gave the first hint of trouble. The guards had been long overworked, their legs like brittle twigs supporting layers of chainmail and plated steel.

In the alleys of the city, strange symbols were surrounded by mages and guards alike, and each was baffled by what they saw. The language of the markings was archaic and dead, none knew, and none dared to speak it. The constable of Wulfstan was a man named, Olaf, his forces were pressed thin against forces they did not understand. A true master of the law, Olaf was responsible for the upkeep of civility within the city, ensuring that the dark forces brewing beneath the surface remained from the public's eye, as there would be panic and disorder in that ordeal.

The company and Lafayette split with the knights at the steps towards the palace, their work was concluded, and they yearned to return to their castle to the south. Lafayette bid them a hearty farewell, though they were headstrong and rather foolish, Lafayette had never commanded a more honorable lot of men in all his days as First Marshall of Lorine. "Fate would be kind to cross our paths with theirs once more, they made for excellent company and proved themselves skilled in combat," Cedric said as his party watched the knights' ride across the cobbled streets of Wulfstan.

A servant of the king, adorned in the traditional garb of the north, a long tan cloak covering a purple tunic, the color of nobility. They were led into the main hall of the castle, where many emissaries from a variety of nations stood in council with the king. Behind the whole host of the nobles and the throne stood Adalgott's Stone, where the laws of the Northern Kingdom were first put into writing by the warrior king himself. The chamber itself had lines of columns on each side, elvish in design.

King Oswine had ruled since the time of his youth, unlike many of his predecessors. Since the beginning of his rule, the Age of Small Kings had officially ended. It was the period where the kings of Lorine ruled for short times, never even passing five years before death or mutiny overtook them. The fifth king before Oswine, Edmund, was found dead only the morning after his coronation, from over-consumption of unmixed wine, which had choked him in his sleep. Edmund's son, Ross, was only five when he took the throne, and his first kingly winter brought fever which left him in the grave come spring. Oswine served as a stabilizing factor for the king weary nation, a symbol of strength and consistency.

The guards snapped to attention as Lafayette and Cedric entered the hall. The guardsmen sported heavy chainmail which reached down to their legs, along with a thick belt with golden buckle, and long purple cloaks which were draped over their shoulders. They wielded spears in hand, and blades at their sides, though they bore no shields.

On all sides of the king's court, the landed nobles and merchants of the kingdom presented themselves as the Witan, or council, to the king. The noblest and most influential amongst them was Arrington of Lahyrst, a powerful family known for military might and wealth in the lands of Lorine. Upon their ancient castles and cities, they placed their banners proudly waving the Red Fox of Lahyrst. Their chief among them was William Arrington, the house's great patriarch, and political animal. He was Chancellor of the kingdom and had brought a sense of stable order to the nation's political systems. The other thanes and nobles had long since submitted to the power of the Arrington clan, and their might overshadowed all.

He was an older man, William, but still had a fire of ambition in his eyes, and many assumed his sired heirs would inherit the throne. House Deering was also present for this assembly, their thane, Egbert, Treasurer to the King. He was a plump and near rotund man, with a thick and heavy beard, with many specks of food and wine still present from his latest meal. Many would expect this tax collector to be a cruel and greedy man when he was quite agreeable. With his heavy weight came a certain jolliness and he was known throughout the land for taking the tax of only what was owed.

Next to those powerful men was none other than Lafayette, the youngest amongst the king's royal officers. In only a few years' time, he graduated from the military school at Wulfstan and risen through the ranks from squire to First Marshall. His tale was one derived from the purest spirit of ambition. Born as a bastard to a Wulfstanian whore, Bianca, he was the unwanted offspring of an unknown noble. Bianca was an intelligent woman and knew the trials her child would face if unprepared, and so she only accepted payment in the form of knowledge. The upper-class customers of her would bring piles of books for the young Lafayette, and eventually, he proved himself as learned as the wisest of the magi grandmasters. Lafayette had now changed his appearance to one that of a courtly noble. His hair was smooth and silky, his clothes made of the finest cloth, and his accent was like that of a southern bard. Lafayette still feels the burden of his birth, often seen in the poorest corner of Wulfstan, giving gold and fine foods to a poor old woman.

Foreign emissaries and honeyed speakers came from all corners of the world to parlay with the good king, their accents robust and distinguished, carrying the history of their folk with them. From the Elnish lands, the diplomats had come from their spiraling towers and rural landscapes to secure trade rights. These men were from regions just south of Lorine, where fields of grain overcame the scene, and knights sign of fair maidens to be rescued.

Further along the court, Cedric spotted the most foreign men he had ever laid eyes on. Their skin was tanned, kissed by the sun, and their faces were sharp with trimmed beards. They were Tanari, the southern men of Yennen. Some amongst them carried curved blades, they were the darkest skinned amongst their band, and the lighter ones carried straight swords. The Tanaric lands were a mixing pot of culture, for to the north, upon the Arron Plains, the palest amongst them rode as one with a horse. To the south, the men sail upon dormons with hundreds of oars.

Amongst the foreign nobles present, there was Lady Joanne, the Queen of Lusani Elves. She had only recently taken the throne now and was no more than a young adult, but her mind proved older and wiser in political dealings. She wore a long green coat that was covered in the pattern of a great tree, from which the wood elves were born. Her face was narrow but smooth, like that of her kin and she wore her hair in loose blonde fashion. Even for one of the woodland people, she was exceptionally short and appeared like a human child to some.

At either side, two of her Silver Guard stood like stone sentinels in the landscape. Their spears were sharp enough to tear through the toughest of dweor armor, and they wore polished steel helmets without equal. At their breasts, they wore heavy lorica squamata, armor from ancient forges that was composed of small pieces of metal strung into lines. Upon their belts, they wore symbols of their ranks, with five gold belt buckles on each elf's front.

Their queen was giving an authoritative speech on the rights of those who pass through the sacred elven lands. "I am sorry King Oswine, but your people know the ways of the Lusani, all those who march on those hallowed grounds are marked for death by Kyshnael, the huntress, let it be known that our ancient laws shall not change custom for some caravan of goods. My decision on this matter is final, by our gods we wish you well, but in your own territory." The queen turned and marched confidently away, her point made.

Time had strained the relationship between the two fading lands, only three generations ago, Lusani and Lorine found themselves entrenched in brutal war. The King Dechart had led a vast army through the forest of Lusani, attempting to force the woodland creatures into an agreement in which the merchant guilds of Lorine would be given a new land route to Belfas, guaranteeing fortune to be made. Dechart's forces moved without contact for three days, even coming to think that the elves had vanished. On the third day, the forces of men were greeted by a hail of arrows along the road, and the Silver Guard sliced through the chain and leather of the Lorine people like wetted paper.

None of the regulars of the army were ever seen again, the only sign of the war was the gift of Dechart's head upon a pike along the southern edge of Lusani. From that day on the forest has been closed to all the kingdoms of men and only the foolish dare enter. The queen continued this tradition but had loosened some of the punishment. The queen posted guards along the border, warning any who dared to approach of the coming doom, which waylaid many of the foolish merchants of the south and thus avoided political incidents with the outside world. The other nobles of the court were stunned by this display of power by a foreign lady and looked to the king for a response.

King Oswine rubbed his temple with both of his hands, the day's court had brought before him many issues, and it had worn him thin. Without a worded response to the queen he simply waved in hand in subtle agreement, the merchants would no longer trespass with the authority of the guilds. The king was well worn from his many battles, but now he no longer appeared as a bold warrior but as a dead man. His hair was still black, but it had a gray streak on each side of his head. His goatee was refined and curled, a leftover style from his youth in the court of Essaroth. The king wore a great red cloak with a golden pin which had a ram molded into it. His crown was of pure gold, with four pointed tips, beneath each a sapphire rested. The king motioned to his aid and whispered into his ear.

The servant blew a trumpet, and the court was dismissed for the day. Members of the royal houses talked and convened on the political agendas of the days. The merchants of the major guilds stood by a stone pillar, discussing their next economic venture. The king left the court for his gardens, at the roof of the palace.

As the king exited, Cedric was stopped by a babbling knight, who appeared in full mail and coat. At his side, his helm was slung on his belt along with a symbol of a burning sun. His arms were covered in thick padding, less for armor and more style. His head was clean of hair, cut down to near nothingness. His accent was foreign and thick with style heard in the neighboring land of Ritter. "Good sir, I see you too are of noble birth. Then you understand that this is an absolute outrage!" He said as he writhed his hands along his arms in pain.

Cedric was quite amused by this display, and so inquired more. "Truly sir knight you have been wronged, but by what, some noble lady not offering you her handkerchief?" The knight removed his helmet, revealing a grizzled but refined face, which was none too pleased by the jokes at his expense.

"It is an outrage against my order itself, for weeks the Knights of the Eternal Dawn have called upon the aid of Lorine and Belfas." He paused to take a deep breath. "To no avail. Mark these words, it is the end times in the north, and your foolish kings will do not to stop it." The knight hurried off to the outer halls where more of his order was gathered. The Knights of the Eternal Dawn were the last true chivalric order north of Lorine and had stood the test of time for many years but now seemed like an ancient relic of a long forgotten past.

They were formed from the descendants of Adalgott's companions. They were blessed by the priests of Cinder and given the sacred duty to defend the north from the return of Azrael. They have long waited for the day when the Seer, the heir to Adalgott's Kingdom, reveals himself and take his place as the rightful ruler of the north. Their chivalric castles dot the landscape of Belfas and Midland, each a token of favor for the heads of this order. Their central citadel is located along the cold and biting coast of Midland. Zweleran, the oldest functioning castle of man, built long before the knights were founded, it was the site where Cinder revealed himself in the form of a dawning sun. It was a massive complex of fortresses, halls, and towers, all defended by Theodric's Wall. A spanning wall, with a rushing moat of water, stretching from one side of the Vaalian Sea.

Cedric's party was offered a meal alongside the commoners who appeared at the court while the noble himself was given orders to meet with the king privately. Led along many spiraling staircases, Cedric arrived at the roof, where the greenery of the garden was a welcome sight compared to the stone structure of the palace. The king sat on a bench next to a series of statues dedicated to the elven gods, where the vines gracefully entwined upon the ancient carved stone. Between two of these statues were piles of slightly raised grass, with a stone marker above each, which made it the king's favorite spot to spend his evenings. Oswine was delicately trimming a rose bush as Cedric approach, and the old man offered him a seat next to him.

"This is all the kingdom I could ask for Cedric." The old man said as he smiled a genuine and gentle grin. "I heard of Orford's fate, and I'll have you know I'll give your people warm shelter and good food while they stay within the city walls. I suppose you'll be the one to return with them, rebuild that peaceful little spot." Oswine began to reminisce with the young man. "I remember when you and my lads would go running through these halls, such a gift it was to hear you all laughing as your feet clicked away at the stone beneath you." The old man paused in his story, looking towards the stone markers and sighed heavily, in which Cedric took the time to respond.

"Those were happy days my lord, but we have to move forward with our lives," said Cedric.

Oswine gave an annoyed humph. "You say that, and yet you desire nothing but to go backward," Oswine said as his noble helped him to his feet. "We cannot all live in our garden forever Cedric. I remain as the king of Lorine, not some herbalist. And while you continue as a lord of a village, for now, you cannot always remain as it. I shall give you more time, but know that no one who accepts this position should do it willingly. It is the wise king who fears the power of his crown." Oswine, trimmed a red flowered plant with tiny tweezers as Cedric gave his leave, the lord of Orford had no mind to speak further on the matter.

For so long in Cedric's life, they had been like father and son. While Albert fought in the Green Mountains, Cedric was taken care of by his dear friend King Oswine. At the court in Wulfstan, Cedric was groomed and trained as a son of the king, some even reporting Cedric as his bastard son from the confusing state of the boy. The king's two sons found themselves a faithful companion in Cedric, and the three became quite the nuisance in the castle kitchen.

Owen was the older of the two and built much stronger than his pale younger brother, Waldo. Even though this inheritor son proved the better in combat and strength, he never once laid his hands on his brother, for he was a kind and gentle soul, some called him Owen the Gentle Giant. Waldo was far skinnier and paler than his two compatriots, and he was often found sick in his bed. It was at the age of twelve, that Waldo succumbed to a severe fever, thus creating the first stone marker in the garden. Oswine was seen in black clothing for months, and he wept by his son's grave each time he visited the garden.

It was only three summers ago, that Owen was laid next to his brother, a rogue arrow from a Lorinian archer accidentally found its place in the Gentle Giant's chest during a battle with Emford, a small kingdom to the southwest. As Owen lay mortally wounded on the battlefield, the archer was brought before him, about to be executed, it was a man no older than he, his eyes terrified and he sobbed for mercy.

Owen was confused by his soldiers' actions. "Let no more people die of mere accidents this day, he has done no wrong to me in his actions, let him be guiltless in this course." The prince spoke, raising his hands to the sky as his heart stopped. His army wept greatly for him, there had never been a kinder or braver man amongst them, as he shared the pains and troubles of battle with his men as any common foot soldier. The loss of his last son appeared not even to phase the poor king. He did not weep for he had not the will to mourn another son. Now the last vestment of parental guidance fell on the shoulders of Cedric, an educated youth who had training in both administration and warfare was greatly sought after by the king.

Cedric left the roof of the palace feeling dismayed, as he had scorned one who cared deeply for him, for his selfish desire for freedom. It was in the hearts of the men of Lorine to want both power and liberty, and Cedric did not know which would be his path. He wandered the halls searching for answers, yet he found none. It was growing late in the evening and Cedric retired to the chambers he and his fellow companions had been given. Beorn and the other villagers had returned to the refugees of Orford, where he found his wife and unborn child safe.

The rest of his company, Alfnod, Eadwine, and Aderyn remained in the palace as guests of the king. Aderyn relaxed by the fire of the ornate chamber as Alfnod and Eadwine sat by the table. Eadwine was feasting on the exquisite delicacies the palace produced for its guests. The food of the festival of Orford paled in comparison to the meals of the palace, where each piece of meat or bread appeared as if dipped in golden delight. The elf was overwhelmed by the wines he was given access to, many of which were now disposed of as empty bottles rattling upon the floor. He was nodding his head in a rhythmic fashion, made tired and cumbersome by his eating and drinking throughout the night.

Alfnod was composed and sober in his seat, reading from the works of a historian and his journals on the demonic lords and their powers. Cedric sat next to Alfnod and began reading along on the chapters discussing the influence of Crassus Baal on the world of men. It contained many sketches and descriptions of the trickster lord, often appearing as a refined noble in gaudy colored clothes. Other described him as a massless cloud, but still, others describe a great commander, adorned in golden and black armor, riding atop an enormous dragon. There was, however, no information on Edward's tome. Alfnod grew impatient with each fruitless page stroke, his quest for insight into the plans of the demon failing. Tomorrow they would speak to the king, and explain these visions of Cedric, and the two hoped that this warning would come in time for the next prophetic fulfillment.

Chapter 11
The Secrets of the Palace

Cedric laid for hours in his bed, unable to sleep. "Cedric, are you still awake?" Aderyn called out in a faint whisper as she too lay in her bed unable to find rest. "Yes, here, why don't we go for a walk in the palace grounds? I can show you what I remember." Cedric said as the pair snuck from their chamber, taking caution not to stir their companions. The two walked along an outer hall, where the stone archways were alight from the flames of the torches and light of the stars and moon. Along this walkway, the great banners of the noble houses gently swayed in the cool summer's breeze.

Cedric awkwardly tried to break the silence. "I'm glad you're with me, I feel as though this journey will not stop with our stay in Wulfstan. I just hope we have enough time to set things right again." Cedric peered out into the night sky, spotting the many stacks of chimney smoke dancing with the wind, and hearing the drunken songs of the people in the taverns below.

"How does it feel being back here?" Aderyn asked as Cedric broke from his gazing.

"It's strange, I thought I would never return to this city, and certainly not like this. Oswine's already dogging me for the heir; I can't do it. Why does he want me? I've done nothing all my life, and suddenly he just wants me crowned king? And the other nobles would have a festival arranged for the day they organize a moot to remove me from power. I would not receive support from any of the top members of the Witan, save Lafayette. Tell me, Aderyn, why does he choose me?" Aderyn took Cedric by the hands, and the two stared into each other's eyes as she spoke to comfort the distressed noble. "It is because he sees in you what I see in you, what your friends see in you, you are a good man Cedric that is a title given more rarely than that of a king." Cedric felt comfort in the words of Aderyn and the two held to their feelings and each other as they watched the moon's journey across the sky. Cedric suddenly got an idea of something long ago from his childhood. "Aderyn, come with me, I have a pleasant surprise for you," the noble said as he pulled Aderyn into the grand hallways of the palace and began rubbing his arms and hands along the smooth and familiar wall.

"I suppose all this talk of kings has made you mad?" Aderyn smirked as she stood with her arms folded, unimpressed by Cedric.

"Well, it may not look like much right now." The noble said, his arms still searching for a place he once remembered. He smiled with glee as he felt the rough outline of a stone square and a click that followed. "But not everything is as it appears to be."

The two had rediscovered one of Cedric's favorite

childhood play places, the secrets passages of the palace. They took one of the burning torches from the hall and began their descent into the hidden walkways of the palace. It was not damp or jagged like that of the cave systems of other great keeps, but rather smooth carved stone, with many vaulted ceilings and collapsed doorways, signs of the ancient elven city that once lay here.

Along the smooth walls, magnificent mosaics depicted the ancient elven tales and rulers of these lands. Images of garden festivals and great bathhouses were the most common. Cedric's favorite from his youth was that of Prince Dothriel, the elven clad in a shining steel helmet with a green cloak as his chief body armor. His tale was one of deception and cleverness. In his time, his people were few and Thyrs scattered the lands in hunting parties, killing or taking prisoner any elf they came upon. And so, Dothriel went alone into the forest and laid a trap for Mushag, the most fearsome war chief of the Thyrs. Upon the war party's entry to the woods, the elven archer unleashed volley after volley of arrows, and retreat as the Thyrs approached them, refusing to face them in open combat. This continued for hours until the Thyrs were finally withered down and fled the forest like wild beasts, screaming of the ghosts of the forest stalking them.

They stopped at the end of this long and narrow hallway, to a depiction of the tale of Kendrick and Lady Juliana. Kendrick was a renowned warrior of the Belfan lands, known for his chivalric code of honor in which he spared all who surrendered to him, and for that, his people loved and admired him. Juliana was the great Lady of the Lusani elves, known far and wide as the wisest and most beautiful of all the elves. With his falcon, Kendrick sent letters between the two lovers, of the warmth of the sun and his love for the lady. In his final letter, Kendrick wrote of his illness; he was afflicted directly by Beelzus, the demoness of diseases and famine, for the bitter maiden of foul plagues had grown jealous of the love between the two mortals. When he attempted to eat, his food turned to ash in his mouth, water became like acid salt and could not sustain him. When he wanted to rest, the sound of one thousand marching men rang in his head. Juliana rode to the aid of the one she loved, and found him withered and cold, but still alive. For days, she wept with his head in her lap, praying to the gods for aid. Finally, Loden the Traveler, appeared before her and presented her with a gift of a small flask. With this vial, Loden commanded the fair maiden to find the Hidden Lake, where all life that requires water is born, for only there could the cure for Kendrick's pestilence be found. Taking the flask, Juliana healed Kendrick, who regained his strength three-fold. Upon the wall of the hidden hallway, the mosaic depicted the two lovers standing beneath ancient elven ruins, overcome with moss and vines, with Juliana still holding the flask at her hip.

Cedric and Aderyn held their hands in front of this old image of the golden days of Glanfech and silently vowed themselves to one another. As the torchlight flickered and diminished, they made their way back to the palace, their secret between only the two of them.

Chapter 12
Wizards and Their Towers

Cedric and his company rested well in the palace that night; no dreams haunted the poor noble on this moon for he did not sleep for long. His companions were still asleep when he and Alfnod were summoned to speak before the king at dawn. They were led again to the great hall of the king, where Adalgott's Stone lay. The king appeared from a rear door, and all in the court graciously bowed as he took his place on the throne, thus bringing the day's politics and squabbles to his attention. "We shall begin with the situation regarding the village of Orford."

He boomed as his scribes began translating his words to the paper on their desks nearby. One of these scribes was, in fact, a magi, wizards in service of a royal court. His name was Gaspar, an apprentice to the Grandmaster of Magi, sent as a gifted scholar to the king. His appearance was like that of an alert owl, his eyes were opened wide, and he tried to focus on everything in sight. He appeared neurotic as he scurried through the hall, collecting books and writing down their insights. He and these other magi were here as a trading vessel from Tanari had brought many texts and works on ancient philosophers and technologies and the king had ordered they be transcribed in the palace library.

The king began. "The people of Orford shall be the full pleasures as my subjects done unto them, they shall be given safe shelter and warm food within our cities walls. In the market district, there are many vacant insulae, from the time of Nacian influence in our lands. I decree that these be given, without taxation to the people of Orford, until the supplies have been gathered to ensure a safe and hastened rebuilding and recolonization of their currently destroyed village. On this matter, our Chancellor, Lord William, shall oversee the issuing of my commands. There shall be no debate on this issue further, but we now come to the second ordeal to arrive from the sacking of Orford. I have been informed by the village's lord, Cedric that this destruction was for told of by way of a prophetic dream. He shall be given the attention of the court, and the magi present shall mark his word."

Cedric approached the center of the throne room and stood upon which a small wooden platform gave him height so that all in the court could see and hear him. "It was for many weeks that I was plagued with visions of a burning lake with a glowing white tree too consumed by flames. It was here that I now realize that this was a warning for what was to come to Orford, that it was a vision of ill events to come. On the night of the massacre, the vision was at its clearest, and beyond the glowing tree, I saw a withered corpse with a crown of ten fingers, I saw Azrael."

The people of the court gasped and whispered, and Gaspar

slammed his book onto his table, leaning as forward as his posture allowed, beads of sweat began forming on his forehead as Cedric continued. "If this vision is to be taken as the prophetic truth, then the image that came in the journey to Wulfstan must be taken as a grim warning. I saw this lake and tree once more but witnessed the mutilating murder of a milky white ram, stabbed and gutted by many hooded figures. I believe this to be a warning that Azrael means to strike against Lorine." Again, there was a great shock amongst the crowd, while the Witan tried to remain calm. The king sat, unmoved by this speech in his appearance. "We shall give a full investigation into this matter, rest easy Cedric, I recommend you speak to one of our magi regarding this matter, they shall help to understand these visions." Oswine motioned with a single finger for a magi to come forward, to which Gaspar immediately responded, practically jumping over his small table as he stumbled towards Cedric and bowed.

The court began its long chain of daily duties as an erratic Gaspar led Cedric through the palace library, the wizard, rambling as they went. "You have no idea what this means! By Wodan, this is significant in the very meaning of the word. I have studied the demonic lords and their servants for many years but never in my life expected something like this in my lifetime." Cedric struggled to keep up with the wizard, who ran through row after row of books, collecting handfuls of tomes on Crassus Baal as he went.

Finally, they arrived at a wooden alcove and began scrolling through the many books as Gaspar explained to the best of his ability the full situation of Cedric's visions.

"In the time of Adalgott's victory over Azrael, the gods knew he would return for our king did not wholly slay him.

They devised a plan, to send one who would be greater than that of the first unified king of man, to destroy the false one and his minions. This man would be known as The Seer, one who could gaze at the gods and be aware of their world as our own. You say you saw a lake with a glowing tree at the epicenter?"

Cedric nodded, his mind spinning from this new information. "That is the Tree of Life, the domain of the gods. You are The Seer; this means only one thing. Azrael has begun his return; already his minions make ready his way. You've seen it in our world, across every street in Wulfstan there is a mark of the demon lord Crassus Baal, markers that his domain is fast approaching. We believe this is being done by a man we call the Magus; he is well versed in dark magic, we will need to be cautious,"

Cedric stopped the wizard and began to speak for himself. "Along my route to Arazor, we found a strung-up corpse of a deer, used in some sort of ritual..." The wizard immediately returned his voice to the conversation. "Yes, another sign of Azrael's rising power, we must be quick with our counter to the dark lords, there is no telling what their plans are, and who can be trusted. I have much to research, chiefly, how we would slay this monstrosity if, gods forbid, he manages to return. We must meet later; I trust you'll be busy with your affairs." Gaspar said as he pointed to the door of the library, where a guard waited to deliver a message to Cedric. By the time Cedric had turned around to say farewell to the wizard, Gaspar was rounding the corner of the library with the speed of a bird, carrying a mass of scrolls and texts along with him.

In the days before the Ten Kingdoms of the north, the magi ruled with the power of kings. Their harnessing of the strength of the gods served as both blessing and curse, for any power, no matter how good of intention, can have dire consequences.

The guard waited on Cedric at the door and sent word that Lafayette had requested his presence in his private chambers. Led along a long and narrow hallway, Cedric had arrived at the portion of the palace dedicated to the commanders and political figures residing at the castle. They were smaller rooms compared to the noble houses of Lorine but did not lack in amenities and decadence. Lafayette rested by a roaring fire in his study, along the walls and floors, vibrant and colorful rugs from the far south decorated his room. Upon his lap, he read from The Parmacathen, the first book his mother had ever received as payment. On each page were detailed inscriptions and images of proper combat techniques, from the grip on certain blades to the best form. Lafayette had read from this and many other books on the codes of chivalry all his life, and they guided his journey to First Marshall of Lorine.

"Good that we can finally speak privately Cedric, it has been far too long." Lafayette said as the two shook hands and poured glasses of ale. They reclined in the cushioned chairs of the study and drank freely, reminiscing about their days together at the royal court.

"What do you think of this terrible mess Lafayette? How can we even begin to comprehend what powers are at play here?" Cedric said as he gazed into the fireplace, his eyes consumed by the image of the burning wood.

Lafayette thought for a long time before answering. "We must take it as it comes, if we fail here, it will spell disaster for the whole of the world." Lafayette leaned forward and gave Cedric the most important piece of advice he could think of.

"Trust only those you know, to be honest, Azrael is one for trickery, and I would not doubt his servants infest this city. That wizard, Gaspar, he's an odd fellow that is known to all, humph, wizards and their towers, but I suppose he can be relied on. I must ask, how are you holding up?"

"It seems as though there is nothing to hope for. First Orford, now this talk of demons and kings, it is more than one man can handle. But that is why I can handle it, I'm not alone in this." Cedric hopped up and hoped to ease the tension of the situation. "How could we possibly lose with the illustrious Lafayette de Sailes, the First Marshall of Lorine, the lover of every maiden, the drinker of every wine? By the gods, we'll starve Azrael, his minions will realize what a party it is on our side and simply surrender."

The two shared this laugh together as they spent the night drinking, it would be for the last time for many months that merriment and drink would be shared by these two at the palace of Wulfstan.

"Excuse me, my lords." The strange knight from the previous day was at the door, standing at attention. "I would wish to speak with the Seer in private." Lafayette nodded and left the room, taking an extra bottle of wine with him.

The knight kneeled before Cedric, his blade in his hands and the tip stuck on the ground. Though it was rather warm, he still wore his long sleeves, with thick gloves. He spoke words of oath taking and honor. "My lord, forgive my display yesterday, it was rude of me to subject you to such an outburst."

Cedric sat confused. "You are forgiven, it was no concern at all my dear sir…'

The knight raised his hand for Cedric to pause. "My lord I am Amalric, commander of Telfrost Keep and Knight-Sergeant of the Order of the Eternal Dawn. I am bound to your will my lord, by the Oath of the Sword, I swear it." He bowed his head in respect.

"I'm afraid I have no commands for you, Amalric," Cedric said as he sat there stunned by Amalric's display.

Amalric rubbed again at his arms, which clearly were in pain of some sort. "My lord I shall ride to Telfrost, and alert the knights of your appearance. We are sworn to the Seer, and when they hear of you, the Dawn shall finally break across the sea." He turned and rushed out of the room, practically sprinting for the stables.

Lafayette poked his head into the chamber, smiling awkwardly and holding a half-empty bottle of unmixed wine.

Cedric looked around confused and questioned Lafayette. "Err...who exactly was that?"

Lafayette reclaimed his seat and poured another glass for his friend. "That was Amalric of Telfrost, diplomat, knight, philosopher...and a leper." Cedric quickly wiped the smile from his face. "Strange fellow, no doubt about it. Most lepers keep to themselves, but not this one, think he tried to convince himself he isn't one. Instead of being cooped in his hall, wasting away, he took up a wooden sword and began hacking at a straw figure in the courtyard, and hasn't stopped since."

That night in his rest, Cedric was once more haunted by the visions of the Tree of Life, again he heard and saw the killing of the ram. Hooded men defiled the sacred grove of the gods, spilling and spraying the blood of the innocent ram like dew upon the grass. In the grove, a fire burned a list of one thousand names in the charred dirt, and Azrael and his ten-fingered crown stood triumphant over the tree of life. Next came visions of blood upon a great battlefield, with once-proud banners of men, brought low and smeared in ash and dirt. Around Cedric, the grassy field vanished, now the ground was composed of the dead of Lorine. Brave men lay around him, their eyes lifeless with skin as cold as winter's nights. People would look upon these days and say, here stands the end of Lorine.

Chapter 13
The List

The next morning, as the sun greeted the slumbering city, Cedric was awoken to a sharp rasp upon his door. As he looked around the room, he saw that all his companions had already risen, eaten, and gone out. For the first time in many days, Cedric rested well, and the dark circles around his eyes had faded in his sleep. Again, there came a loud knock on the door.

It was none other than Gaspar, looking nervous and frantic as he entered the room before Cedric even had a chance to say good morning. Upon the wizard's back, there was a traveling pack and a wooden staff in his hands, along with a water sack slung on his shoulder. He stood darting a neurotic look at each empty bed as if trying to will that their owners would appear in the room to hear his news.

"We must leave this city, as soon as possible," Gaspar said as he began gathering Cedric's things for him, stacking his sword and other items in the noble's hands. "I stayed in the libraries of Stormwatch for all of the night researching Azrael. There was no mention of where he would arrive from, but there was a constant bit of information found throughout each tome I scrolled through. In each book, the blade of Adalgott, Geanlaecan, is the only blade able to slay Azrael, or at the least send him back to the realm of his master. Normally the magi would have a record of such a powerful artifact, but that was lost to history. When Adalgott grew ripe in age, he left his court by himself and wandered through Midland and possibly all the way to his ancestral home of Belfas, if we are to stop Azrael we will need to find Adalgott's final resting place, where we will most assuredly find Geanlaecan. The book, the one you saw traded at Arazor? It is the Codex Deadhraegl, the book forged by Beelzus, the demon of plague and dark magic. I believe this book holds the secrets to summoning forth Azrael. Now that we know it is in the hands of the Magus, we shall need to find and deal with that wicked necromancer. I have heard rumors of dark magic residing in the Red Marsh, just south of the Knights of the Eternal Dawn in Midland. This shall be a most difficult task, but if we fail the whole of the North shall fall to kneel before Azrael."

Cedric sat down; his mind was racing from the words spoken to him. He sat in silence for some time before speaking. This was not a decision to be made lightly. "If you truly think this is our best path to defeating Azrael, I'll summon those who accompanied me from Orford. I must speak to the king on some important business before we go. We shall meet in the Great Hall when we have gathered all our things." Cedric took a long look at the restless wizard before him. "Try to get some rest before we go."

Cedric entered the garden once more, as the king was taking a midday rest from the weary work of the court. This time he held a glass of wine in his hand and a flower trimmer in the other. "So good of you to come, Cedric, come, keep a poor old man company." Cedric sat next to his former mentor and began to dictate his decision.

"I still do not know if the blood of a king runs through me, but I shall try, for you, and for all who rely on me. But I must tell you now, I will see this task of slaying Azrael to its end. He has taken one friend from me already, and I shall not allow another to fall while my blade can still be held." Cedric kneeled before the king and drew his sword. "By the oaths like that of our ancient codes of knights, I swear to you this, I shall slay Azrael as a man, not as a king."

Oswine slowly reeled backward in his seat, stroking his gray beard. At last, he smiled and told his loyal lord to rise, "you do me a great honor Cedric. Furthermore, you honor your father and these lands. I hope you will have time for the vigil tonight. We cannot forget the Blessing of Cinder, if you decide to leave before then, I shall pray for your safe journey." The old man gave another smile as Cedric hurried off, blessed in his quest to save the whole of the North.

Cedric met his friends, Alfnod, Eadwine, Aderyn, and Beorn at the refugee homes for the people of Orford. Though their journey had been hard and many had felt great sorrow in the past days, they kept high spirits, for they were finally safe within the walls of Wulfstan.

We'll need to head out today. If we can find this blade, we can stop Azrael once he's returned, cut his head off before he can even get it through the door. I know you've all shared in battle with me, but I would not ask this of you if you are unwilling." He stood with his arms crossed, fearing that some would be reluctant to go.

Alfnod approached first. "For Galdwin." He said as he patted Cedric's shoulder and took his place by his side. Aderyn came forward next with a silent nod of approval. Eadwine sat smoking on a pile of boxes and jumped forward with his response. "I suppose we can't go letting yourself get all the credit for this story, and someone needs to be by your side to tell it properly when we get back."

Beorn remained sitting, giving a slight smile as his companions left to gather their things, leaving only him and Cedric present in the room. Cedric responded with his own smile and spoke. "You know I would not ask this of you unless I knew I needed your help. You've got more of a life here than any of the others, I will not hold it against you if you decide to stay." Cedric could tell his friend was at a serious crossroads. "To be honest with you Beorn, I don't know if I would go." Beorn looked at his dear friend, surprised by his bluntness. "But that's why I need you there, why I need all of you there. I cannot do this alone."

Beorn looked down and weighed his options, taking his time before looking his friend in the eyes and giving his response. "It would be wrong to do anything else." He said as he placed his hand on Cedric's shoulder and the two smiled happily. The group made ready, and the path was set, through Midland and Belfas their journey would take them, to uncover the mysterious resting place of Adalgott. As they made their final preparations, Cedric left to speak with the king when a royal guardsman suddenly stopped him at the door.

Cedric approached the guard at the door and was promptly told his presence at the city prison was needed. Gaspar gave an annoyed look but knew the matter had to be of grave importance, so he allowed it. There at the jail, Cedric found Olaf, the constable of Wulfstan, standing anxiously by the entrance to the dungeon while twirling his large set of keys. He was a tall man, with a great yellow beard beneath sunken and serious eyes.

"Thank the gods. We have a matter of urgency here." The man of the law leaned towards Cedric and whispered. "It has been made known to me that there is a plot against the king's life."

Cedric was both surprised and not. He knew that Azrael's growing influence on these lands would have dire consequences, but he expected that he would have more time to prepare. Cedric responded in a grave voice. "How did you come by this information?"

"Follow me," Olaf said as he motioned with his head towards the door to the dungeon. They descended a broad flight of mossy stone steps, entering a darker and deeper part of the prison of Wulfstan. It was a damp and cold place, where it appeared as if a great storm had just doused each stone. At last, they came to a small door surrounded by a full fighting force of guards, all nervously huddled around the door but were quickly snapped into formation as Olaf and Cedric approached. Turning the key while leaving the door closed, Olaf gave a word of warning to the noble. "Don't get too close to him, don't know what game he's playing at."

There in the small dimly light room, a man sat with his feet propped on a wooden table. The only source of light in the chamber was a burning candle on the table, which reflected across the man's pale and grim face which appeared now as a grim reaper or skeleton. His eyes were a shade of green, with dark rings around his sockets. A black cowl covered his hair, and the rest of his outfit consisted of black leather and a thick dark cloak, shadowing much of his body. In his hand, he spun a dagger, well hidden from the guards as he was stripped of his weapons when they searched him. This display did not amuse Olaf. The man sat spinning this stiletto all the while keeping a steady eye on Cedric, who showed no sign of fear in his face. The dark figure was in an intense stare with the noble and had a slight smile showing on only one side of his mouth.

"It is in the nature of men to be afraid." The hooded man spoke, breaking some of the tension that permeated the room.

"I am not afraid of you," Cedric responded quickly, as he took a seat at the table opposite this mysterious figure.

"Everyone is afraid. The trick is being able to conceal it at the proper time, for there's a time for every emotion in this cruel world." The dark clad man leaned forward across the table, practically contacting Cedric's face. "Because right now you should be afraid, not of me, but of what I know.

"And what is it that you know?"

"That someone in this city is going to slay your king."

Cedric and Olaf both looked at each other, unsure of how to proceed with the stranger in front of them. Cedric decided to speak first. "Why don't you start with your name? I'm Cedric Throne."

"I know very well who the both of you are, why do you think I asked specifically for you two? Only ones I either trust or feel aren't too daft to understand the malevolent forces at play here. My name's Leopold, but you know me better as the Butcher of Kruithia, The Shadow of Boleslav, The Terror of Torvir…"

"You're an assassin?" Cedric said, knowing the answer to

his question

Leopold smiled and motioned a salute with his finger. "Here's someone with a little common sense. Aye, I've killed noblemen from the coldest winter of Belfas to the green meadows of Essaroth, but not anymore. Well...not the killing thing...rather, the doing it for a lump of gold."

"But why, tell us, what's your goal here?" Cedric asked.

"We'll leave it at a change of conscience, at least for now. If there are not more stupid questions, we must not waste any more precious time, something your king is running out of. Captain, be a friend and fetch a pen and paper, I shall give my record of events. It began when I was given contract by a messenger that a noble in Wulfstan requested my presence, I was given a note which demanded I met with him at the Grey Swan Inn, a tavern known for its shady and backward dealings. Along with this letter, I was given five hundred gold pieces, payment for simply hearing the contract from my mysterious benefactor. When I arrived, the fool gave me his official house seal, as the form of proof he was a noble, of which I did not care. He presented me with the offer of ten thousand gold pieces in exchange for the life of King Oswine, I was no fool to deny a bloodthirsty noble, and so I agreed and went on my way, with no intention of truly murdering the king. And now gentlemen, we find ourselves here, the minute before the storm strikes." He pulled from his pocket another concealed item, a small pendant, with the symbol of the Red Fox.

Olaf laughed at the sight of this. "You truly are a fool, thinking you can deceive us? Make us believe that house Arrington would dare such diabolical and deplorable act? I shall have the torturer in here momentarily; perhaps he will enjoy your stories more than I."

Cedric grabbed the captain's hand and motioned to hold as he turned to face Leopold, who sat unimpressed by Olaf's choice of action. "Perhaps we should take this matter into a more serious account. If this man claims to be who he is, he has no reason but the one he has stated to turn himself into our prison. If we fail to act now, it could have dire repercussions. Olaf, double the guard on the king, begin patrolling around the palace with every available footman. Leopold and I shall speak more on the matter of the guilty noble." Olaf changed his skeptic tone, and obeyed, calling for the guards at the door to follow him to the palace.

Cedric quickly turned back to his prisoner, who was now smiling. "Where is this noble who ordered you to kill the king?"

"In the city, not far from here. Gather your friends Cedric; we will need all the help we can muster for I fear this night's work has only just begun." The assassin said as he gathered his things from a nearby table, mostly consisting of daggers and poisons.

Cedric collected his companions along with Leopold and met outside the townhouse of the noble. Each of them gave an untrusting look at the newest member of their party, who acted as if he did not see them as he smiled off into the distance.

Leopold spoke, "he's here, hasn't left since the morning, just like I left him. When we enter, don't kill him." He raised an eyebrow at Beorn. "We need him alive, as to unveil the fullness of this conspiracy, for I fear and know this man is not acting alone."

They barged into the small estate; it was a typical Wulfstan design, a two-floored building, with a small inside. The whole of the structure was of carved wood, with a great stone fireplace as its heat, much in akin to the house of Cedric's family. The house smelled of fine roses and roasted meats, as any noble house of Wulfstan. At the dining table, just on the opposite side of the room from the entrance, the noble sat eating his dinner, with half a bite of an exotic meat stuck in his mouth as he froze from the sudden entrance of unwanted guests. He immediately recognized his paid killer and turned a bright red. All his companions stood while Cedric took a seat at the table opposite to the benefactor of Leopold.

"I suppose you'll want us to leave you with your meal, no worries this will not take much time," Cedric said, offering a friendly smile as he loosened a dagger hidden in his boot, it was unseen to the nervous man in front of him due to the table.

The man attempted to smile but could not as he was so struck with fear as his sweat dripped onto the wood of the table. "I…I assure you everything is in order here… Who are you?"

"My associates and I are merely trying to understand some things; this doesn't have to get hostile…" Cedric said this as the man attempted to leap across the table for his kitchen knife currently lodged in a roasted piece of meat that appeared like beef. Cedric quickly raised his hidden dagger and pinned the man's left hand to the table with the sharp blade. He screamed in agony as Cedric left the table, allowing Leopold, who was still smiling, to sit.

"You aren't in command of this little coup; it's obvious that you have not the resources for such a feat. Why don't you tell us who your master is, let this go nice and smooth, perhaps the headsman won't even execute you." Leopold spoke, he twirled and folded his hands on the table as he spoke.

The pinned noble's face turned red with pure hate, gone was his nervous disposition and in its place, a primordial rage of a rat backed into a corner. "Hail Crassus!" He said as he once more leaped across the table, this time at Leopold's throat. Alfnod gutted the noble as he and Leopold slid across the table and he was dead before even reaching the ground. Leopold sat gasping at his neck as the rest of the party began looking for any evidence of Cult of Crassus Baal. Behind an ornamental table, a small wooden switch was carved into the wall, and as Cedric pressed on it, the wall gave way, revealing a hidden basement.

Cedric felt a rush of cold and stale air as he descended the steps with his companions. At the end of their march, they discovered a room, filled with all manner of things dedicated to the demon lord Crassus Baal. Upon the walls, foul Banners of the Rat, a commoner's identification of the Lord of Tricks, were strung up. On a center table, a poor beggar's corpse had been severely mutilated; his bones had been ripped from his body and placed in a basket, while his prime slices of meat had been removed.

Cedric felt vomit in his mouth at this sight. Gaspar cried out, "By the gods, it was not a roasting beef we smelled and savored!"

Aderyn and Eadwine walked over to a strange obelisk, where magical runes had been carved many millennia ago, before the time when the races of Man, Elf, and Thyrs walked upon the land.

Cedric found a most peculiar parchment on the same table that housed the dead man; it was of a fine grade with names carefully written in a blooded ink pen. Upon it, a great list of officers and lords of Lorine were etched, *Oswine, Egbert, Lafayette*…the list continued, striking its vile hate against all those most valuable to the survival of the kingdom. Cedric saw one name missing from the list, one who would be more valuable than any other leader on the list save the king. "Why is William Arrington not on this list? Why would they save him from this hated scribbling?"

Leopold spoke, confirming the forming thought in Cedric's mind. "A benefactor to orchestrate an operation like this, it makes sense that someone with that much authority is behind it. If these men die, only House Arrington would be left in power, ha, Crassus Baal loves making his little deals. If this is true we must act quickly, focus on saving these on the list. I shall hasten to the homes of Arrington, and make them feel swift retribution like I am the angel of death himself." With that Leopold ran up the stairs, his daggers in hand prepared to strike out against the foes of the king.

Cedric's mind was an absolute whirlwind as he spoke. "We must hasten to Lafayette, the king's guard shall protect him for now, and even if he lives the kingdom will fall without the military tact of Lafayette. Beorn and Aderyn with me, Eadwine and Alfnod, see to it that Egbert and the other councilors on this list are kept safe!"

Chapter 14
Blood in the Water

With a ferocious speed, Cedric and his two companions tore down the streets of Wulfstan in search of Lafayette. First, they passed by the houses of ill repute in the poorer districts of the city, where the proud Marshall often stuck his head for the small comfort of company. Finding no trace of him there, they rushed towards the bathhouses of Wulfstan. The bathhouses were a leftover mark from the time when the Nacian Empire ruled over the North. They were a spectacle to the villagers and townsfolk who passed through the city. With great beams and pillars of stone making up the walled exterior, and high copper doors adorned with ancient tales of the gods and man. As they entered, a rush of hot steamed contacted their faces, and the perfumes and incenses inside billowed out in great clouds of air. It appeared as though the bathhouse was empty, save the muffled sounds of faint laughter. They continued their way through the bathhouse until they finally found Lafayette, bathing, drinking, and laughing with the most loyal of his captains of the army.

Cedric greeted him with a glare of despair at first but soon noticed many clothed men, armed with daggers and Billy clubs approaching. They wore the uniforms of the guards of Arrington and Lahyrst, they appeared brutish and outnumbered Lafayette and Cedric's groups. Cedric quickly picked up a small letter opener next to the bath and shoved it in his sleeve. He smiled at Lafayette mouthing the words. "They are here to kill you." He had repeated this three times before the thugs came too close. Lafayette grew tense as his captains too sharpened their senses, made dull by drink and merriment.

They appeared as relaxed as any other man and called to Lafayette, speaking politely. The largest of them had a freshly shaved head and rivaled Beorn in size and strength, on the skirt of his tunic there were splatters of blood. He had the look of death fixated in his cold eyes as he approached and nodded at Lafayette as any loyal soldier would. "Lord Arrington requests your presence; it shall not take long." He said, still holding to his façade of amiable disposition. He had now approached and stood above the bath directly next to Cedric.

Lafayette smiled as the rest of his captains nervously darted their eyes between their commander and the men sent to kill them. Lafayette drank the last of his sweet wine, either to steady his nerves for battle or to prepare his soul for rest, of which he did not know. Cedric's heart beat like a bellowing drum as he reached for a towel and spoke to Lafayette. "Here my lord." His voice was shaking and trembling with each word as he stuck the letter opener to the inside of the towel, its gleaming metal showed only to Lafayette.

As Lafayette rose from the steaming bath, he reached for

the towel, still holding on to his veil of politeness. When the dagger had been carefully placed in his hand, he went for the throat of the bloodied one, driving it hard and fast through his gullet, soiling the rest of his clothing in the red liquid. The dead thug's companions were quick to respond, drawing their clubs and blades upon Cedric and Lafayette. Aderyn was swift, driving her blade into the back of one standing near her.

Lafayette's captains had too now risen from the bath amidst the chaotic scene, grabbing candlesticks and dinner knives as their only defense for their unarmored bodies. Cedric was tackled to the ground and felt the cold sting of steel run its path through his lower side; it was his mistake not to have been aware of his surroundings.

Beorn saw this and made short work of the thug who occupied him, snapping his neck in one fell strike, and quickly rushed to the aid of Cedric, tearing the spine of his foe in two with a great swing of his axe. Bloodied and exhausted, Cedric's allies rested on the floor of the bathhouse, taking a survey of the newly painted floors and walls. The adjacent pools were now filled with a thick wave of blood, each previously whitened and cleaned towel had now been soaked to the core. Cedric's face was covered with blood which was still spurting from the dead corpses around them. Cedric stood first, stumbling for a few steps but found support on the hilt of his blade.

"Muster your courage men of Lorine, for this night's bloody work is not quite finished!" Cedric shouted as he continued his stumbling way through the bathhouse, searching for a pool untainted by the blood so he might clean the blood from his face. Finally, near the entrance to the bathhouse, they found a clean pool and washed the blood of the traitors from their faces. Lafayette's men had traded in their towels for their gambesons and uniforms, strapping their blades and axes to their sides and backs.

They rallied at the door of the bathhouse and pushed out into the night. The streets were dark, but the sounds of battles and death raged on through the void of shadow. No one in the city could be trusted, all could be the servants of Crassus Baal, Wulfstan was divided. Cedric spoke to take charge of the situation.

"Lafayette," said Cedric, "gather the most loyal men in your garrisons, tonight we fight to take back the city from the forces of darkness. Meet us at the steps of the palace; we shall push out into the city from there, reclaiming each sacred stone of the streets." Lafayette answered silently, using only a slight nod to convey his approval. He motioned to his captains, and they followed him into the night towards the main garrison of the city, their weapons were drawn, ready for any who would strike out of the shadow upon them.

Cedric led his companions along the narrow alleys of Wulfstan, avoiding the roaming gangs of thugs and soldiers dedicated to Azrael's cause, they had no hope of fighting them without the aid of their other friends and Lafayette's loyalists. They stalked and crept upon the smaller groups, often made of three or four brutes, going house to house, slaying all inside. The first hours of the night were quiet and dark, for the coup had not yet been fully discovered. When the moon had risen to its highest point, chaos broke out. Houses and buildings were alight with flame, giving light to the evil forces at play. The city streets became red with blood, whole families cast out into the cold, throats slashed and chests pierced by blades in the night.

They slowly made their way towards the palace, each step bringing the chance of discovery and death. The fires burned with brilliance and heat greater than that of Orford, it was like the belly of a dragon in some parts of the chaotic scene. They passed by a house belonging to a relative of House Arrington when there came a great crash of shattered glass from the window.

It was Leopold, his black cloak now covered in traitors' blood. He crashed through the window with one of the vile House Guards, stabbing him through the air and on the ground. He was breathing heavy and fast, his eyes were wild, darting all into the night. Cedric steadied his newest ally with a hand on the chest, as Leopold was attempting to run to the next home of betrayers, as his eyes were so filled with a furious vengeance they were blind to his companions.

He gasped for air and bent over, and he said. "My work is nearly done, we must head to the palace now, make sure your king is still breathing. I have emptied near all the House of Arrington from this earth. William is still alive, though, I saw him on the Western Docks, he is gathering his forces there, no doubt to try and overwhelm the smaller groups of loyalists still left."

Cedric responded. "Fear not, as we speak Lafayette gathers his men, we shall reclaim the city with our army!" Reunited with the assassin, the group continued along the streets, now opting for the faster route of the cobblestone main streets, where there was a path of violence and treachery. Again, there was a line of dead bodies, stretching the whole length of the streets they hurried along, so long as they stayed where there were bodies, they would not encounter Arrington's men.

"Cedric! Over here!" In an alleyway, Alfnod was calling out to his companions. At the small entrance between two houses, the bodies of Arrington soldiers lay dead. Alfnod was tending to Eadwine's wound, an arrow had landed through his upper arm, slicing clean through, and it was not serious.

"We were ambushed near the docks; we were trying to waylay a ship sent by the mariners. Arrington's men were signaling them, and we attempted to call them off but to no avail. When they arrived at the dock, Arrington's soldiers opened on them with a volley of arrows and bolts, killing each one. When the naval support was dealt with, they turned their bows on us; it was a miracle we made it here alive. We tried to double back, towards the palace, but to no avail, getting ourselves trapped in these alleyways. William as nearly five hundred men with him now, we cannot hope to best them without an army of our own."

"Five hundred...I don't know if even Lafayette will best these dark forces we face...come, to the palace!" Cedric said.

Now all of Cedric's companions had been gathered, they made their way to the palace, now only a few streets away. Their eyes and souls grew distraught when they finally reached the steps, there was no sight of Lafayette, save a few nervous guards barricading the upper entrance to the palace. Cedric ran up the steps alongside his companions, not a moment could be wasted in the protection of the king's life, with Alfnod and Eadwine unable to reach the palace before, all the party was filled with a deep dread and uncertainty as they climbed the numerous steps of the palace.

The ancient halls now were silent, with the blazing torches decorating the stone walls now extinguished. The guards had abandoned their posts, each distant and unseen footstep filled the party with a crippling fear of death as they moved forward, towards the private place of worship of the king. It was a small room on the other side of the palace and served as the house of worship for all the gods' and their paragons. Cedric would catch a glimpse of some straggling guards running by doorways, carrying bags and chests of treasures, fleeing the city with as much as they could, an act who deeper meaning means nothing but troubling news. In the first days of the Ten Kingdoms, a sacred right was introduced to the royal guards of kings; that they may take what treasure they can carry from the treasury upon the death of the king.

Cedric and his companions stopped on the side of a wall, nearly at their intended target. They had not heard footsteps for some time, and this troubled all of them. Alfnod raised his voice to a slight whisper to speak. "If Oswine was still alive, wouldn't we hear fighting, or perhaps Arrington's men coming to kill him? I fear we are too late." Cedric reflected on these words, picturing his failure and the demise of Lorine, it filled his heart with grief and at the same time a burning conviction to save what was left of his kingdom.

As they approached the temple, they found two remaining guards, their pikes shaking nervously in their hands and their armor clinking from fear. Cedric was happy to see the king had not been abandoned; he opened the door to see inside. At the center, the king and his nobles knelt in prayer to Cinder at his shrine upon an altar. It was an ancient stone statue, with a circular base with long waves of sunlight beaming from it. Cedric smiled, and pulled the bloody list from his pocket, just to see that King Oswine's name had not been struck. He saw the great host of hooded figures beside the king and his mood turned. He scanned the list for their names. Their names dammit, their names, where are their names? Cedric thought as he hastened through the list, giving up halfway down he pulled out his sword and rushed towards the king.

The hooded figures surrounding the king drew daggers from their sleeves and pockets; the steel was not of the craft of man. Each dagger was jagged and foul, with all manner of dark rituals and runes being performed and carved into their memory.

They were the blades of Belaewan, or the Betrayers. The blades belonged to those who offered homage and service to Azrael at the time of his ascension. These evil knives slashed and pierced at the weak and old flesh of the king, his face of pure terror as they grabbed at his cloak and tore through both cloth and bone. They pierced his chest the most; its gaping wounds poured out a sea of blood onto the chapel floor. Each stone's gap filled with blood before overflowing onto the main stone squares that composed the floor.

Cedric was thrown into a mad fury; his blade Bayeux tore through the Belaewan cloaks. Each blow grew in strength and speed as he cut them limb from limb. His other companions and guards joined the fray, ensuring that none of the cultists would escape. They proved to be of weak mettle, preferring to strike from the shadow rather than an actual battle. The crumbled like wet paper to the strength and steel of their opposition. Their bodies too added to the ever-expanding wave of blood, as Cedric slashed at their corpses, swinging with such conviction as to make them still feel pain after death. He continued this until he heard a faint moaning, it was the still living king.

He rushed to the aid of the king, slipping in the old man's blood. He put the weary soul's head in his lap and began crying. Oswine would soon be reunited with his boys. He reached up to Cedric, and his bloody palm imprinted on the young lad's face. Somehow still the king managed a smile as he spoke. "It is up to you now Cedric…" he paused to cough up blood. "All that we are as men is in your hands, be what I could not, do what I could not…unite the North."

Suddenly the old man's eyes shifted towards the ceiling as if he saw something other than the cold vaulted stone. "They are there Cedric, Waldo, and Owen. How happy they appear! They are glad for you Cedric that you can fulfill their names and mine. They shall be in your spirit Cedric, as king…" the king breathed his last heavy breath as if falling into a deep sleep, and he was gone. His body fell lifeless in Cedric's arms, and his head remained comfortable upon Cedric's lap.

Cedric noticed the king's hand buried in his, opening his palm he discovered the golden ram of Wulfstan, a pin for the cloak of the king. Cedric arched his back to the sky and let out a cry for his once king, the blood of whom was still fresh upon his face. Cedric stood from his king's bloody floor and looked in utter shock at his companions. He was at a loss, with no thought able to form in his mind. The whole of the party was stunned, their king was slain by those he thought loyal, it appeared all hope had vanished from the world of men.

Aderyn rushed to his side and embraced him, she held back her tears for the king old man, for there was no time for proper mourning of such a man. Cedric felt himself slip back into reality with Aderyn's touch; she was like a lighthouse guiding a weather-worn ship to port. Beorn unlogged his great axe from the skull of one of the Belaewan, ripping out pieces of flesh with it. Alfnod and Eadwine watched the doors, while Leopold searched the bodies of the fallen traitors.

Suddenly a steady click of boots was heard from outside; each companion drew their blades expecting the worst. Cedric's mind went numb once more; he raised his sword in a fit of pure rage, ready to take on Azrael himself. Gaspar slid into the doorway, carrying his satchel and walking staff, he jumped back when he saw his allies with their weapons drawn, expecting to be struck down in confusion. "Oh by the gods you are all alive!"

Gaspar's mouth widened into a smile at their fortune, but was quickly turned somber when he entered, stepping in a puddle of blood, he realized what had happened. "Oh…oh no. Cinder preserve him. But we must hurry there is no time left for mourning, as we speak Arrington gathers his forces near the palace. He has won here Cedric." Cedric stared into space as Gaspar grabbed at his arm to get his attention. "Today may be marked as a defeat, but if we fly now, we can defeat Azrael in the end, rebuild what was lost."

Cedric answered as if he had not even heard Gaspar's voice. "What of Lafayette? Where is he, and his captains?" He said, holding his hand at his side, the wound from the dagger at the bathhouse had begun to sting. "They have been gathering their supporters all night, I shall not quit the city, not while they still draw breath, not while the last bastion of Lorine still lives."

Gaspar was disappointed in this answer and explained. "I have not seen a soul loyal to the king in the burning streets. Lafayette and his captains are no doubt dead, thrown into the harbor or gutted on the streets, the end is the same for Wulfstan. We must not dally if you insist on waiting, be my guest, but I will leave without you if we wait for too long for this hopeless cause."

Cedric and his group hurried to the base of the palace steps, looking in every direction for Lafayette and his loyalists. The streets were empty, save some scattered dead bodies. Cedric began breathing heavily; he paced round and round in a large circle. His face was illuminated by the burning buildings nearby, showing his distress. He collapsed on his knees and sat on the steps of the palace, breathing heavy and holding his face in his hands. All hope of victory had faded from his tried and tested heart. It felt as though he was not awake, as though all the terrible things to happen were only an illusion.

Cedric closed his eyes, hoping to escape this wretched nightmare of reality. Behind the darkness of his closed eyes, he was assaulted with the images of fallen friends, Galdwin, Oswine, and the villagers of Orford bounced in his mind. He once more felt the warm ash of his fallen villagers between his toes, as though he was there again, in that hellish time and place. Cedric felt tears forming in his eyelids as he heard infantry marching. He wiped the salty mixture from his eyes, accidentally rubbing some of Oswine's blood onto his eyes as he stood to face whoever came this way. Partially blind from the blood, he pulled out his blade and pointed it towards him, the footsteps were from an unburned section of the city, meaning no face nor body could be seen through the night's shadow.

The steps grew louder and louder, and from the distant fires, the faces of marching men were illuminated. At their front was Lafayette, along with his captains from the bathhouse. They had traded their towels for full suits of armor that clanged with their steps, each breastplate with the crest of the ram upon the center. Lafayette wore his signature steel plate, with a tunic with three golden lions at his upper chest. In total, they numbered near one hundred, each wielding a painted shield. In some hands, the two vines of Deering, representing the twin vineyards planted in their sacred home of Cafold, a famous city filled with gallant knights and tournaments. On others, the symbol of the sacred ram, and still others had the red fox, turning from their master's service to serve their king. In each hand, they wielded swords, axes and pikes, the traditional weaponry of the foot soldier of Lorine. Some used bows, undoubtedly loyal guardsmen stationed upon the wall at the time of the betrayal. Their gambesons and chainmail were painted with the blood red of those traitors unfortunate to cross their path to the palace.

Lafayette smiled as he approached and spoke while taking a deep bow. "Your army master Cedric, Wulfstan has not fallen quite yet!" Cedric embraced his dear First Marshall; the night still had a faint glimmer of hope.

Lafayette was taken aback when he saw Cedric's blood covered face. The Marshall's face expressed the question, whose blood is it? Cedric gave no response with words; he only placed his hand on Lafayette's shoulder. "I'll address the men, Lafayette. For what you have done tonight I cannot thank you enough. If neither of us lives to see the sunset, let them remember us for our courage in the face of death."

Cedric climbed a small barricade on the steps and spoke with his men. The blood of the dead king still smeared across his face, his eyes were filled with a burning rage. He lifted his sword high above his head and called out to each man still brave enough to stand against the tide of darkness.

"Let all men here know that they are the sons of Adalgott. Each man here has already proven himself in every capacity by answering that most sacred call to arms. Tonight, we reclaim what was once ours; we shall take back this city stone by stone, step by step we shall take it back! I am the Seer, the heir of Adalgott, Lord of Orford and future king of Lorine!" He wiped some of the blood from his face onto his hand, and showed the men his palm, shaking from nerves. "This is the blood that was spilled in the name of their evil master, now then men, let us spill some of theirs!" Cedric looked to Aderyn, and her reassuring presence calmed him. Cedric looked back out to the Lorinian infantry and raised his sword into the night.

The men struck and battered their weapons against their shields, crying out the names of all the gods to gain their favor on the battlefield.

Cedric then joined his party at its center and barked his orders. "Men into schiltron formation, no spear or blade shall break through our shields!" The men braced their shields together in a great circle, so that they covered the whole length of the street, letting no foe outflank them in the rear. The pikemen, one rank behind their counterparts, raised their weapons high above the shield wall. Behind them, the archers took up their positions. They had become like a moving fortress, with their shields becoming likes the great stone walls of Wulfstan. They marched forward towards the docks, where the enemy was most concentrated.

Cedric rested in the middle of their moving formation, his blade and mind were steadied and ready for battle. Upon each flank, the swordsmen held their painted shields, ensuring that no strike against them went unnoticed. Enemy scouts could be seen in the narrow alleyways and streets along their route; they were being led to a trap, though Cedric had his own cunning plan brewing in his mind.

Cedric ordered that his pikemen lower their towering weapons of metal teeth. The sharp edges of the spears, pikes, halberds and banner lances of the troops were hidden along their sides as they marched, ensuring enemy scouts could give no report of them to Arrington.

They advanced further and further into the enemy-held

territory; each man grew more disheartened as they went, their eyes peering into the fire filled night with such fear and uncertainty. At last, they came upon the last streets before the docks, thereupon an enormous pile of discarded wood and stone, Arrington's forces had amassed a barricade.

At its front, a full line of shield and swordsmen, three ranks deep, with the elite and coveted armor of Lahyrst, so flawless and bright in design. Their shields were painted with the Red Fox, often depicted with a herring between its sharp teeth. Arrington stood atop the barricade, giving him sight over the whole of the battlefield. Cedric and William's eyes met, within each man a great burning rage boiled over. Cedric breathed slowly; he was ready to kill. Arrington only looked forward intensely; his very look was a challenge for Cedric to approach his ranks.

"Forward all! Kill the traitors!" Cedric shouted with a fiery conviction booming from his lungs, his scream like that of crackling thunder. Altogether his men marched forward, their shields proudly raised to their chests. They beat their swords, axes, and other weapons of war against the edges of the shields, creating a rhythmic call to battle. The archers in Cedric's deeper ranks began unleashing volleys as they approached, with Arrington returning fire all the way. Cedric knew it was a trap, for it to be anything else was foolish.

Now only near twenty paces from the front of the shieldwall, Cedric ordered to his men. "Kill them all!" Each man broke into a mad sprint, crying out in both prayers to gods and frantic noises like that of a wild beast. Cedric drew forth his blade and prepared to strike hard against the wall of wood and steel like waves upon the rocks of the shore. They crashed against Arrington's men with the sounds of cracking wood and the clinking of steel. Men on both sides were kicking and pulling at the shield walls, anything to break it down piece by piece. The battle was even, with neither side able to show absolute superiority in combat.

Cedric slashed and gutted at many Arrington's men; his blade Bayeux moved through the air with the swiftness of a great bird in flight. He terrified many of the untrained on Arrington's side, his frantic war cries and bloody handprint gave him a certain madness upon the battlefield. Forward Cedric pushed his men, driving them into their foes' shields. All of this while Arrington just gazed upon the barricade, though he was now somewhat smirking. Cedric was repelled in surprise and expectation as he heard horns behind him.

Behind his schiltron, the cavalry of Lahyrst, the noblest of steeds and rider, adorned in steel armor and bannered lances rode in a full charge, their hooves beating hard against the cobblestone street. Cedric was ready for this; he showed no sign of fear, just tactical cunning. His ranks further back were unoccupied with the shieldwall, and more importantly, they carried the polearms and heavy weaponry of his outfit. Breaking away from his intense combat,

Cedric pulled his pikes back towards the flank, now nearly set upon by the Knights of Lahyrst. Cedric could hear the heavy breathing of the horses by the time his men were in position, he shouted his command and let loose his secret plan.

"Pikemen! Tear them apart!" All at once the swordsmen placed at the front of the flank kneeled, revealing three rank deep pikemen, with each sharpened end pointing directly at the charging cavalry. The horses and knights and skewered and torn to shreds upon the metal ends, the steel piercing them like the jagged teeth of a ravenous wolf. The cavalrymen were sent flying through the air as heavy hits halted their steeds in their chest. The knights in the rear of the charge buckled and stalled, hoping to avoid the carnage just steps in front of them, but there would be no hope for them this day.

"Forward!" Cedric shouted, the cavalry became like pigs led to the slaughter, their charge had failed, and now they stood in the streets, their advantage had been sorely stolen from them. Cedric and his soldiers on the flank drove through the ranks of cavalry, pulling off riders and sticking them on the ground with their blades. Beorn wielded his mighty axe, slicing knights across the abdomen, sending them flying from their saddles. Eadwine with his longbow picked off any retreating knights; his aim rang true and none who attempted to flee made it out alive. On the other side of the brutal street war, Aderyn, Leopold, and Alfnod were preoccupied with Arrington's shieldwall, trying to gain any footing they could steal from his treacherous army. Gaspar was towards the middle of Cedric's forces, hoping to avoid any physical confrontation.

With the cavalry dealt with, Cedric pressed his men back into the front of the battle, pushing hard against the wall of wood and men. Beorn was swinging his axe like his days as a lumberjack, splintering the shields of many of his foes, slowly but surely, Cedric army broke down the wall.

Eadwine spied Arrington from across the battle, drawing back his bow, he began firing upon the once-chancellor. His aim was marred by the fight around him, causing him to miss with his elvish arrows, though by chance he struck at the guards around William. The battle now favored Cedric, even with fewer men than Arrington, his army fought with more conviction and had scored a major moral victory with the destruction of William's flanking cavalry.

The shieldwall finally collapsed, allowing Cedric's army to pour onto the barricade and overrun Arrington's forces. They put each man on that barrier to the death; their swords were made dull from the intense combat that ensued.

Cedric moved about like a wild man, his face and hair were now both soaked in blood. With each man he slashed, a wave of blood was opened upon him. His eyes became blurry from the red liquid, and they stung with each droplet entering his eye. A spear had pierced Cedric's abdomen during the battle, and only by his armor was he still alive. His arms were sore and tired. His left arm was torn like tissue paper from repeated blows from a sword's point.

Cedric, at last, reached the top of the barricade, Arrington's forces had been broken and began a retreat through the streets, and Cedric let out a great cry upon the barricade, holding his sword proudly above his blood-soaked head.

All throughout the city, the banners of the ram began to fly once more. Lafayette's men made quick work of the smaller barricades and holdouts; soon no street was deemed safe for Arrington's men.

Aderyn rushed to Cedric's side as he collapsed from his victory. His army attempted to let out a shout to honor their success, but it had been a brutal battle. Everyone panted heavily to catch their breath, and they clutched at their wounds. Gaspar next surveyed the top of the barricade; he was checking each body he passed.

He knelt next to a collapsed Cedric and spoke. "Arrington is not amongst the dead Cedric." He placed his hands on Cedric's shoulders to steady him. "Cedric, we need the book, no doubt Arrington has it in his possession. If the forces of Azrael escape, this victory here tonight will count for naught, we must slay those who follow him."

Cedric looked around. His men were celebrating, chanting the great songs of their ancestors as they swung their swords high. He then turned his head and gazed onto the docks, where many innocents had died. There a ship had set sail and was fleeing the inflamed city.

With the speed and fury of Godric, god of the hunt, Cedric bolted after the ship, Gaspar and Aderyn were the only ones to see him do this and quickly followed. He ran with his blade unsheathed; his blood-soaked boots beat hard against the rough surface of the street. Cedric slashed and swung at the enemies they passed, but his feet did not stop moving towards the docks. By the time the three had reached the docking area, the ship was out of reach. It was a cog of simple design, with a single mast at its center and raised platform towards the back.

Upon this platform, Cedric saw Arrington, the henchman to greater evils was staring out into the city, thinking of what was in his mind rightfully his. Cedric had not given up yet, he gained his footing on the wooden dock and lifted off into the water. Aderyn and Gaspar could not follow suit; they could not swim, nor could Cedric. He beat his arms hard on the water in a flailing motion, unsure of how to proceed. Cedric began to breathe in water, his lungs flooded with the sea. From the cog, Arrington laughed at the sight of his foe brought down by such a trivial enemy, his escape was assured.

Slowly Cedric's vision faded as his head submerged below the surface of the port, the light of the burning city illuminating the waters around him. Suddenly, a great strength surged through Cedric, by powers of gods or of man he did not know. He felt the immense determination to live and began pulling himself back towards the surface.

Cedric caught his arm on one of the ropes hanging from the ship as he gasped for precious life-giving air. He steadied himself along the wooden hull of the ship and began to climb, using his feet against the creaking port ship of the ship. The water weighed heavy upon his armor, and his arms grew tired from the weight, but nevertheless he continued to climb. After much effort, he reached the railing of the deck and pull himself over, collapsing on his knees for breath. Cedric lifted his head to survey the ship; he had attracted the attention of a trio guards making their way towards him, a skeleton crew of sailors hurried along with their tasks, hoping not to be dragged into the conflict.

Cedric panted and spat up water as they approached and unsheathed their weapons. Cedric waited on the floor until the proper time, slashing his blade across the first guard's chest as he rose from the wooden deck. With the speed that propelled him, Cedric went at the second guard behind the first, lifting his blade high and then cutting low, practically butchering the man in two. The third guard stumbled backward, blood from his comrades had sprayed across his eyes, before he could even fully react to what had happened, the cold and wetted steel of Bayeux had pierced his chest.

Cedric steadied himself on the deck and saw the sailors nervously running below deck or jumping off. A group of soldiers on the bow did not move; they were watching their master at the back of the ship. Cedric turned his head to see Arrington walking down the steps of his wooden platform; he was draped in a long bearskin cloak. He seemed annoyed rather than threatened by Cedric's display as he removed his coat, revealing an elaborate set of armor, both of steel and stiff leather, and his blade unyielding. And so, the two men and two blades prepared for combat, for in their minds, only one pair would live to have its name be said again. They began circling each other, their steps precise and without mistake. All the while they poked and prodded at one another's blade, testing for weaknesses in form and position.

Cedric struck first, hoping to catch Arrington off guard with a strike veering to the shoulder but ending at the gut, his opponent was quick to parry and retaliate, clipping Cedric's blade. Arrington's relaxed demeanor had now vanished, he understood the gravitas of this fight and showed no emotion. The chancellor took precise stabs as his tactic, knowing he had the better footwork and precision than his younger opponent. With age came a slower but more tactical duel style, compared to Cedric's quick, brash, and untrained swings. Neither man saw a significant flaw in the other's tactics, they only skirted around each other, like two predators without prey.

Cedric grew impatient, his young heart burned only for revenge and not for his own safety. He struck out on impulse, swinging right past Arrington and stumbling behind his opponent. Time appeared to stop at this moment for Cedric, his flaw in this battle was burned in his mind as he shut his eyes, prepared for the counter strike. His back was torn and ripped as he lay on his chest, with a single slash he writhed in pain and screamed.

Arrington knelt beside his defeated counterpart and spoke. "You fought well, at least until the final swing. It is a fool's errand to resist the power of Azrael. He shall return, it is foretold even by the gods. Mark these words boy, I shall return to these lands with my true Lord, and I shall burn you and all those you love from the pages of history. Your name and all it carries shall be gone. You've accomplished nothing here, just a mild inconvenience to an unstoppable power." Arrington rose and grabbed Cedric's arms, lifted him over the side of the ship and threw his body into the port. Cedric's lungs filled with water, worse than before, and slowly sank to the bottom, crashing against the hard stone floor of the sea. His mind blurred as he felt the life being choked from his body. Suddenly, along the surface of the water, there was the Tree of Life. He beat his arms and surfaced

Cedric plunged through the shimmering surface of the garden, finally able to catch his breath. He gasped for air for some time, taking a full survey of his surroundings, wondering if he was dead or alive. Along the shore of the middle of the lake, the tree still shone its light in a brilliant white glow. Cedric swam to the island, taking rest on its smooth grassy surface. Something was different on this visit to the Tree; he heard the soft voice of a woman singing. It was no language known to Cedric, or for that matter, any man.

Not even the elves of Anitquii, so refined in culture and history from the teachings of Duwel, would be able to decipher the ancient words. Cedric reached for his blade, unsure of his guest was a friend or foe, but he was without his blade in this divine garden. Cedric rounded the trunk of the tree and found a great glowing woman sitting with a lyre, strumming in a smooth rhythm. In her voice, there was a deep-rooted pain, and Cedric noticed a bleeding wound at her side, though she gave no indication of it with her face. Cedric tore cloth from his garments and pressed his hands against the wound. The woman looked up at him and said haunting words. "You are but mortal. What hope is there for this wound to heal?" Cedric awoke at the bottom of the port; he was being dragged up by Alfnod.

The two found safe rest on the firm surface of the

dockland, in a spot where ships would be hauled to shore in times of peace that now seemed so far away.

Cedric coughed up water as Alfnod turned him on his chest, examining his wounds. "You're very lucky Cedric." Alfnod pressed his hands along the wound, causing Cedric to scream. "It may hurt now, but there are no signs it shall be a permanent injury. Lafayette is near complete bringing order to the streets, most of the rebels have either been killed or fled the city, any left are being taken to the dungeons." Alfnod collapsed next to his dear friend, for he had received many wounds in battle as well and required a moment to breathe. Aderyn and Eadwine arrived first, followed by the rest of his companions.

Cedric silently thanked the gods that all of them had survived. By now the city had dimmed, the great fires burning throughout the city had been quelled, and an eerie silence overtook each street and narrow alley. Gaspar peered out into the sea, using a strange telescope to chart the movements of Arrington's ship.

"It is turning north, undoubtedly to regather his forces, perhaps they are on the way to resurrect their wicked master." Gaspar looked down on his new friend, his back torn open. "I shall give you a few hours to rest but we must leave come dawn, we have spent enough time in this accursed city." Gaspar handed a small bottle of a strange ointment to Eadwine. "Rub this where the wounds are most grave." He said as they began to make his way through the reclaimed streets of Wulfstan.

Cedric felt a sharp sting as the ointment was rubbed into his bloody wounds, it appeared to sizzle and then become cauterized. Beorn and Alfnod provided support on his arms, lifting him that he may walk and survey the city. The bodies of the innocent tossed into the cold streets had now begun to be gathered and ceremonially burned, such is the custom of the North. The corpses in the port were hopeless, many had drifted out into the sea, and those who were fished out did not burn well.

"How were we so blind, that Arrington could betray us so horridly? How could Azrael have such an influence on his mind?" Cedric muttered as he surveyed the destruction and burning.

"You act as though evil is only present when in its most severe form Cedric," Alfnod said bitterly, clutching at his side. "Evil is not some intangible thing that corrupts good men. It is found within us all, as well as good. Azrael is not some deciding factor in the world, he is merely a catalyst for evil actions, so that men may follow in his path, simply because they can. You are too young Cedric, for I have seen the world. I have seen lords and ladies act as weak as a common criminal, not because of some evil force guiding them, but because we are all born with evil inside us. This path we take, there is more evil in it than just in Azrael."

"This was supposed to be untouchable," Cedric said, and Alfnod carried through the streets. "What hope is there for the hamlets of Lorine or Midland? A wooden palisade is fit only to keep starving wolves at bay, but what we now face is a full horde of evil. This battle cannot be won by a handful of men, which is what we have." Cedric motioned to his friends, and they allowed him to stand by himself, though he was hunched over due to his injury. "We shall need the whole host of the North, each man who remains loyal to his king and the gods shall be required to spill their blood."

Alfnod spoke skeptically. "And you believe yourself to be that king? Cedric, I believe in your cause, but most men do not take kindly to bowing to a stranger."

Cedric huffed and retorted. "Then I shall become known to them all. In my word, they shall find the word of their king. When I wield Adalgott's blade and command his descendants, then shall I be king."

Act II
The Questing through Midland

Chapter 15
The Departure into Midland

Cedric awoke the next morning in the palace, his wounds had scabbed over and were covered in a foul puss. The sun shined bright from the windows, illuminating the whole of the room in warmth. He ached as he rose from the bed, his arms and legs were near numbed from the battle. He washed his face with his basin and cleaned his blade to a shine.

"Did you sleep well?" Aderyn asked. She had yet to rise from the bed as she stared at Cedric's wounds which had healed partially, puss still formed and stung along his back. "You'll need all the rest in the world to be ready for the journey ahead." She rose and rubbed her hands on his back.

"Well enough," Cedric said as he packed a small knapsack with food and supplies. "How are the others?"

"They are tired, but they are with you... I am with you." Aderyn said as she too began packing their things for the long road ahead of them.

"How peculiar our lives are, it seems every step is not what I expect. I thought we would be safe here, but we found only death."

Aderyn paused before responding, hoping to strengthen Cedric with her words. "In this world, we cannot find safety, only create it ourselves. You can create that security for Lorine, for the whole of the north. When the times comes, I know you will be a great king." Aderyn smiled and looked again at Cedric. "Come, the others will be waiting for us."

Lafayette met them at the door, his forehead was wrapped in bandages, and there was a slash across his cheek, but nevertheless he greeted Cedric with dignity. "Cedric thank the gods you have yet to depart." Lafayette gave a look in all directions and put his arm around Cedric's back and pulled him aside from Aderyn. "With the Witan's members near all dead they cannot and will not elect you king." Cedric reeled back in both relief and disappointment. Lafayette continued, "Now they do not deny your claim, as you are the rightful heir by Oswine's decree. They only cannot vote as a half-empty council. I shall stay in the city, try to hold on to what is left of Lorine. As we speak, I have sent our detachments to Lahyrst, to ensure that House Arrington is purged of its treacherous lot. When you return, which I know you will, you shall be king."

Cedric embraced his old friend and spoke. "Thank you, Lafayette, my dear friend, for everything. Do try not to overthrow me while I travel, it would be quite disappointing to return to see you as king." The pair laughed as they departed from one another, it would be many months before either would see each other.

At the main gate of Wulfstan, they found their companions cloaked and packed for the long journey. Gaspar seemed out of place, his clothes were not broken in, and he had brought less than required for the trip. Eadwine was quick to humor this blunder. "Do you intend to cross the whole length of the north or a picnic by the beachfront? Take your silver and get some more grain for gruel, unless of course you are bound as magi to fast on bugs and leaves."

Gaspar gave an annoyed look, but in the end, took out his purse and went to the market for more food. They had been told to carry essentials, and yet Eadwine had brought his lute, taking up much space on his saddle. The bard claimed it necessary to the moral of the party, as, without his singing voice and strumming, they would surely perish.

The party set out before noon, with Beorn and Alfnod leading in the front. Further back, Leopold traveled, he hoped to appear as a lone traveler as to cover the back flank and to avoid conversation with his new companions. The skies were clear as they departed across Lorine, the weather was warm with a gentle breeze flying across the rolling green hills. They crossed by many villages and hamlets unaffected by the brewing of Azrael's wrath, their pastures and fields grew in splendor under the shining sun. They traveled on a cobblestone road, built many centuries ago by the ancient elves of Glanfech. Along the road, statues to elvish royalty and gods were placed as road markers, some etchings of inscriptions remained, though heavily worn down by the passing of time. The road was covered for the most part in shade, as a line of trees on either side of the road stretched for miles, planted under King Uthgir, grandfather of Oswine. They were planted so that all could enjoy the splendor of nature and to signify the majesty and wonderful landscape of Lorine.

None of them spoke for the first hours of their journey, for there was nothing of importance to say. Each member of the party held on their face a look of terrible discouragement; they were without happiness. Eadwine jolted and shuffled from the silence and pulled his lute from his saddle. He began strumming and hummed a quiet tune. Aderyn playfully threw an apple at the elf, of whom responded by sticking out his tongue, causing the whole party save Leopold to burst out in laughter. They needed to laugh, the previous night's events had weighed heavy on them, but with Eadwine's jesting, it seemed like a distant dream long forgotten. They no longer thought of the dread of the past, but rather the beauty of the present day and the promise of adventure in the future.

They passed by the vast fields of Lorine, rich with grain and other crops growing under the sun. The stone fences divided the land into a multicolored wonder, with each field gently swaying with the passing of each burst of wind. They passed by many farmers seeking shelter from the heat under the umbrellas of the nearby trees, with many more working the fields and tending to flocks of cows and sheep. Each of these rural folks were dressed in the traditional garb of their people, with brightly color tunics, and all manner of hoods and hats. Their homesteads were simple but cozy, many billowing stacks of smoke lifted from the thatched roofs of their houses.

They found rest for the night upon a small nook below a grassy hill, with trees forming a cooling shade where they lay. The party tied the horses to these trees, which they fed with bags of grain brought from Wulfstan. As the night grew late and the moon rose high into the sky, they sat by the fire save Leopold, who was sitting upon the hill as a sentry for their camp. The perishable food from Wulfstan was consumed, the meats and vegetables they brought became a hearty stew that filled them with warmth. The beef and pork were roasted upon a spit first, then cooked along with a warm broth, giving it a smoky flavor. Cedric sat with Aderyn, who was beginning to tire, though her eyes and ears remained alerted. Eadwine sat tuning his lute while Beorn poured himself a third bowl, Alfnod had made a hammock and was smoking his pipe, creating all manner of little clouds. Gaspar caught Cedric's interest, as the wizard was scribbling in a small leather-bound notebook. "Tell me magi, what is it that you write with such conviction?" Gaspar looked up with a confused face at Cedric. "Gaspar...the notebook?"

Gaspar smiled somewhat awkwardly and explained. "Oh, I am sorry my lord, preoccupied with thought." He let out a small laugh. "This is the history of our company. When we return, this will be a history of the realm; each step must be recorded so that future generations can hear of our valor and deeds. As of now, I have been documenting our journey out of Lorine, the weather, our morale, and supplies." Gaspar flipped through the blank pages. "Each of these pages shall have been properly filled and recorded when we return; it shall make for quite the story eh?"

Eadwine chimed in, still fiddling with his out of tune lute. "Books may be substantial for a noble and his court, maybe the lucky merchant who can read on top of counting, but that has no place for the ordinary folk's legends."

Gaspar scoffed at the rural backwardness of his elven companion as he responded. "And what pray you wood elf, is the proper form for history and legends."

Eadwine corrected his lute, laid on his back and began playing as he spoke. "All a hero needs to become immortal is three things. A voice, a lute, and a crowd to listen. The unspoken history has always been a part of both man and elf. Who would know of Grimric's duel with the Manticore of the Burned Waste? Or of the Leviathan of the Vaalian Sea? When we return, the people will not learn of Cedric by the hand of some scribe in Wulfstan, but by the songs dedicated to him, sung by every bard here to the Green Mountains in the south."

Gaspar rolled over on his sleeping bag and attempted to ignore his country friend, and lifted his head for the final word. "Perhaps then, I shall write of those spoken stories, only to spite you."

Eadwine reveled in his victory and drank the last ale in his flask before turning over for sleep. Beorn too fell into a deep sleep; his axe slung over his chest would appear intimidating if he did not snore so loudly. Aderyn slowly fell into sleep, Cedric carefully laid her on her sheet and covered her so that the night's chilly wind would not phase her rest. Cedric was about to sleep himself when he noticed the simmering stew before him. He took up the ladle and poured another bowl, but did not eat of it, rather he got up and began walking towards the hill. He stopped at the top, even under the moonlit night it took Cedric a moment to see Leopold, who was covered in a dark cloak. Cedric sat next to him and handed the assassin the steaming bowl of food. "Here, you must eat something."

Leopold accepted the gift but quickly turned cold. "I already had an apple; it shall tide me over." He said as he placed the bowl on his side, and continued sitting with his arms folding across his legs.

Cedric sighed slowly and responded. "Leopold, look at me. If we are to trust one another, if I am to trust you with those I love, I need you to be a member of our party, not just some loner who cannot even share a meal."

"I shall not betray you if that is what you mean, but I have my ways, and those cannot change." The assassin spoke with a monotone voice.

Cedric grew impatient. "I do not believe you would do that, Leopold I am trying to ask why you even warned us in the first place. There was nothing for you to gain if anything you put yourself in more danger. So, we have left we two paths, you either are recklessly suicidal and care for nothing, or you are hiding good intentions. Please, tell me why. I do hope it is the latter of the two."

Leopold smiled and looked down at the bowl of stew. "Perhaps in time, you'll understand, for now, I think I shall keep you in suspense, more fun for myself." The assassin rose and took the bowl of soup with him, making his way down the hill.

Cedric called to him. "Where are you going?"

Again Leopold smiled and spoke. "To be a part of your band of fools." He began eating from the bowl and made his resting spot alongside his companions. Cedric was left perplexed on his face, as he sat on the top of the hill. Unsure of how to proceed, he sat at the head of the hill contemplating for some time, silently gazing at the moon. His quiet meditation was interrupted by the loud cry of a great beast he had heard once before. There across the night sky, Cedric saw the Griffin of Orford tear across the evening sky in grand fashion, its wings beating hard against the windy sky. It danced across the light of the moon, for a moment shadowing itself it like that of a solar eclipse. Cedric smiled, the last symbol of home was still with him each step of the way, even though it chose to remain distant. He wondered if the griffin followed because it had nowhere to return to and that it chased after the only thing familiar to it, or if fate had some larger plan for the two of them. These thoughts preoccupied Cedric's mind as he returned to the camp for some much-needed sleep. The group rested soundly that night, the crackling of the fire was like a sweet lullaby humming them to peaceful sleep.

Chapter 16
A Company of Dweor

Cedric stirred from his sleep, it was early in the morning, but that sun had already risen to its full yellow majesty. The light blinded his eyes, and he was unable to see, the chirping birds and sounds of the camp were all that guided him. Suddenly he heard a twig snap behind him. Cedric, still stirring, he drew forth his blade and swung around to face whoever was behind him. There before him were two stout dweor, cooking breakfast over the campfire. Upon each of their backs were great cloaks, woven with the designs of ancient dweor art, rigid and precise in nature, though none the less beautiful. Upon their faces, below their fat and red noses, great beards of both gray and brown with metal and stone woven amongst hair strands. Their height was short, with thick little bodies. Both stumbled back at the notice of Cedric's blade; their eyes shot open under their thick eyebrows

"Na not there you oaf! Come now, you've gone and stirred

them before the pork is done." One dweor said as he scolded the other, who was hovering over the fire with a skillet containing sizzling pork. The standing dweor was thinner than the other, with strange runic tattoos on either side of his forehead, at his side was a short dagger, no doubt forged in the great fires of Usham or by the smithies of the Green Mountains. The other was unarmed, save a walking stick fit in size only for a human child, he appeared much younger than his counterpart.

The younger dweor offered the skillet to Cedric, hoping the human would sheath his weapon. He spoke. "Please master human; we meant no harm. In fact, our intentions were the direct opposite. Here, this is for you."

Cedric reached out and took the skillet; it had been garnished with all manner of spices from southern lands, a dead giveaway to the Green Mountains, located between the lushly forested lands of Berhungy and the Tanaria. The pork gave off a pleasant aroma, and Cedric realized his stirring hunger. He rested his blade upon his knee, keeping it pointed at his guests, while he pulled out a fork and began to eat the still sizzling spiced pork. Cedric consumed it all, not even leaving bits of fat stuck to the skillet, the younger dweor smiled at the fruits of his labor and felt relaxed, even with the blade still pointed in his direction. The marked dweor stood thinking, he stared intensely at Cedric's sword, as though he had seen it before. Cedric stood, sword still in hand as he woke his companions.

"Everyone up! We have guests." Each of them slowly rose from their slumber, each confused by the presence of the two dweor. Beorn approached and laid his axe on the ground, as a sign of goodwill, in his mind there was no reason to be suspicious of a pair so small in nature. Cedric bent over so he might be on equal footing with the two, he said. "Now then, master dweor I should like to thank you for the meal with your names."

The younger one eagerly hopped up and spoke. "I am Telgor, sir, and this is my da, Odo, we were only passing through when we decided to rest not a walks distance from your camp. Please forgive our intrusion but we thought that it would be a neighborly thing to do, make breakfast that is." The older dweor nodded slightly and with a deep grunt confirmed the younger's report; his eyes were still fixated upon Cedric's blade.

Cedric noticed this and grew suspicious, lifting his blade towards the older dweor who showed no fear of his sharpened steel. "Why do your eyes wander towards Bayeux, dweor?"

Odo let out another grunt and smiled, though it was barely seen through his thick and gray beard. "I know your blade, boy; it once served my village in the Green Mountains." Cedric's face lit up as he realized why the dweor stared. "Though then its master was not a boy but a man by the name Albert."

"You knew my father?" Cedric excitedly asked.

"Ay, he was a good man, an honorable man. He defended my village many years ago; I had not yet been able to grow my first strands of beard when he rode into our quiet town. Ha, I could tell you were his boy, lot of him in you. If my memory serves your name is Cedric, he told me that the name he and his wife decided on. Such a strange thing for us to meet on the road like this." The dweor approached Cedric and offered him his hand, formally greeting him.

Cedric shook hands with the dweor, and the companies exchanged many stories of Albert and the Green Mountains, all while Telgor worked diligently at the fire, preparing a meal for each person present. Soon the other dweor amongst the trade caravan wandered over, and the whole of the camp was alight with conversation and eating. Odo told of the village and its well-doing, how their fat sheep are the largest in all the dweor holds. It was in the Green Mountains that dweor took up this practice, as the mountainsides were so lush and grassy, that it would be foolish not to establish villages and herds of cattle above ground. Odo was a wise old dweor; he had seen many seasons pass by and had now become a merchant in dealings with the men of the north, a lucrative trade in southern goods was always a constant in the northern kingdoms.

"So Odo, what brings you to Lorine, and from what I gather, the whole of the north?" Cedric said as he went for a second helping of food.

Telgor looked at his father for approval, and the old dweor nodded, then Telgor lifted his voice to speak. "Well lord Cedric, we'll show you." Telgor smiled as he went to fetch their crafts from one of their wagons. He returned with a strange barrel, small enough for a human child to hold. The barrel was overflowing with a strange black liquid, which appeared like the thick sap of a tree in its nature. Telgor lifted a large branch and dipped it in the foul-smelling liquid. He hovered the stick over the campfire, igniting the black liquid. Cedric and his party were all unimpressed; this strange liquid was no different than oil for a lighted lamp. Telgor then dipped the inflamed stick in a nearby bucket of water. The fire was not put out, rather the liquid burned on the surface, and began engulfing the whole of the stick.

"That is Usham Fire, my lord, its ingredients, and the recipe is known and guarded only by the high dweor lords. This liquid can burn for hours, consume any person or structure with lightning speed, and cannot be extinguished by dousing it with water." The dweor all laughed at the stunned looks on Cedric and his party's faces, each was stunned by what appeared as magic before their eyes. "It fetched an exceptional price with the Knights of the Eternal Dawn, they purchased the full wagon trains worth, saving us the trip up to Belfas. Now we are back on the southern route, to our home in the Green Mountains."

The groups both knew they could not linger for long, and so, before the sun was at its highest point in the sky, the two groups parted ways.

"Cedric, I wish you the best of luck on your journey up north, be wary for there are many unchecked dangers in the lands of Adalgott," Odo said as his parting words of advice.

Cedric did not ask further of what awaited him, the warning seemed like a cryptic and distant warning, telling of myth and rumor rather than actual danger. Though it did cause him to think back upon the days of Orford, when merchants who passed through Midland told stories of a masked man, though none had ever seen him, they claimed he had laid waste to countless caravans and villages. Without definitive evidence for the masked man, Cedric took it as a flight of fancy, though now he found the thought of a legendary bandit piercing his mind more and more as they approached the Tyr River. This was the first river to cross to reach Midland.

In the great distance, towards mountains and green forests to the east, the great citadel known as Hearth Keep rested in the mountains. Built by King Adrian the Younger, it was constructed in the first days of Lorine, only a few decades after Adalgott's pilgrimage. The great red towers could be seen from miles, spiraling up to the clouds. It was composed of a light red hue only found in the clay pits of Lorine. The fortress was most famous for its massive hall located at its center, with an open fire pit stretching the whole of the long meeting place. Though this chamber is famous, there are several other, massive feasting rooms through Hearth Keep, a behemoth of engineering. It was built along the side of a cliff, with a lone peak as its base, and a long bridge connecting it to the main road of the mountains.

Its garrison buildings could support thousands of men for many months, though it was never the sight of any significant battle, hence why the towers still appear with the same basic design as when they were first built. The banner of the Ram still proudly waved above its towers and walls, by now news of Oswine's death would have reached the whole of the kingdom. Cedric wished to stay, to help maintain order, but he knew that there would be nothing to stop the destruction of Lorine if Azrael were to be resurrected. This majestic fortress and the others like it would all crumble, their memory would fade into the dark shadow that Azrael would cover the world in.

They came to rest for the night on the other side of the Tyr River, after crossing a narrow and worn stone bridge, clearly a relic of the long-forgotten people of Glanfech. This was the edge of those dead people's domain, for the Twin Rivers Tyr and Relif served as their natural border. This land they were now in was filled with ancient markers of these elvish people, in a time when Duwel, the lord of the sky, walked and talked with his people.

Here where the party rested lay the ruins of Solus Keep, an ancient site dedicated to Cinder. It was a large circle of laid stone that once stretched high as the walls of Wulfstan but now appeared as a simple fence on the grass. They set camp at its center, and the soft grass was like the beds of their former home of Orford. The wind howled and struck hard against the stone of the place of worship as they discussed their plans.

"Cedric, what exactly is our plan for Midland," Alfnod said. "The lords of Midland are stern and unmoving like these stone walls; how shall we be able to convince them of your legitimacy?"

Cedric reached into his pocket and pulled out the brooch of the golden ram and spoke accordingly. "This my dear friend is the ultimate symbol of authority; it should convince any minor lord of my authority. Though, Crawe shall be an entirely different beast to tackle, for that lord, Malcom, is the closest thing to king in Midland. His city is the largest in all of Midland, Prav, the city of Crawe. He controls the largest army, the largest coffers, and hordes of grain. If we are to win Midland to our side, we must convince them of Azrael's return. We will find support with the Knights of the Eternal Dawn, who, with any sliver of luck, will have knowledge of Adalgott's final resting place."

The others shrugged and agreed to this plan, then drifted off into sleep. Aderyn raised a single eyebrow and gave Cedric an unconvinced look. "Cedric, do we put too much faith in things uncertain? The lords of Midland did not submit to the banner of the ram then, and I doubt they will now. We must be ready to do whatever necessary to rally the men of Midland to our cause."

"I know Aderyn, I know." Cedric buried his face in his hands and sighed heavily before Aderyn came to his side and rested her head on his shoulder. The two stared into the fire as their companions slumbered under the star-filled sky, each glittering in brilliant fashion.

"You'll make a fine queen when this is over," Cedric said, not even moving his eyes from the fire. Aderyn too did not move at all, but made a face of uncertainty, for they had never spoken of their lives after this horrid quest.

"How can that even be Cedric? I have no royal blood; the Witan would revolt sooner than see a new king not marry to one of the royal households."

Cedric smiled. "I am king, and I can do as I please." He tackled her to the ground and kissed her. "And if it weren't for me, those royal houses would be bowing to Arrington right now; I think a girl I want to marry is compensation enough." The two laughed quietly, hoping not to disturb the sleep of their friends nearby.

That night Cedric saw the Tree once more, the pale moon of this strange realm reflected off the surface of the pond, giving light to the whole of the meadow. This time the plane of the gods had once again shifted, the stars of the sky above Cedric had been banished from the night's sky, but soon Cedric realized what had happened to them. The moon was shining bright, but a thin veil of smoky shadow had engulfed it and had covered the stars, lesser in light than the moon. Even now he could hear the bellowing sound of the wind; he grew unsure if it was a prophetic sign of the gods, or if the real world breached his mind. The lady at the Tree had gone, not even her shallow pool of spilled blood remained.

At the basin of the forest, he saw the image of twin rams, in heated combat. The stronger broke its massive horns down hard against the smaller one breaking its skull. The runt struck back, and slashed its throat, leaving both in pain and agony with the runt victorious. Suddenly Cedric felt a sharp pain overtake his body like he had been beaten from all sides by some manner of blunt object. He collapsed to the ground and writhed in pain. Now all around him, the corpses of his friends, mangled and torn asunder by the dark forces of Azrael. There they made a pile of rotting flesh, their sides and chests pierced by many blades. At the top of this stack, linen-wrapped boots of a bygone age, with strange symbols painted on the cloth. From there above, a dark flowing cape, covering a rotted body, smelling foul of pestilence and maggots. The neck was opened, a wound had ripped open where a man's throat should be.

At the head, a corpse with beady bright eyes, glowing deep inside his eye sockets, and upon his head the Crown of Ten Fingers. At Azrael's side, the Black Blade of Arazor, forged by the Baphamont when Azrael first came to power. His hands were like that of a long-rotted corpse, with only small sinews of flesh and ligaments remaining. He breathed heavy and clotted, his body unable to take a full breath of life-giving air. Azrael appeared to speak in a soft and distant voice, words unknown by all save the gods. They were sharp and filled with hate, like the daggers that slain king Oswine. Cedric could not understand them, the faint whispers of Azrael were like dripping water on his forehead, edging him to madness. Finally, after what seemed like an eternity, Azrael raised his blade to strike down Cedric, who closed his eyes before the blade fell.

Chapter 17
The Wedding at House Moricar

Cedric awoke violently, flinging his arms around from the wounds in his dream, and gasping hard for breath. His companions rushed to his side, attempting to calm him.

"You strike out against air my friend, calm yourself," Gaspar said as he tried to pin down Cedric's flailing arms. It took a few moments for the lord of Orford to realize his behavior, but he soon calmed his weary nerves. His eyes weighed heavy upon his head and had dark rings around them. He stood and walked away, stretching his arms high into the sky. The day was clouded and gray, with strong winds blowing through the warm and humid air.

Aderyn approached him and placed her arms on his shoulder. "Not to worry, Cedric, we are less than a half day's ride to Luxen, we'll get proper bed and food there, I have no doubt these nightmares will cease then."

And so, the company packed up the camp and set off on

the road to the River Relif. Along the way, they saw the White Spiral, a tower built by King Pestel the Mad, grandson of Adalgott. This deranged king was so preoccupied with defense from his allies in the north, whom he believed to be demons disguised as men, that he built a series of towers along the border between Midland and Lorine. Pestel met his end in an ironic twist of fate, as it was by his own noble lords who conspired against him, that he was dethroned and executed. This tower was the largest and most majestic of those constructed under his rule.

It was a massive spiral tower, hewn of a clean white stone that had now weathered and become a drab gray. Upon its top, the original color remained a brilliant blue cap which looked like a courtier's hat from a distance. Cedric waved to the sentry at the tower's peak, whose arm in returning fashion appeared no larger than an ant.

There they took passage across the fast-flowing river by a nearby ferryman. It was the widest and fastest flowing river in the whole of the north. When the party reached the other side of the mighty flowing Relif, they had finally arrived in Midland. Midland, the rolling plains and lush forests of this majestic realm stretched for miles. Within each stone and scrap of dirt, a story of the land lay. The forests teemed with life, as whole herds of deer jumped and ran through the underbrush. It was also a land of tradition, where men still practice the oldest traditions of the gods, worshipping only Cinder. The wise druids of these lands had long guided both the royal and common bloodlines, their mystic runes and enchantments bringing prosperity to all. But it was not only a land of peaceful splendor.

To the northern coast, the Knights of the Eternal Dawn

have long stood watch, reviled by the common folk of Midland who believed them to be tyrannical overlords. Theirs is the protection of Midland from dark forces which laid dormant for centuries, and now awake. Long has this knightly order guarded the coast against invasions and raids from the continent of Vaal, where the race of the giants in great halls rule. These giants have long plagued the fatted fields of sheep and grain alike, taking what they please, and killing all who dare to stand in their path. The Knights are the only actual defense Midland has against the never-ending waves of these barbarian invaders. The Eternal Dawn were formed out of Adalgott's most trusted commanders, each taking up an oath to defend the north from the return of Azrael.

They passed by many small hamlets hewn of mud and thatch on the way to Luxen, the first hold of the noble landed lords of Midland. The journey to Luxen lasted about two weeks, as the roads were in disrepair most parts of this section of Midland. They passed through the tall grasses of the river valley, where many men passed the day hunting with bow and spear alike.

They were the Rivermen, the original settlers of Midland. Tall but thin in frame, they were not renowned for strength but rather cunning and agility. They fought as the bulk of Midland's auxiliaries and skirmishers, their slings and bows fell as many giants as the blades of others did. They wore no armor in battle, believing it to dishonor their skill as skirmishers. Rather, they wore their everyday clothes; tunics, and trousers which gave them greater speed on the battlefield and while hunting. Some that the group saw was hunting in the reeds of the river, for both fish and deer. Others were returning with bounty, to their simple huts along the riverfront.

Their lords came from the house Moricar, natives to these wetlands, whose sigil is a boar upon green field stuck with a spear in its belly. Moricar's namesake and authority stems from their oldest household tale. King Roi, the founder of the house and once one of the Ten Kings, came to hunt in these tall grass fields. A wild boar, large as a bear, struck out at him from the brush, its tusks ready to gore the man. Upon his name and ancestors, Roi claimed until his dying breath, that Godric, Lord of the huntsmen, had descended upon a golden chariot, and pierced the boar in its paunch. Upon that spot, Roi constructed the castle of Luxen and made a shrine to Godric in his gardens.

From across a distant hill, Cedric could now see Luxen, composed of wooden and stone buildings, with a stone castle at the top of the hill. It was a moderately sized fortress, with wooden roofing and railing along its walls, which connected to a large hall towards the back of the hill. The banners of House Moricar, the Wild Boar, proudly waved on the castle and throughout the town below.

The party rode into town, witnessing the celebration of a great festival. Everywhere they looked men and women were drinking, singing and dancing. Each of the commoners' faces had been painted with strange clay, of blue and white. It was the tradition of a wedding in these lands, the wedding of their lord, Roderic, to his betrothed Gwyneth. The folk they saw were much in looks to the Lorinians to the south, though the men wore their beards longer and with knotted patterns.

By tradition, the king had brought out great stores of food and drink, presenting them to his people for a day of merriment. Musicians played through the town, bringing their pleasant melodies into every passerby's ear. Performers and acrobats amazed audiences throughout Luxen, spitting fire and spinning through the air. Tents and tables were set up on each street, providing a bounty of rich and sweet foods for all to enjoy.

The guards kept steady their blades, for the lords in service to Roderic were feasting in the hall, and the entire hierarchy of their land rested on their watchful protection. They wore heavy chainmail with lightly colored green tunics, embroidered with golden squares upon the shoulders. They also held round shields, which had elaborate designs of spiraling dragons, dancing fish, and jumping boars. Upon their aketons which overlapped the chain, they had badges of brown boars, trimmed with yellow cloth. Unlike that of the Rivermen, these were professional soldiers, dedicated to the service of their lord. Another rarity in their arsenal, their long swords, as most drafted soldiers in these lands fought with pitchforks or sharpened spears. Refined iron was not a cheap or plentiful commodity in Luxen.

Cedric and his party removed their weapons at the gate of the castle, as was custom for any meeting between lords, particularly in a wedding, and entered the feasting hall. It was a tall structure on the inside, with large vaulted columns on either side of the hall. The hall was of even stone, save the back towards the lord's table, which was raised so that all in his court might see and hear him.

Tables were filled with food and feasting lords on either side of the keep, many of whom become drunk and disorderly. Pork and fruit were flung table to table in a tipsy row. This was the case in all the feasting hall save for Roderic's table, which consisted of himself, his wife, and his closest friends and advisors, all of whom had remained respectful in the presence of their lord. Roderic had a look of disdain on his face, not for his nobles in specific, but for their ideals. They were pleased with their lot in life, content to eat their fine foods and wines, never thinking of greater ambition.

He was a young man, practically still a child, his face was smooth and his hair light and wispy, but his eyes were that of a powerful leader, burning bright with ambition and cunning. He came off as arrogant and naïve to many of his vassals, believing him to be a boy in a man's world. He disagreed, for he was a man with the patience and ear for the people and ideas that deserved them. To Roderic, everything else was secondary.

On his and his wife's heads, garlands of flowers were placed as a sign of new life within them. He was draped in a majestic tunic, with purple trimming and an orange flower pattern in the center, at his golden belt buckle, the figure of Loden's face. His wife was beautiful, and advanced in age compared to Roderic by around six years, for she appeared as a fully-grown woman. She was a quiet thing, though her advice was listened to and desired by all in the land. From time to time, as Cedric and his group ate with the vassal lords, he would see this newly betrothed wife whisper to her husband, who silently nodded in agreement to her hushed council.

This day marked another important aspect of Roderic's rule, his official recognition as lord of Luxen. Roderic had only recently taken his seat of power in the land, after his father fell ill with Shiverbone, and died. This was the first time in his rule that all those thanes in service to him were under the same roof, and before Cedric arrived, each swore an oath of loyalty to their young lord with the wearing of a golden bracelet, given to each personally by Roderic.

To Roderic's left, his most trusted advisor, a druid cloaked in his traditional clothing and beard. He was an ancient creature, his skin wrinkled and worn like old leather, and drooped to the point that it nearly masked his eyes from view. To their backs, stood the largest man any in Cedric's party had seen. If he was not in the hall of Moricar, some might mistake him for a giant. His face was mostly covered by a patch of chainmail attached to his helm, though his eyes and the flesh around them were exposed. The eyes were piercing, and from what little flesh Cedric saw, he knew the man was scarred underneath his armor. A burgundy tunic with golden trimming draped over the man as well, hiding his robust frame from view. He was wearing heavy mail, large enough to protect two men. He stood with his arms crossed, taking survey over the whole of the hall, carefully watching every guest. Cedric was quick to turn back around when this behemoth took sight of him, for fear that his stare held the strength of a sword swing. His name was Dag, the bodyguard to house Moricar for many years. He had served under Roderic's father, and like his land was passed from father to son.

Roderic stood and raised his arm, and began a speech he prepared for the day. "Lords and ladies, I thank you all for your presence here today. Today is not only my vowing to my wife, but it is a vow to you, to Luxen. For far too long our house has sat at the end of the table of Midland. For far too long we have been left in the shadow of houses who believe themselves better than us. My lords, I vow to you that I shall raise up our house as your king. Together we shall build a stronger Moricar. The road ahead will be long and tiring, as the return of Azrael shall test each man, woman, and child in this realm. But, if we stand together, we shall arise stronger than before, with the name Moricar, raised to new heights." There was a great cheer for their king, some cheered for genuine respect, others cheered out of duty, but there was no difference in their voice.

Again Roderic's hand was raised for silence, and the hall grew quiet in anticipation, save the sound of sipping cups and the devouring of food. "I would like to personally call forth some from your ranks so that they might be recognized for their deeds, would Joto, Dandel, and Chason please stand and come forth." Three old lords rose from their seats, giving nervous looks to one another as they approached their boy king. They bowed and kissed the ring of Moricar, drowning in anticipation of Roderic's words. "You each have served my father well, and for that I thank you." Each man relaxed, and their breathing calmed. "For this, you should be given the gifts of my house."

Roderic's tone changed. "But for some deeds, you should be punished." The three's faces grew pale and in suspense as their lord spoke. "Some among you cannot stand my rule, proclaiming me to be inexperienced and without the will to execute commands. I have offered all of you a place in my house, with good food and wine, and yet there is no thanks for these gifts." Roderic snapped his fingers, and a scribe brought out a great book of record. "My father was a weak man, none here shall deny that, though they may not have the courage to speak it. In fact, he was so weak, that you, his bound lords took advantage of him." There came another snap, and the book was opened, revealing detailed records of the estate of Moricar. "These three, any many more of you still feasting at my tables have stolen what is rightfully mine. You have hoarded grain and other goods owed to my father and myself, all of which is mine by right as Lord Moricar." Again, Roderic snapped his fingers, four guards, including the half-giant appeared and made the lords kneel. "And so, you have made yourselves no more honorable than a common thief in the night, and must be punished accordingly." Three of the guards drew their daggers and rested the sharp steel on the lords' necks.

But again, there came another snap of the finger, and the guards sheathed their blades and put heavy chains on the disgraced lords. "However, since no blood shall be spilled on a day marked by joy," he said as he smiled towards his wife, who smiled back, "I will have you executed tomorrow." The three lords' faces turned the pale white like that of ghosts as they were dragged away screaming. "There shall be no more stealing from my rightful bounty by any of you. These books of records will forever act as law, neglect it, and suffer the consequences. Now then, a gift to each of you, for your ensured loyalty. Those threes' land and property shall be equally divided amongst yourselves, their cattle, coin, and grain shall be given as my dowry to you, as your new lord.

Roderic sipped from his cup as he watched his former lords being dragged away to the dungeon, this time he snapped his fingers for more wine as he descended from his table to walk amongst the rest of his nobles.

Cedric and his group drank carefully from that point on. They sampled the harvest of Moricar's lands, strong ales and sweet wines were given freely at every table. All the while, their eyes glanced around, seeing if Roderic would imprison anyone else.

Alfnod focused the group's attention and began speaking. "I see no potential for a full army in these men, true they have some soldiers, and even what appears to be a giant standing in the back, but a few men do not make an army. That being said, to have the support of a lord, any lord, would be a step in the right direction for our cause. We must be careful in our negotiations."

"I agree," said Cedric. "We cannot come to be picky when we stand on the brink of destruction; we take what we must. I shall go to stand before Roderic, wish me luck."

Cedric got up and began marching towards Roderic's table; he was twiddling his dinner knife against his cloth covered table. Cedric felt all drunken eyes on him as he walked; apparently news of Wulfstan had spread fast to the north. Some lords appeared afraid, as if this party and their quiet lives were about to be disrupted. Others bore faces filled with anger, as though Cedric had come like an avid tax collector to take what was rightfully theirs. The only one who greeted Cedric with a face of kindness was Roderic, who smiled as he noticed Cedric approaching.

Cedric bowed as the whole of the hall went quiet, eager to hear him speak. "Lord Roderic." He began. "I must talk to you about Azrael's return; it is my duty to raise an army to oppose his evil forces, and to name myself as the heir to Adalgott. I am blunt with you as there is no time for fancy words, we must either act now together or perish alone when he returns."

Roderic did not speak; he was thinking intently on Cedric's words, stilling playing with his dinner knife. Suddenly there was an outburst from the feasting tables. "He plans to take our lands!" Another raised his voice. "He's not my lord, the foreign bastard!" He then shot an awkward smile to Roderic, to prove his loyalty. There was an angry stirring in the hall as all the lords stood shouting, and began throwing food at Cedric.

Roderic raised his hand, his face too was embroiled in anger. He strode down to where Cedric was stand and spoke to his nobles. "It is not your place to decide these matters! By our traditions, we give each guest here the respect and welfare they deserve. You do nothing but make a mockery of yourselves.

There shall be no more talk of this matter in public, until your lord has decided the best course of action. Back to your tables lords, back to the meal I have given on this happy day, the one you have so unceremoniously interrupted, perhaps you forget where three of your kind are currently rotting." He turned and began walking towards a back door. He did not look at Cedric; rather he signaled with his hand as he strode across his hall. "Lord Cedric, with me." Before they exited, Roderic whispered to his wife who smiled and nodded her head lightly.

Cedric and Roderic walked outside along the turning stone wall, surveying all the lands of House Moricar. Roderic held two cups of wine in his hands as he walked, drinking from one of them. At the door to the hall, the half-giant paced back and forth, keeping close watch on his lord. In the gardens of the castle below them, there was a shrine to Godric, as well as a stone statue of a boar.

"It's a strange thing…" Roderic began as he peered over the River Relif to the south. "These nobles," He scoffed. "They are so preoccupied with keeping their petty statuses and land that brings them perhaps half a step above a shit covered peasant. We are left with two options Cedric, hold on to what little we have, only to have it taken away, or dive into the unknown. I choose the second; I choose to put my faith you."

Cedric was shocked by Roderic's willingness. "Really? Just like that, you'll support me. Why?"

"I've already said. If I don't, I will rule these lands for a few more months until Azrael comes along, then I'll no doubt end up dead in a ditch, my skin flayed off. If I join and we fail, I will share that same fate. But if we succeed, there will certainly be a power gap for the new King Cedric, a burden I would be glad to share in. For you see, in my current standing, I can afford to throw a feast like this only a few times a year, if the harvest has been truly blessed. I want to be able to have one every single day. Now, when I say that, I mean I do not intend to have a feast every day, but that I want the power to be able to. These noble lords are content to live their little lives from the cradle to the grave, never thinking of the riches of the world just waiting for the taking." Roderic smiled and reached out to give Cedric the second cup of wine. "Ambitious men carve the future, Cedric, shall we face this unholy enemy as allies, and shall we be able to feast every day, if it so pleases us?"

Cedric took the cup and drank from it much to the delight of Roderic. Immediately, the ruler of Luxen threw his cup to the ground and hurried to the door, calling to his bodyguard. "Dag, summon the census takers and the tax collectors! Moricar is called to the service of the true king!" In a whirlwind, the castle ceased its feasting, and the tables of food were cleared, making way for census tomes and other books of records. Each lord was abruptly lined up, many still drunk, and each was made to give full disclosure on their estates. Roderic was sitting on his throne, taking the hand of his lady, both quite pleased with their worked. Lists and numbers of men, crops, cattle, weapons and iron were struck down into the books on the tables, the food of the feast still fresh and warm upon the floor.

"My lord, how can we put faith in a foreigner such as this man, even if he is of Adalgott's bloodline?" One of the nobles protested as he gave the number of the men able to fight in his lands. Around him, the other nobles began to grumble as their wine and food lost its effect.

Arim, the druid, and advisor to Roderic, stood to and raised his hands to the bickering nobles, calling for silence. Roderic too rose and addressed his council. "This foreign lord you speak of is the heir to Adalgott. My friend, do you wish to imply that you lack faith in the gods? Perhaps your local priests shall not take too kindly to that, even going as far as to spread the word of your doubt to your commoners." The old druid smiled through his great beard; he enjoyed his role in Roderic's land. The noble's face turned a bright red as he apologized and bowed to the druid, and he quickly sat down in the hopes that no more attention would be brought to him.

With the census complete, the whole of Roderic's land was accounted for. Some lords whispered about how strange it was that their lord was so ready to call for an account of their estates at his own wedding.

Cedric and his party were given fresh supplies for their journey, as their work was finished in Luxen, in record time, now it was time to go further into Midland. Roderic saw them off with a full battalion of Rivermen, along with his personal bodyguard Dag and two of his knights, clad in steel and chainmail. The two newly allied lords spoke at the gate of the castle. "I send you with my best men Cedric; they will guide you to the edge of my lands, then onto other houses to spread the word of our alliance." Roderic laughed nervously. "You know this may fail before we even begin. If Malcom decides against our plan, I suppose we'll all hang, no doubt he will conjure up some tale about our lot trying to lead a rebellion." Roderic steadied himself and gave his honest advice to Cedric. "Play into his hand, Malcom, he enjoys thinking himself to be a mighty king."

Cedric saddled his horse and prepared to leave. "Thank you, Roderic, when next we meet we shall lead the greatest army this age has seen."

"And Cedric." Roderic stopped the Seer before he could

mount his horse. "Mind the roads, the tales of the masked bandit are becoming more likened to reality with each passing day. But never fear, I send you with my best man, Dag, the bastard northerner, he could tear through whole ranks of men if I let him."

Cedric was quick to switch the subject back to the masked man. "Does anyone know who he is? Or if he exists, for I have heard only rumors during my time in Orford."

Roderic looked down. "All I know is that if he is real, he is a threat to Crawe, whole patrols and camps extinguished in an instance, like a candle being snuffed out. Although there are some reports of villages sacked, so I suppose he could be just in it for wealth and loot. But that is why I send you with my vast army!" Roderic said sarcastically, as he waved his arm towards the Rivermen to accompany Cedric; farmers and hunters mostly, along with Dag who stood high above them. Cedric could not help but smile; they appeared more like jesters than soldiers. "All I know is that Crawe is more preoccupied with this lone bandit party than the real threat, though I highly doubt that he is in league with Azrael like that of your former chancellor."

At last the final bags of supplies were packed, and the party set out down the hill. Villagers of all ages came to see them depart, for they now recognized and knew who Cedric was. Some mumbled prayers to the gods as they passed, others looked on in fixated wonder at their uncrowned king.

Cedric and his companions passed the final huts on the edge of Luxen and moved into the rolling hills of Midland. They headed east, for the roads to the north had no since been abandoned and overrun by nature. Dag led the party, acting as guard and guide to Cedric who trotted along at his side. Behind them, a whole host of Luxen followed on horseback, numbering in the high twenties, enough to stay any highwaymen wandering the roads in search of unprotected caravans.

The traveling party passed through the land for three uneventful days, filled with foggy mornings and rainy afternoons, it appeared the sun had been banished from the land, for they could not even spot its golden outline through the thick veil of darkened clouds. They passed by dew filled meadows, with all manner of birds singing and chirping through the underbrush and trees. The road sat snuggly between a rolling landscape of hills and a nearby forest which teemed with all manner of life. Packs of deer roamed the land, unfazed by the presence of humans, their majesty was revealed to all who witnessed their elegant prancing through the nearby forests. Behind them, some travelers came and went, passing through to their farmsteads or the markets of local villages, but none came in large number. It rained the first night, and each person in camp awoke to soaked clothes and shivering rain.

To the far eastern plains of Midland, the Ithlon, the largest treed land of the north, flourish in a green blanket overtaking the landscape for many miles. It is in the expansiveness of the Ithon that the folk of Godric make their domain. Men and women dedicated to the god of the hunt, they live in small villages connected by forested paths that only they know. At the center of this network of roads, lies Mileast, their capital and the home of the Hall of Godric, where the hunters gather to feast and sacrifice in the name of the Huntsman. House Sodeer has ruled these lands for centuries, holding the title as the Wardens of the Forest.

Deeper in the forest, where the sun cannot pierce the thick

overhead of leaves, and stretching branches, the ones of many names make their home. The final kin of Trundor, the Unseen Ones, The Awaerian, meaning to avoid, all names given to those created as hybrids between man and creature. In his final creation, Trundor, lord of orc, beast, and monsters alike, created the Satyrs and Centaurs, and creatures like them. They were given free range over the hills and grasslands of Midland and Lorine, and their people thrived and multiplied upon the meadows, crafting great wooden towers to their god. In the time of man and the founding of the Ten Kingdoms, these towers were torn down in place of stone palaces, and the fields were emptied of the High Breeds. In this time, many of their races diminished and ceased to exist, such as the Fauns, a dear cousin to the Satyrs, who were filled with the spirit of peace, unfit for the harsh reality of man. Some of their folk fled to the south, hoping to find rest in the greener pastures of Essaroth, a kingdom ripe with fruit and sunlight. Many others fled deeper into Midland, into the Ithon, thus becoming the Unseen Ones, for even the hunters of Godric, in their crafty ways, have few times seen a satyr in the flesh.

The group trotted through muddy grounds on the second day; their horses struggled through the terrain. They passed by ancient wayward stones, built before Adalgott's rule. They were stuck into the ground, reaching the same height as an average man. Worshiped by the mystic, and carved with runic signs, these stones had long watched over the roads in Midland, a guide for any lost traveler and a beacon for any wizard seeking out ancient signs of archaic power.

Suddenly, there was a great shriek of a wild beast from the nearby hills. The Rivermen's horses reared and jumped at the sound. To the sky, the men saw a griffin gliding across the heavens. The Rivermen cried in terror, some drawing their weapons for battle. "It is a sign from Azrael! He sends death to stalk us!" One shouted as he drew back his bow, taking aim at the beast.

"No, you fool!" Cedric said as he knocked down the hunter's bow with his arm. "It is a sign of the gods! They find favor with us, sending us the Guardian of Orford to escort us. No foul beast of Azrael would dare approach us at the sight of a griffin. The packs of wolves and other crafty beasts will be turned back by the cries of such a predator!" The bowman sheathed his bow nervously, keeping a steady eye upon the flying griffin.

As quickly as the Griffin had appeared, it vanished into the overcast sky above them. Then, a great boom came from the sky, and a wave of rushing water was called down upon their heads.

"Roderic tells me you hail from the north," Cedric said to Dag, who continued facing forwards, never shifting his gaze to the one who prodded him with questions. "Did he mean Belfas or Vaal?" Cedric said nervously, hoping not to offend the half-giant in front of him. There was a long pause in the one-sided conversation.

"I don't know," Dag responded. "Never met me ma or da, so I cannot rightly say if I am a real half-giant, all I know is that these folk calls me it and no one messes with me."

"Did you spend much time in Belfas before coming south to Midland?"

"Ay, grew up there, for the most part, started selling my sword to the highest bidder in my teen years. It was bloody cold up there, in Belfas, can't imagine how the giants can live in Vaal, it makes me understand why they want our land so much. It was like the snow didn't even melt in Belfas, everybody just sat around their huts, hoping they'd got enough grain to last through the goddamn spring, can't even plant in spring there." Dag spoke no more, he was not a man for revealing his past and had done very little in that conversation, choosing rather to focus on the nature of the land that raised him, Cedric's rightful land.

Chapter 18
The Rider

On the third day, Cedric peered over the hills covered in the morning dew; none had yet stirred save himself and Dag, who was sharpening his massive blade. Even the birds had not yet awoken, the whole of the world slept quietly. It was at this moment that Cedric's eyes caught sight of a rider just along the cusp of the hill. His clothes were drab and dull, a dark gray cloak covered his body from view, reaching down to the buckles of his horse. The rider made no motion as he overlooked their camp, a black iron blade and dagger were at his side, and both were battered and worn from use and covered in archaic symbols.

"Don't mind him," Dag spoke up, still sharpening his blade with his whetstone. "Not even a complete fool would try to take us by himself." Dag finished polishing his sword, held it high pointing it towards the mysterious rider. He sliced his finger across his throat, threatening the rider to come closer.

The rider whipped the leather on his horse's halter and rode in the opposite direction. His cloak followed his ride some feet behind him as if he were a phantom. Dag laughed and returned to his blade, making sure it was in pristine condition. Cedric remained laying on the ground, pondering about the nature of the mysterious rider.

Dag kept to himself for the rest of the day, replying to Cedric and others with a mere grunt of understanding. He would have made quite the handsome man if it were not for his scars and lack of etiquette. The road quiet save the mismatched beating of hooves against the ground, which melded into a single unending sound. Eadwine strummed at his instrument the whole way, giving a song to the dreary world around them. His voice sang of ancient tales of bravery, both strength of men and grace of his elvish people.

There again, in the evening when the group traveled under the light of the setting sun, was the rider spotted along the horizon once more. This time he was not alone, at either side he was accompanied by a group of fellow horse mounted men, each cloaked and wielding blades. Next, to the first rider, a man wrapped in a bear cloak was reigning his horse. He had two skulls, placed on spikes on his shoulders, and his face was wild and covered in dirt. They now counted in equal number to Cedric's escort and could easily overtake them, though they remained halted on the evening's horizon.

Dag drew his blade and let out an angry cry. "Bastards! We should have killed that scout when we had the chance. To the plains of Carathras to the north, we shall lose them in the night's shadow!" He barked his orders to his men, and all made ready to ride with the fury of a howling wind.

The Rivermen flew through the grassy meadows, hoping to

outrun and tire the mysterious group who now kept pace and remained at a distance. With each beating of the horses' hooves, the sun's light diminished across the land, as were their hopes of escaping those who pursued them. They had ridden for less than an hour before the sun became only a sliver of orange light across the sky, and the whole of the plains were shrouded in darkness. "There is no hope! They shall descend on us in the night!" Cried Gaspar, who was looking back at the ones who chased them.

"Steady yourself wizard!" Dag shouted, he too was panicking, he was turning his eyes to every direction, and his mind was racing in hoping to formulate a plan. "There! Just north I see buildings on the edge of the hills, we ride there and defend from inside!"

With a pointing finger, Dag commanded his men to the site of the ruins, where he intended to make his last stand. They quickly road through what appeared to be the ruins of a town or village, burned into ruin some many years ago. They made their defense at what once was a hall, belonging to some former lord. It was of fine craftsmanship, with a wooden tower propped up from its roof to watch over lands both near and far. Its thatch roof had not yet collapsed, and the wooden walls and stone base proved as sturdy enough protection for the party of the Rivermen. They took wooden beams and loose stones from nearby and placed them at the large doors of the hall, barricading themselves in for the night.

Cedric and Eadwine were at the top of the tower, searching for the horizon for the pursuing party, but they had vanished from view. Eadwine leaned against one of the support beams. "Who do you suppose they are Cedric?" He said as he gazed at the sky that had now turned dark. "Normal bandits are halfwits, content to charge in headfirst, they certainly don't use scouts."

"I know, there is something peculiar about those riders, I doubt that is that last we'll have seen of them. We should ask Dag about this place, seems like suitable soil, why would the people abandon it?"

Below them, in the great hall, the Rivermen had burrowed in for the night, each slept with spear and bow in hand, ready for their barricade to be smashed down by the pursuing riders. They had relit the fire pit resting in the center of the room with broken furniture and twigs and had cooked their meal over its crackling flame. Dag rested on an old wooden bench, it would normally fit at least two men, though he barely fit himself. Cedric's party rested too, for each was weary from the day's ride. The horses were tied and fed in a nearby stable, which was guarded by the two knights accompanying Dag.

Cedric rummaged through boxes and bags left by the previous inhabitants. From their contents, Cedric learned that the people here were not wealthy in coin but kind. He found all manner of trinkets and otherwise valueless items, intricately knotted jewelry and carved wooden figurines in the chest nearest the throne of the hall. Little dolls made of thatch and cloth were most common, the property of the daughter of whoever once ruled here. There was a peculiar cleanliness to them, as though they had not been used and rather left to the decay of time. Cedric was keen to uncover the fate of the folk that once lived in this fertile land, and he approached Dag in search of answers.

"Who lived here? By the look of it some noble lord, perhaps wealthier than Roderic's kin." Cedric said as he tossed a jeweled doll on Dag's lap. The half-giant lifted it with his hand; it appeared minuscule in his hand. Dag sighed heavily at the sight of the toy, and he paused before speaking.

"People who did Crawe much wrong," Dag said as he turned over to rest.

"But what did they do?" Cedric pressed.

Dag again turned over on his side, clearly annoyed by the questions he thought unimportant. "If it makes you shut up I'll give you the brief version. Once upon a time House Lenich lived here, and they thought it was a bright idea to challenge Malcom's claim to the throne. They lost both the war and their heads, with their lord sent off to the Dweoran mines for punishment, goodnight." Dag angrily said, turning over once more for sleep, all while tossing the doll into the fire. Cedric hopped from his seat and threw his hands into the flames to save the doll. Malcom Crawe was an odd fellow to many, an old and shriveled man, who still had a burning strength within his spirit, though now it appeared dormant to all around him.

Cedric slouched down next to his companions; his mind left half satisfied with the account of House Lenich. He took out his satchel and tucked the doll away snuggly, and he watched the fire burn as he thought of what this hall looked like in its former days of glory. Torches giving light, and banners flying throughout the hall. The sounds of laughter and joy filled Cedric's imagination as he pictured a happy home amongst the present ruins.

"It's strange, isn't it?" Alfnod said, staring into the fire. "Only weeks ago, we were feasting in Orford, now we sleep in ruins, expecting each minute to bring our deaths." He turned his gaze to Cedric. "If I had another choice, I'd still be here beside you, and I know the others would too, even Galdwin."

Cedric responded. "I sit and wonder if would even be on this road. How many hardships will we face here, and can we even survive them?" Doubt and discouragement filled Cedric; he had brought his friends into a land fraught with danger, for a goal now so distant and chance. He looked down at Aderyn, who was sleeping soundly at his side. "I cannot protect any of you from what is to come."

"We know that. We don't need protection, Cedric," Alfnod replied, he attempted to cheer him up. "Well I know I certainly won't be the one to fall."

"And why is that?" Cedric said confused.

Alfnod smiled. "Why because I'm the hero of this story. The tale of Alfnod the Brave, and his heroic adventure with the humble second in command known as Cedric, who would be lost without his constant guidance." Alfnod struck a pose as though he were a performer reciting ancient tales, stretching his arms to the roof in dramatic fashion.

Cedric smiled and for a moment could forget all that ailed his party, for a moment he was once again happy. That night each of them slept on guard, clutching their weapons at every creak in the floor, thinking it to be from the bandits who chased them. The morning's rising sun beamed through tiny holes in the roof and walls and illuminated the whole place.

Dag was quick to rise and prepare his men, upon a table he crafted a makeshift map of the nearby land, on it were markers indicating the town, the plains, and the nearby forest Ithlon. He had no mind for strategy, and he struggled to plan their next course of action.

Cedric studied the land from both the map and the tower, searching for some undiscovered strategy that would save them. The raiders could not be seen along the horizon, though it was safe assurance that they were merely hiding in wait for the Rivermen to leave the village. The road was far too exposed to take, but the forest, the Ithlon would provide proper cover. From there, they would travel east and then north, towards the next noble house of Midland, while leaving Dag's men to escape south, where the hills keep them hidden from their pursuers.

Cedric informed the Rivermen of his plan, and each of them agreed that it was their best and only option. They knew it would undoubtedly draw the bandits to Cedric and his men, and away from themselves. Their gear was packed and ready, and the barricade at the door was broken down, each made ready to fly from this place. Before they left, Cedric did one last search through the keep and found a dusty old chest; its only content was a worn and ancient banner, that once waved in the name of Lenich. It was the symbol of twin deer, crossing their antlers between one another. Cedric rolled up this old banner and took it with him, placing next to his own in his knapsack.

Cedric joined his group at the door; they would leave first, just moments before Dag and his men. The door was swung open, and they ran to the stables, quickly packing their supplies on the horses and saddling them. They rode as fast as they could to the edge of the Ithon, unable to see what lied ahead through the thick and ancient forest. Before they entered, Cedric turned his sight back to the town, where he saw Dag's group making their exit. Along the northern horizon, Cedric also caught a glimpse of their unknown enemies, giving chase towards the forest. The plan had worked as the Rivermen had hoped, now it was up to Cedric's group to lose them in the expanse of the Ithlon.

Beorn and Eadwine descended into the forest first, swinging their blades through the thick underbrush as they rode. Leopold was next to enter; his cloak danced along the tangle of branches guarding the Ithon. The rest soon followed though Cedric dallied at the edge of the forest, looking back towards the advancing bandits. Aderyn called to him as she entered the Ithlon, though she did not stop riding, "Cedric we must go!"

Cedric was frozen in place, for he saw what none other saw, for they had already entered the forest. He saw the mask of the lone rider. It was a burial mask typical for the folk of Midland, composed of gold and steel, it shined and reflected from the morning sun that was piercing through the gray clouds above. His eyes appeared dead, as though they had long lost the warmth of life, and Cedric felt chills rushing down his back as he locked eyes with this masked man, it appeared time had frozen when their eyes met. Cedric's mind was rushed with fear, "his eyes, by the gods his eyes," he said to himself. The rider's eyes were black and deepening, like a void of existence. He felt the cold of those beady things as he stumbled into the Ithon.

Chapter 19
The Ithon

Cedric was quick to turn back towards the Ithon and spurred his horse through the forest, his mind still chilled by the masked man. Cedric made headway for only a few minutes before he realized he had lost his companions, for the forest was so dense that a man could not see but ten feet in front of him. He turned his horse in a circle, his eyes hoping to catch sight of his missing friends, while his steed became entangled and tripped on the uneven floor of the forest. Cedric's horse threw his master from his back and bolted deeper into the woods, panting heavily from fear.

Suddenly Cedric felt completely alone, he called out to his companions and heard only distant voices in response. The sounds of the forest were made known to him, all manner of foul and evil things seemed to call out to him. The tangled vines and branches of the woods appeared to creep towards him, like a predator slowly stalking its prey. Cedric was panicking, panting as he called out to his friends and tripped over the ground. "Aderyn! Beorn! Where are you!?" He cried as he stumbled through the forest which now seemed to close in on him from all sides. He heard a rustling in the nearby underbrush and drew his blade, and dig his feet into the ground as he prepared his defense.

Out from the bushes, Eadwine poked his head out and sighed, relieved at finding Cedric. "Finally found you, we thought we'd lost you to that group of savages chasing us."

Cedric sheathed his blade and caught his breath as Eadwine helped him to his feet.

"Come now to the clearing; we must find a path through this maze," Eadwine said as he cut through the thick branches back towards his fellow companions.

They reached a small clearing, where the party gathered and planned their next step. The day had only just now begun, and time for traveling could not be wasted. Leopold climbed a nearby tree, surveying the miles of wooded land that stood in their path to the north, back towards the clear hills he saw no sign of the bandits. Back towards the north, Leopold caught sight of white stone columns, breaking out from the tree line, undoubtedly a marker of ancient ruins.

"Is it some ghost that pursues us!? A cursed spirit brought forth by Azrael!?" Gaspar shouted as he paced throughout the clearing, he was breathing heavy, about to collapse from the anxiety of the past days.

Alfnod found a seat on a flat rock, pulled out his pipe, and began to smoke. His face and voice were like a cold hardened stone as spoke; his mind searched for their next move. "Calm yourself, wizard, they did not follow us in; it would be near impossible for them to cover so much land." He blew out an enormous cloud of smoke and leaned back. "He is no more a spirit than myself, and steel will work on him like any other man."

"We should push back towards the hills; our horses will be downright useless in here," Beorn spoke up, propping his back against a tree as he sharpened his heavy axe. "I would rather take my chances with some foolhardy bandits than whatever unknown things await us deeper in the Ithon. There are tales from my traveling days, of standing wolves and tribes of the Unseen Ones, they would not take kindly to us entering their territory."

Alfnod devised a strategy as he rubbed his temple, his pipe creating billows of smoke from his mouth. "No Beorn, if we turn back now we'll be in the same situation as before. They outnumber us, it would be an assured death to go back and an uncertain end if we press forward, so I vote we move through the Ithon. There are villages and roads to the north of this forest, under rule of House Sodeer, if we can make it through this patch of untamed land we can find shelter and possibly more support for our growing cause there."

"I caught sight of nothing for miles, save some strange column protruding from the forest's height, could it be a sign of a settlement, perhaps a southern town of House Sodeer?" Leopold spoke, as he stood on the edge of the clearing, peering into the forest, listening to the sounds of chirping birds.

Aderyn spoke, as she remembered the tales of history once recited to her by Cedric. "No, it is a ruin of the Lusani elves who once ruled here, before migration of the Unseen." Cedric nodded with approval as Aderyn smiled, for he had forgotten that bit of history.

Cedric knew his vote would carry the most weight, and

ultimately would decide the group's path. He took each of their opinions on the matter and chose the path he thought would be safest. "I say we move further through the Ithon, if not only for a few days. That way we should be able to throw off that masked rider and his thugs, and we'll be on a straight path to Prav. We can make it to those ruins if we ride till dusk, and we'll have a nice dry spot for camp."

Alfnod finished off his leaf and stood up. "You heard him, mount up we move through the Ithon." He spoke bluntly, the rider had unsettled his calm demeanor and he wished to put as much distance between them as possible.

Beorn merely grunted and prepared his gear that he had laid on the ground. It unsettled him to descend further into the unknown wilderness. In the Ithon, there were no men or elves that dwelled in the forest, for fear of Trundor's beasts, who stalked and hunted throughout the land.

Each rode slowly, for their horses were untrained for the rough and uneven terrain of the forest. Cedric rode on the back of Aderyn's horse, as they had not found his since it ran. They passed by small babbling creeks on their way, passing by swathes of woodland and glades.

They came to rest at dusk at the ruins Leopold had spotted in his report. There they found ruins of an ancient forum, overrun by vines and broken apart by trees that sprang up from holes in the stone flooring. Around them, bits and pieces of fallen statues made their resting place on the white stone, the visages of elven beauty had been cracked and faded.

The night's sky was clear and filled with flickering stars as the group lit their campfire and rested in the ruins of a forgotten kingdom. The forest around them grew silent, the chirping of birds and other sounds of nature had become muffled. Only one sound could be fully heard, and fully known, the screeches of the Griffin, which had made its nest in the nearby trees.

"We should name it," Eadwine spoke up, he was starved for idle conversation as he tossed bits of twigs and leaves into the fire.

"The griffin?" Cedric asked.

"No, this fellow." Eadwine sarcastically said as he lifted the bust of an elven ruler, before throwing it behind him, smashing it to bits. "Of course, the Griffin."

"Shadow, since the thing never bothers leaving us." Beorn muffled from under his pillow.

"Jarrick," Cedric whispered.

"What does that mean?" Eadwine inquired.

"It was the name of the first guardian of Orford; my great grandfather called it that when it first came to nest in that patch of forest. I suppose this one is that last of its line, so it's rather fitting." Eadwine shrugged in agreement and drifted off to sleep, the rest soon followed, save Cedric and Leopold.

The pair chose a silent company to that of conversation for what seemed like the longest time until Cedric finally raised his voice to speak. "You know now is a good time for that story."

"What story?" Leopold said as he was stretching and arched his back.

"Why you're here with us, why you decided to help in the first place." Cedric pressed, he was staring up at the stars

Leopold took a long pause and then began. "I suppose you might have a right to know. I was traveling not...agh!"

Cedric looked to Leopold and recoiled in horror, on his neck and back was the visage of a massive gray wolf, ripped into his spinal cord and snapping his neck with ferocious power. Leopold was dead before Cedric could draw his blade, his spine was untouched by sheer luck, and blood was rushing from his exposed neck. The wolf snarled through its blood-soaked fangs and fur as he approached Cedric, all the while other wolves jumped from the shadows. Cedric screamed for his companions.

"Wake up! Wake up!" Cedric shouted as the first wolf launched towards his throat. With his blade, Cedric pierced long ways down the wolf's mouth, tearing through its heart. He struggled to remove his blade as another came forward, only to be cut down by Beorn, who sliced its head in two with a swing of his axe. His other companions too joined the fray, slicing and stabbing at the pack of ravenous wolves. The other wolves did not wish to die as their kin, and with their fangs still showing, retreated into the shadow of the forest. Leopold jumped up from the ground and clutched at his exposed neck with his black gloves that dampened with his blood.

"What in the name of the gods was that? Are we cursed by bad luck or has Crassus Baal come to torment us," Leopold screamed as he taunted his blade towards the forest, throwing curses at the pack of wolves. "I mean this is just ridiculous!" Leopold continued his plethora of muttered swears.

Aderyn rushed to his side with a clean rag and applied pressure to the spurting wound. "You'll be alright Leopold, just keep this on."

Leopold winched in pain, like that of a pouting child with a fresh scrape. "Oh all right enough of that!" He grabbed the rag violently from Aderyn's hand, brushing off the act of kindness. "No time for the while I gut every one of those bastards!" He screamed in a great huff at the silent forest.

"Quiet Leopold," Alfnod said as he listened to the sounds of the woods.

"No! I swear I shall gut and hide every one of…" Leopold was cut off.

"Shut up!" Alfnod shouted, raising his hand towards his elven friend for quiet. His pointed ears twitched as he focused on a single sound coming from the forest. It was heavy breathing of some animal, wounded severely, but still in the realm of the living. "Come on!" Alfnod ordered, his companions followed him into the forest towards the source of the strange noise, there was no sign of the wolves.

Upon a grassy knoll, they found a strange creature, breathing heavy from wolf bites and tears in his flesh. It was majestic and mysterious, its horns were curved once round, and his face and legs were that of a ram, and his body was of a man, though it was covered in fur. His yellow beady eyes were only half open; his vision was weak from his wounds. At his side, he clutched a large gash in his side, were blood rushed out like a running river. His weapon was an archaic thing, a stone club carved with many symbols known only to his kin. His belt was adorned with many brightly painted smooth stones and appeared in the same reverence of precious stones to the kings of men. His tail was limp upon the ground, near lifeless, like that of his body.

"Quickly, we'll take him back to the camp and bind his wounds," Aderyn said as she lifted his arm to her shoulder, and began dragging him back.

"We should leave him; those wolves are drawn to the scent of his blood," Eadwine interjected as he held his bow drawn, gazing out into the dark forest.

Aderyn was resolute in her stance on the satyr. "No, the scent of blood is already overwhelming from Leopold, it would have no use to leave this satyr to die." And so, the Unseen One was taken back to the camp, and his wounds were bound. He spoke no words before collapsing into a deep sleep, clearly exhausted from his injuries.

No visions came to the Seer that night, and all he saw in his dreams were blinding darkness.

The morning sun broke from the veil of the tree line and greeted the ones sleeping on the ancient ruins. Cedric was staring at their guest as he stirred from his healing rest, for this was the first time in many generations that the forested folk of Trundor had met with man. The satyr spoke coldly, though politely, a simple thank you or yes was all they could get from him as they ate their breakfast. He made no attempt to move or get up, for he knew his hosts would not let him leave just yet. They had removed his club, and he was not given a knife to take his meal. His eyes had grown wide in his healing, and they were darting in each direction, taking in the faces of each of his saviors.

"Who are you?" Cedric asked he grew impatient of the polite but empty answers that satyr had given. The satyr did not respond; rather he continued to eat his breakfast using only his fingers as utensils. "Why are you here? What brings you this far west in the Ithon, I thought your folk lived in the thick woods to the east?" Again, he did not respond; he did not even look to face Cedric. Cedric grew angry; his face became red hot as he drew his blade on the satyr's neck, who jumped back in fear. "You shall answer me wild thing, or I shall do away with you like the wolves. My companion near died because of you, you led those wolves here, by ill intention or accident I do not know. I only know you shall answer me or die!"

The satyr raised his hands in submission and began to speak. "I am Pike, son of Halke, Lord of the Folk of the Forest.

I was passing through the eastern paths of the forest when my party was attacked by the same wolf pack that killed your friend, of which I am truly sorry." The satyr's eyes grew mournful as he thought back to his former companions. "My friends were slaughtered too by those wild beasts. We were sent south by my father to parley with the one your people call the Lord of Suthon, the forest far south of here. I cannot mention more of my mission, for it is of utmost importance to the welfare of my kingdom."

Cedric sheathed his blade and helped the satyr to his feet. "Go then Pike, leave us and return to your father." Cedric was through with the situation, and he wished to drop the matter entirely.

Alfnod was quick to pull Cedric to the side, and the elf spoke. "Cedric, this beast knows the paths of the forest, with his help we could navigate through the Ithon in less than a week's travel time, we should not be so fast to dismiss him.

Pike interrupted the two's private conversation. "My lords, I am truly thankful for your rescue, if it had not been for you I would have surely perished." He knelt before Cedric, "allow me to repay your service, I shall take you to my father, Halke, and he shall give you many gifts for saving his eldest son, and safe passage through his forest paths."

Cedric and Alfnod exchanged a look of approval with one another and made silent agreement to honor this pledge.

"Thank you, Pike, we need supplies and rest, I shall honor your pledge," Cedric said as he shook hands with the satyr, and the group made their way east, further into the forest.

Chapter 20
The Guidemaster Pike

In the group's days of travel, they passed by paths and roads known only by Trundor's people. The ways were well hidden, not even the greatest hunters in all the land could track the pathing of a satyr or passing centaur. Pike taught them much about his culture in the way he carried himself. He stood tall and with pride, with his chest extended outward, as any son of a wild king would. He was clever as well, finding abundant hordes of berries and wild mushrooms, knowing which were deadly, even to men and elves. He had been taught well by the shamans and wise of his people, who had lived for many lifetimes in their hidden huts.

Over the days they traveled, Pike was told of Cedric's cause and quest, and the return of Azrael, or The Cursed One, as he is known to the Unseen Ones. Pike responded with his own people's tales of Azrael; for in the time of Adalgott Azrael and his servants came to visit the Ithon, and made friendship with the former chiefs of satyrs and centaurs. They each were seduced and empowered by the promises Azrael made to the Folk of the Forest, chiefly, the return of the Lorinian fields to their possession.

For many years, the Unseen fought alongside Azrael's forces, until the day Azrael began to force the woodland folk to worship his lord Crassus Baal. Some took the blood oath and worshiped their new master. Others, Uthlek the Righteous, head of the centaurs, opposed the conversion. This centaur took his best warriors and went through hamlet after hamlet, slaying all those who betrayed Trundor, until he eventually took up the role of king of the forest. With this slaughter, Azrael was banished from the realm, and his years of diplomacy proved fruitless.

They made good time, and in only a few days they had reached the edge of Pike's home territory. The landscape changed around them, for the sun became blotted out by the thick bunches of branches from overhead trees, and the sounds of birds had become more primal, it appeared as a land outside of time.

"Here is the border of my people," Pike said beaming with pride as he reached towards the dirt, marking the etchings and foot trod paths that made a physical border with the rest of the Ithon. "You will find our land to be prosperous and happy, for we have not dealt with outside threat, nor outsiders in general for many generations. Behold Lord Cedric, you and your company, are the first men to walk in these lands since the time of your Chief King, Adalgott."

Now through the mess of trees, small hamlets and huts came into view. The wild creatures of the forest were hard at work, bringing back the fruit of their hunt, or tending to household duties; each was abuzz with activity. The villagers stopped and stared at the passing group led by their prince, for many had never laid eyes on man or elf. Little satyr children, with newly sprouted horns, followed them from a distance, exchanging hushed whispers of excitement with one another. It was dusk, as the little light that broke through the tree line had become a fading orange.

Pike led them to a great hut, with many supporting beams and ornate designs on its huge cloth walls. It was the hall of their king, Halke, and had served his many ancestors before him. They were stopped by two chain-clad guards carrying spears, with closed helmets that masked their animalistic features.

"Make way for the son of the king," Pike bellowed in an authoritative tone as he raised his hand. "I bring Halke dire news from the Suthon, as well as guests from the lands of men." The guards stepped down and allowed them passage, though they shot angry and distrusting looks at all the prince's guests.

They entered the tent and were immediately assault by an aroma of sweet-smelling perfumes and spices. A great council was being held. Many hanging braziers of flames illuminated the faces of many tribe chiefs. They sat in a vast semi-circle, save the few Minotaurs who were too large to sit. At the back of the tent, King Halke took each member's council into account, and he listened intently to his subjects. His horns were massive, larger than any in the hall, and they were covered his black iron. Near and around his feet, a great host of female satyrs, his harem, lay with their young, each imbued with the strength of their father. At Halke's side, Kiltha, his chief queen sat, the mother of Pike. Far in the corner, a man clad in rugged, wild clothes stood with a great staff. He was a magi, like that of

Gaspar, but his power came from a sinister force. His name was Yellow-Eyes, and he was a servant to Azrael. He had come to the forest realm just days before Pike's return, and yet already he had brought corruption and dissent to the Unseen Ones.

Each of the chiefs was dressed with great golden belts, encrusted with jewels and stones. Some of them, hailing from the far eastern regions of the Ithon, came with horns carved in designs and pierced with rods of metal and gold.

"Wait here by the entrance; I will let my father know of your presence, it would be a bad idea to interrupt his council," Pike said as he motioned to the floor for his new friends to sit. He then approached the throne, bowed respectfully, and took his place by his younger brothers who jumped at and wrestled with him.

Halke nodded to his son and resumed taking counsel from an elder of the villages, with horns had been worn by many battles and years. He was a truly ancient satyr, his brown fur had grayed all over, and he had replaced his club with a cane, for he could not stand without it. "It is not in our blood, this fight between man and Azrael. We need not get involved, the forest has been our home, and none can enter it without our consent. Why waste our lives on either side of this war?" Some the older clansmen shook their spears and beat their hooves against the dirt floor in approval.

A younger warchief stood to speak; he had the fire of a true warrior in his blood. Cedric noticed Pike's mood sour when the young warrior stood to speak. It was Melgor, second son of Halke, and half-brother to Pike. In all respects, he was stronger and faster than his older brother, even towering a full foot over him, but he lacked the patience and wisdom needed in a king. "My friends and fellow chiefs, there is no choice in this struggle," said Melgor. Yellow-Eyes nodded with a crooked smile as the warchief spoke. "Our only course of action is to reclaim our homelands. The vast fields of Glanfech where our people once grazed freely, for the first time in our history we are given a chance at redemption. If Azrael is the path to the reclamation of our land, I see no reason for you all to doubt and argue, we must unite now, or not at all." Yellow-Eyes was pleased with this display, and he beat his staff along with the other chiefs who applauded his speech.

A Minotaur raised his voice to speak. H was an ancient being; well versed in history and sought to refresh the memories of his fellow chiefs. Eldest and most respected by his kin, he had been known by no name save the Stag for many years. He received this nickname for his horns, which had been poured over with hot metal in a branching pattern, creating a set of iron antlers. Using no blade in combat, he preferred to gore his enemies on his horns, a sign of ultimate strength to his kind. "My friend, lest you not forget, we attempted to ally with Azrael once in history…" The young-blooded warrior rolled his eyes and crossed his arms at this history lesson, smiling with confidence. "He turned us against one another, made us forsake Trundor, we cannot go down this path again. The only way to truly keep ourselves safe is to ally ourselves with the enemy of Azrael. Man may have turned us from our homeland, but we have found a good life here, a life worth dying for. For hundreds of years, there has been a calm peace, and I will not be the one to break it."

The young chief jumped up to respond, but he was stopped by Halke, who called for silence throughout his hall. He was troubled by the division in his land, and indecision wrecked his mind. He placed his fist on his chin and contemplated what each of his lords had to say, avoiding the inevitable decision that would divide his people no matter what he chose. He suddenly found an exit to his decision, "Pike, please come and give your report on the Suthon." Everyone in the hall sighed in relief, even the young chief.

Pike stood and bowed to his father, and faced his host of subjects, giving them the full report of his mission. "My entourage and I arrived in the Suthon not three weeks ago, when there we were treated as honored guests, and our message was given ear." He took a long pause, for he knew his next words would dismay many in the hall. "The Lord of Suthon has decided to throw his support to Azrael."

Pike continued over the massive roar that broke out in the hall; some lords exited in protests, others like the young one clapped and cheered. "As we speak his armies of beasts march to the north, and are prepared to support Azrael's claim, in exchange for our ancestral lands." Pike raised his voice to a shout so that all could hear what he thought was the most critical detail of his story. "On my return trip, we were set upon by a pack of savage wolves, who killed all but myself. I was on the brink of death when I was saved by the men in the back of our hall. They are led by Cedric, the rightful ruler of the northern kingdom; he has come to make his case before you all, as the sorcerer had done for his master." Pike pointed them out, and all turned their animalistic eyes on them, some with glimmers of hope, and others filled with rage.

Through this loud row, Halke was calm, as though he was the eye of a storm. Halke judged Cedric through one quick glance while ignoring the rest of his party. He stood, and all those still sitting rose as well. He spoke with a booming voice, like cracking thunder in the sky. "There shall be no more discussion on this matter tonight, for it is not in our way to decide on such grave matters in so little of time. I give this order to you all, rest, and gather your minds, for this issue shall take many weeks to decide upon, I do not take the lives of my people lightly. For our guests, no matter what side they represent, they shall be treated as what they are, guests." He looked towards his second son. "That means that shall not be harassed or harmed in any way, Melgor." Melgor had the fire of his ancestors in him, and he burned for the opportunity to reclaim the homeland, anything else was second to him. The council was dismissed and all dispersed to the various huts and carved trees of Halke's hold.

As they exited, Cedric took advice from his wizard. "Gaspar," he said, "what do you think of this lot? Can we find an ally in them?"

"Yes, my lord, I believe we can," the young wizard replied. "We must win them with both our ways and theirs, the way of wisdom, and the way of strength."

Eadwine joined in as he gave nervous glances to some of the larger beasts surrounding them. "So long as they don't throw us in the stew pot first."

Suddenly Pike appeared before them with a small retinue of his close friends and guards. "Come with me, we have much to discuss, and much to drink," Pike said with a smirk as he led his foreign friends to a large tented area, where many of the delegates and chiefs were being served strong smelling drinks and spiced foods. They made their rest at an empty table and were served with the food of Pike's people. A satyr sat on a rug nearby, and he strummed a stringed stick like Eadwine's lute. The satyr sang with his throat, producing a deepening sound which sounded more akin to blown horn than a voice.

A range of berries and other harvests of the forest were brought out in large cornucopias bursting over their wicker tops. Along with this, freshly slaughtered boar meats were arranged on a platter, sprinkled with spices and sweet-smelling jams made from fresh fruit. The drinks they were served matched their heads in size, born in huge wooden flagons. The liquid frothed and steamed in a light green color.

"I would not recommend that my friends," Pike said. "I've seen one of those put a Minotaur to sleep like a resting baby." Eadwine took a pitcher of the green liquid, which frothed and steamed as he held it. He took a deep breath and sipped from the large flask. He coughed and spat out the drink, and his face turned pale from its strength. Pike reeled in laughter as he took the bottle and drank it himself, without so much as a tiny flinch as he poured its contents down his gullet.

Melgor approached staggering, clearly inebriated. Pike's mood quickly soured to that of a stoic guardsman, giving no emotion to the hot-blooded warrior that slammed his arms on the table in a drunken stupor.

Pike greeted him with complete uninterested. "Hello Melgor, I see you've found the reserves."

Melgor wiped the green ale from his furry beard and gave an evil eye to the humans and elves who sat across from him and his half-brother. He put his arm round Pike as he reached for another mug. "You know brother; I could have used your support in there, I know, I...hiccup." He shook his head and took a moment to gather himself. "Pike, with your brains and my brawn, we could convince our father to reclaim our homeland from..." he leaned in and whispered to his brother, "these thieves."

Pike rolled his eyes and tried to disregard his brother's

words, but he couldn't shake his wrapped arm. "Please Melgor, go back to your tent, I'm sure your bed warmers are waiting. Come now we can talk of this later."

Melgor slammed his closed fists on the table, shaking and spilling the food and drinks, and causing all in the tented area to go quiet and stare. He spoke in a deep-seated rage. "You and the whole lot!" He swung his arms, casting his anger at all the council that sat and drank. "All you want to do is sit here and talk. Time for talking is over, we've got a chance to get back our home. And you, you're too afraid!" Melgor pushed his brother into the mud. "It should be my birthright! You are favored only because of birth, not by merit!"

Pike was quick to jump up, and the two brothers breathed and snorted heavily at one another, puffing out their chests. Pike responded with his own words. "It is the truer coward who is afraid to think before he acts…brother." Pike pushed his brother, though he did not fall, nor did he flinch.

Melgor stamped his hooves against the floor and issued a challenge. "There is only one honorable way to settle this, brother, the jousts."

Pike stood firm in his resolution, and he agreed to the terms. There was a great cheer from the surrounding chiefs, who all gathered at the jousting grounds. It was a long strip of dry dirt, surrounded by wooden benches and stands, bearing the banners of the different tribes. Cedric and his group were ushered to seats, and when night fell upon the forest, the match began.

On either side, the two eldest sons of Halke stood, their chests were adorned in brightly colored clays and powders, and their horns painted. Burning torches were placed around the arena, illuminating their faces, which burned with a deep-rooted rivalry.

"There is still time for you to submit brother! Let these people know I am the stronger." Melgor called to Pike, grinning wide. Pike stood unfazed and did not respond as he took the last sip of his ale before throwing the mug to the floor. The crowd began a great cheer, and Cedric's heart started to beat to the stadium's rhythmic chant. The two brothers bowed to the statue of Trundor off to the middle of the arena and began beating their hooves against the dirt, giving them proper footing. Their nostrils flared and let out clouds of steaming breath, and they awaited the call of the horn.

The horn echoed throughout the wooded realm, sending all manner of birds flying, and the brothers charged at one another. They ran upright, gaining speed with every step. When they were not but thirty meters apart, they reverted to their animal form, turning their heads down hard, preparing to ram one another. Their horns and skulls impacted, and the sound of the colliding bones filled the field and silenced the crowd.

Pike was on the ground in an instant, crashing on the dirt with the weight of a falling tree. He clutched in pain at his skull, for it appeared his horns had been struck like nails with a hammer. Melgor stood proudly, he caught his breath and faced the crowd, lifting his arms in victory. But it was a short-lived triumph.

There came a loud booming voice approaching with speed. "What is the meaning of this!?" Halke was in a fury, his face alone was enough to frighten the bravest the warriors present. Melgor's tail threw itself between his legs as he lowered his head in submission to his father, even he was terrified of the great warlord's wrath. Halke pushed his second son to the dirt and stood with his arms crossed, giving looks of disapproval to both of his children. "You are princes of Trundor; this low fighting is not in your blood! Return to your tents the both of you! You are either drunk or foolhardy or both." Halke twisted his body and began to walk back to his tent.

Melgor smirked as he laid on the ground. "I don't think Pike can make it, father, I think I gave him too good of a beating."

Halke turned to his son, his rage boiling to the surface once more. "Then you shall carry him before I hide you myself!" Melgor quickly wiped the smile from his face and put Pike's arm over his shoulders, carrying him back to the tents.

Cedric and his party were led to a larger tent, given expressly for their own party, for none of the ambassadors wished to bunk with the same men who had stolen their home. At the door, Yellow-Eyes waited for his fellow guests, even though his tent was close to Melgor's quarters. He turned his body to block Cedric as the lord attempted to enter. "You had best watch what you say, usurper." The sorcerer spoke with disdain on his tongue. "These folk don't take kindly to sinister outsiders."

Cedric was more annoyed than angered. "Then I'm surprised they haven't flayed your man-bits yet, worm. Run back to your master; I'm sure he could use another chamber pot holder."

Yellow-Eyes made a face like a pouting child. "Watch your words, untrue king, for the mark of daggers in sleep can be untraceable." He felt accomplished with his threat and smirked, only to find that as he leaned back, Leopold placed a knife on his throat from the opening of the tent.

"Strange sorcerer, why did your master not warn you I was going to put my steel through your gullet?" Leopold smirked through the shadow of his cloak.

Cedric leaned in and whispered to the sorcerer who now smelled as though he had soiled himself. "You are right, vile thing, there are indeed many daggers in the night, thank you for the warning." Cedric laughed as the necromancer shrunk away to his tent, muttering curses and foul words in anger. It was then that Cedric noticed the bound book at the evil one's side, with gold lining and missing jewels. It was the same book at Orford. Cedric was moved to anger, and he called to the servant of Azrael. "Sorcerer!" He turned to hear the lord's words. "Now you know I will be expecting that back, what with it being stolen property and all. Perhaps if you return it now, I won't gut you like the slithering snake you are." Yellow-Eyes made no comment, he simply tucked the book under his cloak and continued walking, this time at a more alert and brisk pace.

The group retired on haystacks, the finest bedding throughout this forest kingdom, and they discussed the day's events as the candles flickered on the walls of the tent.

"This is more of a madhouse than a proper country," Eadwine scoffed as he polished and maintained his lute. "Every which way there's a brawl, an argument, a side to pick, not good for recruiting an army. How Halke keeps all these folk together is beyond me."

Gaspar was wiping centaur droppings from his shoulder as he shared his thoughts. "I for once agree with our rustic friend; we should leave, we have the noble lords of Sodeer, Oderyr, and Crawe still waiting to hear our plea. It is important we use our resources where they actually can have an effect."

Cedric lay flat on his cot with his eyes open, watching the flickering illumination of the candles. "If we leave now that rotten Yellow-Eyes will get his claws deeper in these folk." He turned on his side to face his friends. "It is now not so much a matter of gaining an ally, but taking away support from Azrael. If we leave now and if we are lucky, we might be able to convince the remaining houses and the knights of our cause, but we'll have given Azrael an entire hoard of an advantage. The houses are not going anywhere yet, for now, we remain here, and act as diplomats, even if I want to gouge out that squirming rat's eyes."

Alfnod nodded off to sleep, but not before agreeing. "Aye, I would rather be on a battlefield fighting with a Minotaur at my side, rather than it rushing its horns at me."

The group sat around the fire and drank for some time, drinking only of the liquors they had brought. Though there were full barrels of green ale, none dared drink that concoction not made for man. One by one, each drifted into sleep as the fire died out in slow-burning orange embers.

Cedric was hours into a deep sleep when he was shaken awake. Over him stood Aderyn, who had kicked his side. "Cedric, are you awake?"

He responded with a sarcastic tone. "Well, do I sound awake?"

"I haven't been able to sleep. Come on; I found something you'll want to see," she said as Cedric rose from his pile of hay.

Together the pair climbed through winding and wrapping staircases that encapsulated the great trees of the Ithon. It was an outside path, which swung round many high rising trees. Floor after floor, they passed by rooms carved into the trees, where many satyrs and woodland folk drank and made merry in their taverns and homes. The burning braziers and torches along the walkway danced and flickered throughout the trees like the stars of the night sky.

They climbed and climbed until they reached the top branches of the forest, revealing a rushing landscape of treetops that stretched like open plains. The moon was full and brightly shining as the two made a nest of leaves and branches on top of the trees, and watched the moon's journey across the sky.

Cedric watched as the moonlight danced across his love's face. The white glow was radiating in her pupils as she stared in beautiful awe at the huge full moon.

"Does the full moon seem different in this place?" he asked as he stared at the glowing moon.

"What do you mean?" Aderyn responded.

Cedric struggled to explain. "I don't know; it seems different like we watch it from a different angle…everything seems different outside of Orford."

"We'll rebuild it one day; the folk will have a home again because of you." She encouraged him.

Cedric was unsure. "That's if we can even make it back, and even so, how many will return? I should have never brought you all here."

"We came of our free will. Cedric, you must stop worrying about us. You think I came all this way to be treated like some gentle maiden, fit only to sit in a tower and swoon over chivalric knights." She turned his face to meet her own. "I came to fight for you; someone has to show these northern fools how to fight." The two smiled and kissed as the Griffin, now Jarrick, broke through the tree line, making a nest on a jumble of sturdy branches.

"Why do you think it follows us?" Cedric asked both himself and Aderyn.

"I think he is clinging to something familiar, the whole lot of Orford and the forest burns, and all he's left with is the image of a human who dared to challenge him."

"Perhaps it will approach one day, maybe to kill us, maybe not. We won't know until it happens." Cedric rose from the branches, and they headed back towards the tent. "I know we'll make it to that day."

They descended from the skyline and returned to their hut where all were fast asleep. Cedric went out from the tent and took in the sights of the campsite, where even the hardiest of drinking warriors had now fallen into an inebriated sleep, spread out on both grassy knolls and tavern tables. Cedric spotted Pike, who was sipping his last drop of wine, the two gave no word to one another. Pike simply raised his bottle and nodded, before returning to his tent, where his harem awaited him.

A guardsman, dressed in chain and armed with a glaive approached Cedric and gave word that Halke requested his presence in his tent. Cedric was led through a long dirt pathway, towards a well-guarded and well-lit tent, larger than the council chambers of before. At the door, Yellow-Eyes appeared smirking as he exited the tent, revealing a few of his remaining and rotted teeth. "You are too late, False Lord Cedric, your words will not change Halke's mind now that I'm through with him." A guard scoffed, shoved the sorcerer aside and allowed Cedric in.

It was a swath of rugs and fine pillows scattered throughout the tent. All along the walls great forged weapons and heirlooms rested on wooden and steel racks. Halke's bed was massive, but on this night, it was empty of his harem, only the satyr king sat on its edge, taking small sips of wine in stoic contemplation.

"Welcome Lord Cedric, will you drink with me?" Halke

changed his mood to that of a receptive host, and rose and opened a fresh bottle.

"Of course, King Halke...I must thank you for the hospitality; I know there are some here who would rather see me flayed than drinking with their king."

Halke laughed as he poured another glass of wine. "Then the same goes to that silver-tongued snake; he's right set that I'll support his lord." He Cedric took rest on a carved oak chair, gilded with gold, while Cedric sat on a little wooden stool. Halke reclined and let out a long sigh. "So here we are Lord Cedric, I shall hear you as I heard Yellow-Eyes, and perhaps you shall be more convincing than he was." Cedric paused nervously as Halke looked unimpressed.

This silence continued, for Cedric had no thought on what to say. Finally, Halke broke the silence, realizing he had off put his guest. "They say Azrael's forces are due north of here," he sipped from his glass, "If that is true they are undoubtedly laying siege to any village in the land of House Sodeer. I know of those men well, though they do not know me. The hunters of Godric they are called, keeping close to the forest always. I have never had cause to fight them, for they are respectful of the woods, as we are, taking what we must, holding sacred the unspoken law of nature. Now I hear stories of villages left to starve, their hunters slaughtered and fields salted. But they are starved, not killed. No, the dark one leaves the weakest of the folk alive so that they would have a slow death."

Cedric grew angry from this story, not at Halke, but of his real enemy. "And what say you Halke? Would you side with the one who starves and cruelly mocks those you respect?"

Halke bitterly retorted, "And you would have me betray people? Leave the land we once ruled unclaimed and defiled? I am at a crossroads, human. Either path I take it will lead to the death of many of my friends and kin." He turned to dourness as he hung his kingly head low. "There is no right or wrong in my choice, for in both there is good and evil. Now Yellow-Eyes has spoken well, and he has given me much to think about. In an instant, the king was back to a sour mood. "So far you have yet to impress me."

"You know what to do," Cedric said, causing the satyr king to lift his head in confusion. "Before you, there is a good choice and an evil one." Cedric took a tone as he had never before, and spoke with an ancient authority rooted deep within him. He remained calm; his voice was steady as a ship in calm waters. "You know what the right course is, but you are afraid, afraid not only of failure but victory, that you will be detested and hated by many of your people." Halke stood angrily, his chest puffed out and attempted to make Cedric cower, but to no avail. Cedric matched him in standing, and refused to back down, again he pleaded to Halke, "If you join me, and we are victorious, I swear your people will write your name in their songs for generations to come. They would sing of the king who brought peace to their lands and ended the feud with kingdom of Lorine. Do I need to tell you what happens if you side with Azrael?"

There was a long silence, and Cedric remained calm as Halke breathed violently and twitched his head. Cedric had taken control of the situation. "You expect me to come here and beg Halke? No, rather I expect you to make the right choice on your own and prove you're worth anything as a king. How long would peace with Azrael last in your perfect world? If you chose now, in this darkest hour, to side with Azrael, he would enslave your people. Those green fields he has promised you will turn black from his shadow. Your shrines to Trundor will be torn down and in their place, foul and pestilent effigies of Crassus Baal." Halke appeared angrier with each statement; his mind whirled as he tried to decide. Cedric remained stoical, holding back his fear and body from fidgeting. "If you join me, I cannot promise the full return of your people's land, but I swear I shall try. If you side with Azrael, he will lead your people to death and ruin, from which there is no return, you stand to either keep or lose everything. You know this way is the only path that your people can survive, do not be the coward I think you are." Cedric had struck a chord uninvited and reserved from all; he could see Halke turned red with anger. "You ask for this council and call all your chiefs together to debate for days what could be decided in an instant. You have long past weighed these options, you hide behind the decisions of others to mask your indecision. I tell you Halke; you must act now or you will be remembered as a coward."

Halke smashed the bottle of now emptied wine with his closed fist, sending a mix of glass and blood flying across the tent. "Get out…you impudent man filth!" He raised himself higher and higher, as if on command, but Cedric did not waver. "I am king of this realm; I waver nor bow to no man!"

Cedric's heart was racing, though his exterior remained calm and collected, he feared Halke could hear his thundering heartbeat.

Cedric turned as Halke swelled up with rage and the young lord quickly scurried out of the tent hoping to avoid his wrath. Cedric caught his breath outside of the tent and thought on what he had just done. Though he had won the engagement and held fast in his place, he could not shake the feeling that it was all for naught. Had he doomed everything in a burst of pride, for who could know how Halke would react? Cedric dwelt on this and on what to do next as he hurried back to his tent.

Cedric returned to the tent and paced frantically in circles. He kicked the lot of his companions and stirred them from their sleep. "Wake up, we must speak, all of us," he said with haste.

Eadwine, who was clutching a bottle like a mother with her child, was annoyed by this rude awakening. "What are you talking about Cedric?"

Cedric sat and placed his hands over his face. "I was invited to Halke's tent, where I saw Yellow-Eyes had been as well. I may have either just won over their king or insulted his legitimacy; I am not entirely sure which."

"Well it might be important to make the distinction before kicking my head," Alfnod said sarcastically. "What exactly did you do?"

Cedric responded. "I told him the truth, what would happen to his people if he joined Azrael…though I may have also called him a coward."

Eadwine spoke both seriously and in humor. "Well at least I know I won't have my head by tomorrow night!" he said as he drank the last contents of his bottle. "Thank you, Cedric, at least now I know when my hour is!"

Gaspar raised his hand to Eadwine to silence him. "Wait, Eadwine, we may still have a chance." The wizard then pointed his finger at Cedric. "Now you may have indeed insulted Halke, but it does not guarantee he will kill us. You have goaded him into action, and perhaps to prove he is not coward he will play right into your hand. If you had left it with a logical argument, it might win over a king of men, but the Awaerian are not so easily tempted. They require strength in diplomacy, something you may have shown by challenging his authority."

Cedric was relieved to hear this. "So? How can we know which is which?"

Gaspar appeared ready to answer but paused. "Well…I am not sure."

Beorn chuckled. "Some advisor you are Gaspar," he switched his tune as though he was a high-pitched wench calling to patrons, "Oh I don't know Cedric it's only the bloody reason you brought me along!"

"Quiet you, empty-headed oaf!" Gaspar was turned red by the mockery. "When last I checked the greatest contribution to this party you have given is a swing that can hardly split twigs in two."

Beorn turned serious and pulled out his axe. "Oh but I reckon it could slice through your brittle bones any day scholar boy."

Soon the tent was in a roar of bickering as the party rapidly devolved into chaos, with insults and rumors of pig breeding were thrown to one another.

"Enough the lot of you!" Cedric silenced them all, and Gaspar and Beorn both held a face of shame at their actions, holding their heads low and with respect for their lord. "We cannot bicker like this, I know I am to blame for this so stop aiming for one another. We wait here until morning; I'll head out to the council chamber first, I have no doubt Halke would want to make it public. If I live, you can come after me, if not, I hope you'll put as much distance between this place and you."

Each slept that night with their hand at their blade; each snapping twig was perceived as an approaching guard, coming to make an example of them. They were exhausted when morning broke out through the tree line.

An arm broke through the veil of the tent, it was Pike, wearing a grim look on his face. "You are requested as the king's council tent." Cedric got up and went to the door; he saw Pike wearing two bracelets, each a swirling of gold, showing loyalty to his king. "I was told all of you are requested." Cedric froze and looked back at his friends, who gave one another unsure glances. They all joined Pike and marched to the tent, where once more the chiefs had been gathered and taken seat to give counsel.

Halke sat on his throne, his harem of wives had left and he was sitting with his hands clutching at the ends of his chair, his face was expressed by slight discomfort, with the smallest curving of his lip. The whole host of the tent fell silent as the humans and elves entered, this silence followed by hushed whispers that muffled together into one sound. Pike led his friends to empty seats before he took his seat by his father. Melgor sat opposite Pike, on the left of the king, as is the custom of the second-born son. He sat exchanging grins and excited squirms with his sorcerer who stood like a shadow along the wall.

Halke twirled his fingers along his wooden chair as he made decisions in the solace of his mind, he bit his lip as he finally decided, raising his hand for silence. "After council with yourselves and our foreign diplomats I have decided our course of action, it came not without heavy contemplation, and I could not have decided without your wise words, I thank you all." His chiefs leaned forward, awaiting his word for war, Pike looked down, waiting for the worst to pass quickly, like pulling out a splinter. Halke meandered on, "it is in our people's destiny that we reclaim our home," some of his chiefs rolled their eyes and leaned back. "Both paths that are before us will lead us to our home, in one way or the other, but for how long, that is their difference. Is it nobler to hold our home for only a generation or two, or to find our destiny of our ancestors in a different hearth that has served us well for so long?" Melgor's smile vanished, he was now on the edge of his seat, staring deep into his father's eyes, who only glanced at his second born, before speaking again. Halke's final word was brief and to the point, getting his say in before the council erupted in shouting from both sides.

"We side with the Northmen."

The room burst into energy with the word of war. Some cheered and beat their walking sticks and weapons against the ground in approval. Others sat with mugs of anger and disappointment, though none dared to challenge Halke's authority, all save Melgor. The second son jeered in his seat, pouting like a spoiled child whose toy has been taken away. Pike breathed a heavy sigh of relief and nodded to Cedric, who too relaxed in his seat. Yellow-Eyes tried to make a quiet exit but was pushed around like a stranded sailor in a storm by the massive Minotaurs and others that surrounded him.

Halke steadied his kin and smiled for the first time in the day. "My chiefs, rally your warriors!" He stood like the proud warchief he was and raised his fist, stirring the unified spirit of his people that for so long sat dormant. "We march to war! Let everyone who can carry a spear bring honor to their father, let our cry be heard..." Halke was cut off, and he winched in pain as he collapsed in Melgor's arms. The chiefs were stunned at what they saw; Melgor, with a grim face that lacked all emotion for his act, held his dying father in his arms, drawing his dagger from Halke's back, causing it to pool and spurt all over his throne. It is said that at this moment, a whisper, heard only by Melgor was uttered by the dying king. "Not…you." This whisper said just moments before he collapsed, and Melgor rose to claim the usurped birthright.

Melgor was shaking violently, wiping the blood of his father from his blade and stained arm. He looked around the room in full circles, like a child lost in the forest, scared and alone. Pike stared without saying anything, filled with disbelief and mourning. Yellow-Eyes rushed to Melgor's aid and steadied the second son. Melgor shook his head, and suddenly he was as himself, filled with a burning rage. "I am king! And we kill the Northmen!" He shouted with a commanding voice that outweighed his father's in gravity. He pointed his dagger at Cedric, "the first to bring me his head will be my second commander!" Some of the chiefs formed a line around Cedric, unwilling to betray the final order of their true king. The young-blooded amongst them began drawing their weapons, a bloodbath was inevitable.

"Murdering…second born…scum," Pike murmured as he held the corpse of his father. Melgor looked down with a wicked look in his eye.

"What did you say to me?" Melgor said in disbelief.

Pike rose, a fire that burned bright and hotter than in Melgor was stoked that day in Pike. "I said that you are a murdering, second-born, scum." His voice rose in volume and strength with every word. "You are not the king, and you will never be king!"

Melgor threw his arm to stab down into Pike's shoulder, but the older brother blocked the blade by grabbing Melgor's hands. Cedric rushed to Pike's aid, drawing Bayeux and placing its tip at the usurper's neck. "You move that dagger one more inch, and I'll have you bleeding on the floor." Pike nodded to Cedric.

Pike had a deathly serious tone in his voice; he knew his next move from the moment he rose from mourning his father. "Shall we end this the proper way, brother?" he said with a half smirk. "No more jousting, no more fist fights, we end this for good."

Melgor dropped his dagger and spat on his father's corpse, now turning cold and pale from blood loss. He looked around the tent and saw Yellow-Eyes nod in approval. "Very well Pike, we end this the old way." The chiefs sighed in relief and sheathed their blades, though they kept their hands readied to draw them once more. "Tomorrow, we fight for the right of kingship, to the death."

Pike rushed to exit the tent, and Cedric with his band followed. Pike hurried to his personal tent, where he threw tables and chairs in a fit of rage, one barely missing Cedric's head. The prince collapsed on the ground and buried his hands in his face. "It should not have been like this," he said somberly. "Now I am left with two options. Kill my brother, the arrogant pile of dung he is, which will not be easy, mark you, or die." Pike stopped feeling sorrow for himself, he steadied himself and gathered his weapons, laying on a table an assortment of knives and axes, running his hands over each to measure their worth and craft. "What do you recommend Cedric?" He lifted an axe, crafted from polished stone, tied to a golden handle.

"How many weapons are permitted for this type of duel?"

"Three in total: a spear, a ranged weapon, and a blade, of any make," Pike said as he practiced swinging with a long spear. "Though a shield is also given...I think I'll take a dagger for my blade." He lifted a bone carved dagger; it was from a Behemoth, a great beast with hide like that of steel armor, and bones larger than whole men. Cedric did not know what to say, so he left Pike alone in his tent, plotting the battle for many hours of the day.

Cedric returned at night, while the chiefs and their parties were drinking and playing in the fields, Pike and Melgor prepared for death in their tents. Cedric entered the tent and saw Pike giving precious gems to two fauns dressed in exotic silks and strong smelling perfumes, beautiful by the standards of Pike's people. The two looked at Cedric and giggled before exiting the tent. Cedric broke out with a joke. "Did I interrupt your battle planning?"

Pike smiled, the torchlight of his camp barely illuminated his face and leaving half in sheer darkness. "No, no…well actually yes." He lifted a small pouch and shook it, causing its contents to clink and shake. "These are their reward when I survive," he said as he tossed it to Cedric. He opened it and saw an assortment of gold and gems.

"What exactly are they doing?" Cedric asked confused.

"They are on their way to Melgor's tent," Pike said as walked around his tent, "To keep him occupied, a gift from his supporters who wish him luck and fortune. With any luck on my side, he'll be tired and sore when they are done with him in the morning." Pike motioned to empty chairs, and the two sat down, opening a barrel of the green ale. Pike shook as he took small sips, being sure not to drink more than he needed to calm his nerves. "Never been in a real fight before." He took another drink. "Are you supposed to be this nervous?" He looked at Cedric with such uncertainty and fear, the fear held by men who knew death was coming.

"You'd be a fool not to be. It's a good thing, means you're

not ready to die yet."

"I suppose. I feel I always knew this sort of thing would happen, Melgor and I, it just was unavoidable." Pike got up and paced around the room nervously but slowly. "I've got my armor laid out at last...that took up a lot of time." He pointed to a black breastplate, decorated with golden satyrs dancing on opposite sides, along with a chainmail cuirass.

"I like it, light enough but it will block a stray swipe if need be," Cedric reassured Pike, who went for another glass of ale. "Steady with that, don't want to end up like Melgor tomorrow morning." Cedric stopped Pike's pour, leaving it as a glass half full.

"Thank you...I suppose it's time for you to head back, I'll need my rest."

Cedric patted Pike's arm. "Rest well Pike, and you'll fight well tomorrow."

Cedric left the tent, and caught sight of Melgor with his hands wrapped and tangled around the waists of Pike's escorts, drinking barrels of green ale with his compatriots. He was preparing his body for glory, to meet Trundor in the afterlife or to serve as his vassal king. Pike meanwhile, sat alone on the edge of his bed. He clasped his cup with both hands and silently prayed to Trundor.

Cedric returned to his tent and collapsed on his straw cot, with his head facing toward the branches of the trees that masked the starry sky. "It is as my dreams showed me," he said to himself, though his companions all heard him.

"What do you mean Cedric?" Alfnod said as he diced a wheel of cheese with his dagger, eating bits of it from the steel blade.

"I saw it in my dreams, two rams dueling, with the smaller

wound but victorious. For the length of the fight, the odds were in the larger's favor, but in the final moment victory was stolen from him." Cedric said with confidence. "Pike will win tomorrow; he has to. If he doesn't, we must be ready to flee.'

"Those visions haven't been the keenest help so far, giving you veiled views of the future, too late to do anything about what foul thing's to come." He cut off another chunk of the wedge.

"Maybe they grow stronger, if you remember they started as nothing but screaming shadows, now I see fully fleshed images."

"Very well could be," Beorn interjected. "But there's no way even with the gods' help that that whelp of a satyr is going to win."

Cedric continued to stare upward. "He will win because he must win, or else we are all doomed."

Chapter 21
The King of the Forest

Cedric and his group were led through a massive and still growing crowd to the jousting arena. There the banners of all the clans and chiefs were waving, some on Melgor's side, and others on Pike's. The group was brought to a free section in the stands, just next to the fighting ground. A full regiment of band players came breaking through the crowd in rhythmed march, adorned in flowered horns and golden wristbands. They came beating on heavy drums, signaling the beginning of the tourney. The drummers led the two brothers, who walked side by side, carrying tokens of favor from their harems stuffed in their armor. Pike wore his blackened breastplate, and his chain skirt jingled and danced as his legs kicked up dirt. Melgor appeared as a tortoise, his armor, thick and brightly polished steel, enclosed the whole of his body like some noble knight in Lorine. Melgor was tired; Cedric saw it in his dull and baggy eyes, which were red from his drinking and whoring. Pike was well rested, and remained calm and collected as he walked beside his foe.

The drums stopped their beating when the brother reached the dirt field, where the wise elders of the tribes had prepared each their tables of weaponry. Both Pike and Melgor kneeled before the elders, who anointed both with holy oil, which dripped and soaked through their tufts of fur. The oldest of the elders came forward, his hair white and long flowing as a magi of the court, and he spoke. "Here Trundor! We come before you with two sons, both worthy of kingship. May you guide their spears, to sovereignty or your side, only you know!"

Pike and Melgor stood and took stock of their weapons for the duel. There were three parts to any duel in the Ithon, the ranged, the far, the near. The ranged was any thrown or drawn weapon. Pike chose a large sling, with three smoothed gray stones hard enough to crack through a knight's steel helm. Melgor chose the javelin, three with bronze tips. They then both lifted their shields, circular and only modestly larger than standard bucklers. These shields were the finest in the armory, composed of many layers of hides and metals, with patterns of forestry and running beasts of gold and silver.

They took places opposite each other until they were roughly twenty meters apart, and the horn sounded for combat to begin. Pike loaded his sling, but not before Melgor loosed his first javelin. A complete miss, his arm was sore from the previous night's debauchery, and his spear near hit the sitting crowd.

Pike threw two rocks in rapid succession, striking and deflecting off Melgor's shield. Cedric and his friends held their hands fast against the wooden railing that separated them from the fight, and they cheered along with half the crowd for Pike.

"Keep your shield high! Don't give him any rest!" Cedric shouted advice from the stands, hoping to give Pike word of some unseen advantage.

Melgor let rip his second spear, tearing through the many layers of metal and hides on Pike's shield. The older son's shield fell to the floor leaving him defenseless as he looked in shock back at Melgor, who now threw his third shot. It tore through Pike's lower leg causing the crowd to cheer and boo. It narrowly missed the bone; it was only by his scheming the night before that Pike was still alive.

"Oh gods!" Gaspar reeled and swayed like a princess in a storybook as Pike collapsed to the floor, clutching his leg.

Pike appeared beat, and Melgor knew it, for he held his shield high and beat his hand against his chest. "Get up Pike! Get up! You aren't beat yet, get up!" Cedric screamed from the sideline; the fear that his vision was untrue rushed through his mind.

The satyr was breathing heavy and fast as he broke the javelin in half, leaving the wood that pierced him lodged in his leg, to keep it from bleeding. His supporters cheered as he dragged himself back to his feet, and was given a new shield and his spear for the far combat. Melgor picked up a massive club from the weapon rack; it was shaped like a spear with metal ribs along its steel surface. He twirled it and produced a sound like a songbird as he smiled, causing the crowd to cheer.

Pike was on the defensive, he lowered his legs for his balance, keeping the weight off the one still stuck by the spear. Melgor continued spinning his club until the very last moment, before bringing it down to strike Pike's shield. Pike jumped out of the way rushing to the side as the club boomed and appeared to break the ground as it crashed and rang against the ground.

Melgor immediately lifted the weapon, swiping hard to the side and cracking open Pike's breastplate, all while launching Pike into the air.

Pike laid on the ground, his spear thrown clean from his reach, and Melgor approached to finish his work. Melgor raised his massive club and threw it down to end the fight, but Pike raised his shield with both his hands, which cracked and broke under the immense force of Melgor's swing. Pike grabbed dirt and threw it at his brother's eyes, giving him a moment's time to roll towards his spear.

Melgor quickly whipped the dust from his eyes and lunged at his brother, who had grasped his spear firmly in his dirt covered hand. Pike rolled back over to face Melgor, and raised his spear towards the sky, skewering Melgor on its sharp end as he jumped to swing his club. Melgor screamed in agony and stressed every muscle of his face in pain as he was standing with Pike's spear through his gut. He grasped at it and ripped it from his lower abdomen, and it began to bleed and pour over his once shining armor.

Pike jumped up and caught his breath; both were panting and torn to ribbons as they were handed their blades for close combat. Melgor called to his brother. "Pike! Submit now and spare us this trouble, we know how this will end!" To the crowd, this seemed as though the young warrior was still in his headstrong mood and mocking his brother, but to those seated closest to Melgor and Pike, it was a plea to end the violence, for there was still a part of Melgor that did not wish to slay his brother.

Pike said nothing, he simply strapped on his third shield and took up a short sword, along with a dagger he placed on his lower back. Both brothers were turned light brown from the dirt of the arena, and when they shook piles of dust came flying off. Melgor quickly cauterized the wound by having his aides hold him down and prodded a hot iron into his gut. He screamed and roared, causing the crowd to go silent. They rose again in cheer when he lifted his shield and sword, ready for the final round, the one that can only end when one of the two laid dead. The brothers beat their swords against the steel rims of their shields as they approached, and rushed at one another with their blades, and the final round began.

Both were exhausted and swung only when they had the strength to. Their steel shined brightly through the cloud of dust that had been kicked up. The arena itself had now changed its hue, for the blood of both brothers had mixed in with the dirt, and creating small running rivers of red water.

Melgor threw a good hit, hitting Pike right at the hilt of his blade. Pike collapsed as his sword flew from his hand, Melgor had beaten him. The blade flew at the crowd, near where Cedric was. Pike landed his head on a stone that stuck out from the ground, and his younger brother hatched a plan. He grabbed Pike's horns and placed them on the rock, to the crowd's horror. He raised his heavy boot and threw it down hard between Pike's horn and the rock.

The crowd was stunned, and Pike was screaming in pain. Melgor raised the right-sided horn of his brother in victory, it was cracked and broken, leaving Pike with a nub left on his head.

"Come now brother, you are beaten," Melgor said triumphantly as he panted, "submit now, and I will spare you."

Pike looked over to Cedric and his group, ready to surrender, and he realized their fate if he was to submit. Pike pulled his dagger from his back and lunged at Melgor. Melgor caught Pike by the wrist, a reversal from yesterday, and crushed his hand until he dropped the dagger.

Cedric was suddenly compelled to intervene. He pushed through the crowd and found Pike's lost sword, and shouted to his friend. "Pike!" Pike looked over with a look of complete conceding, but his face lit up with new life when he saw Cedric holding the blade.

Cedric threw the blade back into the arena, for he could not directly give it to Pike, as it would break the sacred honor between the two opponents. He flung it just towards Pike's feet, and Melgor reached for the fallen dagger to finish his brother. Pike, still held by his brother, gathered all his remaining strength and struck Melgor's chest with a closed fist, freeing him from his grip.

Pike fell onto the ground once more, but immediately dragged himself to the sword, and gripped it in his hand with conviction as Melgor approached wielding the dagger. Pike was on his chest as Melgor approached and surprised him, turning his body around as he swung the sword.

The crowd went silent for the final time in that fight, they saw Melgor clutch as his throat and watched as blood dripped down onto his steel armor. The young-blooded chief collapsed on the ground, his eyes wide open but dead, and his throat was gushing out blood.

Pike stood hunched over in shock at what he had accomplished. He looked at his bloodied blade and let it slip from his hand, clanging as it dropped to the dusty ground. He looked up at the crowd, who had fallen silent and stared at him in awe. "I am king! We march to face Azrael!" He beat against his chest, shouting with such volume so that the whole of the Ithon could hear his cry.

The crowd erupted into cheering, as by the will of Trundor their king had been revealed. His supporters broke down the wooden fence and rushed the field, and lifted their king upon their shoulders and carried him throughout the camp. Barrels of ale were opened, and songs were sung, all in honor of their new king, Pike, son of Halke, the firstborn and chosen champion of Trundor.

Cedric managed to find Pike hours later in a medical tent, where his doctors attended to his many wounds. They were stitching up his leg when Cedric entered the tent.

"Leave us." Pike beamed with happiness as he saw Cedric, and waved his hand for his doctors to stop. He hopped up and hobbled on his good leg over to his savior of the duel. "Ha-ha! We've done it, Cedric! Come, drink with me." Halke collapsed back on his cot and struggled to uncork a barrel of ale. Cedric noticed two empty barrels just along the frame of the bed.

"I see you've been enjoying your victory."

"Should I not?"

Cedric smiled and laughed. "No."

"I'll make this oath to you Cedric, that tonight I will drink every drop of ale and bed every faun in the whole of the Ithon tonight." He said as he opened the barrel and drank straight from its nozzle.

A guard entered the tent wielding a spear and bowed his head to his king. "My lord, the sorcerer Yellow-Eyes has fled the camp, his belongings and horse have gone along with him."

"Good riddance," Pike said as he looked to Cedric, "shame, though, I would have enjoyed taking off his head, thank you, you are dismissed." The guard bowed once again and took his leave.

"No doubt he's gone to stir up trouble somewhere else,"

Cedric said.

"I will send a message to my scouts and fringe chiefs, to be on a careful watch for that worm."

"And send another message to mobilize their armies," Cedric added.

"And that of course…where will you head now? I assume you need more than a herd of satyrs to win your war?"

"North, towards Prav and the other houses, what support I have with their lords already will do me well in the capital. Then its north to the Knights, who I believe will gladly support my claim."

"If you want to beat that slime to the other lords, I recommend you leave tonight, no telling how much distance he has on you already."

Cedric made his way to the exit, opening the flap to see his friends drinking and singing with the rest of Pike's people. "Thank you, Pike," Cedric turned to face Pike who was clutching the barrel of ale like a child to his mother's breast. Cedric burst into laughter, and Pike rolled over off the bed in a fit of tears.

Cedric finally stepped over the threshold of the tent and made his way to his companions, and he saw that night had fallen over the camp. "Cedric!" Pike called to him, the king had crutched himself on a branch and made his way to Cedric. "A memento, so that your line never forgets what we accomplished here today." He handed him one of his golden braces, and Cedric placed it on his right hand. The two exchanged no words, but only shook hands before departing, respect to one king from another.

Cedric found Eadwine inside a barrel, being rolled down a hill with the others cheering him on in drunken slurs. "Would you rather stay here or come with me?" Cedric called to them. As if on instinct, Eadwine cried out as he rolled, "Stay here of course!" Just before he smashed into a stockade at the bottom, splintering the wooden barrel and sending him flying.

Beorn and Aderyn were the only ones not drunk of the company. "So, it's time?" Aderyn said stoically.

"I'm afraid so, let's gather what supplies we need and ready the horses."

And so, the sober amongst them gathered their inebriated friends and gathered the last bits of their supplies. They took the northern road out from the camp, heading straight in the direction of House Sodeer. Cedric turned his head to face the camp one last time as they reached the top of a hill. He saw the torches and braziers burning brightly, piercing through the green roof of the Ithon, and heard the many songs and cheers coming from the partying Awaerian. The group soon lost the sounds and light of the camp, left to travel north through the forest in both silence and darkness.

Chapter 22
Reavers and Knights

The group wandered through the Ithon for many days, passing through uncharted lands, unknown to both man and the folk of the forest. As they made their way north, the lush and green tree fields grew into expansive hills that poked from the tree line, rolling and waving through miles of terrain. To the east, the Hirdland Mountains, covered in blankets of icy white snow, with bases of gray stone that appeared to travel upwards for miles.

"House Sodeer will be a great help in the war," Alfnod assured the group as they rode. "I have met some of their rangers on occasion, the best fighters this side of the Tyr if you ask me."

Cedric joined in the praise. "Aye, Azrael will have a difficult time once the rangers on harassing him, moving like shadows through the tree line, he won't be able to march his army one step without an arrow flying at him."

On their way, Eadwine strummed and sung of his people, chiefly of Dothriel, the Prince of Geladhithil, who wandered for years through the Suthon as ranger and sentinel. He sang in his traditional tongue, taught and passed down his father, and his father before him. His language was known only by Alfnod, and little by Cedric, from the time in Orford where Eadwine taught Cedric the legends of the Lusani folk. These tales of crafty woodland creatures and ancient palaces rang throughout the whole of the Ithon.

The expansive hillsides of the Ithon Forest soon faded, and the trees diminished in number and size. The group had made it to the edge of Sodeer country, where the noble house has long stood watch as the wardens of the forest, ensuring that no Awaerian force could surprise Midland. The party grew cautious, for they passed many hamlets and huts, but saw no view of peasantry on their way. Missing too, were the rangers of Sodeer, draped in grim cloaks with the brooch of Godric's silver horn. These men were a common sight to any traveler in these lands, though now they caught sight of none.

"Hark! What is that on the horizon?" Eadwine cried from atop his horse, pointing towards a billowing pillar of black smoke, which appeared like a dark tower in the blue and sunny sky. They pressed their steads forward and hurried to the edge of the forest, where they found a burning town.

It was Mileast, an important trading stop for any traveling merchant in Midland, often seen as the journey's middle ground between Lorine and Belfas to the north, and more importantly, the capital of House Sodeer. The great mercantile houses, hewn of smoothed stone and redwood, along with glimmering glass windows, had been burned and left to smolder. The stone walls were in ruin, and the spiky pillars of logs had corpses of guardsmen thrown about them.

Cedric and the others dismounted their horses at the gatehouse, which had been completely smashed in, the gilded steel doors, composed of silver and gold were dented and strewn about on the muddy and bloodied ground. The many market stalls that once drew grew crowds had been smashed in, with their tented roofs of ornate design now covered in brown mud, and sunken into black puddles along the road. Dogs and freed chickens ran through the streets, they appeared hungry, as though they had not eaten for a day or so in length.

Sacks of grain, still ready for selling, were cut open and their contents were thrown about on the ground, though there was not a sight of a loose piece of silver throughout the whole market. The smaller houses of the lower district painted with blues and whites had been thoroughly picked over, and nothing of value was left.

There came a slight rustle nearby; a wooden post had collapsed. Cedric turned and pulled out his blade. "Come out! We can hear you!" He called, but there was no response. He looked back to his group. "Keep on your toes; we are not alone."

The group marched up the hill towards the castle of House Sodeer, all the while their paranoia mounted with the growing feeling of eyes watching them from afar. Crows and other birds had come by this time and had begun to pluck away at the decaying corpses that littered the streets. Amongst them were highborn and merchants, artisans and farmers, folk whose life did not know such violence, a life that could never be prepared for such a brutal attack. It was skeleton force that defended Mileast, for most of the fighting force was drafted into the rangers, keeping the borders safe, though leaving the heartland completely exposed to assault.

The muddled through the ruins, and Cedric knelt to inspect the road. He saw the marking of horses, too many in number to count, which had ridden all throughout the town. "The attackers were on horseback no doubt. They not only had the element of surprise, but they also had mobility…it couldn't have been more than a half an hour before Mileast was completely overrun."

"Do you think they'll be back?" Gaspar said nervously, holding back vomit, as he turned over a corpse to check for signs of life. He muttered silent prayers the whole walk, praying that someone would be alive in the piles of the dead.

"No," Alfnod said, his face turned pale by the destruction laid before them, "if this was a few hours ago, perhaps, but these corpses are beginning to smell, they will be miles away by now."

"I'll make one last sweep through the village," said Leopold, in a strangely somber and dire voice, "make sure we aren't missing anyone that might still be here."

They, at last, reached the flat top of the hill, where they found the castle burned out, its insides charred and battered. The banners of dancing deer had been torn and thrown on the ground, and the feasting hall was in shambles. Next, to this sight of destruction, the Hall of Godric, remained standing, though none less damage was dealt with it. The hall's great burning hearth, which spanned the whole of the main hall in a thin line, had been broken and chipped at. The chairs of bones, carved and cleaned by each member of the hall, had been broken and their fragments had scattered across the floor. Shifting through the piles of animal bones, they found no corpses, as the hunters of Godric were enlisted as rangers, and no doubt died in their forest as they would have wanted.

Upon the back wall of the hall, the monstrance that once held the silver horn was desecrated, and the horn lay defiled in two splinted remains. Its silver rim, which once called the nations of the north together under Adalgott, lay broken, never to be called again.

Suddenly there was a cracking of bone towards the doors of the hall, Cedric turned to see the shadows of two thinned framed things rushing past the pillars the supported the building and flying into a nearby closet. Cedric silently signaled to his group, and they took their places by the door, bows drawn back and blades in hand as Cedric reached for the handle of the door. He could hear breathing, light and frightened.

He threw the doors opened, and saw the figures of two children, clutching at each other for safety, with faces covered in dirt and the look of hunger on their lips and eyes. The group relaxed and were filled with embarrassment for drawing weapons on little children. It was a girl, the elder of the two, and a boy, both with golden blonde hair, and simple clothing. Aderyn knelt and approached the two shaking children, speaking in a soothing voice as to not frighten them more.

"Hush children, do not be afraid, we are here to help." She placed her arm on the elder's shoulder, who jerked back in a panicked and mousy breath. "What happened here young one?"

The child said no words; fear had taken the voice from her. "Why don't we find you something nice to eat? Would you like that?" Aderyn smiled reassuringly. "I think I spotted some sweets in the kitchen, would you like some?" The children nodded and stood, and held hands as they followed Aderyn to the kitchen of the hall.

Nightfall had come quickly, and the smoking ruins of

Mileast, at last, began to cool and subside. The sky remained clear through the night, and the stars were in full view, illuminating the remains of Mileast.

The group had relit a small portion of the long hearth, which illuminated the gilded wooden roof. They had salted pork roasting with herbs received at the Ithon by Pike. The hard bread of the Awaerian was coarse and dry but had a slightly sweet taste to it. Mixed ale was brought up from the cellars of the hall, along with wines and any meat that had not yet turned.

They ate a small feast, and the children gobbled down whatever was presented in front of them, their stomachs growling like a mad dog at the sight of sizzling meat and fresh drinks. They still spoke no words, though the young one now appeared calm, and his eyes regained some charm of innocent beaming.

Beorn was plucking at a chicken breast when he broke the silence. "You know lad," he nudged the boy with the handle of his axe, "I have one just your age. Little fire starter that one, would you happen to be a little devil like him?" Beorn smiled like an old and jolly man, and the child held back a grin as Beorn joked with him.

The girl stared with intense eyes at Leopold, who pretended not to see her. Leopold would give her a little glance every few minutes, as though it were a small confirmation for her wondering mind. At this moment, Cedric realized the two had met before, for why else would a child be so fascinated by this black-clad man.

"I'm Gwen, and this is Atticus." The girl suddenly said, even she seemed surprised by the sudden burst of words that sprang from her mouth. She too had finally begun to feel relatively safe and grew to realize the nature of her elder friends.

"They came in the morning before the dew had yet to down. My mother, she was a maiden to our lady, and I was playing in the gardens when I saw those riders coming up from the market. I grabbed Atticus and took off to the shed, and they started killing everyone. Dragged the poor lord out into the muck, and cut off his head. The one who did it, he had two heads on his coat and acted like they were taking to him. Cause right before he swung, he said his brother told him to let the lady of the castle live, but I didn't hear anybody say that." She went silent again, and her throat began to swell, and her eyes grew glossy.

Cedric felt the pain in her words, and would not press her to tell more. "Come morning we'll be on our way out of this town."

Gwen continued to stare at Leopold, who had begun to grow red-eyed from the story, a truly peculiar thing for his demeanor to this point. "Will we be safe...Leopold?" The girl uttered in a small voice, near a whisper.

Leopold matched her tone, giving faint confirmation. "Yes Gwen, you're safe now." Everyone looked at Leopold with confused looks as the children breathed out in relief that the worst had passed. The group gave them their cloaks as blankets and moved down the hall to talk without disturbing the little ones' much-needed sleep.

"Leopold, can you please explain how you know these children?" Cedric asked demandingly, for he realized this was the story Leopold had yet to tell."

Leopold sunk against a wooden pillar and lifted his cold and distant veil. "It was only a few months ago...I arrived in Mileast on a job, some fat merchant who had been taking up too much space in the market. Easy enough, in fact, I was on my way to leave when the lord and lady came before me. They said they needed help, mistook me for a sellsword. They offered me a bag of gold, less than the payment for my job, to go and clear out some pesky bandit hideout. Was going to tell them to choke on the gold, when these two little ones came up and begged me, tugging at my cloak until I promised to help. The young ones told me no knight would not help the helpless…they mistook me for some noble knight." Leopold was smiling as he looked back at the sleeping children. "So, I took the job, killed the bandits who had cobbled a few kitchen knives together for weapons, took the gold, and went on my way. I didn't even collect the payment for the merchant, just rode straight to Wulfstan to get drunk enough to forget about those people. That's when I got the job to kill your king, decided right then and there I would be what those kids thought I was, maybe to convince myself there's more to me than the flick of a knife."

Cedric and his group fell silent, for so long they had been convinced the man who confessed his deepest thoughts to them was nothing more than a swindler, content to use whatever and whomever to his own advantage. Cedric quietly gave a look of approval and thanks to Leopold, for he knew the assassin had been through enough embarrassment.

"There can be no coincidence in this matter, the reavers that sacked this place were the same who pursued us weeks ago through Moricar land," Gaspar said to break the tension, turning the conversation to the riders from the other side of the Ithon.

"I agree with Gaspar," The rightful king said, "The lass' description of the skull-adorned one matches what I gazed upon as we entered the forest, a rider with two skulls placed on shoulder spikes. We can only wait to see if those two have more to say," he said as he pointed to the fast-asleep children, "we must know if their leader, the cloaked one, was here as well." The very mention of that beady-eyed rider sent chills through the hall, and a great gust of wind came through the broken windows, filling the hall with the night's frigid air, and extinguished the candles and brought the hearth's fire to an ember's glow.

Suddenly there came a great noise from outside the hall, the steady rhythm of approaching horses through the muddied road. The town was dark, and only the shadowy figures of an odd twenty riders could be made out through the veil of shadow as Cedric and his band took up arms at the hall's door. The riders drew forth blades, which appeared to glisten from starlight, for they were of the finest quality steel.

Their leader, chiefest amongst them in rank and title, boomed in a loud and commanding voice. "Let those who serve Azrael come forth and have the justice of Cinder executed upon them!" Cedric and his friends were confused. "We have seen your light and horses! Come out, so that Amalric may achieve his king's justice!"

The riders revealed their nature; they were a patrol of knights, down from the northern winds of Telfrost. Cedric jumped out into their view, and his face was dimly lit by the fires they had going inside the hall. Amalric's knights prepared their blades and drew back their bows at the sight of the one they did not know as their king, all save Amalric.

The leper knight immediately dismounted his horse when he recognized his king, and bent his knee in the muddy mixture, staining his white cloak. "Hold back your blades all!" The Knight-Sergeant ordered to his men. "Here before us stands our king, Cedric, the heir of Adalgott!"

The knights fell before Cedric as though he were a holy relic, and threw their blades in the mud and each offered their steel in his service. The band of knights then joined the others in the hall and were given portions of the ale and food that was left over. In the candlelight, Cedric took note of each of their faces, for they were from all walks of life but had arrived at the same destination. Their kite shields and long white tunics bore the same symbol, a blue sea, with the golden red sun rising from its foamy surface, the symbol of Cinder's Dawning. The knights wore many different styles of helmets, some of Ritter origin, with beaked fronts, and other like that of the North, with flat plating. Their armor was the finest of quality plate and chainmail were interlocked, providing mobility and protection in unison.

Gwen and Atticus had woken from the shouting of Amalric and staring in awe at the chainmail clad warriors who sat and ate before them like they had appeared from the pages of a nighttime story.

Amalric was clad in leather straps along his arms, covering his disease-riddled hands, and he appeared in less health than in the palace at Wulfstan. Another change was his blade, for he now strapped it on his right side, meaning he would draw into his left hand.

Cedric was intrigued by this and spoke to his Knight-Sergeant. "Amalric, I did not notice you were left handed when last we spoke."

Amalric smiled awkwardly, and he did not wish to speak with shame to his king. "Oh yes my lord…well my right arm just hasn't been acting on the up, so I decided to work on my left-handed practice."

Cedric would not press further, for he realized he had embarrassed one so loyal to him, and he now knew the reason behind the sword's switching. Amalric had lost strength in his right arm to his affliction, for it had begun to shrivel and blood no longer flowed through its veins. To any other knight, this was a death sentence, the death of the lifestyle that is. Amalric laughed in the face of his disease, switching his practice to the left, to extraordinary success as his retinue agreed. In only a few weeks' time, Amalric had grasped the basic motions in his left hand and had begun relearning the most skilled moves in the arsenal of the Eternal Dawn.

Miro, a knight in Amalric's service, was of Tanaric descent, originally from the Plains of Arron where the vast fields are filled with wild stallions. His hair was jet black with a smooth and trimmed beard which covered his tanned skin. He bore small shields upon his shoulders, bearing the image of a three-towered castle as red as blood. At his hip, a curved blade, with overlapping designs of beautiful symbols and flowers from hilt to tip. He had served as Amalric's squire in his earlier years but now had officially taken oaths to Cinder.

"My king, why have you come to this forsaken township, would you not have more luck in Prav, where I am told that Malcom gathers his armies?" Miro asked in a slight accent that had been degraded from his constant interaction with the blunt tones of the Northmen.

"We spent the last weeks convening with the folk of the forest, and their new king, Pike, has thrown his support behind us." Amalric and his knights were stunned, for such an alliance, nor any sort of meeting had ever been assembled between the two people.

"Truly, my lord?" Amalric was on the edge of his seat, like

that of a child waiting for a story.

"Yes," Cedric turned serious, "but we were not the first to send emissaries, for Azrael's sorcerer Yellow-Eyes, had beaten us there and a significant minority amongst them supported his claims."

"Hmm, yes we have received reports of such a character roaming Midland as of late," Amalric said in a grave tone, "though none have managed yet to capture that rat."

"What news of lord Roderic, Amalric? Does he continue to support my claim?"

"Yes, my lord, when we received our last report, he fields near two thousand Rivermen, though the numbers grow by the day."

Alfnod raised his voice to speak amongst the nobility of man. "How long a ride to Telfrost? We'll need fresh supplies, and way to send word throughout Midland to the other lords."

"It is not far," said Amalric, "only a few days' journey, and we'll be safe behind her walls. We can find someplace for the two children as well; they'll be well taken care of, perhaps the boy may grow to train as a squire." Atticus' eyes lit up at the mention of becoming a squire, for he often played in the gardens of Mileast as though he were a noble knight or even Adalgott himself.

"Amalric," Cedric asked, "why have you come this far south, to chase after some group of bandits so unconcerned with the knight's chapter castles?"

Amalric answered gravely, and with the utmost seriousness. "My lord the bandits we track, the very same who sacked this town, are in the employment of Azrael. Their leader, a man known as Sibi the Brother, has taken a full warband across Midland, slaughtering and capturing innocents that cross their path. These captive prisoners have yet to be accounted for, and we are trying to discover where they are being held, for I fear the meaning behind these attacks is of the utmost severity. For in these times, the Rat grows in strength, and his influence has already begun to corrupt this peaceful land."

Amalric continued, describing how the folk to the east had come to reave and rape the countryside. Beyond the mountains east, to the Hirdland, many men had come westward. Many of them mercenaries and sellswords now in Azrael's service. They came in ragged clothing, sewn together piles of fur, and their faces were grim and uncivilized. At their fronts, great men with chain armor, with faces painted by blood splatter, their brutal clansmen devoted to their evil master. In a long-forgotten time, their folk served Azrael in his first wars against man; it is now that they remember their ways, and take up the sword against the people of Midland.

"We'll accompany you back to Telfrost, and then to Prav, where we can finally meet with King Malcom, and devise some sort of grand strategy," said Cedric as he imagined the savages from the east.

The conversation slowly dimmed between the two groups, and the knights established a perimeter of guards along the ruins of the wall while the other slept in the hall. Amalric was sitting perched against one of the pillars, clutching at his hands covered by bindings.

"Does it hurt much?" Cedric asked in a hushed voice, to not wake the others.

"No…I can't feel them, but every now and then, I get a small feeling, as though I'm getting better, but it vanishes as quickly as it came." He continued to writhe his hands. "Telfrost is my birthright you know? Not even the grandmaster could remove me from it. I could have rotted away in my chambers, getting fat and lazy, but I chose this over that. I would rather struggle to lift my blade than feast and rest all day; there's no honor or challenge in that lot."

Cedric was engrossed in Amalric's life story. "But it isn't as though you were forced to become a knight; you did it out of duty."

"Aye, I was not about to be the first in my house who couldn't ride a horse into battle…but the truth is I barely can nowadays. He revealed the skirt of his tunic, lifting it so Cedric could see similar wrappings along his legs. "It has spread through my legs now, every step is unsure, every time my horse bounces as it runs I fear I will not have the strength to hold on. But here I am still, and here I shall remain. I swear I will tie myself to my horse before refusing to follow you into battle, you're the true king, and I'd be happy to die for that and not in my bed not able to lift a finger."

Cedric was impressed by Amalric's loyalty, but he required more than loyalty in his allies. "Thank you for the bout of confidence, but remember, we aren't out on that field looking for a glorious death, we try to find our way home."

Amalric looked down at his mug that was still half filled. "Thank the gods they did not take away my feeling in my tongue," he said as he downed the rest of his ale and turned over for sleep.

At the dawning hour when the sun appeared orange across half the sky, the knights and Cedric's party departed for Telfrost, taking the northern road out of Mileast. The children, Gwen and Atticus, rode respectively with Aderyn and Beorn, and both little ones cried at the departing horizon of Mileast.

The knights rode in silence, for they had no natural

charisma for conversation that did not involve prayer or training. Their life was a simple one, but one that brought peace to those who could aspire to the tenements of The Eternal Dawn. Justice, Honor, and Wisdom, the three virtues held sacred by the order. Many common folk believe them to only focus on battle and to train their bodies only for the sword, but it is not their real goal. For in the order, every warrior must also be a scholar, an administrator, a judge, they must be a beacon of hope for the hopeless. For in their minds, there is not a righteous path to holiness without the balancing of a man's life.

For three days, the group rode throughout the day, while also taking rest for lunch when the sun was highest in the sky. They rode through open hilly fields and light spots of trees, where the first of orange leaves had begun to turn, though none had yet to fall from their branches. The air had turned to a temperature that could not be felt, for it was neither warm nor cold, much time had passed these lands while Cedric parlayed in the forest.

On the third day, they were in a particularly wooded patch of Sodeer land, and they could scant stay in a single line due to the trees. The group heard the snapping of a branch nearby, and each drew their weapons in anticipation of those who had torched Mileast.

"Who goes there!?" Amalric boomed through his helmet as he waved his sword. From out of the bushes, three figures emerged. Their leader bore a long and scraggly beard with dirt about his face. He wore a long open coat, which revealed a shirt of chainmail underneath. His companions bore separately styled clothing, which had a badge of Sodeer at the chest. They each carried bows that were drawn at Cedric's company, along with longswords at their hips.

Their leader spoke, "I could ask you the same." He took a moment, and then answered Amalric's question. "We are rangers of House Sodeer, sworn to these sacred woods to which you make your journey. State your business and be gone."

"We are Knights of the Eternal Dawn, with the company of Cedric, the true king of these lands and of your lord," Amalric spoke with gravitas.

"My lord is dead; his people litter the dirt," The ranger spoke brashly, and with a hint of anger in his voice, "This man you travel with is no king of me or mine. Begone. These woods remain as ours, these tracking paths our sacred home. Mileast has fallen, the late lord, and my Sergeant-Commander of the Rangers as well. My folk answer call of arms to no lord now. Again, I say, begone."

Amalric was about to speak, but Cedric waved him off, there was no point to it. Cedric and his troop pressed onward, leaving the rangers to their business.

Upon the fourth day's ride, they passed through the lands of Owain Sigberht, proud lord of Gwent. It was snug upon a hill, with many halls of stone with wooden roofs. Banners of the coat of arms of Sigberht, a single tower upon a green field, waved proudly upon the battlements of the walls. Cedric and his companions did not stop to see the city, only to glance at it from the distance of a hill. Gwent was the second largest city in Prav, and yet it was completely emptied of all life save the rats scurrying about its streets. Everyone had made way to Prav, and the tracking of cart and foot could be seen well in the distance, dark and embedded into the roads. The many tall stone buildings of the city were sharp as a blade up their tops, shaped like obelisks of the Tanaric peoples.

On the fourth night, the group was starved for

entertainment, for the only interruption of the days' monotonous rides were the brief gusts of wind and sprinkles of rain. As their campfire crackled and the last bit of pork that had yet to turn was cooked, Eadwine tuned his lute once more to sing of ancient tales.

"Tonight, I shall sing in your common tongue, so the knights may also hear and understand." He said as he strummed his instrument for tone. He was a true master of the silver tongue, for the tale he told had no translated form in common language, so Eadwine translated as he sung.

"Forsooth my dear knights I know many tales of my kin, I can tell you of little elves and tall elves, wise ones and daft ones. On this night, I tell you the day of the cleverest of them all, the tale of the Prince Dothriel."

In the days when Glanfech still stood tall, and their culture thrived, their Prince Dothriel set off to ride the countryside of bandits and highwaymen, armed with only a purse of coin, his trusted bow, and his wits. In these times, he traveled as a beggar, appearing as though he had a limp, and wore mudded clothing to hide his princely looks. He went amongst his people, and lived by their charity, often sleeping in barns and damp cellars.

For weeks, he hunted through the deepening woods of his lands for the bandits who sullied his land. Upon a clearing, he found their camp, and they were drunk on libations and pride. The campfires were wild and unkempt, and so Dothriel hatched a cunning plan. When the last of the bandits fell fast asleep in their tents, their fires still burned brightly in the night. Dothriel snuck into the camp and took up burning branches, tossing them at the tents that went up in a fire like kindling.

The bandits ran from their tents, clutching at their inflamed cloaks and screaming through the night like wild beasts. In this panic, Dothriel hid along the tree line, picking off the panicked band with ease. Upon the morning, Dothriel returned to the village, where a vast number of his people had come to see the commotion. He threw down the brooch of the bandit's leader, and the people let out a great cheer. Dothriel, not a seeker of pride or glory, left without lifting his hood, and his bright face was not revealed to his people. Later, on his deathbed, after a long and prosperous rule, Dothriel revealed himself as the hooded vigilante. His people were stunned and brought many gifts to his tomb, adorning it in the rustic goods that thrived in the land he defended.

Eadwine finished his tune and downed the last of the ale, for they had only brought a few pouches worth from Mileast. The knights sharpened their many axes and blades, not allowing for a single speck of dust or rust to disgrace their holy instruments.

"By tomorrow we'll be safe behind the walls of Telfrost, about time too…can't do without ale on an open road." Miro said with an angry stare at the elf who has swindled the last of the brew from the camp, all the while sharpening his curved blade to a razor's edge.

When the sun broke out upon the sky they took their breakfast of oatmeal and simple dried fruit, for they had officially run out of meat and finer food from Mileast. A short time after noon, they reached the final hill before Telfrost, and they set their eyes upon the outpost of the Eternal Dawn.

It was of basic design, consisting of four straight carved walls, each holding a tower at its end, and a keep towards the back of the castle. The small hamlets of Telfrost sat snugly upon the open fields of the land, dotted between squares of growing grain now close to harvest. They rode past the moat which was only half filled, making it appear as nothing more than a pit of mud. The drawbridge was closed as they entered and their horses were taken to be fed and rested at the stables. Many folk of the castle, the servants, and guardsmen alike, gathered to greet their lord Amalric, who in turn greeted them all by name. From the main keep, a woman clad in purple garments appeared to float down the stone steps towards the lord of the castle. It was Josephine, wife of Amalric and Lady of Telfrost. Her hair was a dark red, near auburn brown, and her face was pale, a common sight for the ladies of the north. In her arms, she held a baby boy, yet to be named, for it was the custom of the knights to name their sons and daughters on the eve of their first birthday. Amalric rushed to his wife, and embraced her, though they did not kiss, for fear of spreading his pestilence. The leper knight took his child in his hands but again did not touch without a layer of clothing.

The knights disbanded and returned to their quarters, to retire from their muddied chain and tunics. Cedric and his party were offered fine but snug rooms in the castle's main keep, where Amalric prepared a large meal for them. They ate red meat and drank from steel goblets, a personal gift from the grandmaster to Amalric. The two children, Gwen and Atticus, stuffed their faces with the food before them like dogs going for fallen table scraps.

Miro entered the room, now wearing an elegant silk tunic in the style of his people, carrying messenger scrolls from Castle Zweleran. He presented them to Amalric, who took and read from them diligently.

"How old are these messages?" Amalric asked shocked.

"Two weeks by now, could be coming for us soon," Miro responded gravely.

Amalric crumpled letters in his fist and slammed his palms on the dinner table, before collapsing his head into his gloved hands.

"Amalric what has happened?" Cedric implored the Knight-Sergeant.

Fear gripped the knight, and he struggled to muster his words. "It…it appears as though the outer rim of castles has been sacked. Plymford Keep, the castle nearest the Hirdland, has been burned to ash. There is nothing between Azrael and a direct path to Zweleran. If we do not act quickly all we have done so far will be for naught, as Azrael will burn everything the knights have spent centuries building." He continued deeper into the letters' contents. "As I suspected…it appears the riders from Mileast orchestrated these sackings." Both the children at the table stopped eating, and their minds were called back to that dreadful time. "There are only a handful of operating castles now; we cannot track Sibi and his men without outside aid…we need the spies and songbirds of Prav."

"Something tells me finding Sibi will lead us to Azrael." Cedric said as he imagined the skull-adorned savage in his mind. "I say we ride tomorrow, if we can reach Prav in less than a week's time we'll be in good shape to hunt down Sibi and prevent him from raiding any more towns."

"Agreed," Amalric said as he resumed his meal of roasted pheasant, downing the last of his wine. They ate in silence for the rest of the dinner, both out of hunger and the dread of being thrown back into the fray.

After the meal, Amalric led the two children to their quarters with the servants, he told them of their new life here, that they would be safer here, but the children appeared distant and stared off into nothing as he left them tucked in their beds.

Chapter 23
Loden the Wanderer

That night while Cedric rested, visions once more appeared in his dreams. He heard a slight whisper coming from the woods surrounding the water. "Come through the trees." It spoke in a manner soft it was as though it was but a thought in the mind, whom none but Cedric would be able to hear. "Come…" It spoke again, this time holding on the single word for what seemed like an eternity. Cedric walked through the forest, brushing against the thick bundle of branches and twigs.

Before him lay a blue and ethereal landscape, where blades of long grass danced and swayed in the howling wind. Out before him, a long road reached out beyond the horizon. Cedric was compelled to march forward on the mossy stones of the road, and he ran his hand through the grass, which felt cold to the touch. Above him, the moon beamed as it always had in his dreams, though this time its light reflected across the whole of the land, in a distorted appearance of daytime.

At his side, a leather sack of ale was filled to the brim and bounced off his hip as he took his strides. He felt a great thirst building in his throat, which appeared parched as if from nowhere. He took a few full gulps of the ale before placing it back at his side, all the while continuing his walk along the road. Soon buildings in the far distant came into view, towers of a bygone age, built by those not of his world. The towers floated in the sky, their foundations were torn from the ground and suspended by nothing. Others lay in ruins in the field, and none appeared inhabited. Cedric took another drink and had nearly emptied it when he heard a sound not far from him.

From over the hill, there was another voice, not like the previous whispering, for it appeared warm and welcoming. The voice sang a tune far from the common tongue, and the words seemed mumbled and without meaning. From over the hill, an old man in a great pointy hat and a dirty robe was walking hunched over, his beard nearly at his feet.

He almost passed Cedric before looking up at the young king who stood before him. "Oh hello my dear boy, how goes your journey?" He smiled through his silky white beard that covered his face, and his eyes were filled with wise kindness.

"Who are you?" Cedric said surprised, for he had yet to converse with one found in his dreams.

"I am but a lonely wanderer, willing to share idle conversation with another who takes this road." Cedric looked back toward the road, taking his view off the old man for only a single moment. When his eyes returned to the old man, he had vanished. "Do you have something to drink my young man?" Cedric turned his body around and saw the old man sitting by a campfire that had appeared before them. By the fire, the fields of grass grain had vanished and become a rushing river, which frothed into a white mist as it broke against the rocky shore.

Cedric slowly and cautiously sat down, for he realized this old man was no ordinary traveler. The old man smiled and stoked the fire with a stick. Again, the old man asked his question. "Do you have something to drink my young man?" At this moment, Cedric's throat was once more dried, and he felt a great need to drink. He looked down at the bottle by his side and opened the top, seeing that there was only enough for one to be satisfied. Without a word of complaint, Cedric hesitantly handed the last of his ale to the old man, who quickly snatched up the bottle and drank it whole.

The old man laughed in a sweet-sounding voice. "Thank you, my dear boy; I was truly beyond thirst when you found me." He saw that Cedric too was thirsty, and his face turned witty and wise. He handed Cedric back his flask. "Take that and fill it in the river, I swear it will satisfy you."

Cedric appeared skeptical, but nevertheless rose and took the pouch to the rushing river. He waded into its icy cold current and filled the bottle to the brim, before bringing it back to the fire, where the old man smiled at Cedric. Cedric looked back at the flask and saw that its color had changed, and he when drank from it he tasted the sweet ale of Orford, the reserve that was by fate, never to be drunk. He consumed it all in his thirst to be at home, and with each drop that passed by his tongue, a fond memory of Orford was engraved in his mind.

Cedric opened his mouth to speak but found that no sounds came from his throat, as though he was deaf to his own voice. The old man shook his head and spoke humorously. "It is not wise to talk without the proper words." His muteness was clearly a jest by this strange and sage-like old man. The bearded man pointed towards the river. "Catch something to eat." Cedric turned and saw a great salmon swimming against the current of the mighty river, its rainbow coat glowing brightly through the crystal-clear water.

Cedric once more approached the raging river, where the salmon calmly resisted its current. He wrapped his cloak up to his elbows and plunged his hands through the surface of the frigid water. His hands struggled to grasp the fish, which began thrashing wildly with each touch. It made a great splash in the water, and its long tail smacked Cedric in the face, before finally being pulled from the frigid water.

The young king threw the salmon against the rocks and broke its head against a jagged stone. He returned to the campfire, where a smooth and thin plate of rock were heating over the flame. Cedric gutted and placed large strips of the gigantic salmon on the stone, where it cooked and sizzled with speed.

When the fish had been cooked properly, Cedric lifted a piece in an offering to the old man. The old man slowly waved in hand in rejection. "That flesh is not for my kind."

Cedric took the chunk of fish already in his hand and ate of its flesh. The fish's taste was typical, and there was nothing to distinguish it from one caught on the shores of Lorine. Suddenly Cedric felt a rush of energy tingle up his spine, reaching the back of his head and his mind was opened by the taste of the rainbow salmon.

He knew that the old man before him was Loden the Wanderer, the Father-Son, Father of the Children, and First Son of Cinder. "I greet you Cedric, son of Albert, heir of Adalgott and king to the Northmen. I believe you know who I am?" The old man smiled a warm smile; he had not had company for some time.

"Why have you brought me here Loden?"

"So you can understand," The old man said as he struggled to rise. Cedric rushed to his side and helped him to his feet. "This world is fading, as is yours. For in the darkening shadow of the Rat, our power weakens." The two began to walk again on the stone road. "Soon the moon that guides our steps will be clouded, and nothing shall be known. It is only by your will that any of us can survive."

"How can this deed fall on my shoulders, are you not a god born of Cinder?" Cedric asked impatiently and confused.

"I wish it did not, but it is the only way. For the battle of good and evil cannot be decided by gods and demons, the lords of those two opposites." He stopped Cedric and placed his finger where the young king's heart rested. "The battle of good and evil is decided by the lesser ones, by you and your foe Azrael."

"You say this as though Azrael is a mortal man."

"He is my dear boy, no less flesh and bone than you."

"How is that possible? They say his flesh is torn from his bones, and that he rides like a wraith across the night's sky." Cedric was distressed, for he knew not how Azrael, born of hate, could be of his same flesh."

"Here," Loden said, as he pointed to the river, which now produced a memory of a time now distant and faded, "see what Azrael is wrought of."

Cedric leaned close to the glowing pool of water and saw the image of a nobleman, adorned in golden chains and bracelets. He rested beneath an oaken tree, just outside a mighty hall in fatted lands, where cattle and crop grew rich. At his side, his blade, used for justice rather than greed, along with a flute, where his people's culture rested. This was a lord filled with the blessings of the gods, given what men envy, and yet, in his heart, there was a small flicker of ambition that could not be quenched. In his great hall, the banners of a golden blade, which was wrapped by two stretching vines, which grew fat with grapes for harvest. It was the banner of Clan Frisin, a noble house only remembered by the wisest magi in their record books.

In the dead of night, as this lord's courtly duties were winding down for the day, his guardsmen produced a hunched over cripple, with a dark cowl covering his head, caught cursing the blessed statues of the gods, which lay out in the green fields. The lord's wife and children sat next to him, and they were filled with fear by the sight of this stranger. His people were terrified of this dark figure, and pleaded for their king to do away with him so that they might receive the gods' favor.

"No, my lord," the wretched creature spoke with broken and screeching tongue. "You do not need the blessings of your gods. I was doing you a favor, my lord, for the gods only tempt your magnanimous power." The king's ego had been stoked, and the embers of ambition within him were set alight, and so he bid the foreign thing speak more. "Allow me just three days in your court my lord, and I shall offer that your enemies fall and you rise in splendor if I am false, then may you cut my head from my neck." The king smiled smugly; it was a deal that had no chance of losing, as he would be entertained by how this foul thing's head rolled from the chopping block.

In three days' time, the stranger had been hard at work in the laboratories of the hall, and in three days' time, the neighboring kings had all fallen ill and died. As any king would, the ambitious lord let out his armies, and overcame his neighbors, bring their lands into his fold. When he returned, the stranger was waiting with chests filled with golden coins, minted in the lord's likeness, for the stranger knew the ways of alchemy and had produced the coins from heaps of mud. The king was pleased by all of this, and gave a golden chain of office to the stranger, inviting the gift giver into his council.

Now there came a day in the following months when the lord's oldest child fell sick, and all feared he would die as he was as a pale as milk and coughed blood throughout the day. The king's magi prayed and gave him medicine, but to no avail. The stranger once more appeared before the lord, "Lord Frisin, you must send away your courtly magi, for they only worsen your son's health by worshiping deaf gods. Burn those wooden statues I so graciously once tried to rid you of, and your son shall be as healthy as the spring's morning." And so, the king cast out his magi, sending them down his roads in ragged clothes in disgrace. Next, the king burned the wooden markers of the gods, all to the pleasure of the stranger, who in return, cured the son of the king.

In the years to pass, the kingdom grew in wealth, and the hall of Frisin was ornate with golden splendor. The king grew old, his hearing began to fail him, and his eyes deceive him, but his burning ambition grew brighter with age. With shaking hands, the king called in his trusted advisor and told him of his growing fear of death. "My lord you do not need fear, for I shall give you the answer you want, as I have for so many years." The stranger leaned in and whispered in foul voice, words of absolute evil now made dull by the years of blasphemy. "The blood of kin is the only price for this gift of immortality, the blood which will sustain you forever. I see it now my lord, your wise rule shall outlast the false gods themselves, and you shall inherit the whole of the earth as your golden kingdom. Bring forth your two sons, and your wife my lord, invite them to feast on poisoned food and drink, then I shall speak of the next step."

And so, the king did as his advisor told, and prepared a large feast in his family's honor. Each of his kin fell on their food, choking on the ground in agony, their faces turned purple and eyes red. The foreigner was pleased by this display, and next ordered that the king dig a great ditch in his most bountiful field. The king did this, and then threw the bodies of his now deceased family into the pit which appeared like a void under the moon's dim light.

It was at this moment when the king believed he was at his most powerful, that the foreigner took off his cloak, and revealed his real face. It was Crassus Baal, for his head was that of a rat, and his tunic underneath his cloak was adorned in royal splendor. The demon clicked his hooved feet with glee as he shoved the last Frisin lord into the pit to rot with his family.

The trickster tossed piles of dirt onto the king, who had broken his legs from the fall and was writhing in agony at the faces of his family. When the last scrap of dirt had been placed on the tomb, the deceiver knelt and cursed the soil with foul whispers to forever bind the king to his will.

For one full year, the king decayed in that pit, his flesh mixed in with the bloodied dirt of his family. Weeds overran his fields and died, for none were left to sow them. His hall was divided up by his neighbors, and the golden details were cast into coinage. His banners withered and grew dust until their golden image of a vine had faded both physically and from memory. On the same date as the last year, the king emerged from the tomb, his withered arm sending dirt flying from the mound. He pulled himself out, now less man than any alive, for his body had decayed and now he was left with mere sinew and bone. It was at this moment that his friend, the Rat, returned to him, and offered him news since his departure. "Your fields lay barren, and your neighbors grow fat off your gold, take up the sword, and claim what is theirs in my name, and I shall give you back your kingdom."

And so, Cedric saw the tale of the last king of Frisin, who is doomed to walk the earth as a servant to Crassus Baal, never to have his true name known by any.

"And now you know your enemy, my child." The old man said with deep sorrow, his face had turned down and wrinkled. "He was once a man, but now what is left is just a pale imitation of life. You must end his animation, for, with every step he takes, his lord's dominion grow, for he offers the same to each man as he did that day. You must hurry to gather your forces, for not by the knights alone can this battle be won. Travel to Prav, and summon the Witan of Midland, for as we speak the remaining lords gather their defense. Awake now, Lord Cedric, for your hour draws near, and the tides of temptation swirl round like the tempest."

Suddenly Cedric's eyes were forced open, and he lay in a cold sweat on his bed. He leaped from his room dressed only in his undergarments, carrying a candlestick and waking his friends and Amalric. They gathered at the main hall where many tapestries hung in vibrant color, and Cedric revealed what he had learned in his dreams.

"For Loden to appear to you…such a thing has never been heard of," Amalric said in shock, though he did not doubt the word of his king for one moment. He too was still in his sleeping clothes, though he had draped himself in a long bear cloak

"We must heed his word," Cedric implored. "Amalric, I know you trust in the strength of your order, but we have seen that even they cannot stand alone against this rushing tide. We need the other nobles of Midland, with Roderic already behind us we may yet have a chance to persuade them."

"I know you think you are king," Amalric warned, "But Malcom Crawe does not see it that way, as with most of the other lords. To them you are a foreign invader, you must convince them otherwise." Amalric paused and strategized their next move in his mind. "…We will ride to Prav, seek out whoever will join us. But we must return to Zweleran as soon as possible, Midland in support of us or not." Cedric smiled and nodded in approval; he would not squander his one chance to seize Midland. "We ride at dawn, gather what you must now, for it shall be a dangerous road." Amalric turned, spinning his brown cloak, and headed back to bed.

Chapter 24
The Dogs of War

Upon the dawning of the sun, Cedric and his merry band packed their horses and prepared for the road. Out of the keep, Gwen and Atticus came bounding from the door, well-rested and in good spirits, though saddened by their friends' departure. Leopold felt ashamed that he had forgotten to say his goodbyes to them, and with red cheeks on his face, he hugged them into his black cloak.

"Will you come to visit us again Leopold?" Atticus said, his eyes welling up with glossy tears.

"Of course, I swear on my life." Leopold smiled to assure to the young boy. "Here," the assassin reached into his pocket and produced a small token, a rune stone from the Ithon, painted in yellow and blue symbols. "When next we meet, I expect this trinket to be clean and safe, can you do that?"

The young boy nodded, thrilled by this mystical little gift. Leopold patted them both on the head and mounted his horse.

Eadwine smirked as he leaned forward on his horse. "Where's my token Leopold?"

Leopold simply rode forward without looking at the elf while giving his retort. "How long did it take you to think up that little joke?"

Eadwine was pleased his with own sense of humor and gave a look to see if any in their party had found it funny, but found only the focused faces of those ready for war. Their journey had steadied them, and their hands were eager for their blades' handles, for their feel had become second nature to them.

The knights took the lead of the caravan, riding in full armor and carrying the banners of their respective houses, with Amalric at the head wielding the sigil of the Dawn, given to each Knight-Sergeant of the order. Cedric carried his household banner, the proud griffin flying freely in the breeze, released from its long slumber. Its golden and red designs were the paramount of royal splendor, and the fields of simple farmers they came across were in awe at its passing.

The many fields of Midland had begun their harvest, and everywhere the party passed wagons were being filled with grain and barely, to be shipped to castles for the coming tide of war. The lesser houses of nobles had frozen in place like dogs to the sound of a thundering storm, cowering in their hovels rather than acting against the oncoming horde. Content to vanish with a whimper rather than a crackling climax.

Prav, the city wrought of the vine. Founded by Scallion Crawe, an Eln man with no title, no land, and no wealth, only a handful of Iceberries in his pocket, names for their pale blue exterior. He came up from the south, a trader with an ambitious mind. In the land where men knew nothing but beer and ale, he intended to bring culture. His Iceberries could grow tall in stalk in even the mildest of northern winters. Upon where his family's palace stands, in Elnish splendor with columns and courtyards, he planted three rows of these berries for his winery, which soon multiplied into numerous fields throughout the land. His wealth rivals even that of the first Erastrian kings, and his officers are donned in polished steel, with three golden vines along the breastplate. Long has this city stood growing like their vines, unchallenged by all. Now in this dark time, the might of the wine king shall be tested, and his fields will be thrown against the mighty storm that comes with Azrael.

They made good pace to Prav, for the roads had been cleared of common thugs and highwaymen, now too afraid of Sibi and his roaming savages, who kill criminal and commoner without restraint.

They passed by the Red Swamp, the swath of marsh just south of the northern coast of Midland, where Vaal and their ships come in the springtime to raid and reave. It had been many years since the last. The swampland was famous for its red lily pads, whose sweet aroma seeped into the murky water, turning its color to bright red in the summers when it grows.

On their fourth night of travel, they had near reached the hills before Prav and stopped in a small town known as Harfield, where the peasantry made their final preparations for the capital. From the road, they saw a great stone mill across the town's snug houses and expansive fields and vineyards. Within the fields themselves, great stone and wooden carvings of the gods lay for blessings of a good harvest, their stoic faces frozen in a blank expression across the landscape.

At the edge of the township, Cedric's party tied their horses by an inn called the Giant's Delight. In the dry grass to the back of the tavern, a decently sized host had pitched tents and were in a loud row of music and drink.

Cedric and his friends entered to find the bar filled with all manner of sellswords and brigands, and the inn was near filled with their company. They sat sported in aketons and tough leather jerkins, standard for such a group. Even from a distance, they could be made out as Elnish, preferring the company of wine to ale, and the captains of the company dressed in fine flowery armor. The knights scoffed and held their cloths to their noses, and found a small booth enclave where they slunk from the noise and spilling of drinks. At the host's bar, they found a fat bald man manning the tavern, running around in a frenzy to refill the drinks of his unruly guests.

Cedric approached and found an empty stool, while his companions stood behind him, darting nervous looks at the crowd of guests. "What's the fare for twelve road weary travelers?"

The man looked up for a moment in a daze and immediately went back to pouring more beer and ale, shaking his head left to right. "No no no, don't have any more room. These lads have seen to it." Cedric looked back at the crowd of ruffians who spilled their drinks and threw their food, with the occasional fist thrown as well.

A man approached from this row, appearing as though he were not a part of this rowdy lot. For this man wore clean and refined clothes, a leather jerkin embroidered in design, and slick trousers with a gilded belt which held a shining steel rapier with a thick blade. His hair was pulled back, and his beard was trimmed fresh.

The man clicked his boots all the way to the bar, where he took the stool next to Cedric and snapped his finger for the fat man's attention. "More schnapps this way, Thoron, there'll be a gold piece for you when we reach the capital." Cedric tried to hide his face, and turned the other way, for he had no way of knowing this warband's intentions. The suave one looked at Cedric and reached for a glass of ale. "You heading to the capital too, friend?" He said in a warm voice.

Cedric was brief and answered sharply. "Yes."

The man leaned in closer, and placed his hand on Cedric's back, "what business could some noble, a band of misfits, and chain-clad knights have together?" Alfnod grasped the hand on his blade, showing its steel. It was as though that steel against the sheath was as loud as a storm, for the whole of the tavern fell silent, and stared at Cedric's group.

"What's your business?" Cedric retorted, his hands growing wet with sweat as he thought of how much time it would take to draw his blade.

The man smiled wide. "Why to rape, pillage, and cause an amount of general chaos."

There was silence as the two groups had been fully absorbed in suspense. Blades were ready to be drawn, and throats to be slit. The suave man broke into laughter, soon followed by his entire party, who removed their hands from their swords and returned to their drinking.

"I am Tarquin," the man said extending his hand to shake Cedric's, who steadied his hand and relaxed. Cedric's party unwound and breathed a heavy sigh of relief, and the tavern keeper poured a whole mug of ale down his gullet to calm himself before returning to his work. "These men here are the Dogs of War!" He shouted with pride as each of his men raised their cups in toast of their name.

Alfnod pushed past some of the brutes to where Tarquin

was sitting, his long ears perked by the mention of their title. "The mercenaries from Kruithia?"

Tarquin was polite to the elf and answered while nodding his head. "The one and only. Yes, we're up here on business to King Malcom, promising a lord's fat stash for service in his name. We've been helping this village gather up their grain, and making sure they get to Prav without any harm. Can't well win a war but not have anyone to farm next year's crop. Come, we'll have room enough for your party." Tarquin said as he pulled up more chairs, and ordered another round of drinks. "So, what brings you on the road to Prav?"

Cedric alone answered for the others did not know if it was wise to reveal their mission. "I am Cedric, and this is my retinue accompanying my way to that city, where I will take counsel with Malcom."

Tarquin was pleasantly surprised by this news and downed another flask of drink. From the kitchen, a faint scream could be heard, and the tavern keep scurried away to investigate. "Oh yes, the southern bastard as his grace so eloquently puts it." Cedric turned dour; he was already on poor terms with a man he had yet to meet. "But I'd prefer the company of a bastard to some high-born dandy. Less frilly rules to follow." Cedric and Tarquin drank to those terms, and the rogue leapt over the counter to procure another bottle.

As Tarquin leapt back to his seat, the back door to the kitchen burst open, and a member of Tarquin's group came rushing out, getting cutlery and pots thrown at him. The screaming from earlier was from the tavern master's daughter, who had been preparing pies and meats for the guests in the back room. The girl was not yet a full woman, and she had flour in spots all over her face and in her stringy and frizzled hair.

The tavern owner protectively held his hand over his daughter, and he was wielding a butcher knife.

"Back you scoundrel before I take your man bits off!" The bald and sweaty man said as he swung the knife in wild fashion. The scoundrel in question was red-faced, and he carried a great sword at his side. The man reached for its handle, and pulled in out menacing the tavern owner.

Just as blood appeared as good as spilled, Tarquin stepped between the two groups, holding out his hand to calm his frenzied companion. "What's the meaning of this?" He implored both men.

The innkeeper answered first, spewing out his words quickly. "My lord he meant to take my daughter in the cellar, he's a savage I tell you, I won't serve him again."

"A lie!" The companion shouted, his cheek had been bloodied from feminine nails.

"Now Grif," Tarquin said soothingly, "we don't take what our hosts haven't offered." Tarquin patted him on the back. "Apologize now, and I'll let you sleep in one of the tents outside." Tarquin turned and face the innkeeper. "My good sir this man won't be problem for tonight. He will forfeit his room and board, he will sleep in the tents in the field, and by my honor will not step through this establishment's doorway."

The innkeeper nodded in approval, though he did not take his eyes off Grif until he had departed with his gear. The daughter was sent scurrying back into the kitchen, curtseying to Tarquin as she passed. The men returned to their drinking, for it was a common thing for one in their party to be scorned by their commander, for discipline was the Elnish way of war.

The night was passed with drinking and stories, tales from the small city-states of Kruithia and the Elnish people. The sellswords were quite welcoming when properly drunk, and they treated their guests like members of their own band. Slowly the Dogs of War exited the inn, each left when they had had their full fill of wine and food, returning to their tents and campfires. Traquin's group of captains left for their beds in the inn, mats of hay that appeared like the silk sheets of a noble's bed, compared to the sleeping sacks outside.

"Lord Cedric, it appears you and your illustrious companions have space in the inn for tonight. For we have left many of our company in the tented field," Tarquin said as he motioned upstairs. The knights stood and shuffled up to the common room, for they were tired of resting on mudded meadows.

Eadwine, being one for jests, did not give his new ally any quarter. "Fancy yourself some noble born Tarquin? Talking like some flowery tart in court?"

Tarquin responded as he reclined in his chair and crossed his arms. "None more than yourself master elf, practice with such words is but a means to an end with those flowery tarts."

Cedric was last to climb the stairs, but he was stopped by Tarquin, who sat with his legs on a now emptied table, pouring another glass of wine. "Lord Cedric, do have one last drink with me." He said politely as he gestured his arm to the number of freed chairs of the inn. Cedric took him up on the offer, and pulled up a chair to the table, and took a glass of wine to both their health.

"So how does a band of Elnish mercenaries end up in the frigid tundra of Midland, fighting for a foreign king?" Cedric said as he took his first sip of wine. He realized it was a Kruithian vintage, and reduced the taste of Iceberry Wine to that of foully made moonshine. "You brought this all the way from Kruithia?"

Tarquin nodded. "Yes, my favorite winery that place, the Magi's Elixir." He twirled the half-filled cup in his hand. "Well since Malcom still has so many connections in Kruithia, thanks to his heritage, he naturally found out about the great Pit Fighter this side of the world."

"You fought in the Pit?"

Tarquin reminisced. "Oh yes, for what was about a full year's time. The Pit...that ultimate example of Kruithian justice." Tarquin referenced the lowest level of Kruithia, as the city stands by itself in a ring moat, which stretched down near seventy stories. At the lowest level, now called the Pit, prisoners are made to fight for their freedom or the other option of enlisting in the military. "I was a merchant's son you see; we had a spectacular villa overlooking most of the city. I just happen to find myself in the bed of the wrong noble's daughter...completely by her choice no less. Her father had none of it, bribed damn near every official until I found myself in the Pit without a trial." Tarquin smiled and brushed his fingers across his blade's handle. "If it were not for this steel by my side, I would have wound up at the bottom of the moat. I won every match I was in for that year until I was finally granted my freedom, but not without trophies." Tarquin revealed many slashed scars across his chest, gifts from his most worthy opponents.

"I was not always from the cesspool of a city, the mercenary continued, "My family is of southern Elnish descent, from where the fields are golden and the histories filled with noblemen. I was born in Modelo, along the shorelines which were perfect temperature for swimming all year round. It was by sheer luck I immigrated to Kruithia. My father was embroiled in a scheme against the Dux of Modelo, how you say, Duke, in my tongue. He was exiled, and took my family north to Kruithia where he still had a few allies…" Tarquin paused, he had spilled his entire life's story to a stranger, and his face began to turn red from the silence.

"And this brought you up north?" Cedric burst to break the silence. He had been enthralled in the story the mercenary had woven. Cedric eagerly awaited the rest as he poured another glass of Kruithian wine.

"Aye, the Crawe's have many who serve them in the free city, with plenty of coin as the incentive for such a long journey." Tarquin leaned in and bragged his lump sum of wealth. "I've already been given near king's fortune just to guard these vineyards and peasantry; I can't imagine what riches Malcom has stuffed in his coffers of Prav." Tarquin reclined and placed his hands on his head as though he had not a care in the world. "Who knows? Perhaps I will return to that fair southern city; I'll be richer than that noble who imprisoned me…maybe even bribe his passage to the Pit, see how long he lasts."

Suddenly there was a great shouting from outside, muffled by the wooden and thatch walls of the inn. Grif burst through the door, and the cries came amplified with the slamming of the door against its post. "Riders from the other side of the village! Nearest the windmill!" He was clutching his blade, his aketon dangled on his chest, for he had not had time to properly fasten it.

With this warning from Grif, the knights and captains, along with Cedric's friends, leaped from their rooms with their weapons. Tarquin took a brisk walk out of the inn, taking survey of the village, now partially engulfed in raging flames which had spread from the half-emptied grain fields.

Cedric and Tarquin ran to the tents, where the sellsword gathered his men to mount a defense. Suddenly a rider came out from the night's veil and rode hard towards the suave commander. As though it were an effortless thing, Tarquin picked up an angon from a pile of weapons nearby and threw the barbed javelin with such grace that it appeared as an arrow flying through the sky. It struck the chest of the rider with such force that he was thrown backward from his horse, and Cedric stood in awe at the warrior's prowess and calmness in battle.

Tarquin turned and faced his men that had gathered their gear for battle, each carrying a beaming grin of pride for their company. Tarquin smirked and drew his blade to the starlit night, and rallied his men to battle. "Live up to your name, Dogs of War!" They raised their various weapons and gave a great shout as they charged through the village, taking the riders in small groups, so the horses became overwhelmed, buckling back in fear of the savage-faced men.

The Knights of the Eternal Dawn mounted their horses in full chainmail and with their lances in hand, rushing to aid the mercenaries. Their bannered spears scored many a death that night and gored upon both the horses and riders of those that burned the town of Harfield.

Cedric and his band found themselves rushing to the defense of the villagers and farmers, who had gathered at the town square and cowered in their barns and halls. Coming out from the red smoke, a man with two spiked skulls upon his shoulders rode atop a black horse, accompanied by full escort of men with the blood of the innocent upon their blades.

It was Sibi the Brother, chiefest of reavers to Azrael, and the scourge of the peaceful towns of Midland. He bore a wild look, and his hair and face were covered in a thick brew of warm blood and dry dirt. In his hand, a huge axe, double-sided, and sharpened to a shine, was dipped in a black sludge, which dripped from its edge. The raider has not expected a host of sellswords, and he realized his mounted party, no matter how brave or fast, were heavily outmatched in this battle.

He whistled to his sergeants, who quickly waylaid orders to round up whatever villagers they could, tying them to the backs of horses, or a worse fate of being dragged along the dirt behind the steeds. As Cedric and his companions were occupied with some bandits by the square, Aderyn found nothing but empty night air between her and Sibi. Drawing back her bow, she aimed true, and struck at his shoulder, just below where his brother, Sven, had his head spiked.

Sibi reeled in pain, clutching at his shoulder which bled profusely and spilled over the visage of his brother. With a kick, Sibi ushered his horse forward, and raised his axe to Aderyn. He took a mighty swing, nearly taking her head off. By mere chance, Aderyn had been grazed by the blade, though it plunged deep through her thin neck. She spun through the air as the blow threw her from her feet, landing with a thud against the hard stone floor of the town square.

Cedric went deaf as he rushed to Aderyn's side, and the world around him seemed to slow and fade into the dark of the night. He knelt beside her and laid her head in his lap, and pressed his loose cloth of his clothes to her gashed neck, which was covered in the black ooze of Sibi's axe.

"Gore and searing death upon you Cedric!" Sibi shouted from his horse, just as he rode along the horizon of the hill. "I will burn your false gods! My brothers demand blood, and I will give it to them!" His black horse bucked and reared against the night's black veil.

Sibi beckoned that his riders follow his lead back out of the town. As quick as the raiders had come, they had too left, leaving nothing but burning fields and scatters clumps of the dead or near death. Tarquin and his sellswords were quick to gather the remaining villagers, who huddled together like a flock of sheep against the fangs of wolves in the night. Many were missing, hogtied and taken by Sibi's lot.

Dawn was not far off now, and a light hue of orange had begun to pierce the furthest corners of the sky. Cedric stayed by Aderyn's side through the remainder of the night, for her breathing had become shallow and the wound had turned a black red, darkening the whole of her neck. Her face had become pale, covered in a layer of cold sweat. Her eyes were bloodshot red and slowly rolled round as she lay awake.

"She'll need to rest while we travel," Cedric said to his companions, "prepare a place for her on the carts." And so Beorn lifted the pale-faced Aderyn into his arms, and gently let her down on a bed of carpeting and bags of grain that were gathered on one of the carts being driven out of the village.

The dawn had come and with it a rainstorm which clogged and mudded the road ahead of the people. Now the people of Harfield were being led to Prav by Tarquin's remaining men, whose spirits had downed from the sudden attack in the night. They marched only on the road, opting for a long and narrow caravan of people and carts, which stretched out across the hilly and forested landscape. Cedric and his band rode out along the front of the camp, keeping constant watch over the horizon. Tarquin's sellswords marched on the outside, the first line of defense, along with any of the villagers able to carry blade or sharpened stick. These peasants were truly Crawe's people, for they had not known such hardship in their life, always use to the delicate taste of wine and feel of luxury clothes upon their backs. War had come to them all the same, for it gave no prejudice by wealth or birth, for Crassus Baal did not care for such trivial things.

They did not stop to take their lunch, nor to wipe the grim and muck from their boots, for fear that they would be set upon in their rest. At midday, Cedric turned his horse round to face the caravan behind him, where he trotted along until he came upon the cart where Aderyn lay. As her wound festered and turned darker, her skin became all the paler, as though it was sucking the life from her. Cedric turned grim as he saw this, for his hope was fading quickly. In the afternoon, they set up camp for only an hour, so the young and old could rest their weary feet, as their boots had been weighed down in heavy mud.

"What can we do for her?" Cedric said as he brought Gaspar to look at her wounds. Gaspar peered and squinted at the black rot that had taken her neck. The magi took a small scalpel from his sleeve of tools, and snatched a sample of the foul-smelling ooze.

"It is Basilisk Venom; these symptoms give away its source." He said as he placed a droplet of the stuff on his tongue, before immediately turning to spit it out. "We need antivenin, and soon, for no medicine I know of can cure a case this severe." Gaspar pointed to Aderyn, who had appeared to stop breathing, before finally taking in another shallow breath. "It will turn her insides to stone, and she will stop breathing."

Cedric grabbed Gaspar by his cloak. "What can we do?"

"This is Northern Basilisk Venom, a good thing for us. In my studies at Prav I researched Sir Cantelot the Lore Master, he concluded many of these beasts reside in caves along the

Belfas Mountains."

Cedric turned and prepared a sack of supplies on his horse, and fastened his blade to his traveling bag. "We go there now; I'm not taking any chances with that venom spreading through her body."

Alfnod raised his head from the campfire where he was resting. "You can't go alone, Gaspar and I will accompany you." Alfnod raised a nod to the others in their group, for he knew their place was to protect these people and keep Aderyn safe.

"Not without me you won't." Eadwine raised his voice as he sat arms and legs folded. "Who else will regale you with stories for the dreary trip, and who will sing of the firsthand account of Cedric the Basilisk-Slayer?"

"I'm afraid the story would end up being how we had to pull an elf's corpse from that creature's teeth if you came along," Alfnod said bluntly, but with a small smile. He rubbed Eadwine's head and silently agreed to the bard's decision.

Cedric gave orders to his remaining companions. "Beorn and Leopold…" his face turned grim and pale, "keep her safe."

Beorn extended his arm, and the two shook as brothers. "We will." Leopold sharpened his knives and gave a look of oath keeping.

Gaspar poked his head up, and interrupted the sweet moment, for he appeared to turn as pale as Aderyn, "are you sure such bloody work is fit for a magi? I could certainly keep Aderyn safe as well."

"We'll need you to make the cure Gaspar, and you'll know where to find these creatures," Cedric said in a pleading manner, he did not want to force Gaspar's hand.

Gaspar swallowed his fear and took a deep breath. "To the Belfas Mountains then."

Cedric then summoned his council of knights, whose tunics were damped and browned by the constant downpour. He placed his hand on Amalric's shoulder and entrusted him with a sacred task. "Amalric, take half your knights and ride for Castle Zweleran, we cannot hope to win without them." Next Cedric turned to Miro, who sat on a rock polishing his curved blade. "Miro, take the rest and double back towards Telfrost, from there you must ride to the Ithon. By now Pike will have gathered his army, tell them to march straight for Prav."

Amalric took his blade and placed it through the mud, and kneeled in the presence of his lord. "With the speed of Godric's hounds, we shall cross the land, Lord Cedric. The whole host of knights shall prepare for war, and the castles will be garrisoned twice-fold." And so, the knights took their leave, hurrying down the road they had come from, and soon they were out of sight, for the rain was thick and veiled the horizon.

Tarquin bid Cedric luck, and the sellsword bore a grim look on his face, gone were the days of merry drinking in taverns, now came the true fight for his reward of a coin purse. Cedric, at last, took to his stead and prepared to set off with Alfnod, Eadwine, and Gaspar.

Chapter 25
In the Lair of the Basilisk

Cedric, Alfnod, Eadwine and Gaspar rode hard throughout the whole of the night, taking note of how the landscape began to change around them. The green trees and abundant crop fields now became barren and stony hills across the landscape. The Belfas Mountains were not far off now, for they lay as the fourth wall for Prav, and many castles along the ridge of hard stone.

They came to the edge of the Red Marsh, which spanned the land between Midland and Belfas. To the north, the stone bridge road to Castle Zweleran lay before them, protruding from the bubbling surface of the swamp. The Red Marsh was given its name for the red lily pads which rested upon its wet surface, and whose petals turn the landscape a bright blood red. It was a greater defense to the knights than their wall, for the marsh had but one route through it, the bridge that lay before them. None had ever taken the bridge, not while the knights stood watch for the Eternal Dawn.

Upon the knoll of a hill, they established a small camp, where they lit a fire and cooked some rabbit they had hunted in the nearby burrows. The rabbit haunch was dry and rough, like salted provisions for the road. Eadwine was bored by the day's ride, and squirmed under his blanket, reaching for his lute. He began to strum, as he had so many nights before.

"What's a good one for tonight?" He whispered to himself. Suddenly his fingers began to dance along the strings, and the steady rhythm of The Twiddle and Whittle began:

Oh the farmer had a pig
A hog so fat and full
It snorted and twiddled
While the farmer sat and whittled
And the pig did laugh and the pig did jest
For it knew not why the farmer whittled
While he did twiddle
Then came the day
When the farmer had whittled
A spit for the pig
That the pork did no longer twiddle!

The lot from Orford smiled and gave a laugh to this folk song. Any lad who lived where the fields grew grain knew that tune, and Eadwine had played it many times in the Green Devil. For only a moment, as the fire crackled, they felt at home, and their grassy beds were like the cots of yore, their ale pouches like the strong liquors of Cedric's manor. They sighed and dreamed of their home, but only for a moment.

From the distance, there came a faint sound, which began

to grow with the howling wind that picked up in the night's sky.

"There above the dark of the horizon!" Alfnod screamed as he pointed towards an orange ember appearing on the horizon. This ember soon grew into a full-fledged flame, and from the flame, an out of control fire. But it was not the pine nor grass of the land that burned, it was torches, and oil braziers wrought of mannish craftsmanship.

Across the horizon, this sea of burning fire swayed and moved across the landscape. Amongst some of the torches, banners of gray cloth and blooded sigils swayed in the wind. The drums of war beat to the rhythm of their march, foul drums that heralded the coming tide of death.

Cedric looked out in horror at this army, and immediately back to his own little campfire, which he stomped out with his boots.

"What are you doing!? The rabbit!?" Gaspar cried as he struggled to wipe the dirt from the meat still stuck on the spit, which had collapsed from Cedric's frantic rush to extinguish the fire.

"Those men shall see our fire!" Cedric cried out. Cedric called out to Alfnod, "Go, move closer to their ranks, but make sure not to be seen. We must find out if they come as friend or foe."

Alfnod silently moved through the brush, vanishing into the night. The group had waited for ten agonizing minutes before the bushes rustled again. Alfnod burst back into sight, out of breath. "I had the fear they had seen me," He spat out with a shallow breath." I have seen those banners before," Alfnod said, "They come from the Hirdland, that expansive steppe that remains untamed. Look." The elf pointed back towards the ranks that swelled in the valley. "There are some banners from Belfas, marching in better order and rhythm than their counterparts, for they have been drilled in the art of war. By their ranks, men of Usham, those former slaves now turn their hate upon any in their path. They come bearing dwarven weapons, steel forged, sharper than any blade of man. Even more so I saw symbols from the south, men of the Elnish kingdoms, wielding steel shields and riding atop horses. This horde shall test the folk of the vine…let us pray their harvest is not found lacking." Alfnod stood on the knoll of their hill, his foot placed against a high rock, peering over the ledge towards the flowing sea of men that swelled the valley below them.

The small group took refuge in their hill and under their blankets, silently waiting for the horde to pass them by. For hours, the rushing tide of doom did march, and by the light of the dawn, the last of their host had come through the valley. The four pressed further towards the Belfas Mountains, and their horses slowed and climbed against the rough terrain that overtook their hooves.

On the next night, Cedric dreamt of the hidden garden once more. Here he found himself in a darker world than before, for the stars had gone black, and the pool had turned to a black ooze. Aderyn rested on her back upon the surface of this tar, and her body was half submerged, reaching near to her lips

At last at near midday they did arrive at the base of those rising spirals of stone. So jagged and narrow that they did appear to pierce and shatter the sky. Upon the expansive tops, snow had stood for thousands of years, dancing and blowing with the movements of the frigid northern wind.

For a short while they took a path alongside the mountain base, for Basilisks they hunted for were cave dwellers, preferring shadowed and smoothed walls to that of open fields. Crafty and powerful creatures they are, dwelling as near blind creatures of acute hearing and smell, able to hunt a shepherd's lone sheep from miles away. But it is the foolish man who mistakes these beasts for mere pests, for their poisoned fangs are sharp, and can pierce the finest steel plating as though it were a lady's handkerchief.

They came upon a cave, whose insides howled and bellowed with damp and cold air, and to which the sun gave no light to its contents. "I would bet my last silver on this as a Basilisk's Lair," Gaspar said as he leaned over the cave's entrance, trying to make out its end.

Cedric lit a torch, and descended first, followed by Gaspar, next Alfnod, with Eadwine bringing up the flank. Each took their steps slow and calculated, for the darkness of the cave did not reveal their footing, and the ground was covered in wet moss. Soon they had turned many corners and crevices, and all natural light had faded from view, leaving their torch as the only light source.

Gaspar took a small orange stone from his satchel, and when he clasped it tightly in his hands, it glowed with light. "An Emberstone from Usham; got it from a dwarven merchant," Gaspar explained as he beamed with pride at his clever purchase.

"Give no voice to our presence," Cedric whispered, "We do not know what lurks with us." They continued down a narrow hall, which led to an open standing cave, filled with a still pool of water. They made their way across the mossy pathing, and their eyes darted in every which way in search of a slithering beast. The cave made no sound, and all was dead quiet, so much so that breathing gave sound like a blowing horn.

They had crossed this mossy bridge, and found themselves at a doorway, carved by human hands. Cedric held the flame to the runes that had been etched at its top, it was a strange language, with little logic in its patterning. Gaspar proclaimed in learned tone, "This is the text of the ancient ten kingdoms, before the time of Adalgott."

"Can you read any of it?" Eadwine asked as he darted his gaze back towards the moss, sure he had seen something dart away from the corner of his eye.

"No, it has been weathered severely, and there is no sense in the structure remaining," Gaspar said disappointedly.

The group pushed forward, now passing through ruined halls and long bridges over chasms that showed no floor. It was a labyrinth of intersecting paths, and the companions feared they would be lost in the maze. They took a long flight of stairs downwards, to where the architecture faded, and the cave began reemerged.

Cedric slipped as he went forward, the stone in front of him was wet. As he fell, he felt cold water. Luckily, he had the reflexes to catch their torch, and he could see a large pool of water reflecting the flame's light.

"Where do we go from here?" Gaspar said in a hushed but frantic tone. There was no footing on the walls of the cave, only the calm pool of water lay in front of them. Cedric paused to think but heard a sound from the other side of the water, the sound of slithering upon stone.

Suddenly the water began to stir, and steady beats of waves, so subtle and calm that it went unnoticed by Cedric and his friends, began to dance along the stone. A great crash of water came behind Cedric, and the lord drew his sword to face what monster lurked behind him. Gaspar had plunged into the pool, for he had placed his foot on a loose rock and had come unbalanced.

Cedric and Alfnod both sighed, and looked at Gaspar with smirks upon their faces. Gaspar tried to hold back an embarrassed smile as he pulled himself out of the pool, his robes now drenched and his traveling pack filled with water. From out of the shadow of the pool, there was another wave, and from it, the horror of the cave emerged as Gaspar recoiled and jumped back in fear.

In full display, with neck and head of thick scale like that of steel, and a slithering body with a long and twirling tail. Its eyes appeared like that of a shark, black and with nothing but primal power infused within. Its teeth, thin and sharp as spear points, had many rows to them, and it revealed them all as though it were smiling. The basilisk let out a great hiss, which seemed to dwarf the sound of a bear or lion's roar.

Cedric and Alfnod stumbled back as they swung their blades at the magnificent beast, which made a slow approach, all while dodging their blows with quick movements. Gaspar grabbed hold of the torch, which had fallen onto the wet stone floor, and shouted to his companions. "Run!" Immediately Gaspar turned and rushed back towards the cave's entrance, taking their only light with him.

They scurried through the many halls and passages, unsure of where they had been and what spots were unknown. The basilisk hissed behind them as it plowed through pillars and jagged rocks alike, which did nothing to hinder its steady advance.

Suddenly a faint light passed by the doorway and the sound of heavy footsteps that clicked sharply against the stone floor.

It was the magi, who nearly slipped as he stopped to see his companions. "No!" Gaspar shouted as a scolding teacher, "To the entrance, it's the only way!" And so, the company ran from the room and followed Gaspar through the narrowing

Cedric and Alfnod followed behind Eadwine and Gaspar, and they could feel the breath of the beast against their necks as they stumbled towards the light of the sun. Back out of the cave, they once more heard chirping birds and blowing wind. This moment of idle beauty was short-lived, for the basilisk came crashing out of the cave's entrance, its scales shining brightly against the light of the sun.

Gaspar had worked a miracle of brilliance by guiding them out into the open. The basilisk had weak eyes, and it was slowed by the beams of light which pierced its black eyes. It darted and glanced in every direction and hissed as the trio took near ten pace distance from the beast, each in opposite directions. The creature was confused, and it did not know which man to kill, and so it spun in a circle.

Now Cedric could see it clearly the shadow no longer hid the full body of the massive beast. It was not as gray as he thought, rather a light blue, with a body which twisted and coiled in a woven pattern that seemed never to end. Its eyes were yellow with black beady pupils. Its fangs glistened in the light of the day.

Cedric locked eyes with the basilisk, and the beast had found its mark. With rapid speed, it picked up its lower side and struck out at Cedric, revealing its sharp teeth. In an instant, it was on top of the young lord, and it bit and snarled as Cedric struggled to hold its mouth at bay with nothing but his bare hands.

Gaspar and Alfnod let out cries and threw their blades

upon the back of the basilisk, but to no avail. Their steel was nothing to the scaled hide which appeared now like stone. With ease, the basilisk lifted its tail and threw the two attackers from its side and into the air.

The basilisk closed the distance between its sharp rows of teeth and Cedric's face, which was red and tense as the lord tried with all his strength to hold back his certain doom. The beast appeared to smile, and widened its mouth, preparing for the final blow. Cedric closed his eyes, and let his arms loosen for a moment, and with a great yell, pushed and heaved with all his strength, turning his face bright red with rushing blood.

Suddenly there was a cry of another legendary beast, and the basilisk's heavy weight was lifted from Cedric. The lord opened his eyes and saw the basilisk being tossed back through the air, with Griffin claws digging hard through its scales. Jarrick had come, and the beast plucked and slashed at the basilisk's eyes, which were torn clean from their beady sockets. Suddenly Jarrick beat his wings hard, flying upwards into the sky and descending just as quick, taking his claws to the basilisk's exposed throat, which bled like a rushing river. Cedric struggled to his feet in awe as he saw the Griffin proudly stomp on the body of its foe, its red coat of feather waving proudly in the sunny day's wind.

When Cedric had risen back to his feet, the griffin met his gaze, its eyes unyielding and filled with recognition. The bird beat its wings hard against the ground, and launched back into the sky, before disappearing over the horizon.

"By the gods, we are lucky to have such a beast as guardian," Gaspar said as he took a curved dagger from his satchel, and knelt while he carved into the venom sacs of the Basilisk's mouth. He was careful at his work, to cut the pouch at too low a point would cause it to leak. The black ooze around the sac was itself harmless, but the contents within could melt a man's hand to the bone.

"Why does it come so close, yet run every time?" Eadwine said as he rubbed his back, which was sore from being tossed through the air.

"It is in their nature," Gaspar said as he fumbled back, a black sack of thick gelatin now rested in his hand, and its contents oozed over his sleeve and arm. "Hold this," Gaspar spoke in exhausted breath as he slung the sack into Eadwine's open hand. "Griffins are proud beasts, the noblest of the wild creatures. It would not bow to a man sooner than a lord gives up his title."

"I heard your ancestors rode them," Alfnod said as he wiped his blades on strings of grass. "Adalgott is said to have crossed the distance of Belfas in less than a day, riding on the back of an emerald coated griffin."

Gaspar prepared some vials and tonics from his knapsack and placed them along with a few dried herbs in a mixing bowl. "Aye, though no real records remain of griffin riders, there are of course folk tales of such men." Gaspar took to pile of gel from Eadwine's hand, and mixed the slime with the herbs and strangely colors tonics. Suddenly the mixture became a balmy paste, with a light green hue. "Aderyn's last hope," Gaspar said gravely as he poured the stuff into a bottle, and sealed it tightly before handing it to Cedric for safe keeping. Cedric clutched it to his breast, near to the point he feared he would crush the bottle, he would not allow it to fall from his pocket.

The road back to Prav was fast and uneventful, filled only with downpours of rain which turned more chilled with each gust of northerly wind that rattled the land. The days appeared to grow shorter, and grass began to turn dull in color and dried in the gray sun. On the fifth day of travel, the band of four came to the Sundering Hills, which lay barren of crop or settlement. They were drab fields, unfit for the grapes that the Crawe household had brought north with them, so the land was not cultivated.

Small forts and towers appeared along the horizon as the group made their way south. Hewn of wood and base of stone, they were temporary and thrown up with haste, each bearing the vine banner of their regent and king. The guardsmen they came upon had the bearings of gold and silver metaled into their hard leather plates of armor, and they came carrying long spears, bannered in purples and greens. The captains amongst these folk barked and gave orders with grave looks beneath their golden helms carved with the images of dragons and wolves, for they knew their hour of doom fast approached, and not even their coats of chain and royal cloaks could save them.

On the seventh day, they finally passed through the valley into the fields of Prav. The sun shined bright on that day, though much of its summer heat had no faded into memory. There stood the wealthiest city of the north, Prav, the gem of the chalice. Fields stretched for miles bearing fresh fruit, ready for the press, in turn, ready for the happy bellies of the citizenry. Great towers of stone decorated the walls, which stood some eighty meters strong in some sections. Outside of this mighty wall, stood a smaller one, with a dug moat and stone supports. No tower nor ladder could reach the main walls because of this.

Upon many small hills, burgs of larger homes, like that of Wulfstan, stood tall with rising vines and mazes of gardens at their bases. The homes of the wealthy nobles and merchants of the city, who had retreated from their summer homes in the country back into the city, along with the rest of the common folk, who now swelled and filled the city. Many towers of silver dotted the city, carrying musical bells upon their crownings. A distinctive trait of this city was the many domed houses and buildings, a remnant of the Crawe family's southern legacy.

Cedric and his companions entered the city through Scallion's Gate, ornate with golden vines and bronze doors some three meters thick. Through the gatehouse, they came upon the market districts of the city, now flooded by refugees from the countryside, who lay on piles of their belongings in tents and the open. The roofed markets had been mostly taken down, leaving room for people to sleep, with only the barest of goods still on sale. Guards rushed by, hurrying to one barracks or the next, handing out spears and helms to any man conscripted to fight in the Vine Guard.

The faces of broken men and women littered the streets as Cedric, and his companions rode through on their horses, faces covered in dirt, yet strangely still filled with an endearing hope. The people of Midland were forged in hotter flames and were not willing to surrender. Minstrels still sang their songs and hummed tunes, keeping morale across the city as high as they could, being paid in scraps of bread rather than coin. A sense of community was felt throughout the city, each man was an equal, in the coming wave of doom.

Suddenly Cedric spotted Leopold's face amongst the unending mob of peasants; his pale skin was like a drop of milk in a bottle of ink. Immediately Cedric jumped from his horse and pushed through the crowd, and greeted Leopold with excitement, clasping one another's hands.

"Where is she?" Cedric said with concerned eyes.

"Right this way." Leopold bobbed his head and ushered

Cedric through many alleys and backways, towards a smaller looking insula, where Tarquin and his men had established their quarters. Cedric gave Beorn, who sat sharpening his axe, only a small look as greeting, for his mind and feet were set on finding Aderyn. In a nook of a room, Cedric's heart sank as his eyes fell upon his love's thin frame and he fell back against the wall, feeling a buildup in his throat. She had fevered in the time he had gone, and her condition had spiraled sharply. Her neck was consumed in the foul black poison, and her breathing was shallow beyond common sight.

Cedric rushed to her bed and placed her head on his lap. Taking the vial of cure from his pocket, Cedric gently lifted her head and poured its contents down her throat. It appeared some color had already returned to her pale face, and she breathed a heavy, but congested breath as the last of the green potion past her lips.

Aderyn's eyes opened, and Cedric's heart raced at the sight of blue pupils as he had so many days and nights before. She gazed deep at him, and a faint smile escaped from her ghost white lips as she whispered in a weak tone. "I had dreamt of you."

Cedric smiled and held back tears of joy which now appeared to escape from his eyes like water from the darkened sky. He laid his lips upon her cold forehead and held her. "And I of you." He responded as the two sat in the empty room, united and in bettering health.

Cedric emerged sometime later, with Aderyn left to gather strength and rest under blankets that the lord had replaced. He met with his original company in the courtyard of the compound, where they had gathered and planned their next move. Alfnod stood with his arms on a table with maps sprawled across its surface, where they had placed mugs of beer and ale from barrels brought by Tarquin's company. Alfnod gave the latest word from the front.

"Word has reached Prav that First Marshall Lafayette has quelled the last of the chancellor's forces…he marches across the Tyr as we speak, and should arrive soon. Yet we have had no word from Miro, nor from Amalric. Crawe has sent many scouts to his furthest holdings, though I doubt much will be learned from their reports, for the enemy in the field is beyond number nor camp. The Vine Guard have done battle with small regiments of raiders, though none beyond the size of a scouting skirmish. If they march on Prav, they will take the city." Alfnod struggled to strategize their next move as he rubbed his fingers across the ink-stained paper of both local and large maps.

"I will speak to Crawe as soon as possible; he will listen to a fellow lord, even one he thinks is a foreign threat," Cedric said with a firm authority; he would need such a disposition to stand equal to the Wine King.

"Don't do anything to upset him," Alfnod warned as he grabbed Cedric's arm for his friend's attention. "Malcom is an old and stubborn man, play into his hand, make him your superior, and he may just follow your word."

"What would a king be without diplomacy?" Cedric said with a light heart. The lord of Orford was given a private room amongst the apartments and changed into smoothly woven silks for his audience with Crawe.

Cedric was accompanied by two Vine Guard officers and full company of spearmen, regaled in full plated armor and cloak, along with his own royal retinue of Alfnod and Gaspar. They were led along the Root, a huge boulevard which served as the main street of the city, which was spotted with flowing fountains and hanging vines which covered the marble laced buildings. At last, they reached the second city wall, which served as a decorative divider between the main quarters of the city, and the king's own palace.

Upon entering the gates, they were stunned to see the number of knighted lords and noblemen who stood gossiping in the gardens of the palace. They had come from all over, just as their subjects, and they too were afraid.

"If Crawe has half a mind he'll face them in the field before they've got enough to sack this city," one voice raised.

"Why not wait them out? Come winter there'll only be stock in the city, and Azrael's armies will starve."

"I hear they've started eating those they captured…for idle pleasure."

"Hush…there goes that southern lord." Their great host of landed folk went quiet as Cedric walked by. Some looked in disdain, others with bright looks of hope. Even the noblest of the citizens were terrified in the truest sense, for they knew nothing differentiated them from the refugees when the horde comes for them in their beds.

The gates of the great hall were opened, and Cedric was led inside. It was a cold feeling building, so different from the design of the rest of the city. None of the braziers that adorned the walls and sides of the columned hall were lit, so only the faint light from transparent windows filled the room. It was a long and narrow hall, with a massive table at its end, where a great burning fireplace resided, carved of pure stone and gilded with vines.

Seated at the table, Malcom Crawe, Owain Sigberht lord of Gwent, Theodric Oderyr lord of Swamp Rock, and Cedric's only courtly friend Lord Roderic, sat eating a fat boar that had been roasted, along with a whole crop of grapes. They appeared as three shriveled old men, their faces well-worn and fixed with a perpetual scowl. Malcom wore an elegant purple robe, which was fastened with a golden grape pin, and a seven-pointed crown rested on his head representing his seven vineyards.

The guards behind them matched the ones that had brought Cedric, dressed in plate that protected them from head to toe. The rest of the army had not been given such equipment; most wore leather with golden badges and decorations, useless against a proper enemy.

Roderic gave a small nod of encouragement as Cedric approached, and he gripped his hands in anticipation. Towards the wall of the hall, Cedric spotted Dag, who was adorned in his helm which covered the whole of his face.

Cedric approached and bowed deeply. "Lord Malcom Crawe." He said as he awaited response.

Malcom appeared to shrug with his eyebrows and took a deep breath before recognizing Cedric. "Well…this is the lord from Wulfstan then? Would you have me lay like a kenneled dog, or should I just melt my crown for your grace?" Malcom was unimpressed, and his sour attitude filled the room with a cold disposition.

"No, my lord I would not, for you are a king in your own right, just as I am. I did not come to take your crown, I came to defend the whole of the North," said Cedric as Lord Owain turned and whispered into Malcom's ear, who nodded with approval.

"Words can be proven empty lord Cedric; actions cannot." Malcom signaled to his steward and motioned for another course to be prepared. "Come, eat at my table, I'll not deny a man their guest right."

Chairs were brought out, along with a roasted duck and three golden chalices filled with sweet smelling wine for the Vine King's guests.

"I may be old Cedric, but I'm not some withered corpse…at least not yet." Malcom burst out as he choked down the last of his wine, snapping his finger for the pitcher to be brought forward. "I will not stand idle while this demon's servant ravages my country, killing my people, my own flesh, and blood. I need your armies same as you need mine. We have mustered ten thousand Vine Guard to our defense, and with your supporters, we will have a large enough army to take the fight to Azrael. I will lead this force, with you acting as one of my chief commanders."

"I'll have peace on those terms, Malcom, I truly want what's best…" Cedric said begrudgingly.

"You shall address King Malcom by his proper titles, or by silence!" Owain of Gwent barked. He was a patriot to his country, and most importantly, fiercely loyal to Malcom, his friend who had shared many a battlefield with him.

"It's all right Owain, let the boy speak his word." Malcom leaned in towards Cedric and spoke with a softer demeanor in his words. "Good, there will be supplies for that Lorinian army when it arrives." Cedric raised a brow; he had thought Malcom was unaware of his army's movement. "Did you think I wouldn't know you've sent scouts to call them up? I know everything that goes on in my country." Crawe shot a glare at Roderic, and the vine king threw a chunk of boar meat into his mouth, growling like a hungry wolf. "I've emptied every granary from here to Belfas. Without food, your men won't follow you or me, and without your men, you've no more claim to the throne to a beggar in the streets."

"They have men," Cedric said, "The enemy, more than either of us. I have seen their numbers swell the whole of valleys. At their helm, wise strategists from Lahyrst beckon orders with precision and without mercy. They come marching with mercenaries from east and south, trained to kill, and armed to the teeth. If you march your army out of this city, you'll be blindly throwing away our one chance to survive. Azrael will not offer quarter, he comes to kill us all, you cannot treat him as a rabble-rouser to outwit, but as a doom-bringer to outlast. I will fight by your side, Malcom, but understand this; we should not march out of the city."

King Malcom grumbled with a grin, drawing out each of his words, "Good, good." He downed a glass of wine. "Then it's settled! Wine!" Malcom burst with such thunderous voice; his cupbearer nearly threw his pot of the drink.

The cupbearer approached and poured another glass, this time in an ancient cup many times used. It was a simple thing, made of wood, but had the finished insides of fine copper. Malcom took the glass and drank half its content. "The pact making of my kin," he said, "This cup, the first my forefather, Scallion Crawe, ever owned." Malcom leaned in close to Cedric. "Remember your roots boy, no matter what, it makes for good crops." He took the cup and offered it to Cedric, who took it and drank, sealing their pact as allies.

"Now off to rest with ye!" Malcom bellowed, "I'll have no man claim Malcom Crawe denied his allies the finest silk sheets this side of the world! Ha-ha!"

Cedric stood up from his chair, followed by Alfnod and Gaspar, before turning to leave the hall. Gaspar awkwardly fiddled with his sleeves and bowed to Crawe. "My lord, any questions you have regarding our alliance please direct at me, for I am advisor to the good Cedric, who is clearly exhausted from the day's travel, excuse us." Malcom simply waved the magi away. Gaspar put his arm over Cedric, beckoned him away from the table and through the many halls of the castle.

Cedric was given a full room in the palace, complete with silk sheets and soft pillows, so unlike the cold hillsides, he had become accustomed to. He washed himself with a fresh water basin as Alfnod entered.

"Well, that went better than I expected," Alfnod said with a sigh.

"Truly?"

"Yes. Cedric, you've just added double the strength of your army, with a man who now trusts you as much as its possible for Malcom Crawe to trust." Alfnod raised a confident smile.

Cedric sank onto his bed and folded his hands upon his face. "I suppose this is the last of it, not much more to do but fight."

"It seems that way…and we're ready for when that fight comes. With Amalric, Pike, and Lafayette we'll have one of the largest forces ever assembled in the north, all fighting for you. It won't be easy mind you, but the fights worth fighting never are."

Roderic entered the room, regaled in his red vestments and with his nose held high, wearing a leather strip crown with golden beads. "My king." He said with a cunning smile.

"Those are treasonous words, Roderic," Cedric said gravely as he peered out into the hall, making sure no guards were posted within earshot.

"Is it treason to fight for the welfare of the North? If Azrael doesn't slice Malcom in two himself, old age will take him soon, and with no male heirs, you have the next claim by all rights.

Now then, I've brought near three thousand Rivermen up from my garrisons, they've got bows and slings for the most part, along with spears and short swords. They may not be the Vine Guard, but they'll do for fodder."

"I will use them well Roderic; an arrow can kill as well as a blade," Cedric said as he looked over some maps sprawled out on his desk, taking note of the latest sightings of Azrael's forces.

"None have yet seen the rotted one himself, some say this is all a ruse by your chancellor, and his mage Yellow-Eyes."

"And what news of they?"

"Up north, near the Red Marsh, but again, those reports are unconfirmed." Suddenly a sharp noise pierced the air. "By the gods what is that?"

A horn's blow was heard through the window, and Cedric rushed out with his companions to discover its source. The city waited in anticipation as the gates were swung open, and guards and commoners alike were filled with awe at what they saw.

Gleaming in full shining armor, and adorned with feathery tops, the Knights of the Eternal Dawn had arrived. They came in columns of cavalry with squires and auxiliaries carrying luggage. A full regiment of knights had come, measuring near a fighting force of around one thousand full. The carts they came with were stuffed with Usham Fire, barrels filled with the black tar.

Lord Crawe and his supporters came out to the courtyard, where they received a grinning Amalric regaled in full plated armor, with the image of a dawning sea's horizon upon his breastplate and kite shield.

Amalric bowed his head and saluted his feathered cap to Cedric and the other lords. "My lords, I bring the friendship of my order to our true king." Amalric looked to Cedric, all to

Malcom's own displeasure. Amalric then pivoted his horse and addressed his host of knights. "Azrael sends a fighting force of near fifty thousand to Prav, he intends to sack the city within the fortnight, but we shall reveal the dawn to him!" The knights raised their swords and lances to sky, and let out a great rallying cry.

The Wine King merely scoffed and turned to rest in his hall. "Well go ahead and make yourselves at home, Amalric, as though I have a choice."

Amalric hopped from his horse, but collapsed upon his knee and sighed in agony. Cedric rushed to his knight and lifted him by his shoulder. Cedric could see that Amalric's left leg had completely gone, for it rested lifeless on the ground.

"I thought I had more time, my lord." Amalric had a look of melancholy on his face, and his eyes appeared tired, accepting of his fate. "But I fear leprosy does not wait for men."

"Can you walk? Gaspar may yet have some cure in his pouch." Cedric spoke in a soft voice, to console his captain.

Amalric waved off this gesture. "None such this exists, it would be but a delay to the inevitable. That's what men must do Cedric, accept when their fate has arrived." Amalric turned grim, his face washed of emotion as he limped with Cedric to the palace, where the defensive plans of Prav had begun.

Chapter 26
The Siege of Prav

Three days had passed now, and the Knights, along with the mercenaries and Vine Guard had settled in for a siege. Battlements were constructed, and the last grain stores were finally filled. Cedric planned the siege with the rest of the lords, with Amalric overseeing the construction of strange containers for the Usham Fire upon the towers of the walls.

By the third night, Azrael's army had come, their torches and campfires were so numerous it appeared as if the fields were engulfed in burning flame. The horde set up small sets of barricades and wooden palisades, they did not intend to stay in the field for long. Cedric stood as a sentry on the wall, and by the torchlight, he saw the construction of siege ladders in the enemy camp.

The moon reflected this doom, for it was full in the sky, and with the hue of blood. It appeared near three times as large as other nights, stretching full across the heavens, filling the men of Prav with unspoken fear.

Malcom came to join Cedric's watch, and the two shared a meal of chicken and wine as they were consumed by the ever-growing tension of the coming battle. Malcom had dressed for battle, wearing heavy chain which draped down like a tunic, along with a thick black cloak fastened by a silver brooch.

"I suppose this is what I'll be remembered for Cedric," Malcom said with his signature scowl as he looked out to the enemy besieging his city. "For fifty long years we've had peace with my rule, but this is my defining moment. The scholars won't remember the many winters I fed my people, or kept them safe on my roads, doesn't make for exciting reading. If I'm to fall, I will make it something to remember." Malcom paused for a long time, and the bitter old man fiddled with his chicken which stuck to bits of his snow-white beard. "I'll take my place on the wall." The ancient king said with a heavy grunt as he heaved his body from his seat, and walked with his hand along the wooden railing of the side of the wall.

Tarquin was climbing the stairs from the town as Malcom left, and the mercenary took the place where the king had sat. "Are you nervous?" he said.

"Of course," Cedric replied. "I'd be a fool not to…yourself?"

Tarquin reclined and placed his hands on the back of his head. "I have trained myself not to think of such things. I'd prefer to think of the green fields of Kruithia, my home, or the taste of sweet wine, to the freight of battle. I'll be sent down to the gate for the fight, held up like a cornered rat."

"You should stay with us upon the wall, much safer." Cedric implored.

"In battle, I do not care for safety, it is the one in the most danger, who fights the hardest. Any day of the week I would take a fight in the muck and grime than in the open field. Give me a dagger rather a lance and horse. How fares your lady love, I had seen her carried in the city with the caravan?"

"She is recovering, safe in the city."

"Remember her when the enemy comes for the wall, the bound of a good memory can rally man better than anything on this earth."

Suddenly Cedric spotted a rider approach from the field. He rode a black horse, whose eyes were a bright red, and was draped in a long dark cloak. Cedric recognized him as the rider who had chased him into the Ithon, for his eyes were as cold and void like as they had been on that day. From the height of the wall, Cedric could also spot Sibi amongst the company, along with Yellow-Eyes and Arrington, the chiefest commanders of Azrael's forces.

The rider raised his hand forward, in it, a banner of black with a red rat's head. The whole field turned a dark red as the moon brightened overhead as though by some foul magic. A chant of unintelligible phrases went up in the enemy camp, accompanied by a beating of spears against shields.

Cedric spotted patterns of shifting in the enemy camp. "Crawe, look out to the field!" Cedric said as he leaned forward on his seat, and placed his hand upon his blade.

The beady-eyed rider raised his arm, which was too covered in black cloth, and gave a command to the horde. The great camp outside the wall suddenly appeared to move, for the torches and men now swelled and rolled across the landscape, directly towards the walls.

Cedric jumped to his feet and rushed to alert the others. "They are moving to the walls! Hurry! Sentries to their positions, Guards to your feet. Now is the hour, to your work!"

"Let them come!" Crawe shouted as he drew his sword, which was ornate with golden vine upon the handle. "Let them come and find the Vine King's blade!"

The Vine Guard assembled on the wall, wielding long spears and heavy shields of many layers, and some were armored in their standards of thick leather jerkin with golden vine pressing upon the breast. The other levies of Midland bore metal helmets and greaves, but only tunics upon their torsos. The Rivermen, adorned in light leather and rich tunics, took arrows into large baskets, and each made ready to loose their flatbows against the enemy. Roderic was at their helm, with a crown placed upon his head which held the figure of a bronze boar. The Knights moved into position, taking hold of strange bronze canisters which contained the Usham Fire, and were decorated with the images of dragons.

Cedric took command by Amalric's side, and the horde advanced, carrying ladders. Their standard bearers blew on dark horns and beat large drums, marching the horde forward at a brisk but steady pace. The chanting morphed into a single note of wailing, as though the spirits of dead marched with the enemy ranks, and it filled the defenders on the wall with a dread that gripped tightly to their hearts.

The archers began their volleys, scoring ranks of hits against the lighter dressed Hirdmen in the horde, who often came with light leather or fur as their only protection. The rushing enemy's movements were thrown together and unorganized, throwing themselves against the first set of walls like falling rain against a rock. Amalric held his knights at their position, for the horde was still out of place for his strategy. From the towers, the Rivermen rained arrows down; each volley called down by Roderic's booming battle commands.

It was near midnight when the horde had broken through the first gate, placing battlements and ramparts so that they might cross without the fear of arrows. Tarquin and his foreign mercenaries were holding the gate, throwing up lances and shields as a makeshift wall. Many had fallen, and yet more came to replace them, making it seem as an unending chain of bodies. It was at this moment that Amalric unleashed the master plan of the knights. He flung his mangled arm down in command, and torches were lit upon the end of the copper canisters, and the pumps were pressed back and forth. Suddenly a stream of the black tar and bellowing out of the nozzles, and burst into a cloud of flame as it passed the torch serving as the pilot light.

The flames engulfed the horde trying to scale the walls, their skin burned as they screamed in agony, and the smell permeated and fouled the air. The fire soon became a huge billow of black smoke, which covered the view of the ground from the battlements on the wall.

From the ladders, Hirdmen came up bearing long shields and blades as they scaled. Cedric saw one jump from his ladder, and directly onto the pike of a Vine Guard who cried out in humor to his companions as he saw the man cough blood from the end of his spear. "Look Lord Crawe! By the gods, this one has lost his supper!" The young lads at his sides laughed as he threw the Hirdman back off the wall with one mighty heave, soon a great cheer started throughout the ranks of archers who volleyed down at their foes.

More and more of the horde poured off the ladders, and soon they matched in the number of defenders on the wall. Cedric was on the vanguard, accompanied by Alfnod and Beorn, who guarded at his sides. The heat from the Usham Fire bellowed and overtook the stone of the walls, causing ash and sweat to form upon the red faces of both defender and attacker. Cedric rushed into a cluster of Hirdmen, who had begun to enter the gatehouse in an attempt to lower the iron wrought door.

"Don't let them near the gatehouse!" Cedric cried as he stood vanguard over the door, packed tightly with a battalion of Vine Guard who raised their shields as tight as the shell of a tortoise. They fought slowly, taking precise moments to strike out, lifting their shields and plunging their spears into the exposed ranks of wall climbers. Even with this caution, wounds were unavoidable, and Cedric and his companions felt the sting of sharpened steel against their flesh.

Crawe could be seen from the gatehouse upon the higher ramparts of the wall, accompanied by a compliment of silver and golden guard, adorned in jewelry and armed with fine blades. The Wine King had made his stand, and gave a grizzled and bitter war cry, plunging his golden handled blade through a swath of the enemy.

From the gatehouse, there was news of a break, and a great host of the enemy rushed through, near swallowing up Tarquin's band whole. Amalric saw this, and he descended from the wall, with a full escort of knights.

Cedric cried to the leper knight. "Amalric! You cannot hope to turn them back! We can fall back to the palace!" The lord pleaded and begged, but he knew Amalric's mind was set.

Amalric and his knights mounted, though their commander cried out in pain, for he could not feel either of his legs as he saddled, and his arms had become nearly completely void of life. "By Cinder's light, I will not be left out of this fight!" Amalric boomed as he thought of a plan. "I spit in your face Beelzus, queen of disease." Amalric spotted a nearby squire, tending to the wounded. "Lad! Come here and tied my legs to the horse, for I have no strength to hold my lance." His knights watched in awe as Amalric became wrapped in a mess of straps and leather, suspending his back upright against his horse, allowing him to hold his lance proper.

Taking firm grasp of his lance with the last of his strength, Amalric pressed his horse forward. Flying down the streets, he charged at the horde of the enemy near the gate, who had begun to pour into the city. He drove his lance through near five ranks deep, and his horse crushed the bones of the unfortunate in its path. The Knights were quick to follow, pushing the enemy back through the gate. The battle was won there, but not without cost. For many Hirdmen carried spears and struck and pricked through Amalric's shining steel. His gripping disease kept him from feeling their blows, and he continued swinging his sword madly through their host.

Finally, his horse was struck, and he collapsed beneath it. Prod upon many pikes, he bled from all manner of places, his chainmail and white cloak turned to a dark red from the pouring of his blood. Cedric rushed down from the battlements, and with a small band of Amalric's knights, secured the gate.

Cedric collapsed to his knees and attempted to drag Amalric from the bottom of his lifeless horse. He had not the strength, and fell backward as Amalric coughed, his throat congested with blood. Cedric took off Amalric's helmet. He could see clearly the knight was dying fast.

"Amalric hold on! The doctors will see to your wounds; you won't die today…"

Amalric lifted his right arm and stretched it out towards the sky. "This is what I want," He cooed, coughing more violently than before. "I die a knight of Adalgott, a knight of Cedric." His arm fell, and his body became limp.

Soon the fighting devolved into madness, for the Vine Guard and Hirdmen alike grew winded, and soon broke from rank and training. The smoke had filled both sides' lungs, and their faces and eyes sweated and burned from the smell and feel of the fire. For hours, the burning raged without end in sight, and the moon, now veiled by black smoke, had waned and fallen in the sky.

When the fire had subsided and the cloud dissipated, there came a great cheer from the defenders. The horde had broken, and now they fled back across the wooden ladders of the first wall, and across the horizon, their army routed and scattered. The Vine Guard rattled their spears against the stone flooring of the walls and cheered with booming voices in victory as their enemy fled in disorderly chaos.

"See how they run!" Malcom cried out, his armor was dirtied and has many holes in it, though the old man did not bleed. "See the cowardly forces of Azrael! More fit for the gallows than the marching ranks!" The old man grinned and growled like an old grizzly bear as he patted Cedric on the shoulder, who was now stretched against the wall. Cedric had collapsed on the wall when the retreat began. He was exhausted from the hours of fighting and couldn't even stand. He clutched at his side as blood ran down from his forehead from a spear point which had slashed at his hairline.

Cedric heaved, and pulled himself to the battlements of the wall, and took stock of the fields. Many bodies littered the place, but by no means a full company of the enemy. Most had broken and fled before even reaching the walls, for fear of the consuming fire which spewed down upon them. Upon the furthest hill, Cedric spotted a figure that once more sent chills rushing down his spine. The beady-eyed rider was once more upon his eyes, and his horse was kicking its front legs in the night and cried a terrible and blood boiling cry. From, this distance the rider's eyes appeared red, matching that of the full red moon to his rear, which loomed over the landscape in horrifying fashion.

Cedric felt his body weaken, and his eyes grew heavy as blood swelled around them. Soon he was fast asleep on the wall, and he did not stir till the morn had fully come.

Chapter 27
The Child of Lenich

"Come on get up." A voice called to Cedric, along with a sharp kick to his side. Cedric saw that it was Eadwine, who had been bandaged along his arm and side. As Cedric slowly opened his eyes, which were filled with the radiant light of a bright fall morning. Cedric was filled with urgency and sat upright against the rubble and wall.

"Are we all safe?" Cedric said with a dry throat.

Eadwine smiled reassuringly. "Well Leopold still can't seem to wipe his dour mug off his face, but other than that plague we've all done well for ourselves. Come now, I have a surprise." Eadwine slumped next to Cedric, and pulled a gilded glass bottle from his cloak, with the reserve of Crawe's wine within. "The lords and captains had such a row when the battle was done; they had not the wit to place a guard at the cellar, leaving swift hands to their work." He uncorked the bottle and began to drink, before offering some to Cedric, who took it gladly.

The wine tasted crisp and refreshing as it rushed down his dry and hoarse throat.

"I feel like I was trampled by a horse," Cedric said as he clutched at his side, and lifted his tunic of chain, which revealed a bruise black and purple. "I think I was actually trampled by a horse."

Eadwine gave a small laugh, and with one gulp, finished the bottle of wine meant to be savored and sipped. "Let's get you back to the palace. Lords and captains are assembling to plan our next step, Azrael's beaten but not finished." Eadwine hoisted his lord to his feet and placed Cedric's arm slung over his shoulders as the pair made their way through the city, where jubilant people celebrated and sang in the streets.

Back at the palace, a party had raged through the night and morning, with both sleeping lords and bottles of wine were littered across the great lawn and scattered in the maze gardens nearby. Cedric and Eadwine crossed through the threshold of the central courtyard and entered the hall where Malcom sat at his table, accompanied by a full host of lords feasting and drinking merrily.

"Come! A place at my table for every brave soul who shared the wall with me that night!" Crawe cried out, lifting his glass with a wide grin to toast Cedric. "Ha-ha! Did you see how we beat them?! They'll sing songs of that night till the end of the world!" The lords burst out in cheer, and too raised their glasses in celebration, ignorantly spilling their drinks and tossing their food like children. Only Roderic, who still was adorned in his boar helm, did not drink or eat, nor give shouts of merriment. He held his hands at his bruised chin, pondering deep in his mind.

Cedric was helped into his chair by Eadwine, who took his

place next to him. "What news from the barracks? Did we lose many?"

"For every one of us that lies on the ground, ten of the enemy do as well, so our scouts say," Malcom said with swagger, as though by his work, and his work alone, that they had won the battle.

"Have their forces begun to reform ranks? We will need to chase down those who routed, so they cannot muster another attack," Cedric said concernedly.

"There is no need, Cedric, they have completely scattered. Some head north, some south, others east. Come the first snow they will starve, why waste men on such a benign task?"

Roderic winced and rolled his back on his chair in annoyance. "I did not know that one battle wins a war, my king." He said with a bitter taste in his mouth.

Suddenly the laughter and merriment stopped, and all lords looked to Malcom, whose faced has been wiped clean of any faint sign of joy. The scowl returned to the old man's visage, as he took the last of his wine, placing both of his hands on the table. "In this case, it does young man; age teaches you such things."

Roderic sat with a smug look on his face, fit to prod at the old man just enough to rile his bitterness. "Have we any news from our lord Cedric's allies, the Unseen?" Roderic quickly changed the subject while twiddling his fingers on the table.

"None but that they muster." Malcom gave an old man's unique grunt. "Bah, by the time they've mustered, the enemy will have frozen in the next ten winters!"

Cedric was quick to defend Pike's absence. "Only because they lack our order, your grace, which they make up with unmatched strength in battle. When they are ready, they shall come, by my honor."

"I'll hear no more of fairies of the forest." Malcom had bitter feelings toward the Unseen, as he had for a great many people. "We must take them in the field." He pointed to the map which lay at the center of the field, across it, wooden figures had been placed where the enemy was in number. "There." Malcom pointed to a large crag upon the map, surrounded on either side by stony hill. "To the Sundering Hills, they have their greatest force, where your chancellor is certainly helming his rally. We take the fast road, through the valley of rocky terrain, and we'll gut through their many force, dividing down the seam."

Roderic raised his voice in protest. "We have no idea what number they field, nor their entrenchments. We should wait come the spring when they have starved."

Malcom was resolute, unbending in his decision to one so young. "If we wait then, we shall have no idea what damage they will have done to our countryside. Whole fields salted, villages burned, come the next winter it would be us who starve. No, our course and fate are set upon that valley. Men may win battles, but supplies win wars. We will show the north menfolk do not need the help of flowery southerners, nor woodlands beasts." He gave a small chuckle, satisfied by his own wit.

Malcom waved his hand and considered this business done. "Our scouts report the enemy is broken in the field, traveling in fractured ranks towards the north, by the Red Marsh…" The seated lords became distracted, and their gaze had followed the figure who approached in the doorway. Cedric turned and saw a young woman standing in the doorway, with red hair with a tint of rose petals, as her father once had in his youth, and her skin was pale as Malcom's white beard. Her face was no less dour than her father's, but where his was filled with a quick anger, hers was covered by sadness. "The joy of my joys. Come and be presented at my table." Malcom beckoned her over in a jolly voice, and each lord, including Cedric, was fixated by her motion, as though they had an unspoken connection. "My lords, my daughter, the Lady Beatrix."

The girl gave a small courtesy, and her cheeks began to blush with redness as though a fire had been stoked. She took her place by the wall, accompanying the other lesser nobles with sat there. Cedric noticed Dag by Roderic's side, and through his chain mask, the half-giant gave Cedric a strange look

Cedric gazed at her, not by desire, but by interest, for the remainder of the Witan, which droned on with circling debates of defense or offense. The lords were in a strange place, for some spoke only to impress the lady, giving empty rhetoric which had merit only in sound. Others sought to impress with bravery, suggesting that they move their armies directly into the fray.

Their efforts of the day were fruitless, and when the court had dismissed, Cedric rushed after Roderic and Dag.

"Why did you give me such looks in the court Dag? Have you gone smitten for the lady yourself?" Cedric said lightheartedly, which masked his growing interest in the affair.

"No my lord," he spoke in his deep and monotone voice, "if I gave and such gaze, think of it as nothing."

Cedric was disappointed, like a child excluded from a friend's secret. From behind, Beatrix approached, her hands folded by her hip, accompanied by full escort of handmaidens and courtiers. The two lords and their companions bowed for the lady as she approached.

"Lord Cedric," she spoke in a soft mousey voice, as though

she was frightened by every sound. She was near opposite to Aderyn in every respect. "I have been told you fought well upon the wall."

Cedric turned to his friends, who had unsure glances, before turning back and mustering the first line he could think. "As well as a man can fight, my lady." The two exchanged small and awkward smiles with one another, lightening the mood some.

"I was told by my father to welcome you to the city…" She struggled for her words as she fumbled and twirled her fingers. The court had not been her place for long, and there was a certain rustic charm to her ways. "I hope to see you safe when this war has ended."

"Thank you, my lady." The men once again bowed to bid the lady well, and she took her leave with her retinue.

"I sense a sadness deep within her," Cedric said to Roderic.

"And there is much cause for such; her mother has recently passed, leaving only Malcom as her family in this city, for her father died long ago, in the place you and Dag passed through." Cedric turned to Roderic with a confused look. "Half Lenich for certain, half Crawe possibly. Her mother, Beatrice, the prize of every lord from here to Belfas in her day. Her hand was offered in the tourney of Malcom's father, Mathon. Lord Lenich rode honorably that day, best his opponents in graceful shined steel. The young Prince Malcom did not fare as well, not an exceptional warrior in his youth, he was always more bookish than martial. He was promising once, Malcom, had the wit of a weasel, and the knowledge of good and evil. Though Malcom was beaten in the tournament, his heart grew in passion for Beatrice, though she had none for him. That night at the tourney, Malcom lost every good virtue he held. He tried to advance on Beatrice, but she spurned him. Malcom struck her for that, and Lenich struck him in return. Malcom left disgraced, laughed at by his father's lords; he vowed revenge that day."

Roderic paused and looked around the palace halls, making sure none were listening. He leaned in and whispered the story forbidden in Malcom's court. "When Malcom was crowned king, his first act was to ride to House Lenich and demand the lady be turned over to be his wife. Lord Lenich refused, and Malcom ordered them all to be executed, save for Beatrice. It was not a day after her husband's head rolled off the block that she wed Malcom, who was quick to do his marital duties…though rumor has always testified that Lenich had also and that the fair lady was already with child. To this day none now know, for Beatrix holds defining features only from her mother. The hair, of Lenich, the face, of Malcom, it is anyone's guess. To think, Malcom was once respected by all; now he is but an old man, bitter at the world for hating him, not because they do, but because they do it justly. What man butchers his own vassal for lust?"

Cedric felt the girl's sadness, for her loneliness radiated and filled whatever space she occupied. Last child for either House Crawe or Lenich, a fate unknown by all.

Cedric and Eadwine returned to their quarters, where the other licked their wounds from the previous night. Aderyn had remained bedridden, and she was now cleaning her black wound with a water basin.

"How are you?" Cedric said as he placed his hand on her wound, careful not to touch the exposed bits of flesh still festering in black ooze.

"Better." Aderyn was still weak, and her voice was tired.

She gave a small smile to Cedric, who responded in kind.

"This war should be over by the spring, at the pace of this." Cedric placed his hands in hers. "It will be a distant memory when we have ruled until we reach ripe old age. Greeting flowery lords and ladies every afternoon." Cedric gave a chuckle. "Grey-haired, children and grandchildren bickering over their rivaling estates."

"I'd rather be at war," Aderyn said as she dried her face.

"Look at me." Cedric turned Aderyn's face to his in a gentle motion. "When this is over, I vow, we will be together. We'll be wed at Wulfstan…or Orford; both will be our home. I promise." Cedric took Aderyn's narrow face in his hands, and kissed her forehead, smiling to comfort not comfort her, but himself. Since the black axe had near taken her from him, nothing could relieve his mind of her safety.

Cedric paused, and his smile was wiped away as his mind was dragged back into the field of battle. "We need to send word to Lafayette, for he still has yet to cross the rivers, by our latest reports." He turned to Eadwine and Leopold, who appeared ready for the task. "My swiftest allies, you must get word to Lafayette, tell him we march north, and he should avoid the road to Prav, lest he is slowed or thrown off proper course."

"Sure…" Eadwine rolled his arms back and stretched with a loud yawn. "It seems as though you get all the honor, while I get a long and tedious ride with the dreariest man in the world."

Leopold fetched his knives which were lying out on the table, and stuffed them in his boots and long sleeves. "Good idea to send to riders when this fool goes and falls off a cliff I can still deliver the message."

Cedric clasped hands with them, and bid them farewell at

the main gate, where rubble was still being hauled away. The ornate metaled gates had been completely bent from shape and lay strewn across the ground. Cedric watched as his two friends disappeared over the horizon of the overcast day, which carried a warm feel with a cool wind blowing down from the north. It would not be long till the first snows graced Midland in thin and gusting waves.

Aderyn appeared beside him, dressed for travel, with leather boots and a long cloak. "I'm coming with you to the Sundering Hills."

Cedric was filled with a dreadful fear. "Your place is where it is safest, please Aderyn…'

She cut him off. "You say we will be together? Then let me be with you now."

The two wrapped their arms around one another as the sun graced the top of the sky, in the next days the armies of Midland would make their leave of Prav. The Vine Guard prepared for a light journey of only a few weeks, for they assured themselves the enemy would be dealt with swiftly. As the night fell on Prav, the first cold clouds of winter arrived from Belfas and brought with them a light brush of snow, light as a bird in flight. When the people of Prav woke the next morning, they did not find their breath in the air, for it was still only cool in temperature, even though snow had lightly blanketed their homes.

Chapter 28
At the Sundering Hills

Thus, the armies of Midland came to march out of Prav, heading due north in a rhythmic and merry march to the Sundering Hills, where their foe was in greatest, but scattered strength. Their wineskins swelled with rations, and each was made red-faced by their drinking and singing. The drink kept the newly forming cold at bay, which had now turned much of the green grass brown and dry. The Vine Guard sang to Domovoi, the gold-bearded god of wine and hearth, whose laugh roars louder than the strongest wind, and whose feasting table leaves the richest lords in envy. They sang.

A toast to the guard of the hearth!
A toast to the one that makes his mark
On the fields so ripe
And press so full
A toast to the god of wine!

The little man
So clever and so drunk
With unkempt beard
And locks of gold
Let's raise our glass to him
So that our glass might always brim!

Cedric and his companions did not drink nor participate in the merriment, for they scanned the horizon in nervous glances. With the king, Beorn, Alfnod, Gaspar, and Aderyn traveled, their drinking sacks filled with mixed wine, near wholly watered down.

The landscape of open fields faded as they made their long journey north, passing into the Sundering Hills, gray and inhospitable lands. On their final day of travel, they came to a great split in the earth, surrounded on either side by massive stretching mountains. It was Sundering Pass, the sole role through the rough terrain.

Malcom rode to the front to assess the situation with Cedric. "We should press through the mountain." He said in his signature gruff. "It is near week's travel to cross otherwise, by that time we will have lost the enemy." He had drunk freely, and his face red was and fierce with confidence.

Cedric did not wish to take the pass, nor any route for that matter, the safest way was back to Prav, behind the walls. "Are you sure the enemy has emptied out of this valley? It would make for a perfect ambush."

Roderic rode up beside them, adorned in his helm with a bronze boar. "I agree with Cedric; it would make for an ambush. But the enemy is scattered." He looked intently at Cedric, giving counsel to the one he knew as his king. "They have not the strength or wit to muster such a strike. When we have ridden through the valley, we will be at their heels in less than two days and overwhelm them, my king."

"It is settled then, thank you, Roderic, for your support," Malcom said ignorantly. "Forward all! Steady march!" With that, the Vine Guard and Rivermen, along with the remaining Knights, pressed through Sundering Pass.

Soon the grassy brown hills turned to rough stone, as they had for Cedric the last time he ventured into this land. The valley became more pronounced as they traveled, and the sides around them grew in height. This was the Valley of Sundering Hills, where many armies of yore had passed and had battle. The gravel-filled rode the Vine Guard marched upon was rumored to be wrought of weathered bone, from former fallen companies. In the walls that surrounded them on either side, small alcoves could be seen, where figurines of deities and ancient figures were carved.

Many of the marching soldiers offered prayer to The Children, and to Duwel, elven god of sky, that their heads were clear of cold northern rain. They marched in a long column, four across, with cavalry in lead and rear, along with Rivermen at the most central point.

By the afternoon, a heavy fog had rolled through the valley, so thick it appeared as solid matter able to be sliced by blade. Cedric was in the front of the company, with Tarquin mounted beside him. The two could not see ten feet in front of them, and torches had to be lit.

"My rapier could cut clean through this dense veil!" Tarquin joked, pouring down more of his wineskin's content. The mercenary then motioned the wine to Cedric, who took a turn himself, it was a fine red from the king's cellars.

"This cannot bode well for us," Cedric said only half as humor, he eyes glanced and darted around the valley, making account of every nook and rock.

"Let them come in this valley, and see how they fair. At the gatehouse, I held them, dagger in hand and courage in my heart. Let them come, and I will hold this valley." Tarquin gave a loud sigh and grinning smile.

Cedric gazed out into the endless road ahead, and he felt as though he was being watched. He turned his head side to side, the upper parts of the valley were out of view. The statues were near twenty feet in height. It seemed only Cedric noticed this grave gaze, for the Vine Guard continued their merry chants, ignorant of the mighty stonework of their venerated ancestors.

From out of the fog, Cedric spotted once more the vilest of all portents, and his horse kicked back its front legs in startled fear. The young king's eyes zoomed and focused upon a rider in the fog, wearing a burial mask of silver and gold, with dead, beady eyes shining through the dense cover.

"Everyone cover!" Cedric shouted as he ducked beneath his horse, and a hail of arrows from all sides was unleashed upon the marching army. Cedric's horse was dead in an instant, shot through the brain, and it collapsed on his legs. Beorn rushed to Cedric's side and began pulling him from the horse.

"Tarquin! Get your men to the flanks and upon the hill! They are upon the hill! Upon the…" Cedric was cut off by an outpouring of blood which smacked across his face and in his eyes. Tarquin was struck with an arrow through his throat, which had torn through his windpipe and main artery, and he gasped and choked in vain at the wound, for there was no hope for him.

Cedric struggled by himself to free himself from his horse,

and he caught sight of the rest of his now panicked army. Hirdmen and others in Azrael's employ had come down from either side and crashed against the Vine Guard already riddled with arrows.

"With me!" Cedric cried. "With me!" Aderyn, Alfnod, and Gaspar rushed to his side, and they were distraught upon finding Beorn dead.

"What do we do Cedric?" Gaspar yelled from under a heater shield, which had the emblem of the Vine Guard.

Cedric scanned the narrow battlefield, finding death in every direction he looked. Finally, he spotted Malcom, riding forward with his noble lords including Roderic and his bodyguard Dag. Dag, adorned in his helm of steel and mask of chain, swung his heavy bastard sword side to side of his horse, cutting down ranks of Hirdmen who dared approach the half-giant and his lord.

Malcom called out to Cedric, his blade bloody in his hand. "They have overwhelmed the rear; there can be no turning back at this point." An arrow struck Malcom's horse, who in turn threw Malcom from the saddle and onto the ground in a thud. "Oof!" He cried. "I will kill every one of these savages for that!"

Roderic remained calm, even in the face of this onslaught. "That is all well and good my lord, but let us save your foolishness for another day." Roderic pointed forwards, towards where the rider had first been spotted. "We must press out of this valley, into open pasture where we may match them in strength."

So the lords rallied together the remaining Rivermen and Vine Guard near them and made a push through the rest of the valley. For near an hour they ran, arrows flying and whistling past their heads. Many fell as they fled, for the Hirdmen had filled the valley and overrun much of their force.

Finally, the valley began to smooth, and the fog seemed to dissipate, for they could once again see clouds and the sun.

"Thank the gods!" Roderic cried out as they neared the end of the trap.

Cedric collapsed from exhaustion as they found themselves on grassy terrain, and he grasped bundles of the root with his hands to make sure it was real. So many had fallen, now only near five hundred remained, collapsed and panting from exhaustion and fear.

Cedric rallied himself and drew his sword to command. "Vine Guard! To the valley's entrance, let none through, we've got the advantage now!"

Now all the sudden from behind, a host of cavalry appeared, wielding spears and axes in hand. At their head, the beady-eyed rider, accompanied by Sibi, Yellow-Eyes, and Arrington. The horsemen quickly surrounded the few of Prav, who could not muster the strength to put up a fight. Cedric himself dropped his blade as well, knowing there was no hope for victory, and he quickly took place next to Aderyn.

The rider whispered to Sibi, in a foul and distant voice, as though words did not come from his mouth but the rushing wind. Sibi called to his raiders. "Pack them up!"

Suddenly the Vine Guard were seized and bound in heavy metal chains, around their necks, arms and legs. Cedric, the fellow lords, and his company were thrown into iron wrought carts, with thick bars. Those who were not in carts were led in a single file, through the cold mud common to upper Midland.

Now the merry songs were sung by the Hirdmen and the others accompanying Arrington, who sat with a smug grin on his face as he rode. For two weeks, the carts dredged through rugged and soggy terrain, and it rained cold and hard water for near every day they traveled. Their route took them north, towards the Red Marsh, where the frigid landscape mixed into a wet muck. The road became narrow, and many fell in the travel, cut loose from the chain and let to rot. Cedric's clothes, like the others, were completely ruined, soaked and muddied, turning his fingers and toes blue from the cold. Many marching Vine Guard caught fevers and were cut loose from the chains to die. While the enemy feasted, scraps of rotted and burned bread were given as prisoner rations, leaving men with the frame of skeletons and walking corpses.

During a stop, Sibi rode his horse next to the cart and revealed Bayeux to Cedric. "A beautiful blade, lord Cedric, not use to holding master craft steel." The savage said in a condescending and bragging tone. Cedric was silent. "I think I'll stay with my axe." Sibi took the heirloom of Cedric's house and placed the blade on a sharp stone, and with a swing of a hammer, broke the blade in two. Sibi then took the blade to a fire and watched the steel blacken and spoil in the charcoal heat, before giving out on last vile grin.

Cedric could not muster any strength for emotion, though he wept bitterly in his mind…the last tie to his family, other than in name and banner, was lost.

Cedric shivered and shook in his cage, and his face turned pale as milk. Aderyn was at his chest throughout the journey, resting her tired head.

"Cedric? Are you awake?" She whispered in a hoarse voice during one of the nights.

"Yes." He said in a broken will.

"Had you seen a vision of this?" She asked not hoping for an answer.

"No…they've abandoned us." Cedric had given up any hope, and he lay there limp, unwilling even attempt to move. "I will not try to see that hidden pool tonight, with what little strength I've left there is no chance. What strength of arms have the gods given us so far? Nothing but faint warnings that do no good! We were all fools to think them stronger than Azrael." Now Cedric cursed the gods for his own pleasure. "What strength is there is wisdom compared to Azrael's horde? Wise words and good deeds cannot stop a lance's pierce."

They came to an abrupt stop on their long dredge. It was now nighttime, and the winter's cold bite hard at the prisoners. The Hirdmen made camp along the dry edge of a vast forest of redwood and was situated just below a rolling hill. Torches and campfires were lit, though the Vine Guard and carted prisoners were given no provisions or place by the fires. Yellow-Eyes and the beady-eyed rider came up to the cages, and the magus clutched the ancient tome of golden wrapping close to his chest. The magus gave a crooked smile.

"We have special plans for you Lord Cedric; I will pay back in kind for each insult you hurled at me." The magus received no response from Cedric, who lay silent in his cage, broken and beaten. "Though we have no use for him." Yellow-Eyes ushered Hirdmen to Malcom's cage. The Vine King was bruised upon his head, and blood had dried around his left ear from wounds sustained. The sorcerer's men grabbed the king from his cell and brought him from his cage and onto his knees.

The beady-eyed rider, for the first time heard, spoke. "Surrender your titles; you are beaten, my master offers much for such grace."

Malcom lowered his head, as if from shame, and whispered so none could hear. The rider knelt so that he could hear the surrender. Rather, Malcom spat on his face and gave an angry growl. "I will never bow to your master Azrael, and his master before him!" The grizzled old man was resolute in his stubbornness.

Yellow-Eyes fetched a cloth and wiped away the spit from the rider's cowl. With a snap of the finger, a broadsword, black with a serrated blade, was summoned for the beady one, and Malcom was thrown face first upon a smooth and large stone.

The rider commanded to Yellow-Eyes. "Begin the reading."

With a swift nod of the head, the sorcerer flipped open his tome, revealing pages upon pages of strange writings in no language known to mortals. He rested his hand on a page with archaic symbols, and the red visage of a devil, with huge fangs and horns, and a foul grin. It was the Codex Deadhraegl, a book of foulness written by fallen man. In its myth, a traveling holy man sought knowledge of the gods, only to be tricked by Crassus Baal. Condemned and deceived, the man was forced to write the book, till the end of his days, without rest or food or drink.

"H*iz sha, follen lis*...come now, dark one..." Yellow-Eyes chanted in dark and quiet tone; his glossy eyes turned milky white as the words filled him with power. The torches flickered as the wind picked up as if from nowhere, and the air became colder than it had in any deep winter. The rider rubbed his clothed hands against the stone where Malcom was held; he breathed a deep breath before speaking. Yellow-Eyes placed his hand upon the chest of the rider, a surge of energy flowed through the mage, to that of his master.

"You mistake me, Malcom, for I am not a servant of Azrael." The rider swung his blade in a fell and mighty hush of wind, slicing Malcom's head clean from its place. The Vine King's blood poured upon the table as his lords cried out in terror. In a scene of pure horror, the rider threw away his cowl, tossing it through the wind which seemed to howl in fear. Upon the head of the rider, a skull with gray lumps of hair, and his flesh was rotted and mangled, leaving only sinew of ligaments and bones in some places. Azrael had revealed himself to the world; his return was complete.

His beady eyes became fiery, though none the less lifeless. Yellow-Eyes came up with the Crown of Ten Fingers as it had been before, and crowned him. "Hail to you Azrael!" The sorcerer took up the blood of Malcom and anointed Azrael with it. "Rightful King to the North, and harbinger of Crassus Baal!" The Hirdmen bowed and repeated the words of binding. "Hail to you Azrael! Hail to you Azrael!"

Azrael mounted up upon a black horse, accompanied by two-thirds of his army, and he made ready to depart into the Red Marsh, where he was keen to wipe out the Knights of the Eternal Dawn, his most ancient foe on this earth.

"I give you leave of the army, Arrington, do well to march through Prav, and the rest of Midland," Azrael commanded to his general with a confident swagger.

"Of course, my lord, a feast shall be prepared in your honor, a coronation for the true king!" Arrington grinned wide, for his place of power had been secured.

Owain, lord of Gwent, wept bitterly for his king, and the tears froze as they dripped to his mustache, which had lost its emboldened red flame. He was starved as the rest, his eyes with sunk deep with dark blushes below them, and the whites of his eyes had now turned bloodshot red.

Cedric had been broken wholly, and he spoke no words to

his companions, he could not come to bear what he had seen. Cedric shuttered, and his teeth clanked together, and his breath moved through the air clear as dragon's fire. His mind slowly drifted from the world, and he fell into a troubled and shallow sleep.

Act III
The War for Spring

Chapter 29
The Final Dream

Again, Cedric awoke in the garden of the gods. The trees had now withered, and their leaves had dried and fallen to the ground, where the fields lay barren. The pond was disturbed, its water stirred and had been muddied. Now even the stars in the sky had faded, and in their absence, a consuming and eternal darkness had taken shape.

Cedric stood in awe at this silent scene, whose silence rang and beat in his ears, for it was the silence from the lack of all life. Cedric then gazed upon the Tree of Life, a husk of its former self; its branches were white as bone, and its immaculate glow had turned inward, and reflected no light, as though in deep hibernation.

There came again, as there was had been, the weeping of a woman. Cedric tread through the water of the pond, and once more discovered a bleeding woman. Her hair, once blonde it seemed, had now turned gray. She gave a small and bitter cry, and her white and golden dress was tainted in blood.

This time Cedric felt no sympathy for the woman, and he grew to a red-hot rage. He grabbed the woman by the arms and held her close to his angry face. "Why!?" It was all he could muster. "What strength do you lack that you abandon us!? I was supposed to lead them, and now they are dead…why?" Cedric collapsed onto his knees and held his head low, and began to weep. Tears were rolling down his face when he felt the woman touch his hands. She knelt next to him and wiped away his tears, and when she touched his face, he knew her name. She was Arian. The goddess of land and all life, the firstborn of the Children, kindest in heart of all gods. Her strength had subsided, and her face was hollowed and thin.

"The power to fight evil is not mine, nor my kin. It is sealed in you, man, for only the one so easily corrupted and so common to failure, can combat such force. Pureness cannot drive out the evil; it is in the common things that such strength is found." Arian comforted the weeping lord greatly, and he felt shame for his red-faced acts. "You do not fight because you are our pawn in some game, but because you know it is right. You will always know it is right, and so you must always fight." Her strength was fast fading, and she near fell to the ground, if it were not for Cedric who steadied her. She breathed shallow, but she moved with a purpose, sticking her hand in the muddied water.

Suddenly the water where she touched turned clear, and Cedric could see. A weathered citadel in the north surrounded by snowy forest. It was built from the base of a gray stone mountain, and it spiraled and pierced through the clouds. The image in the water now changed. A deepening stone face, with such stoic look as Cedric, had never seen before. Next, blackness, a darkness which was all-consuming. Suddenly, fire, a flame began in the darkness, bringing light to everything it touched, and in the flame, a steel sword forged centuries ago. Suddenly the vision faded to black, and the cry of a great beast filled Cedric's ears, a cry he had heard at Orford and the lair of the Basilisk.

"What is that place?" Cedric asked.

"The place where your forbearer forged his own legend, now you must forge yours, King Cedric, lord of Lorine, Midland, and Belfas, the heir to Adalgott, and Seer of the Garden. Go now, for my strength is gone, and I cannot keep you here." With this word, the garden grew dim in Cedric's eyes, and he found himself once more in his own realm.

He was once more in chains, and Aderyn, along with his other companions rested alongside him. By now, Azrael's portion of the army had marched out, and the camp seemed almost deserted compared to a few hours ago. Guards were stationed by the carts and were drinking of unmixed wine. They feasted on pork and beef, rations from the Vine Guard supply wagons.

Cedric whispered to Aderyn. "Are you ready to die here?"

She awoke confused, but his serious look gave her understanding. "No." She replied.

"We can distract the guards, have them approach, then hold them against the cage." Cedric plotted in his mind and became engrossed in strategy. "We will have only moments before their companions notice, so we will need to rush to the armory, grab our weapons, and free the others. If we..." Suddenly an arrow ripped through the sky and lodged in the head of a guard. The guards around him visibly shook in fear, before they too were riddled with arrows.

Cedric held his hands to the bars, and gazed out into the night, trying to spot the archer who had such skill. Another guard approach, and saw his dead compatriots. "Oi! You there," He pointed his blade at Cedric. "What foul magic you usin'? He brandished his weapon and was ready plunge it through the metal bars. "Oof!" He was struck from behind, and he collapsed forward towards the cage. In his back, a throwing knife had lodged through in a clean hit.

Out of the shadow, Eadwine and Leopold leaped forward towards the cells. "Thank the gods they've left you alive." Eadwine whispered as he drew his bow once more, standing sentry over Leopold who rummaged for keys on the dead guard's belt. Leopold found a small copper key and plunged it into the lock, and with a turning of a gear, the prison cart was opened. Taking the key, he opened the other carts of the camp.

The lords and knights stretched and sighed heavily as they used limbs unused for many weeks. Cedric took the blade of one of the guards, and slid it into his hilt, the steel scrapping against leather sounded like heavenly music. Owain, the most important lord other than Malcom, had died in his cage, along with many of his vassals. His body could not withstand the winter, his eyes and skin were blued as the sea's water from the cold.

"How did you manage to find us?" Cedric said as he embraced his two rescuers, who both smiled and Leopold gave full testimony of their travels.

"Upon the road, just past Luxen, Lafayette had camped his army, and we relayed your message as promised. And as promised, we marched past Prav and directly to the north, where we came upon the Sundering Valley. Lafayette went into a rage when we found that field of dead. He personally combed the bodies to see if he could find you. When we failed to produce your corpse, he ordered double-time march up north to find you."

Cedric was warmed and inspired by Lafayette, the noblest son of Lorine to be born a bastard. "Where is this army now?"

Eadwine cut in front of Leopold and smiled wide, a lit torch in his hand. "Waiting for the signal of vengeance."

Cedric took the torch and drew his borrowed blade. "Men of Midland, your lord Malcom died tonight, shall we have revenge?"

Grins and chuckles rose in the host of nobles, armed to the teeth with stolen armaments ranging from clubs to great halberds. Cedric rushed forward towards the main garrison tents of the camp, and flung the torch through the air, landing atop the main granary tent.

The fire spread from the outside of the tent, and soon engulfed the barrels and sacks of food, which billowed and spiraled towards the sky in a huge swath of flame, which could be seen clear across the night sky. In the distance upon the hill, a horn was blown, and a cry was heard. From the hilltop, a full army of Lorine plunged down to destroy the Hirdlanders consumed by the chaos of the flame, which jumped from tent to tent where men were still waking from disturbed sleep. Cedric and his band rushed through the tents, taking out scores of smaller groups that were running around in panic at the sight of their camp in flames.

Roderic took a hammer and pounded away at the chains of his River Folk, who stood more like skeletons than men, withered with their flesh hugged against raw bone. Roderic led his bowmen away from the camp, for Roderic knew his men were not able to fight, they were too tired and weak. He ordered them to stand upon the hill overlooking the burning camp, where they provided support as archers, picking off any Hirdmen who attempted to break and flee.

Now from the hill, a full rank of cavalry rode down the hill, sweeping through the base of the hill with ease and precision. Upon their shields and banners, there was a red falcon, the Red Gyrfalcon. The knights were in regal armor, full plate with helms which were feathered in a rainbow of color which stretched down to their saddles. Their thin lances pierced through the hardest of armor like tissue paper as they rode through the camp with speed swift as lightning.

Following the horsemen, the Lorinian infantry, adorned in thick aketon and chain armor, went through and overwhelmed towards the northern edge of the camp, where most of the tents were now blackened ash upon the ground. Cedric hurried through the main pitches, towards the center where Arrington's main tent was set.

"To the chancellor brave men of Lorine! Now that traitor shall see the harvest of the havoc he has sown!"

The flame had not yet consumed Arrington's tent, and it stood towering above the smoke, a series of wooden towers covered in thick cloth, with roomed tents connecting into a rustic palace. The chancellor had a full host of men from Lahyrst in his retinue, adorned in steel scale armor, dark and pointed helms, and long flowing black capes marked with the sigil of the red fox. These guardsmen were overwhelmed with arrow fire which pelted them from all sides, tearing through the flames and nearby tents. When the last of them laid slain, Cedric and his followers rushed into the tent, where Arrington made his stand.

The inside was broad and tall, like a lord's feasting hall, and it was adorned with chandeliers which hung from high standing wooden supports. The main tent was floored with wood, and a great map of northern Yennen lay sprawled across the table, along with figurines representing cities and armies.

At the opposite end of the table, William Arrington was half dressed, still in his sleeping garments and cap, though he had steadied a longsword in his hand. Cedric was filled with a vengeful rage as he crossed the wooden floor, ready to end the Fox.

The two scuffled, and neither had the advantage with the blade, for Cedric was not used to the balance of the Hirdland weapon in his hand. They resorted to the oldest form of fighting, drawing blood from fists and elbows all while Cedric's companions gathered around and watched. For a moment, Cedric was on his back, receiving fists directly to his face, rupturing the veins in his nose, sending blood flying across his face. With a swift move of the legs, Cedric threw Arrington upon the table and felt his hands move into rhythm as he mercilessly pummeled the chancellor into a bloody pulp. The chancellor's legs kicked up and up as he struggled to survive, all while Cedric gave no motion of slowing his brutal rampage.

This went on for some time, until Cedric collapsed onto the floor in a complete mess of sweat and blood, panting heavy and holding his nose which was now cracked and broken. His hands had become numb, and his ears were ringing as his head seared in pain. Arrington was dead, his head nearly caved in, swollen and red like a piece of crushed fruit.

Aderyn rushed to his side. "Cedric…" She said in a muffled voice, which sounded distant. "Cedric." It came again this time clearer. "Cedric!" Now her voice was there with him, and

Cedric looked up in confusion, still panting, as she examined his hands. "Gods, look what you've done." His hands were nearly torn open, bits of exposed flesh showed the outline of bone and muscle. Aderyn quickly took cloth and wrapped his hands, turning the makeshift tourniquet a dark red from blood.

Cedric rose and steadied himself on the table, where Arrington was now sprawled lifeless across scattered the maps and battle plans. The largest map, representing Midland and Belfas, had yet to be disturbed. "Here," Cedric said. "We can gather some knowledge of Azrael's movements."

"Hurry," Beorn said as he peeked out the tent with the handle of his axe, "the flames are rising in the eastern quarter and are crawling towards here."

Alfnod straight the map with his hands and took account of each army. "Azrael is marching northeast, towards Zweleran, it seemed he intends to crush the only ones still able to challenge his claim."

Cedric spotted a strange carved marker on the east, towards the Ithon, it was of a stag. "Ha-ha! Pike must be marching. Look, he is just on the cusp of Midland, Miro's lot have done their part well."

"Come, Cedric, we must leave before these flames take us with them," Beorn said in a concerned voice as he ushered his companions out of the tent. The camp had been emptied, a decisive blow to Azrael's forces. The group marched through ashen mounds as they reconnected with the Lorinian army. They marched upon and over the hill to the east, where they were met by a host of cheering soldiers, chanting the name of their king, Cedric.

"Hail! Hail! Hail!" Thrice they chanted, each time with more vigorous strength, all the while rattled their blades against shields, lifting pikes and spears high into the night sky. Lafayette emerged from the crowd, adorned in his typical red cloaked armor, and he bore a wide grin.

"My lord!" He embraced Cedric, and the two were at last reunited after months away.

"Took your sweet time I see." Cedric joked.

"Yes well, there was this particular maid in Lahyrst." Lafayette shrugged his shoulders sarcastically. "It just didn't feel right to leave her so soon."

Cedric turned his face to one of absolute seriousness, and in a small and timid voice, he could only muster. "Thank you." Lafayette exchanged the same look and nodded; he knew the gravity of the war they wrought.

Cedric was led to a large red tent, where new garments were waiting for the remaining Vine Guard and Cedric's companions. Alfnod giggled like a child with a birthday present as he slipped new socks and boots on his callused and bloodied feet, which had near turned full purple from the freezing cold. Cedric dawned a heavy bear pelt cloak, which warmed his bones and gave color back to his flesh.

They then were offered a commander's meal, a full soldier's ration, plus dried fruits and freshly caught game, along with a hearty reserve brought up from Wulfstan. The companions scarfed down the food, taking paused only for breath or drink. Beorn ate two full chickens, and he plucked his teeth with their bones as he reclined in his chair sipping at his wine glass.

When they had supped, the table was cleared, and battle maps were laid out, detailed images of Belfas and Midland. Esmond, Knight-Commander of the Red Gyrfalcon, entered while removing his feather helm, and knelt before Cedric.

"My lord, my horses are yours to command, their lances

yours to give issue." Esmond appeared more aged than the last time they had met, and his hair was now gray with only shades of black left in some parts.

"Thank you, Esmond; I will need a Commander of Cavalry, you would do well at it."

"My lord." Esmond took his place amongst the captains who had entered to discuss the war plan.

"What is our next step?" Alfnod interrupted. "Without the armies of Midland, we've still been left in dire straits, for Azrael still holds two-thirds of his strength." The two spoke as they walked towards Lafayette's tent, where maps had been laid, and supplies accounted for.

"What numbers do we have here?" Cedric asked.

"Nearly two thousand, many were left in Lorine to keep watch over Lahyrst and Wulfstan."

Cedric looked at the detailed map of Belfas, where every mountain, river, and village was shown. It was an ancient land with much history and lore. Upon the coast of Stirlen, Loden is believed to have wept upon the sand, forming man from the clay he made. From the southern city of Ponstow to the coastal castles of Canterbrick, the Belfan Lords rule their petty kingdoms, never fully united, though never fully divided.

Lafayette interrupted Cedric's thoughts. "We seem trapped on this hill front." He pointed to the map and dragged his finger across Midland. "To the north, Azrael campaigns against the Knights, though with our victory here, his attention will inevitably turn to us. To the east, if we march, we would be overrun before reaching the Ithon. If we move south, Azrael will send his cavalry forward, who near double our own infantry numbers. To the west, Belfas, we would have no supply chains or friends in that land."

Cedric pondered over each detail, hoping for some sign of advantage. To cross in Belfas, they would take either of two roads. The redwood forest north of the Red Marsh, snug between a mountain pass. Or to Green Rock of the south, home to house Oderyr, whose liege lord, Theodric, and all his troops, had not been present at the Sundering Hills. The castle of Green Rock was just upon the edge of the Red Marsh, nestled at the basin of the Belfan Mountains, meaning no attack could come from the south or the north.

"If we march west we may yet find a friend in the Swamp Lord," Cedric said with uncertainty.

Roderic was not convinced. "Bah, an old loon that one is, ruling over his pile of mud and dung. Did you see his banners at Sundering Hills? No, he abandoned us for his own safety. An unreliable vassal if I've laid eyes upon one."

"It seems as though from our report, it is our only chance, unless of course, you want to face Azrael head-on, Roderic," Cedric said in a lighter tone as he raised his eyebrow smugly.

"The way is not wholly safe, Azrael still controls the easternmost patch of that swamp. It could be another ambush like Sundering Hills."

"We'll just have to take that risk then, no avoiding it. Captains, ready the men come the dawn, we march for Belfas."

The captains and Lafayette bowed, gave a, "yes my lord," and exited the tent.

Cedric walked by himself out of the tent and wandered through the grassy field. His legs felt freed for the first time in weeks, and he took delicate time to stretch and breathe fresh air. His bloodied knuckles had been wrapped and cleaned, though they still stung from the nip of the cold air. He held his bear cloak close to his skin, folding it over his arms and neck as the wind howled and sped across the grassy hill. Cedric stood and tried to remember the feeling of a warm summer breeze, gentle to the touch. His mind searched and searched, but was given only the present sting of cold, even under his many layers of clothing. Cedric stood and feared, feared that he would never feel the touch of a summer's breeze. He took it is an ill omen, a memory never to be recalled.

Upon the furthest distance of the horizon, Cedric saw his companion from Orford. Jarrick had caught a goat and was playing with its meal like a house cat.

Cedric stood watch over the field for a full hour, mesmerized by the griffin just on the cusp of his vision. The first snows of winter had come in Lorine, as Cedric would be told, the time for a conventional war had passed, for the coming battle would be a war for survival, a war to see the spring.

Chapter 30
Castle Green Rock

The army marched through the grassy fields of Midland for a week before finally reaching the full extent of the Red Marsh. The muck reached up to the thigh and was textured like a rotted stew. The only saving grace of that swamp was the red water lilies, which emitted a pleasant aroma which filled the air in the form of visible clouds.

From the hill above the swamp, Cedric paused to take a full view of the marsh which stretched endlessly into the horizon. It was covered with trees which had thick branches and vines which wrapped around one another. Many of the trees were shaded red as the water lilies, giving it a beautiful, yet ominous hue.

"Gaspar," Cedric said to his wizard, "Do the magi know why this swamp is painted with such brilliant red?"

"Only that this marsh was swept up by a great rainstorm some thousand years ago, filling this once-valley whole. It was a blood red cloud which bore the water, making many believe it to be an omen rather than a natural event. The red water lilies have no origin behind them, for nowhere else has such a species been recorded. Some magi theorize the storm came from beyond the eastern shores, to the Greendawn Sea. That would mean the storm came from the lands where no men dare sail, where people wear stones in their ears and lips and have purple teeth." Gaspar spoke no further, the land across the Greendawn had often been the apt story for parents trying to get their children to sleep.

Once King Baudoin, founder of the Erastrian people, sailed there with a fully crewed ship. Upon his return, he was mute, and his crew was missing. It was in his private journal his courtiers discovered details on a savage and terrifying land, guarded by stone giants and forests filled with men who hunted their own kind.

The Lorinian army slugged for two days through the swamp, taking makeshift rafts across, before they reached the beginning of Oderyr territory. It was marked by ancient rune stones and wooden posts sunk deep into the murky terrain of the Red Marsh. Only a single road, hewn of cobblestone, was raised above the marsh. The men marched in rows of two across the narrow road, which winded and stretched across the landscape.

This area of the Red Marsh was much fairer in weather and look, with littered trees across the mostly clear water. The red lily pads which decorated the landscape were in full final bloom before winter and had an assortment of reds in their pedals. On both trees and rocks, a green moss was growing strong, engulfing near ever surface in sight as though it were grass upon a prairie.

The army was met by soldiers loyal to Oderyr, dressed in the garb of both Midland, in their cloaks and brooches, but also that of the swamp, with many rugged furs and brown colored clothing. Their faces were fierce and near wild, for they had bits of mud and leaves in their long flowing beards. They wore kettle helmets which reached down to their noses and had slits in shape of eyes for clear sight. Their shields were pavise in design, with furs and pelts of animals strung over some, while others had painted images of a green tower. Their spear points were sharp though jaggedly made of low-grade steel.

"Hail to Oderyr," Cedric said from his horse as the guards approached, "I am Cedric Throne, heir to Adalgott, we come seeking safe passage through your land."

The guardsmen grumbled and spoke amongst themselves, till their captain, who bore a heavy axe and heavy chain coat, approached to give an answer. He slung his axe's handle upon the road and looked up at Cedric. "We will take you to Green Rock; it is less than an hour's march."

And so, the two groups now made their way to Green Rock. Cedric caught sight of fishermen going about their business, paddling along on long and narrow boats filled with their catch of the day, catfish, and trout amongst the lot. As they went, more clusters of guardsmen to Oderyr arrived and joined their caravan, coming from small forts of stone, tree huts, and caverns filled with garrisons of swamp dwellers. Some of them came bearing banners, bearing the sigil of Oderyr; a single-towered castle perched upon a muddy hill, whose stone had turned green at the basin. Their armor was mixed, with few matching uniforms. Most bore simple leathers with studded straps, others came with full breastplate, though the craftsmanship was poor and rusted.

Finally, they reached the Moss Bridge, curved as a semi-circle above the still and clear moat, which reflected the green bridge in a perfect image. Across this bridge and canal, Castle Green Rock, an ancient testament to architecture, built sometime in the first days of man and maintained and built up by the family of Oderyr ever since. It was an island surrounded by a single circular wall, with the keep and other buildings upon the central hill. The central keep was of basic design, though no less effective, and on all sides, a design of vines and moss clung to the walls, as beautiful and filled with history as a woven tapestry.

This description is not to take away from the overall magnitude of the castle, for it was larger than most in Midland. The island substantial enough to allow four separate halls, along with a few towered buildings which stretched above the canopy of the swamp.

Cedric's army was given camp just on the outside of the moat, where there was enough dry field to hold them, while he and his companions crossed over the Moss Bridge. The main courtyard was composed of gardens and ancient fountains, which poured out water from faucets in the shape of fish and other animals. The guardsmen led Cedric and his retinue to the main hall, where lord and lady Oderyr awaited their king and guest.

The couple sat in wooden chairs around a large fire pit, which was laid at the center of the hall. Theodric and Elanna, ancient as their own castle, were both of white hair and wrinkled skin. Theodric turned to greet Cedric, his lips were curled beneath a long white beard and he raised his gray eyebrow high on his brow. His eyes were wide and appeared near insane. "My lord! Come and sit by the fire. Ha-ha,"

Theodric and Elanna burst into crackling laughter, their age evident in their voice as they bellowed and warmed their shaking hands at the fire. "Come now Cedric; I'm only half as mad as they say!" Theodric's mind seemed to wander as Cedric pulled up a chair, and the old man was deep in disconnected thought.

"Thank you, Lord Theodric, the road has not been kind to us, I am here to…" Cedric was cut off by Theodric, who suddenly jumped out of his thoughts.

"Why are you here Cedric? To snatch away one of my daughters as a bride, hmm?"

Elanna, with white and wispy hair, was rocking back and forth in her chair, hard at work at embroidery which had no clear pattern or reason. "We haven't got any daughters Theodric. He must be here for the tourney, why all the pretty young lads come for our tourneys."

"Why yes, we have daughters, my wife, that one lovely lass, hair red as…"

"No, no daughters at all, Theodric."

"Oh, yes that's right my dear wife, no daughters at all…must be the tourney."

Cedric sat befuddled in his chair, unsure of what was happening. He turned to his companions who were equally confused. Eadwine hid behind the rest of them, trying desperately to contain laughter behind a widening grin.

Cedric decided to test the old man. "Theodric…do you know where Malcom is?"

Theodric turned deadly serious and leaned in close to Cedric. "If you are here, of course I know. He's on his way just now! The king wouldn't want to miss our tourney! Even have that lass with the red hair…"

"We don't have any daughters Theodric," Elanna interrupted again.

"Oh yes, that's right my dear wife, no daughters at all."

"Theodric!" Cedric raised his voice and startled even himself. He took a gentle tone for the rest of his conversation. "Malcom and many others were slain at the Sundering Hills. I lead what remains of our forces with Roderic; you know Roderic don't you?" The old man nodded. "We need passage through the Marsh. If we cannot reach Belfas, your people, and all of Midland will be in great danger."

Theodric turned to his wife, and attempted to whisper, though Cedric heard. "What is he talking about dear?"

"Why, the tourney my dear."

"Oh, yes the tourney, well tell him to see that lovely girl with the red hair, win her favor so pleasantly."

"Of course, dear."

Cedric had no words, he had heard rumors of the Oderyr withering age, but nothing on this level of sheer madness. The captain of the guard who led them to the castle approached and knelt beside Cedric to whisper. "My lord, their health is not well, follow me."

Cedric alone was led up a spiraling tower as his companions were given room and board in the guest wing of the castle. He climbed the steps with the captain until they reached a large wooden door, where two guards kept keen watch, spears, and shields at attention.

The captain beckoned them aside and opened the door with a heavy iron key, which rattled as it slid through the lock. The door screeched open and revealed a rather plain bedroom, with a red-haired woman sitting upon an arched windowsill, looking out at the expanse of the sunlit marsh.

It was Beatrix, her face was pale, though it had gained some color since the last they met. Her face was filled with sadness but also hope.

Cedric stood and bowed before her. "My lady…your father did not make it."

"I know," she said quickly, almost not giving Cedric time to finish his words. "A rider came just two days after bearing that news. I have no more tears for such mourning, for there is no time for it." She flattened her dress with her hands, stood, and crossed the room towards a large chest. She opened the iron box and lifted another, smaller box, wrapped in an elegant purple cloth. "I fled from Prav just hours after I learned he died; I knew I would not be safe there. The Oderyr, though they are mad, are sweet and kind, and more importantly, unable to remember why I am important, so there is no chance of betrayal." She began unwrapping the cloth, revealing corners of polished gold and gems decorating the box. Cedric leaned forward, his interest mounting by the second.

The cloth fell to the floor, as if in slowed reality, and Beatrix opened the box. Inside, a crown of gold. It was thin and had many pointed tips, each with a single red ruby. The main part of the crown was etched with magnificent craftsmanship, many swirling circles and designs akin to the most ancient of northern kings.

Beatrix carefully lifted the crown and rested in on her lap. Cedric knelt and bowed his head. "My lady you honor me…"

"I do not," Beatrix said in a stern voice, while Cedric lifted his head with a confused look. "I do this to secure my birthright, not only to Prav but to the lands and titles of Lenich. I was raised as the child to Crawe, but my blood, as far as I can tell, is of Lenich. I will give you this crown, give up my claim as

Queen of Midland, but only if you grant me the title of my twin fiefs."

Cedric was distrustful and questioned her motives. "Why give up the royal crown, for one of a vassal?"

She brushed off his doubts in a swift word, "I've no mind for battlefields and supply trains, but I have quite the skill in politics, why scrape by as commander when I can thrive as councilwoman, advisor, and landholder?" And yet Cedric was still unconvinced, both in look and mind. "I know the title is but honorary at this point, Lord Cedric, but the few that remain, they would rally, the captains of the Oderyr banners for instance…'

Cedric doubted, yet held no intention of denying the offer, and so he gave his decision, "It shall be tonight, in the gardens of Green Rock."

Beatrix nodded her head and gave a smile, "Of course my king, it shall be done."

And so, the local lords of the swamp gathered, as the sun fell and the moon rose, to await the Witan. Torches with sweet smelling oils were placed surrounding the gardens illuminating moss covered statues and overgrown hedges. A stone table was brought out to the center of the garden from the main hall, and pen with paper was placed upon the smoothed surface.

Cedric was led out from the main hall of the castle, now bathed and dressed in a purple silk shirt, with the faintest embroidery of grapevines, as befits the King of Midland. He was given a golden ring which held the coat of arms of Midland, the ring once worn by Malcom at his coronation. He sat, and the lords took seat around him in a great circle. Many of the men were of little land and wealth, though their title satisfied that they sit on the Witan.

Behind this sitting council, Cedric's companions stood, dressed in finer clothes. They had laid their weapons at the guest hall, where they had received food of various fish and wetland crop. Beorn looked like a jester, for he wore a tight brown shirt, two sizes too small, with frilled shoulders of bright orange.

Gaspar then approached, his long gray hood over his head, and he wore many chains of clergy over his neck. His face was stern and serious, as it was a significant honor for a magi to preside at a coronation, an event for historical record, one Gaspar would gladly write about. His familiar face comforted Cedric, who had sat in the stone chair with a nervous look. Gaspar was given a wineskin and a finely made glass bottle filled with oil.

Gaspar spoke with booming and confident voice, "Kneel, my lord, see yourself prostrate before the gods and your loyal subjects." And so, Cedric knelt and placed his hands at prayer by his chest. Gaspar took the wineskin and poured out the wine upon Cedric's head three times, blessing Cedric each pour. Next, the magi took up the bottle and placed oil upon his palms. He rubbed the oil on Cedric's forehead with his thumb and put his hands on his lord's shoulders.

Gaspar looked up from Cedric and turned his head to the council around them, "What say you men of Midland?"

The lords rose, and Theodric stood to give the council's word. Cedric bore a grave look; he knew not if the man intended to announce his kingship or the extraordinary sight of the lilies in the garden. The other lords all leaned in and awaited the old man, who had begun to mutter and shake under his breath. "We…the council…" Theodric looked back towards one of his vassals, who quickly gave a muffled whisper of instruction. "Submit to Lord Cedric…my, would you see the daisies bloom…" His voice was drowned out by cheering, and the lords quickly beckoned that he sit before any damage be done.

Gaspar boomed once more, "Rise a new man! Cedric, son of Albert, of the name Thorne, whose founder is Edric. Rise and be called King of Midland!" The vassal lords now came forward one by one, and each was made to kneel and kiss the plain ring upon Cedric's hand. Each said to him, "My lord, I humbly swear my fealty and loyalty, in the most dreadful winter, and pleasant summer, I will always have ready my table for your arrival, and your cup shall overflow at my feastings." Cedric gave his own oath to these lords, etched for eternity in word and pen. With the sigil of Thorne, dipped in hot wax, Cedric signed the paper upon the stone table, which had his own oath written upon it. The oath to uphold the rights and liberties of all his people.

When the swearing of oaths had been completed, a great feasting began. Full roasted pigs with appled mouth came from the kitchens, which spewed out heat and steam from their hard labor. An assortment of sweets, custards, pastries, and cakes, were laid out on tables in the gardens. Bouquets of fruit had also been laid next to freshly gutted trout, which simmered and steamed as guests took their fill.

Music too was played throughout the gardens, and Eadwine himself strummed his lute in rhythm with the musicians. It was fit for good dancing, and the lords began to partner with spouses and maidens of the hall. Cedric saw Aderyn sitting by herself, and slowly walked towards her. On the way, he picked a white tulip, long in stalk with milky white petals. He twiddled the flower in his hands and exaggeratedly knelt before Aderyn, reddening her face with embarrassment.

Cedric spoke in rustic accent, "Shall we have this dance, my lady?"

Aderyn crossed her arms in protest and sarcastically pouted, "I didn't realize the king wanted to die at his coronation." Without word, Cedric grabbed her from the seat and rushed her to the main stretch of grass. They swirled upon the grassy knoll of the castle's courtyard, their heels clicking sharp against cobblestone which patterned the ground. The two danced till guests had returned to bed, and torchlight grew dim as the orange sunset. When the candles had burned out, the two retired to the keep, happy, for the last together.

Cedric awoke to find that Aderyn had already risen and left his room, and he looked out the window to find the chirping of birds greeting his waking. He rose, and rather than wear the stuffy clothes that befit a king; he dawned his usual traveling clothes. His weight felt shifted; he had yet to grow accustomed to the new, heavier sword on his hip. He sorely missed Bayeux.

His room was situated a full story above the main hall, and he made his descent to join his other guests. When he turned the corner of the hallway, he saw that his friends had begun their breakfast, along with a few of the remaining vassal lords, for most had already left for the road home.

Lafayette had his feet upon the table, sipping at a brandy snug in his hand. He said, "To the king's health!" Lafayette raised his cup in toast and downed the last of the liquid courage. "It seems the party is truly over my friend," his tone turned serious, "look, the candles have run their length, the feasting tables emptied of their bounty and left as scraps for the dogs, the wine has run dry, the reserves as well. We must march to war." Lafayette donned a long flowing coat of red fox skin and ushered towards the door. He added to his own words, "These last lords of Midland have pledged their men and supplies, supplies enough to reach Belfas, the time has come." Lafayette gave a sympathetic shrug to his king, who had yet even to reach the bottom of the staircase.

Cedric looked down, uneasy at the prospect, for he knew the last feast had been done, the last wine drunk, he could feel nothing but the cold of the coming winter, which seemed to barrel towards him in growing speed.

Cedric took an empty chair, reclined, and began putting food on his plate. Cedric gave his last joke, "Well I've never heard of a good general who didn't have breakfast before the battle."

Lafayette smiled and said, "Very well my lord," conceding the breakfast meats and leftover cakes to his lord as final break before the road, and he left the hall to ready the horses.

Cedric was greeted by Theodric and his wife Elanna, as well as Beatrix. "Oh, the tourney is over so soon!" said Theodric, his mind was truly like gruel.

"Oh my dear," his wife said, "But what a tourney it was! Lads all clad in armor, see them there at the camp."

Beatrix stepped forward to interrupt, "Yes my lord and lady, truly…a riveting tourney." She pulled Cedric aside, "I supposed it's the western road for you then?"

Cedric responded dryly, "Yes, we'll be taking rafts across the marsh and onto that path into Belfas. Thank you for everything Beatrix."

"Remember, it is not a gift, it's a deal." She was headstrong and proud as her father.

Cedric mounted his horse and rode to the front of the marching lines, where Oderyr infantry carried long rafts upon their shoulders. Beatrix would stay at Green Rock; it was now the safest place in the north. Meanwhile, Cedric marched to where the danger was greatest.

Chapter 31
The Second Stone

So the camp was packed, and the fields emptied, the road was once again the home for Cedric's band. The journey out of Oderyr territory was done by boat, for the westernmost reaches of the marsh were the wettest. By rows and rows of longboats, they paddled across the wetlands, pierce through patches of thickly fogged land. When the army had docked upon the western ferry, they took their packs and supplies upon their backs and began marching for Belfas.

The western road was much wider, and in most places the army found themselves marching on dry grass, rather than muddy swamp. Soon the highland of Belfas revealed itself, in majestic whited mountaintops, and vast green valleys, where bellowing winds greeted the packs of grazing sheep. The signs of winter were abundant in the highlands, for grass lay browned and dead, and the days grew shorter and colder with each one that passed.

The southeast of Belfas was mostly uninhabited, for the men preferred the warmer, western coast, where fish and game were plentiful, along with fertile land for sowing. The only men they saw were shepherds who had come down from villages on mountainsides hewn of rock. The Belfans were dressed in heavy winter clothing, a mixture of beautiful furs and thick dyed wool, woven into intricate and colorful patterns along their shoulders and sides.

At the front of the army, Cedric rode a white steed, which had spots of brown, with flowing mane of milky white. Upon the horizon, Cedric caught sight of a great smooth stone which jutted from the ground like a mountain. He bid his army rest when they came upon the base of the rock, which was shaped like a carved square, standing taller than most castles or towers. Upon the rock above the basin, Cedric noticed many carved patterns and words, along with depictions of the gods and mortal men.

Gaspar approached and dismounted his horse, and ran his hand along the stone. "This is an ancient place of power…Adalgott's Second Stone," He said as he turned to Cedric, wonder, and amazement fresh upon his eyes. "It is the only evidence that Adalgott went north when he abdicated his throne, for it was carved after his time in Wulfstan, but before the time of his descendant kings. Look," he said as he pointed out an etching of a crown adorned man wielding a flaming sword, "There is Adalgott himself, snug between the depictions of Loden and the map of the North."

"Do you know what the words say?" Cedric asked.

"None now do possibly save some master magi deep in their studies…my, what it must have been like, to stand here those fateful years before." Gaspar was enthralled by the stone, both the religious and the historical merit it held.

Cedric approached the stone slowly, as though he approached in reverence the gods themselves. He removed his riding glove from his right hand and touched the cold stone. His body jolted with an incredible energy, profound and ancient, which stirred from long winter's slumber with his touch. Cedric heard a great bellowing in the mountains and especially in the stone, though none else besides him could perceive the sound. Like a thousand beating drums and blowing horns, it pierced his ears and rang incessantly in his head.

Suddenly there was a sharp sound. "Caw! Caw!" A full flock of crows ascended from the grass and small bunch of trees, their wings black as night clouded the ground that their shadows passed. Cedric felt a great tremble at his feet, as though the world would crack in two, and yet his hand kept steady on the stone, compelled by a subconscious will. His hand grew hot, hot as the sword when at the blacksmith's forge, and the stone his hand touched appeared to turn a molten, white-hot red.

Cedric lurched back, afraid of what strange thing he had awoken, and his companions looked at him with glances of confusion, for they had witnessed none of it. "Could you not hear those booming sounds?" Cedric said with fast pace. He looked at his hand, expecting horrific burns, but he saw only his hand, still cold from the stone. His friends grew in their concern.

"The wind is but a typical sound," Leopold said, "Does it boom in your ears?"

Cedric looked back at the stone, looking at it longingly, for it now appeared old in his memory. He spoke, "Never mind…it was nothing." It appeared the stone visage of Adalgott, with eyes so cold and stoic, now looked back at him.

Cedric's army made camp upon the valley of the standing stone between two climbing mountain peaks, whose peaks could not be seen through thick night's cloud. Cedric sat alone in his tent, the wind biting at his cloth home, which furled and flapped in the wind. At his desk, candles were lit, and the young king looked over logistics: grain, arrows, and horses, all vital for the war he waged. The army was well supplied, thanks to the support of Oderyr, who sent a full supply train of fresh food as tribute. They could push near halfway to the northern coastline of Belfas, where ancient cities could provide shelter for many months, possibly years.

Lafayette entered with a scout by his side, garbed in brown clothing fit for stealthy riding. Lafayette spoke, "My lord, this man has come from the eastern front, on mission to track and gain information on Azrael's forces."

Cedric beckoned the scout forward, and the candlelight of his desk revealed he was a young lad, with first beard and freckles fresh upon his face. Cedric took a pitcher of wine, and poured a glass, and offered it to the boy. The king spoke, "For the cold," the boy happily accepted the wine, drinking it greedily, "Now then to the meaning, your report?"

The scout put the cup back on the table, "Oh yes my lord." He loosened his belt buckle and produced a small satchel with sketching and tally marks done with charcoal. He read from the list he presented, "I first spotted their scavengers and sentinels upon Karak Makath, the second largest castle of the Eternal Dawn." The boy's voice went gravely serious and he gulped down air to steady himself, "Azrael had sacked the castle, its billowing black smoke could be seen well into the sky, and I had healthy fear that it would blot out the sun. Their host in near eighty thousand, as I counted from a nearby hilltop…"

The scout stopped to gather himself. "I snuck into their camp, under the veil of night, and took number of their men and supplies. They come with raiders from Hirdland, as we already know, but there are mercenaries from Dradania, adorned in heavy steel armor, which shined as they passed by torchlight. There too, they gather strength of Elnish men, bearing heavy halberds and crossbows from their southern realm."

Cedric leaned in, his face was filled with dread, and he spoke, "By what number do they greet us?"

"They come nearing twenty thousand, possibly more, for I was compelled by fear to flee the camp when dark glances were given as I counted."

Cedric reclined in his chair and rubbed his temple. His head raced with thought of such a force. "Very well," he said as he gripped both arms of his chair, "See yourself to a bed and hot meal…'

"That is not all my lord," Lafayette interrupted. The scout fumbled with his words, and finally, Lafayette spoke for the boy, "They have made camp only ten miles away, and they have gained ground in the past weeks. Soon, very soon, they shall overcome our camp, even if we marched all day and made no permanent camp."

Lafayette beat his foot against the tent floor, and ushered the scout away, thanking him for his service. Now it was just Cedric and Lafayette in the tent. The wind howled outside, bringing in a cold gust which raged against the candles of the tent. Cedric felt utterly defeated.

"That was it, Lafayette," Cedric said pathetically, "Our final chance is gone."

"Battles have been won against worse odds than that," Lafayette said optimistically as he grabbed two glasses and a pitcher of wine. He took the cups and poured wine, and the king and his commander drank together.

"We had a good run," Cedric said, already reminiscing on his life. "You would've made an excellent First Marshall for the whole of the north." The wine soothed his throat and calmed his nerves.

"There is still a chance." Lafayette tried desperately to rekindle his king's courage. "I remember when I was just a youth, nothing more than a squire in Oswine's court, I was sent out with Sir Jerald, do you remember him?"

Cedric smiled and spoke while sipping his wine, "Yes, he had a great curled mustache if I stand correct?"

"Yes, though it had grayed by the time I was his squire. He took a small band of knights, and myself out for a ride through the countryside. We passed by the Elthine Forest, where we came upon a whole regiment of cutthroats. Jerald fell in the first wave, an arrow right through his eye, his body near crushed me as it swung off his horse, clanking in his fine steel. I was sure I was done for, they had us surrounded on all sides, closing in fast, and me, without armor or a horse. You know this story Cedric, I was the talk of the kingdom when I returned to Wulfstan, Oswine gave me a ring and name, and I was taken as his ward, just like yourself. I did not get where I am in life by ease." Lafayette went deathly serious, and he took away Cedric's glass, so he was at full attention. "I fought harder that day than any other day in my life. It was a mess of bodies and horses, I took up Sir Jerald's sword and fought, fought until I could see the other side, the side with the honor and truth… Cedric, you have united the armies of Lorine and Midland, you've rallied the Folk of the Forest, you're the bloody heir to Adalgott. You cannot give up now not because are won't, but because you can't." Lafayette stood and gave a bow, "I have followed you for years as friend and captain, now let me follow you."

Lafayette exited the tent and vanished into the cold of the night, which crept through the open flap of the tent and bit at Cedric's flesh. The king was in deep thought, and he laid both his hands, shaking, upon the table to steady himself. Cedric stood and gazed over the map. Suddenly his fists slammed against the table, and he knocked the pitcher and glasses from the table. He rushed from the tent, and his guards gave attention as he went.

He saw the whole of his camp, as his tent was on a small hill above the rest. Hundreds upon hundreds of tents organized in neat rows, with dots of brazier fire to warm the watchmen greeted his sight. Cedric saw the stone just upon the edge of the camp, which again appeared to call out, crying for his namesake. The king marched towards the stone, with a slight stumble from his wine and lack of rest.

Cedric collapsed as he reached the basin of the stone and laid both his hands upon its smooth design, searching for answers within the rock and himself. He spoke to himself, and to the gods, in whisper so quiet it appeared as loud as a solitary thought, "Show me…give me a sign of strength." The stone was silent, only the wind gave an answer, cold wind against his face.

The king began to weep, mourning not for himself, but for those who followed him. For those who had not the strength to follow, who sat by their fires in winter, unsure of their fate come the spring. Again he whispered, "Give me a sign," and again the stone was silent. Finally, Cedric grew angry, and his face turned red. He screamed and shouted at the tree, "Show me the way! Do not abandon me now!" His fist pounded hard against the stone, and he could feel them already beginning to bruise. He heard a faint sound, the second stirring of the stone. This time there was no great booming noise, nor shaking of the earth. The noise was like a whisper, and it soothed Cedric to hear it cry to him.

Cedric gazed deep through the stone, and his eyes were made clear. Within the stone, there was cold darkness, and yet at its center, a flame.

Cedric was filled with the warmth of the fire, and he jolted up from his knees. He went running at full sprint back towards the camp, a broad smile of hope on his face. He rushed towards the quartermaster's tent, where Beorn was sharpening a heavy axe against a whetstone. The enlightened king came through like a storm, without so much as a hello to Beorn was gave a raised eyebrow. Cedric took a large chisel and pickaxe from the supplies and hurried back to the stone with them under his arms.

Beorn rushed after and called to him, "Cedric! Where are you going? What are you doing with those tools?"

Cedric was in a satisfied grin now, "You shall see my friend! You shall see!" Cedric reached the stone and took the pickaxe in both his hands. He paused for a moment and turned around to see that many his men had gathered to bear witness.

Gaspar cried out to him, pushing through the crowd, "Cedric no! This is sacrilege!"

Cedric steadied the pickaxe in his hands, "No Gaspar," He turned back to the stone and swung the tool back, "It is gods who guide me." He struck at the stone, sending chunks flying, and Gaspar nearly fainted as a maiden in a poem. Cedric chipped away in steady rhythm for some time, gradually working his way towards his vision of the flame. At last, he knew he drew near, and threw down the pickaxe in favor of the more delicate and precise chisel.

The stone slowly gave way, and Cedric's heart began to beat in rapid order, his eyes filled with a wild and burning passion, stirred by the stirring of the stone. Cedric jumped back at the final strike, in the stone he saw the pommel of a sword. It was of simple, but elegant gold, circular, with a pattern of overlapping curved triangles upon it. Next came the handle, which was of many thin wrappings of steel, a grip much longer lasting than that of leather. The crossguard was the shape of a curling snake, bent opposite horizontally on either end. The bottom edge of the blade was decorated in a column of runes, which stretch half its length. Forged by the smith god Welund, these were the words of power which gave its fiery legend.

Cedric took a gulp of air, wiped the sweat from his brow, and took firm hold of the sword's handle. He breathed deep and began to pull. There was some resistance, but Cedric felt the sword starting to move. He placed his feet against the stone to give himself proper footing and pulled with all his might.

As the sword was drawn out from the stone, it struck against its rocky tomb like a flint with proper stone and became alight with a bright glowing flame. The power of eternal beings made solid matter in the blade did spew out its flame in wondrous fashion. Cedric lifted the sword above his head, pointing the tip directly into the sky. In a sudden burst, the flame reached high into the clouds, as thin as the blade's shape, but brighter than one thousand suns.

It was called Geanlaecan, meaning unity in the long-lost tongue of Adalgott's folk. None could wield it, save for his heir, as the power would consume and destroy anyone else. Cedric felt this power course deep through his spirit, and he had thought he would be killed. He steadied his mind, and slowly the flame that spit across the sky began to recede into the steel. In a great hiss like a serpent, the flame completely vanished, Cedric was at one with the blade.

Gaspar rushed up to Cedric while his arms and legs shook from the power he had witnessed. Gaspar looked in absolute wonderment of his king, and the two smiled in hope. Gaspar took Cedric's free hand and raised it as a champion, and shouted to the army, "If Azrael has returned…then so too has Adalgott!"

The men raised their swords in unison, and cheered and shouted cries of victory, for they were filled each with the strength and will of one hundred men. Cedric's worries and fears melted away with the heat of the blade deep in his heart, and he felt tears welling up in his eyes. Cedric began to raise Geanlaecan to the rhythm of his soldiers, and he cried out, "For Lorine! For Midland! For Belfas!"

Aderyn rushed up from the crowd, and her arms wrapped tight around Cedric, who returned the embrace. She spoke into his ear, "There is still hope…there has always been hope."

Cedric could not help but contain the spirits of his army, who went through the camp opening their reserves and fine meats in celebration. These fine foods would do them no good, Cedric thought, for he knew they would not reach a week's travel before being met by Azrael. Cedric's mood lessened from jubilance, but he was still filled with fierce determination and set himself and his captains upon the maps in his tent.

He placed his open hands upon the table, and spoke intently to his commanders, "We have the morale, and we have the sword to slay Azrael, let us not lose them now." Cedric turned to his marshal, "Lafayette."

Lafayette snapped at attention with beaming pride, "Yes my lord," he answered with courage in his words.

"We march tomorrow morning, double paced." Cedric ran his finger over the map; he had made his decision. His hand hovered over an ancient citadel, not garrisoned since the time of the first kings. The image had a tower, though it was broken, and appeared as shattered teeth from an equally broken castle as its jaw. "At Broken Fang, we'll make our stand," he looked up for the approval of his commanders, "It has the best defenses for making our armies equal in strength on the battlefield. At the front, we can bottleneck their army, turn their fifty thousand men into but a minute number."

Lafayette approved with a nod and spoke, "We can establish perimeters in the forest surrounding the castle…it is our best choice."

Esmond, the captain of the Red Gyrfalcon, raised his voice, beaming with the pride of his order, "My lord! Give me the van on the battlefield, you have no better leader of cavalry in your service. I would lead by my order, and the Knights of the Eternal Dawn sworn to you if you so will it." The knight knelt and let his long hair droop at his shoulders; it had been let to grow since the beginning of the war, as a sign of his honor.

Cedric was glad to see such men still loyal to his cause, "Rise Esmond," He joked with the knight, "I am still your younger there is no need for so much courtliness. I will have much to learn in cavalry tactics back in Wulfstan. Go, assemble both forces of horsemen, and prepare them for our journey tomorrow."

Cedric looked back at the map as Esmond left. The king took a golden pommeled dagger from the table, and pierce the map directly over Broken Fang. "This is it, Lafayette," He said with such strength never heard in his voice, "Here is our victory or defeat, and here I am...ready for it." His hands were steady; fear had washed over and consumed his soul for the last time the previous night. Like a baptism, the fear had cleansed him and made him whole once more, finally ready for the crown.

Chapter 32
The Rain at Broken Fang

The camp was disassembled and made to march through the highland of Belfas. They marched not five miles before their first riders caught sight of Broken Fang. Beyond a high hill, the castle lay in a valley of wooded land. Built tall as mountains, for it had many levels of walls and keeps, though much of it was in ruin. Upon its crown, a longhall of stone, surrounded by smaller keeps upon lower levels. The twin towers of the castle were both shattered, and their once tall frames could be seen overcome with moss and dirt upon the ground.

Once those towers were built as a testament to man's strength, by Ballomar the Proud, whose hair was wrapped in many golden knots. Ballomar ruled before Adalgott, in the lands stretching from Prav to Broken Fang. He thought himself a descendant of the gods, and his people labored to exalt his name, forging numerous temples and holy places for his honor. His final work, Ballomar poured all his wealth into Broken

Fang, so that he might reach the clouds, and take his place amongst the gods before old age took him.

When the gods saw what Ballomar was doing, they said to themselves, "We must cast him and his people down, for they think themselves with pride unending and hunger for power unyielding." And so Duwel, lord of cloud and all the sky touches, took a mighty wind from the northern sea and made low the Tower of Ballomar. Ballomar collapsed for fear of the gods, and shaved his golden beard, and threw off his jewelry, and repented.

Now twice in history, Broken Fang would be the last defense, the last hope, against the coming tide of Azrael. Cedric ordered his men enter the castle, and they established camps at various levels of the castle. Cedric resided in the central keep, snug deep within the thick stone walls. There were remnants of statues and relics aligning the alcoves of the hall, though none were in full form.

By this time, it was the late afternoon, and the sun began to turn a dark orange as it dipped into the landscape. Stakes had been driven deep into the ground surrounding the clear field in front of the castle, and sentries of Rivermen were in the woods. Cedric took meal in the hall, alongside the lot of his companions. It was a simple affair of salted fish and some scavenged roots, which made for a light broth for stew he also took, along with a small loaf of dark bread. The wine they had was from Lorine, brought up with Lafayette's personals.

Eadwine picked between the bones of his meal and rubbed his finger around the edge of his chalice. He took his drink, and raised it, saying, "I propose a toast, to our journey and the friends absent and present." Each of them clinked their glasses and drank, thinking hardback upon their journey, and the road they endured. "And what an unexpected journey it is. The next time, let's let the nobles deal with second comings of evil."

Leopold humorously raised his cup, "Now I will drink to that," he said as he poured back the rest of his drink. They laughed and drank the meal away, their faces glowing with happiness, as though their war had long faded into memory. Cedric looked around the table and felt as though he was back at Orford, in the corner room of The Green Devil, exchanging stories of the faraway lands of Midland and Belfas. He stared intently at Aderyn, memorizing each detail of her face, and how the candlelight reflected off her milky white skin and black hair. He could not help but smile softly, for he was at this moment, genuinely happy.

When dinner was over, Cedric took Gaspar into a doored cloister of the hall, which was adorned with ancient tapestry and stone furniture, an official's chamber of Ballomar's time. Cedric talked with the magi, "Gaspar, I may need your help later tonight."

Gaspar was thrilled, though also nervous, "With what my lord? Do you need some man to lead the vanguard of the woods? I shall!" Cedric tried to explain, but Gaspar was engrossed in himself, "Whatever the daunting task I can handle it! If you asked me to slay Azrael with but a wooden stick, I would only ask when!"

Cedric sighed, "Gaspar it is nothing of that matter."

Gaspar breathed heavy in relief and flung his hands dramatically, "Oh thank the gods."

"Just make yourself free tonight. I will explain later." Cedric left the small room to deal with final battle plans.

As Cedric and his captains dealt with final preparations, the sun finally faltered and collapsed beneath the horizon. Braziers were lit upon the levels of the castle, and sentries patrolled the walls and towers with torches in hand. Cedric wandered the many inner halls in search of Aderyn. It seemed to Cedric as though Ballomar had built himself a labyrinth rather than a castle, for the rooms interconnected in bizarre fashion, and gave no indication of true direction.

Cedric jolted back when the door in front of him opened, and he sighed when he saw it was only Aderyn. She was carrying an old tome, written by the magi to Ballomar, which described the affairs of Broken Fang's courtiers after Duwel's mighty storm destroyed the towers. She gave a warm laugh at his fright, and she jested with him, "Good to see our brave king brought so low by a door's screech."

Cedric replied with a laugh, hoping to subtly deflect the jest, "Well...it was a loud screech in my defense. Why are you wandering through these halls?"

"Boredom, anxiousness, take your pick. It was not all for waste, look." She flipped through the pages of the book and revealed many tunnels and caverns constructed under the castle, secret routes for escape or incoming supplies during a siege, or the possible night raid upon the enemy camp. "We should send men in the morning to see if any of these routes are still standing, it could be a key advantage."

Cedric took the book, and flipped through more pages, revealing more detailed descriptions of the castle's defenses, an invaluable stratagem for any defending commander. "Even now I would be lost without your guiding hand," Cedric said lovingly.

"Aye, you would no doubt be dead in a ditch somewhere if not for my wisdom...the question is, why were you wandering through these halls as well?"

"Looking for you," Cedric said slyly.

"Oh?" Aderyn crossed her arms and leaned against the wall.

"Come with me; there is something you'll like."

And so, the two climbed the western tower, whose rooms and staircase were still intact, save the top which had been cut down. They came to a room which overlooked the whole of the castle's landscape. It had some ten arched windows, now long without their stained-glass insides, and torches had been lit on the wall. Inside, Gaspar and the rest of Cedric's closest companions waited.

Cedric and Aderyn stood before Gaspar, who recited ancient hymns and prayers in a soft voice, "Loden, God-father to all, see that your people have gathered in this place to give witness to your intelligent design. Let these two be joined as one so that they might guide one another to your healing house, where a table is prepared for us all. Now, swear before the sight of the stars and moon, those ancient sentinels of Cinder's light, and be made as one."

"I do so swear." Cedric and Aderyn said in unison. Sealed with word and kiss underneath the light of the eternal heavens, the two were married by the blessing of Loden. Retiring to Cedric's chambers, the flesh was made one, and souls became like the interwoven nature of silk clothing, forever connected in an unending pattern.

Chapter 33
The Battle of Broken Fang

Cedric awoke lying next to Aderyn, who was on her front sleeping face first in her pillow. He rose and stretched as he gazed out his room's window. The clouds were a dark gray, fit to burst open in thunderous rain. From the distance, he could see lightning cracking over the mountain range. He knew it would not be more than an hour or two before the armies of Azrael arrived in the valley.

He sallied into the other rooms of the king's chambers, where a squire awaited his command. Cedric was dressed in a thick hauberk, and a tunic was wrapped over his armor, which in turn was covered in plates of hardened leather. The tunic bore the symbol of his house, a proud Griffin, pouncing in ready to take flight. As he was dressed, thunder broke out above his head. It was so loud and powerful, it seemed to shake the foundation of the castle, and noise of heavy rain came directly following it.

Lafayette entered and gave his report, "Cedric, most of the tunnels and secret ways had been completely destroyed, with too much rubble in the way for them to be cleared. However, a single tunnel remains intact, leading out to the western forest…If we fail here, you should take that route to safety."

Cedric clipped on his scale pauldrons, which bore two circular sheets of metal at his upper chest, with the visages of Adalgott and Loden on each respectively. He fastened his sword and replied to Lafayette, "I will not run anymore. For months I've been on the road, never once facing Azrael in full pitched combat. No more, I face this day as my first as king, or last as the lowly lord of Orford."

Cedric and Lafayette walked along the battlements of the walls, inspecting the Rivermen who were gathering bundles of arrows and javelins. At the lowest level's gate, Beorn saw to the barricading, and he had two massive beams of logs on his shoulders. The lumberjack called to his lord, "These gates will not fall Cedric I will see to it." He let the timber drop, and other soldiers placed them against the gate.

Cedric clasped hands with Beorn and held his head as he would a brother. "We're almost out of this Beorn," he said welling up with emotion, "By the spring you'll be back with Hilde in Orford…we'll rebuild it together. So try not to get killed."

"Ha-ha, I will try my friend, I will try." Beorn went back to his work manning the gate, and he lifted a brimming pot of burning oil next to the machicolation. He was in a joking spirit only for a moment; his smile quickly was replaced with dark look, one of uncertainty seen in the eyes of dying men.

Lafayette and Cedric continued their march along the battlements, and Lafayette gave report of the woods surrounding the castle, "We've stationed Rivermen along the western and eastern portions of the forest. From there, they are in range to fire on the grassy field leading to the gate." Lafayette pointed out to the field, which was muddied and had puddles of brown water scattered about. Nearest the castle, wooden stakes were being hammered in, save in front of the gate. By doing this, the enemy would be funneled into a small zone, unable to rely on their superior numbers.

Alfnod approached, dressed in his usual armor of thick yellow jacket with metal beads, along with an additional chain shirt underneath. He had a barbuta helmet in his hand, and he nodded to Cedric, saying, "The Rivermen are secure in the forest, they've dug in and set traps lest the enemy tries to overrun them. My lord, I have no place with command. Let me fight by your side, as your bodyguard and standard holder."

"I wouldn't have it any other way Alfnod." Cedric took his sword, and said to his dear elven friend, "Kneel as Alfnod, adventurer from Orford." Cedric placed the blade on Alfnod's shoulders. "Rise, Sir Alfnod, a knight of Lorine." Alfnod barely contained his excitement as he stood and faced Cedric. The elf joined the king and the commander as they surveyed their defenses. As they inspected, a flat sounding horn could be heard, echoing from over the muddy hill.

From the hillside, banners appeared all along the horizon. They came bearing a plethora of color, ranging from the navy blue of Elnish mercenaries and princes to black and red symbols of Hirdland and Azrael. Beneath these banners, an army appeared, strong as Cedric feared, and their blades glistened and shined, even in the fading light of clouded day.

Cedric took position with his commanders upon the second story of the wall, where the whole battlefield could be surveyed. Just outside the gates, a full regiment of Lorinian spears was placed, so the enemy could not destroy the stakes. Beorn was with the van, wearing his hangman's mask and brandishing his heavy axe. Above them, the Rivermen not in the forest were ready, with arrow fastened to the string of their bows.

Some of the men shook at their posts, for the wave of foes enveloped the horizon. The battlefield was silent as the enemy took their positions, only the howling wind could be heard. Both sides waited, waited for the moment to strike.

"Alfnod," Cedric said with daunting conviction, "Prepare the order to fire at my command, if any man shoots without permission, there will be hell to pay." Cedric gazed out to the enormous waves of enemy that now swelled the hillside in front of him, and his heart pounded as he looked to the mudded field, his grand strategy.

Alfnod shouted out to the ranks of captains and bowmen, "Prepare to fire! Let no arrow fly before the order!"

Cedric gave his final round of encouragement as the enemy began to taunt and cheer, "Be brave on this day! Be heroes on this day! Do this, and I swear your names shall always be remembered!"

Enemy cavalry began to form ranks, and they mustered out just at the edge of the field. Azrael could be seen on the top of the hill, mounted upon his black horse, with Sibi and Yellow-Eyes by his side. The taunts and cheers from both sides faded, and all became dead silent. Yellow-Eyes beckoned his horses forward and rode out to meet the defenders.

"Shall we fire my lord, kill his second in command?" One of the captains said.

"No," Cedric scolded him, "Why waste arrows on one who

matters so little?"

Yellow-Eyes stopped before the gate defenders; his horse struggled through the mud, which had covered the whole of its legs. "Surrender lord Cedric! The battle is hopeless!" For a moment, it appeared there was genuine compassion in his voice, but Cedric knew it was but deception. "Let your men go home! They shall be given safe passage; my true king proclaims their innocence in this matter! If we overcome you, none shall be spared, the whole of your villages and cities burned, temples ruined, fields salted, your women made as concubines for my lord's brave army!"

Cedric gave but one word in reply, "If!" Cedric drew his blade and shouted at Yellow-Eyes, "Come! Let your master feel his bane for the second time!" Yellow-Eyes made a sour face and kicked his horse back towards his side. The sorcerer struggled through the mud the whole way.

A horn was blown, and banners were raised. The enemy cavalry advanced at blindingly mad pace, ripping through the field, kicking up mud and patches of wet grass. They were well in range of arrow fire, and yet Cedric did not waver or show fear. He raised his arm, but let it hang there, even as sound of hooves grew ever louder.

"Let fly!" Cedric threw his arm down, and the captains in unison repeated, "Let fly!"

The first volley was devastating, wiping out in full the first riders, whose flying bodies and dying horses clogged the path for the rest. Next came the arrows from either side of the forest, their flatbows so heavy and arrows so sharp, that the cavalry armor was like cloth sheets. The enemy did not even reach the stakes before being routed back to their hill. Scores laid dead or dying on the field, littered with arrows, sinking into the thick mud.

Cheers erupted from the Rivermen, who jeered at the enemy now exchanging unsure looks between one another. Again, a horn was blown, and a wave of infantry with rectangular shields and swords moved forward. They were mercenaries from the Elnish kingdoms, sporting brightly colored uniforms and elaborate banners which depicted unicorns and all sorts of mythical beings. Their proud songs began, and they hummed tunes of drink and hearth, strengthening their will to fight.

Soon, this merriment died down, for once they stepped onto the field, their fine metal and cloth boots were consumed in piles of mud, bringing them to a slow struggle. "Fire at will!" Cedric commanded from the battlements. The Rivermen took another round of arrows and began to pepper their foe, who fell and screamed in the muck. Only a third of the Elnish mercenaries reached the dry ground of the gate, where they fought with the defending Lorinians. The mercenaries did not fare well, as they had already been exhausted by wading through the mud, and so they struggled to gain any foothold at the gatehouse.

A runner came up from the back gate, bloodied with torn armor. "My lord!" He cried out to Cedric, "They've taken cavalry into the western forest, and begun to turn back our archers! Roderic remains there, but he cannot overcome the enemy."

Cedric was quick to act, "Saddle our remaining knights, I will lead the counter-attack in the forest. Lafayette! You have the command of the castle. To the woods!"

Cedric mounted his stallion and took off through the back gate of the castle, hidden by the dense forest so that the enemy could not know of its existence. He led a band of some hundred knights through the forest. Accompanying him were Alfnod, Eadwine, and Leopold. They rode fast to the aid of the Rivermen, who they could already see fleeing from their position.

Their charge flanked the enemy cavalry, bring swift blades down upon their bodies. Cedric was thrown off his horse; a lance had struck his right shoulder and nearly broke through his now bent pauldron. With Geanlaecan in hand, he lit the blade with his will, striking terror in the eyes of both rider and horse. His sword had no equal in precision of cut, making whole men seem like firewood against a woodsman's axe.

Esmond, the captain of the Red Gyrfalcon, was slain as he rode, a lance drove deep through his upper chest, and he was dead before he fell off his horse.

Eadwine rode swiftly through the forest, scoring many hits with his bow, while Leopold stalked by tree roots and hidden crevasses, ambushing any he came upon. Rivermen grouped with the companions and their king, forming tightly to ward off the horsemen.

Alfnod fought with only one of his blades, the other hand occupied with Cedric's banner. In half an hour's time, the western forest was secure with the enemy routed, though they themselves had taken heavy losses. Only a few knights were still on horses, making them ineffective as a charging unit. The Rivermen too were badly bloodied, their bows lay broken on the dirt, left with only daggers and short swords. Roderic was alive amongst them, his leg had been driven through with a lance, and his boar crown had been bent out of shape.

Cedric grabbed at his shoulder and struggled to the edge of the forest; he could see now that another wave of the enemy had reached the stakes. It was as Cedric feared, the Rivermen atop Broken Fang had now run short of arrows, there was now nothing to stop Azrael's forces from reaching the castle. The bent metal of his pauldron rubbed harshly against Cedric's aketon, so he removed it, leaving him with a single piece on his left shoulder.

"Hurry! Back to the side gate, they will need us at the gates!" Cedric gathered up his men and hurried back to Broken Fang. They had only just reached the side gate as they heard clanging swords and sharp battle cries pick up in the wind.

Another wave of the enemy, Hirdmen, had thrown themselves upon the gate, burning down the old and dried wood with torches. The Lorinian forces outside the gate had been wiped out, and now the defenders mustered inside the gatehouse. From the top, Aderyn aided the Rivermen throwing down rocks and pots of boiling oil through the machicolation. She called out to Cedric, "They're near through the gates! Call the archers back a level!"

And so, Cedric ordered the Rivermen flee upward, towards the second level of the citadel, while the Lorinian men at arms and last of the Vine Guard held the gatehouse. It was hot work once the gate had been burned, men were thrown against one another in such tight conditions, blades and spears could scant find space to swing. Cedric stuck was towards the back of this mosh pit, and he feared he would be trampled under the massive weight.

Beorn was towards the front; the man struck fear in all the foes who dared look him in the eyes through his mask. He made room for his axe, shoving even his allies so he could properly swing. He scored many kills in a mad rage, sending Hirdmen scurrying back to the field.

Soon, Beorn tired, and his guard began to falter. A spear was thrust through his side, and he screamed in agony before breaking it off with his arm. Beorn was then cut at the upper thigh, and he collapsed onto his knee. Just as a Hirdmen intended to finish him, Beorn rose and cut the man in two with one swing. Again, Beorn was pierced, this time on his shoulder, and once more in his side.

Finally, the lumberjack fell again to the floor and was struck in the neck by a blade. Yet Beorn still, by magic or will, was alive. He struggled to his feet, only to be met by Sibi the Brother, who had pushed through and even killed ranks of his own to reach Beorn. With a terrible cry, Sibi pierced Beorn's heart with his sword. Beorn had breathed his last.

Cedric cried out with unintelligible pain and rushed through the ranks with reddening eyes. He tackled Sibi to the ground, and the two beat against one another as their armies fought above them. Cedric was on top of Sibi, beating his face into the mud, but soon, Sibi's brute force knocked Cedric on his back.

The savage Hirdlander, with wild eyes, began beating Cedric's face inward. The first. Cedric tried to grasp his sword, but his hand was stomped on by passing feet. A blow was shattered across Cedric's eye socket, and the pain was so stinging he thought he had lost his eye. He could no longer see from his right eye, either it was gone or filled with blood. Another fist to his face, this time across his cheek. Sibi then wrapped his hands around Cedric's throat and began to squeeze. Sibi's face turned bright red as Cedric purpled, and bits of violent spit dripped onto the king's face.

With one last effort, Cedric struggled to his feet and knocked Sibi backward into the enemy. Sibi could not rise, for he was consumed like a rock in a rushing wave. The chieftain of Azrael screamed as he was crushed from all sides, his men did not even notice, for the battle had made them numb to hearing. He fell deep into the mud, so deep his face submerged fully, and he drowned beneath the boots of his comrades.

The king hurried backward through the ranks; he was bloodied all over his body, both of his own, and of others. His face was severely beaten, and his nose bled, along with a large gash in his forehead. He supported himself against his sword and spat out blood.

Cedric collapsed against the battlements, his heart in a deep pain and his head ringing. The battle seemed to grow more hopeless by the second, as more and more of his troops fell at the gates, while the enemy continued to pour throughout the hillside. Suddenly a small battalion of Rivermen came through the back gate, and were brought to speak before Cedric, "My lord," a captain of them said, "The eastern forest has fallen! With many stalking swords and rushing riders, they tore us apart! None but us were left alive, and we fear they may have followed our trail back to the hidden gate!"

Cedric felt the weight of Azrael's power closing fast upon him, like the clamping of a beast's sharp and mangled fangs. "To the second level, all! We can hold that gate a while longer!" Cedric ordered his men back up the curling stairs of the castle, leaving a few braves to keep the gate long enough for them to make their way. He did so with no light heart, for he knew he had condemned his men to die, only so there might still be a chance of victory for all.

Even with this sacrifice, it was not enough to save all his companions. Azrael ordered his men to fire upon them, for much of his force carried javelins and bows, unused until now.

As they climbed the stairs, Cedric heard the sound of an arrow tear through armor and flesh. He turned and saw Alfnod's surprise face. The armor that covered his heart turned red, and he began to spit up blood.

Alfnod collapsed into Cedric's arms; there was an arrow sticking out of his back. Cedric felt numb, and he almost lost the strength to carry on up the stairs. Propelled by his remaining companions, they pushed upwards.

Alfnod was laid down in the upper courtyard, and Gaspar, who had up until this moment been tucked away in the hall, appeared with an assortment of oils and medicines. The magi acted faster than he had ever, quickly tearing open Alfnod's armor and removing his chain shirt. The arrow had narrowly pierced through the other side, a good sign.

Gaspar took the arrowhead and broke it at the tip, all while Alfnod screamed. "Put this in his mouth," Gaspar said without looking up, he handed a long piece of cork to Cedric, "for the pain," Gaspar said as he went to his surgeon's work. Cedric did as he asked, and held Alfnod down from thrashing about.

"I need something to stop the bleeding," said Gaspar as he struggled to pressurize the wound. Cedric looked at his sword and hatched an idea.

"Hold him down for me Gaspar," Cedric flickered his blade alight, and took the metal to Alfnod's chest, singeing the wound. It smelled foul, but it would do for cauterizing the wound. Alfnod screamed as the hot iron touched his skin, and he fainted from the pain.

"Smart thinking," Gaspar nodded to Cedric, "I will take him into the keep, see if I can give him something for the pain, and clean up these burns."

The defenders huddled against the walls and battlements of

the second level; their brothers lay dead just feet below. With bellowing chants the enemy flooded the castle, turning some to tears and others to final prayers to the gods. The whole host of the enemy entered the castle, Azrael himself rode in, his men offering favors and praise as he went. Cedric clutched his blade in hand, ready to die with blood fresh upon it. Aderyn was next to him, and the two were prepared as one.

The sun broke through the gray clouds, and its radiance shined upon the muddy battlefield and tinted the color of puddles of blood. The beams of light revealed the corpses in the muddy field and drying their tomb. Cedric looked up for a moment and saw a red figure race across the sky, the old friend from Orford was observing the battle. He closes his eyes, breathed a deep breath, which did more to his soul than to his lungs, and willed his blade to light with flame.

Cedric cried out, "Let them see the King of Lorine, Midland, and Belfas yet stands proud against this evil! With me men! Now is the hour of our death, let us face it like the men we are!" The last defenders huddled at the entrance to the final level, bearing war faces and battle cries, they made ready.

Chapter 34
The Horns of the Ithon

From the hill, a horn was blown, causing both defender and attacker to pause and look. It was no horn from either camp; it came with a rustic tune, unsung in green fields of Midland for many, many years. With the sun at their front, Cedric spotted Miro, accompanied by his band of few knights. They rode hard, as though they had the strength of the whole world at their backs.

Azrael burst out in a deep laughter, "Ha-ha! The fools, to our bloody work my braves, leave these worms to fester in the castle a while longer! We've a proper foe in these foolhardy knights."

Azrael ushered full ranks out of the castle, and well into the field, which had finally dried since the sun's shining. Yellow-Eyes smirked widely as the knights approached. He was sent out as the emissary to them.

"Knights of the Eternal Dawn, have you come to

renounce…" Yellow-Eyes tried to begin.

Miro spoke with swagger, "Surrender now you impudent vagabond, for you and your men will be given no quarter in battle, for the justice of Cinder waits for no man or foul beast! I say again surrender, or you shall be destroyed!"

Yellow-Eyes could not contain his laughter, "Ha! You come before us, a band of road-weary knights, and ask us to surrender? No."

Miro did not falter, "Very well." Miro took his knights and rode back, while the enemy jeered and swore at them. The knight took his horn from the saddle and blew it. It was not the same tune as the one that had rung just moments before. From over the hilltop, a force of shapes and sizes appeared. They came with horns and hooves and screeching voices that rang true through the cold air. They had all manner of banners under their command, unity among many different peoples.

At their head, the proud king of the Ithon, bearing his dark plated armor, and metal horns now encrusted with gold. It was Pike, he came with a host of nearly forty thousand of his forest, of all races, satyrs, Minotaurs, centaurs, and many other beasts now far from their woodland realm.

Pike rode out in front of his lines, mounted on a brown steed with white spots, who had been outfitted with horned blinders. He himself was crowned with a golden wreath, which sat snug between his horns. In his hands, he held a horn, carved from the root wood of the oldest tree in the Ithon. He raised the horn high above his head, and its iron mold shimmered in the sunlight. With all his breath, he blew life into the horn. It was a high pitch thing, sounding like the cry of an animal.

The Hirdmen were shaken, but they remained in their formation upon the field, hoping the same muddled fate would befall the beasts as it did their brothers. The men formed up in three ranks, brandish pikes and spears from a wall of long shields.

Pike rode back to his ranks and dispatched orders through the number of his warchiefs. Pike's forces moved forward, with a brisk and steady pace, chanting and beating their shields as they went.

Slowly, Pike's forces began to pick up speed. By the time they were halfway across the field, they were in full charge. The Minotaurs came first, screaming in mad bloodlust, with their hooves beating hard against the ground, their crude weapons of club and axe ready for battle. Behind them, centaurs raged like cavalry, moving quick, some carrying lances and others, bows and javelins. Further back, where Pike commanded, the satyrs moved as infantry.

Then they came to the mudded field, and Azrael felt confident, letting his enemy go through the same hell his man had waded through. But when Pike reached the mud, he found it as dry as sand. The sun had dried the field since the morning rain, and now Pike had free range to charge.

Azrael's forces were filled with a great fear, and locked their shields together tightly, bracing for the charge. Minotaurs beat their chests and went down on all fours, breaking directly for the frontal lines. The front line put down their pikes and braced for impact. At the last moment, the Minotaurs broke off to either flank. For just a single moment, the front lines were distracted, all Pike needed was a moment. Directly following the Minotaurs, the Centaurs came rushing with their spears, plowing through the ranks that had raised their spears in confusion.

It was to great effect, for Azrael lost nearly two-thirds of his front ranks to the first charge. The Hirdmen were given no break, as the Minotaurs who had feinted now came from either flank, pincer striking through the second rank. The satyrs came next, wiping out the remnants of the two front formations, while the third already began to break away towards the castle. This charge was finally slowed and pitched combat began between the Hirdmen and the Unseen Ones.

It was not long before Pike had driven through the melee of the field, and brought his band of bodyguard up to Cedric's level in the castle. The king in the forest dismounted from his noble steed, whose iron antlers were now bent and broken from the charge. Pike embraced Cedric as he would an old friend. "We had not thought to be here Cedric! For weeks I was bogged down in the land where the Ithon and Suthon meet, near the city of Eadburg. There I grappled with the Wolf King of the Suthon, who gave me this," Pike lifted his right arm, which had long claw marks running up its frame. "I would have come at once, but to leave the Suthon to raid and reap in my lands, would be unacceptable."

Cedric could not help but smile as he spoke, "There is nothing to regret, you did as any king would do, it was a wise choice." The two steadied themselves and turned their full attention to their armies. Pike had overwhelmed the castle and was winning in the field.

Azrael was beaten, and he knew it. With his personal band, he took off riding towards the western forest, hoping to flee back to the Red Marsh. Cedric saw this, and though he was wounded, he took off after him. "Come with me, any who can fight! To the hidden tunnel!" Aderyn, Alfnod, Leopold, and Eadwine joined Cedric, along with a small band of Lorinian troops. Lafayette and Gaspar remained behind, knowing that they may need to aid Pike's advancing forces.

Through the tunnel, Cedric's band moved with conviction. Their king led with torchlight at the front, clutching in agony at his many sustained wounds. They came out of a large tree's basin and found themselves near where the Rivermen were attacked. Leopold spotted Azrael's fleeing horse, along with his captains, "Quick! Eadwine, with your bow!" Eadwine took aim at Azrael's steed and followed in unison movement across the forest floor. At last, his arrow flew, and pierce the beast's heart, sending both the mount and the rider crashing to the fallen leaves.

Azrael's company turned their horses and rushed at Cedric's band. The king ducked to the side and sliced through the horse of one of the riders. It was an indecisive battle, neither could get the advantage.

While the skirmish raged on, Cedric approached Azrael's horse, only to find the dark one had already fled. Cedric turned back and ushered to Eadwine, "Eadwine! Get a horse and find out where…" Azrael appeared from behind a raised tree, whose roots tangles all along the forest floor. In his hand, a curved dagger pointed at Aderyn's neck.

"You will surrender your army, false king Cedric." Azrael began to cut, just enough to draw blood, "Or I take what you hold dear." Aderyn struggled, her fierce will never wavering, even in the face of death. Cedric didn't know what to do, his mind rushed for any strategy until he heard the snap of a tree branch behind Azrael and the image of an old friend. Eadwine drew back his bow, "You move the knife but an inch, and I will cut you down!"

Cedric shouted, "Enough!" He ordered Eadwine and his men lay down their weapons. Cedric stood tall, held his hands high, and dropped his sword on the ground. He slowly approached but stopped at where the exposed tree roots began. "There is no need for more bloodshed Azrael."

Azrael was not convinced, so he took a step back and again threatened with the knife, "Stay back! My master will never let you win!"

"He has no power here; I've already won…now drop the knife." Cedric was calm and relaxed; his heart did not even increase pace.

For a moment, it appeared there was refrain in Azrael's cold and rotted face, a lapse in his faith for his master. It was not enough, "Very well Cedric." Time appeared to slow as Azrael moved the blade across her neck. Cedric began to run up the roots, while from behind an enormous beast leaped through the tree branches.

It was the Griffin of Orford, with bloody justice raging in its wild eyes. Its razor-sharp claws tore at the back of Azrael, who screamed like a monstrous beast in the night. In a cloud of shadow, Azrael fled through the forest, swifter than any animal or man could ever move, his scream still echoing around them.

Aderyn was safe, and she grabbed at her red neck and coughed violently as she fell to the ground. Cedric knelt beside her, and touch her hand with his palm. "Do I look like some maiden? Go!" She scorned him for wasting time, and Cedric could not help but grin.

Leopold looked out into the forest, and shouted at Cedric, "Azrael flies with the speed of a wraith! We cannot catch him with simple horses! Look here, a trail of foul black blood." Leopold pointed to the ground with his blade, where Azrael's open wounds had spilled drops of the liquid.

Cedric looked to his Griffin, who matched his gaze with

the recognition of being. The Griffin knew Cedric was his king and arched his body close to the ground. Cedric stood with a blank face and wiped the blood and tears from his face. Taking his sword as a walking cane, he approached the Griffin, and without resistance, brushes his hand along the red and yellow feathers of such royal beauty.

Cedric gripped at the neck of the beast and wrapped himself tightly across its back. The two breathed in unison, and their spirits were intertwined as king and subject. The Griffin jumped like a horse being broken, and its beak sniffed at the dark blood, and its eyes dilated as a lion with bloodlust.

Suddenly Cedric and the Griffin flew above the tree line, as Cedric held on for dear life. His eyes were closed due to the ferocity of the wind, but when the Griffin steadied himself, Cedric opened his eyes to see. They were well above the battlefield, and Cedric could see the full image of Broken Fang and the battle. The Unseen had done their part, sweeping through the castle's first level, laying waste to the final remnants of Azrael's forces.

Then the Griffin dove, bring its wingspan just above the height of the trees as it followed the scent of the dark blood. They flew for nearly an hour, and the sun began to orange as they went. At last, the Griffin landed, its wings gusting wind as a horse would slow its legs. Cedric awkwardly patted the Griffin along its slender neck, and he could swear he heard the noble beast coo as a common sparrow.

Cedric dismounted but stumbled as he went for he was still weak from battle. They were in a wooded grove, and the blood trail had stopped in a final pool. Cedric looked all around, his mind both afraid and filled with rage. The Griffin had its head at attention, listening to any sound the forest produced. Cedric listened and heard a snapping twig, and a running stream of water.

Mustering his courage, Cedric ignited his blade and drove through the shrubbery, where on the other side, Azrael awaited him.

Cedric crashed through and stood with his sword high to strike down his foe. He found himself in a little clearing, where winter flowers were in full bloom, and a stream poured out from a nook of stone. The orange rays of sunshine danced across the surface of the water, turning it to the appearance of liquid gold.

Azrael was there; he was laying down by the stream's source, clutching at a grizzly gash in his rotted side. He breathed heavy, and simply gave of look of complete emptiness to Cedric. Cedric was shocked that his foe had been brought so low, and lowered his sword, though he did not loosen his grip.

"It's over Azrael, your master, and you, have failed," Cedric said with disdain and grief stuck in his throat.

"A thousand curses on your name Cedric, I am the true king, and I will take that title to my grave." Azrael was stubborn and foolish in his mindset.

"Oh, I know you are king Azrael," Cedric said with slyness, "The last Frisian king to be correct." Cedric had struck a chord, his foe's eyes, for only a moment, seemed human. Azrael's breathing quickened and grew shallow; death was approaching as a once denied adversary, ready for the final victory.

"Please…" Azrael turned to pleading, "Take pity on one so unjustly betrayed and damned. It was not in my will, for any of this!"

Cedric gave no pity to the wretched one; he knew it would do nothing. He shook his head side to side, and spoke, "You knew well what you did, and yet death comes for you, in the end, your final promise from Crassus Baal, left unfulfilled."

When Azrael knew his pleading had failed, he revealed his true nature; his voice turned harsh as stone against glass, "One thousand plagues and curses upon you! I would have myself die one thousand times if only see you fall!" With that final word, Cedric raised his sword and swung down, hard as he had ever struck.

The blade burned through the rotted flesh and clanged as it hit the stone lying beneath Azrael. Flocks of birds flew at the sound, and the day grew dim. Cedric collapsed to the grass, and lay there for hours, silently mourning all the war had brought to his lands. Azrael's corpse had withered and turned to ash, as his mortal age had, at last, caught his body. The sky turned orange, and Cedric breathed a sigh of relief. The air felt cool through his throat, not bitterly cold as it had been before, spring was at last in the air. Cedric rose, and with the water of the stream, he washed away the surface wounds he had sustained, though no amount of water or magic would undo the deepened wounds he had sustained. His breath would be shallow upon a random sigh, his leg would feel pain in a random step, evil had done its work, and yet good had conquered.

He walked back to Broken Fang, for his winged beast had already left him, though Cedric could see clearly the beast headed southward. Back at the ruined citadel, Azrael's forces had been gathered up, and they were brought before Cedric as his own men celebrated. Cedric was merciful to the prisoners, declaring them free to leave for their respective homes, but demanding all stolen goods be declared forfeit.

Alfnod was conscious and limped over to Cedric. Alfnod bore a pained look but was turned happy when he saw Cedric's relieved look. With unspoken exchange, Alfnod and Cedric collapsed upon the wall of the castle as soldiers passed by. The two burst out in laughter, tears of joy flowed from their eyes as they wrestled and jostled one another.

Chapter 35
The Waking Spring

The sun broke through the gray clouds of the dawn. Upon the grassy fields, now returning to their green hue, a light sprinkle of dew graced their individual stalks. Birds had now returned to their nest, chicks hatched and chirped incessantly. Fresh cut timber was placed, and the beating of hammers was a constant sound throughout Orford. Men rose to meet their honest work near ten hours of the day, taking nightly rest in pitched tents where their children play, and wives cook. Winter had, at last, come to pass, the burned ash was swept away, and in its place, new life.

Cedric stood out upon his hill, to where his home once stood. His hair had begun to gray at the side, not from age but the weariness of travel and war. Where once his face was cleanly shaved, now a small beard, with twirled mustache had begun to form. At his head, the golden crown of Lorine, bejeweled with bright emeralds and sapphires. His figure had thinned since the beginning of his journey, the happy weight of his time in Orford had vanished. Geanlaecan was at his hip, covered by a long red cloak which lifted with each passing gust of spring wind. He stared out to his village, searching through the bank of memories in his mind.

Upon that hill, he had rolled down to his father's arms in the happy summers of his childhood. In that inn, he had had his first drink and first hangover. Upon that gleaming shore of the lake, his first love. He did not even remember the burning of Orford, for what could that painful memory compare to the happy ones of youth.

A month had passed since the Battle of Broken Fang. Cedric courted in Prav for that time but had now returned to his native land, to his capital of Wulfstan. Declared king of both lands, he ruled more land than any northern king since the time of Adalgott, though Belfas remained an untamed beast. Cedric now gazed out to the countryside of Orford, a place he could return to at any time, but now felt as though this should be the final time his eyes would beset upon it. He wished for nothing more but to stay, abdicate the power he had gained, yet he remembered the advice of the good king Oswine. By hating his crown, he would know he was a righteous king.

Alfnod joined his watch; he too bore the weary marks of travel. The elf had the markings of a chancellor, adorned in a thick red cloak, along with a badge of office bearing an encrusted eagle. He now used a walking cane with a golden handle, for his wounds had not healed properly. He often found himself gasping for air, and clutching at his side.

Behind them both, a full royal escort. Many knights, bearing flags of vassals and noble houses, along with roofed carts of courtiers, including Aderyn, whose hair picked up in the wind, and danced as though in ballet. Her marriage to Cedric had stirred many nobles in dramatic gossip, yet it mattered not to Cedric, he was happy.

Cedric saw Alfnod but gave no word. Instead, the king simply began walking down the hill. He passed by Beorn's hut, which sat empty. His wife could not bear to return to that place without her husband or first born. She went far to the east, to Ritter, to the village of her ancestors. Though she did not blame Cedric, the king never again heard from her in missive or in person.

Eadwine was by his cottage, packing the last of his traveling gear back into his snug hut. He had been offered a council position in Wulfstan, Master of Game, but his heart was in the forests and hills of Orford, where green fields lay unhindered by the rigidness of stone walls. His soul belonged to the country, as he told Cedric when he refused the offer, a common saying of his elven kin. The bard's tale would continue, as he oft found himself traveling the roads of Lorine, spreading the tales of his feats with the good king Cedric. Though sobered by the quest they undertook, Eadwine was fated never to lose his sarcastic tone.

Leopold had already left their company, headed north on route to the city of Dulfen, where a ranger of Belfas awaited him. This ranger had sent word to Cedric, requesting an agent to support his cause, of which he divulged no information. Intrigued, Cedric sent the slyest of his company, one who could discern what this Belfan's true intentions were.

There was little word from the Knights of the Eternal Dawn. Azrael had purged much of their order, their castles lay in ruin, and networks of agents left dismantled as a man sweeps away the web of a spider. Cedric had dispatched Miro, his

Knight-Sergeant, to investigate and give report.

Cedric had forgotten all these courtly duties as he went through the town one last time. Cedric hurried towards the grassy fields where they once feasted under lantern-lit night. He wandered aimlessly in the field until his boot was caught on a rough patch of dirt. Lifting the block of grass, he saw the handle of a practice sword. His heart swelled from the yearning to return to those times and he reeled back, almost collapsing. He curled his fists and closed his eyes as he rocked back and forth.

Suddenly he took the sword, tucked it underneath his long flowing red cloak, and took off running towards the forest. He ran and ran, till he found himself short of breath and he collapsed to the ground in a wheezing fit. He steadied himself on a tree, and laughed; he was not the fit young lad he once was.

Cedric suddenly heard a horse's galloping nearing, and he turned to see the rider. It was Aderyn, who was concerned for why Cedric had vanished into the woods. Alongside her horse, she had brought his own.

"Off for one last adventure?" she teased him as in their youth, "Sorry, those are for the handsome, dashing ones who can run without collapsing."

"Just taking it all in," Cedric breathed the fresh country air and threw his arms up. "We won't be here for a while; there's much to be done in the capital."

Aderyn turned somewhat somber but kept her smile. Her words comforted Cedric, "I know," she said so softly.

Cedric turned back to the pile of stones and pulled out the practice sword he had taken. With the strength of both his arms, he plunged the blade through the rocks. He placed his hands upon the rocks and whispered several blessings and prayers. Cedric headed back, leaving the practice sword lodged in the stones.

Aderyn grew a mischievous smile. "How long do you suppose it would be before the escort realized we've already started riding to Wulfstan?" She threw the reigns of the free horse to Cedric, and he matched her smile. Cedric hopped on the horse, and the two raced through the forest. Overhead they could hear the screeching of the Guardian, now returned to its nesting grounds.

END

A Collection of Tales and Ages
from the Lands of Yennen
and other Continents

The Age of Glory

The Birth of the Gods

In the beginning of the worlds, before the existence of time and space, there was only Kryn, the all-knowing and unknowable. He is a massless and omnipotent being, from which all life is connected and tied. Kryn presided over his barren landscape alone, and from his consciousness, the gods and demons were formed. His first sons were Cinder, the Father-Son whose flame turns across the sky in golden fashion, and Baphamont the chief of all demons. From this, Kryn's children gave shape and matter to the world. From Cinder's great light, the gods were born. The first and wisest amongst them was Loden the Wanderer. From his power came the gods of man, known as the Children; Godric, the Lord of animal life and the hunt, Arian, the goddess of nature and is known by many north men as the Lady of the Lake, and Welund, the god of earth and craftsmanship, whose great fiery bellows gave the earth its warmth and fire.

The offspring of the Children grew in number in the days when the world lay barren. From Godric came the twin brothers of Baldag, the god of law and justice, and Sigberht, the god of war. From Arian, her daughter Bryanna, the goddess of alchemy. Welund wed himself to Boethius, the god of knowledge whose libraries record all of history, and fathered Domovoi, the hearth god who lives beneath the floorboards of all those who pour wine as an offering to his name. Domovoi and his wife goddess, Veria of fertile soil, gave birth to Trundor the Slayer-God, who forged all animals and wild things to be hunted.

The gods together formed and molded the earth to their liking, and sculpted distinct continents divided by great bodies of water. The Moonlands, where the gods did do battle on the Earth. Yennen, the largest of its brothers, and filled with all manner of mythical races and sprawling kingdoms. Erastrius, the smallest of all the lands, dwarfed by Yennen, where the first of Baudoin's line sailed from.

Loden the Wanderer

In the days when Cinder's light burned brightly in the sky, but life had yet to fill the surface of the earth, Loden wandered alone on its barren surface. For years, he traveled alone, his gray cloak became browned as he walked through the dust, longing for companions. When he had traveled the distance of Yennen, the largest continent of the world, he collapsed by the seashore of Belfas, the frigid tip of the north. He wept for his loneliness, for there was no one else who could be at his side. Upon his tear, his magical soul was streamed, and the single tear of Loden fell from his silky white beard and mixed with the sand of the beach.

When the foaming waves of the sea came and swallowed up the sand infused with the god's tear, Loden was amazed to see a great beam of light pierce from the sea's surface. He was blasted back onto his face, and from the bright light, the Children were born. Three beings, born from Loden, designed to bring companionship to the world. Godric, Welund, and their sister Arian filled the world with their creation, spreading man throughout the world, and Loden looked upon this and saw that it was good.

For many passing years, this trinity satisfied Loden, while, to the south, Duwel and Trundor ruled with their offspring. Yet his soul still yearned for companionship, and so he spoke thus to his offspring, 'My Children! What world is this that we are left so lonely, to the south my Brother Duwel is content with his creation, let us be like him.' And so Loden gathered wet sand from the northern shore of Belfas, where he had once made true the image of his children. He took up handfuls of the mud, blessed it with his breath, and handed it to the three Children, that they might become a creator like him. In their father's image, they molded man, strong, wise, brave, but also mortal, cruel, and easily tempted.

The Demons

These races of creations lived together in harmony for many years, giving praise and bounty to their respective gods and civilizing a once empty world. But this all was much to the displeasure of Cinder's brother, Baphamont, who believed he and his demonic rulers should have dominion over the world and the creations of the gods. Baphamont, being brash and unthinking, attempted to strike down his brother Cinder, whose ever-consuming flame, burned the wicked demon, who was cast back to his domain beaten and disgraced. Baphamont's offspring, known as Crassus Baal, Lord of deals and trickery and the most cunning and deceptive of the demons, came to his master's aid and offered his skills of smoke and dagger to rid the world of the gods' rule. Beelzus was formed shortly after, the demoness of disease and famine, hers was the silent and slow moving doom of the mortal races. Together, these demons forged their domain of hell, void of the gods' very essence of existence, a land which is made in total mockery of creation itself.

Regarding the First Kingdoms of Man

In the first era of man, the people were scattered throughout the earth by their divine lords. In the Mist Lands, also known as Erastrius, the Erastrian people settled and established large cities, with massive ships and armies to support them and their noble lords became known as Sea Kings.

In the northern tip of Yennen, the lands of Belfas, Midland, and Lorine, the Northmen thrived in spirit and hearth, forging smaller but nonetheless powerful kingdoms, referred to as the Ten Kingdoms of the North.

In the lands below the freezing winters of Belfas, the men known as the Eln thrived in their little hamlets and green growing fields, content to live with beautiful music and rustic culture, to that of city building like their southern folk.

In the south, where green hills turned to seas of sand, the

Tanaric, also known as Sun-Kissed to the Northmen, rule the trading roads and watered cities. Their skin touched by the heat of their homeland, they are wise traders and fierce warriors, who can survive the desert as their camels do. Some of the Tanari exist as nomads, traveling the expansive desert like ants across a field, and are the most well-known to the outside world. However, most settled in the Sancti Lakebed and Arron Plains, where they live as any ordinary folk in Yennen. There they established many cities, including Sulita, the largest city in the south of Yennen, where clean water runs in equal in abundance to sweet tasting wine and exotic spices. The pride of the Tanaric people, Sulita was built by master engineers who labored over three generations to complete the groundwork of the city. Comprised of three walled sections, Sulita was built to withstand any prolonged siege, and a foreign power has never managed to sack it.

To the northeast, the Hirdmen grew in number and wealth, both in cities and sweeping herds of cattle. Living in the grassy Hirdland, where sheep can graze for miles in any direction, the shepherds have ruled as rustic lords, living in wooden palaces and great tents. To their southern border, along the eastern seaboard of Yennen, live the Dradanian folk, broad in frame and taller than all others. Thereupon the northern coast, the Falklands rule with unprecedented knowledge of engineering and sciences.

The Forging of the North

To the North, the Ten Kingdoms arose, where noble knights swore oaths to smaller barons and dukes, owing their loyalty to that league of ten. It was here where Seax, Lorine, and other great noble kingdoms began their history. Rich in song and silver, the countries thrived and made great temples and shrines to their gods, carving out the mountains and massive stones in their honor. But it was all for ending, as Azrael, Prince of Crassus Baal, and defiler of man rose to power in the late days of these kingdoms. He slew the bravest sworn shields in pitched battle, and his blade was unmatched by any mortal man. He slew the ten kings of the north, from each taking their index finger, and forging himself a crown hewed from their skeletal remains, known as the crown of Ten Fingers, or Degsedd.

In these days, hope grew dim in the land, and shadow covered and clouded the minds of the people, reducing them to servants of the evil one. It was by Adalgott, son of The Huntsman Godric, and Mable the lady of Canterbrick, that the north was saved. His mother sacrificed herself so he could live, for the agents of Azrael had tracked them to their homestead. She stood at the threshold of their home and outstretched her arms so none could pass. The assassins killed her, but her moment's distraction had done its work. Adalgott's father, Godric, swept down from the sky upon a golden chariot and placed him in Sulita, far away from the evil one's influence. Son of god and man, Adalgott had the destiny for greatness, for either right or wrong, for Azrael could easily tempt one only half born of gods.

King Uzmet, lord of the Tanari, educated Adalgott at Sulita, and he learned the ways of the sword and strategy, as well as the knowledge of stewardship. When he was sixteen, he was informed of his heritage by a vision of his father, who bid him return to his people. Adalgott did as instructed, and with a band of loyal courtiers, departed for the north. Godric bid his son not go without protection and ordered that his brother

Welund forge a blade. Welund did so, lifting entire mountains to contain to the power of the flaming sword, Geanlaecan, meaning unite. Godric descended to his son the final time and presented the sword to Adalgott.

On his journey, Adalgott was thrice tempted by Crassus Baal. The trickster came to him and his, offering them water, for they had none and were upon the hottest patch of the Tanaric desert. Adalgott shooed the demon away with his staff, and when he had done this, he struck it against a rock, springing forth water blessed by Godric.

The second temptation came when Adalgott came to Nacia, and his mind was made known to pleasures of flesh. Crassus Baal bid him walk through the gauntlet of harems in that land, to prove his resolve and will. Adalgott did not abide, and rather, took a ferry across the sea of that land, for he would not allow himself to be tempted nor subject to the whims of a demon.

The final temptation came as Adalgott arrived in what is now Lorine. A great crowd had gathered to see their chosen champion return to his homeland, and they waited to hear his voice. Crassus Baal appeared to him as a rat upon the ground, nipping at his heel. The rat promised this kingdom without bloodshed, installing Adalgott as the new Azrael if the half-god would but kneel. Adalgott refused and stomped on the rat's head, crushing it into the dirt.

From here, Adalgott's rebellion spread like fire upon kindling. The liege lords and their armies flocked to the banners of Adalgott, the image of the flaming sword. Though not only men joined Adalgott, a griffin, thrice the size of a man, bowed before the rightful king, and rode into battle alongside its master. Azrael was challenged and eventually defeated at the

Battle of Broken Fang. From this victory, Adalgott forged his kingdom, and he came to rule each of the ten as one, creating the Northern Kingdom. His people were codified by his law, which he recorded on stone for all to look upon and understand, and their culture thrived in the years to come.

Adalgott ruled long, supposedly living beyond one hundred years. Without a word, he vanished from his court, leaving his people in disarray. The Ten Kingdoms returned to power, dividing the north into lands unable to unify since their schism.

Morthwyl, Kingdom Across the Sea of Stars

Once there was a folk who ruled where the Belfans now thrive, known as the Deanglians. The Deangli were born of Welund, god of smiths, for he descended to the mother of that race, Gweneth ard Moss, the wisest and fairest of all humankind. Her visage was pale as milk, though her skin was warmed by the fires of her forge. She was a modest smithy's daughter, and she forged many fine pieces of jewelry and weapons. Welund gave himself to her entirely, for he was struck by her genius with metal, which rivaled his own.

This period of love between god and man fell when war raged between Welund's people and Baphamont's legions. Baphamont learned there had been sired a second son of god and man, and so sent his minions to strike down the baby in his crib. Gweneth proved her strength, and repealed the host, losing her life in the process.

Welund was struck grief, and, in a fit of burning rage, threw Baphamont across the Sea of Stars, towards the unnamed continent of the west. There the smith god hammered away at Baphamont, striking his frame so hard on the ground that the craters can still be seen today. For a year, Welund chased and beat Baphamont across that continent, till the demon shrunk to his domain far away from the realm of men.

Welund returned to Yennen and took his orphaned son to that land he had hammered. When he had set foot upon the continent, he took a patch of dirt and sprinkled it upon his son's forehead. Doing this, Welund named his son Pwyll, and granted him lordship over this land, giving him leave over the entire west. Welund also took the tribe of Gweneth and placed them as the vassals and oath bound to his son, blessing them and naming them the Deangli.

Welund could not stay to educate his son or to raise his kingdom, for the war between gods and demons carried on. Welund plucked a tribe of Dweor, known as the Greys, and gave them the power over the mountains of the Moonlands. In exchange, the Greys guarded Pwyll and educated him to be a ruler in his own right. Until his sixteenth birthday, Pwyll was brought up in the halls of Zanula, where he studied under wise dwarven tutors and learned from the books of his mother's people.

When Pwyll had come of age, he was robust and tall, but still retained the wisdom of his mother and father. Pwyll was educated of his heritage and knew his father was Welund. Upon his birthday, he claimed the continent as his de jure kingdom. He forged his crown, and founded the city of Pwyllfeld. With this done, he named his new kingdom, Morthwyl, after the glowing hammer of his father. Welund returned to Pwyll upon his seventeenth birthday and granted his son a winged helm named Doeth. Since this time, Pwyll's descendants, and the Deangli have ruled this land and worked the fields, creating a kingdom which thrives as the faithful to Welund.

Pwyll was an accomplished statesman, and divided up his land into smaller baronies, to delegate the administration of his vast tracts of land. The Baronies of Afon, Blodeuyn, and Zirnhor, were given the lands to the south of the capital. These counties serve as the breadbasket of the kingdom, rustic and tame as the Lorinian countryside across the sea. To Pwyllfeld, Pwyll decreed the kings would rule the northern half of the country, the twin lands of Eirwen, an area blanketed by white snow and stone castles. Beyond Eirwen, the Duchy of Farcyle is a land of perpetual winter, snug across the freezing northern shore. The kings were also granted the Moonlands to the eastern coast, named due to the hammer marks Welund left, as well as the gray sand upon the beaches, resembling that distant rock.

Since its founding, Morthwyl has thrived as a land undamaged by the wars of Yennen. Traders always stream into Pwyllfeld, bringing beautiful works of dweor and human craftsmanship, along with excellent wines from the Barony of Blodeuyn.

Beyond Morthwyl, to the Howling Winds

To the west of Farcyle, a freezing wind has blown since the dawning of time. The White Mountains are the savior to Morthwyl, for this wind would roll over every hamlet in its path, leaving land unfit to sustain life. Rangers of Morthwyl once journeyed out into that tundra, and claimed to have discovered a great palace composed of ice. They had fear they would be killed by some foul force, but found instead a jolly king of that castle. Father Winter, they dubbed him, an ancient spirit composed of cold, though he had a warm heart to his guests.

His jovial song is the winter's howling wind, which spreads in harmonious orchestra across the world.

Tales of the Hlútrian People

In days when the Children walked amongst their people, Duwel, god of the sky, came to form his people. From his silky white clouds, he shaped and molded his people, light and pure as the stuff of their creation. The Hlútrian people were born, with sharp features and pointed ears, they came to conquer the lands between Eln and the north. The two surviving kingdoms of these people are The Golden Court and their eastern cousins the Silver Hlútrian who survive in Geladhithil. These folk, though bright in wisdom and beauty, never grew to the numbers of their human counterparts, and rather found strength in their solitude.

To the common tongue, they are elves, for Northmen and Elnish alike mistook the bright folk of Duwel for that of woodland fairies, reducing the true majesty of their creation to pesky creatures clad in leaves for clothing. In the kingdom of Geladhithil, the elves rule as with a rustic disposition, keeping faithful to their origins in the green realm of Glanfech, known for its wooden halls and numerous vineyards. To the Golden Court, the elves live mainly in the walled city of Evrand. Evrand is the largest city in Yennen, consisting of three isles upon the Lake Evrand, as well as a walled section upon the banks of that country. Ruled by a council, the elves take pleasure in their exclusion from the world, often refusing emissaries out of sheer contempt for the world beyond their stone walls.

The Lusani

In the early days of the Ten Kingdoms of the north, the Lusani, known as the woodland elves to man, came to thrive in the land between Lorine and Belfas. In the Lusani Forest, their kingdom grows shaded from the blight of the outside world, much like the Awaerian of the Ithon.

The role of government typically falls to the women amongst the noble families, with the men of the houses overseeing warfare and agriculture. Another distinction between the Awaerian and Lusani is that the Lusani are masters of engineering and architecture, forging great rustic halls and shaping the earth according to their plans. Their chief god is Duwel, though the Lusani also give plentiful worship to their huntress, Kyshnael, the wife of Duwel, who taught the elves how to hunt with bow and spear.

Conflict with the kingdoms around them has been constant, with man slowly encroaching further into the forest. The woodland elves are not kind to outsiders, often whole bands of simple villagers are found dead upon forest roads. When a batch rangers from Lorine were butchered along the southern border of Lusani, King Dechart marched his whole army into the woods for revenge. His army was crushed, and his head placed along the forest's wall upon a spike. Since this event, none have dared enter the woods, and the relation between the Lusani and men is nothing but ruined.

Kendrick and Juliana

In the oldest days of man, when bards still wrote the great tales of love and courage, the greatest tale of love in the north was born, born from the love of a northern warrior and a

Hlútrian lady. Kendrick, lord of Canterbrick and most brave and kind of the lords of Belfas, found himself in the woodland realm of Lusani, where the elvish folk live in the splendor of culture and hearth.

Kendrick traveled through the forest alone, tearing his majestic cloak of gold on the spikey twigs of the numerous trees. It was when his face was covered with dirt, his clothes torn, and his hands thick with tree sap, that he found a clearing where Juliana rested on an old oaken stump. Dressed in elaborate lavender, with metal working of gold and gems across her thin and pale neck. Her hair was a bright brown, like that of her kingdom's landscape, and her face was smooth with eyes as blue as the sea on a sunny day.

Kendrick knelt before the fair maiden Juliana, whose beauty had overwhelmed his senses, and he was struck with a profound and sincere love for the lady. The man Kendrick had little to give as a gift, and so offered his chestnut colored steed, the cunning Fairfax, as a gift. Juliana, so refined and elegant, blushed red when the noble lord knelt and placed his hands in hers, vowing to love her for all eternity. Kendrick came to live with her for many weeks in the forest, where they promised themselves to each other under the light of the Northern Star for all time.

The day came when Kendrick was called home, for his neighbors had come to war in his land, and his expertise in battle was required on the front. He left his lady in tears, and with his torn golden cloak, so that she would always remember their vow to one another.

In the wars of his homeland, Kendrick was brave and fought well upon the field, and each night took to his tent, to pray the gods deliver his war-weary body back to the arms of the one he loved.

It was in this time of strife and doubt that the demoness Beelzus appeared before the nobleman, clad in her disease-ridden vestments, and rotted flesh. She too had fallen in love with the mortal, and outstretched her mangled arms, saying, "my lord your maiden cannot love as I do, for she is but mortal, while I am forever. Join in my embrace and become immortal as I."

Kendrick spurned the advances of the foul Beelzus, "get out dirty thing! For I could never love one such thing as long as I still draw breath!"

For this slight, Beelzus cursed Kendrick, spewing wicked words upon his fate with dark magic. For the days that followed their meeting, Kendrick became afflicted by an undying plague. When he reached for bread or meat, it became like ashen chunk in his hand, and when he thirsted and tried to drink from his chalice, the water turned to dried salt upon touching his tongue.

He fell ill upon his bed, and his frame became thin and weak, and his eyes filled with dark rings from lack of strength. Life seemed to seep out of him by the minute, and with the last of his will, he took and pen and paper to write to his fairest love. Sending the swiftest bird in his renown, the letter of his failing health reached Juliana in record time. The fair maiden was distraught by the news, but her heart was too fill with the strength to save him.

Julianna set off on a quest, riding day and night upon the horse of her lover, through the kingdoms of man in search of a cure. She visited wise magi, earthy sages, and all manner of learned folk. On her journeys, she learned of a cure to all illnesses, the Weeping Stream of the Falkland, surrounded by flaming mountains and guarded by a great green dragon.

Julianna climbed the fiery peaks of the Falklands, and cleverly snuck past the dragon. She found a cool blue stream hidden in the mountains and took a vial of the holy water back to Canterbrick. Here she saved Kendrick's life, becoming engraved in the myth of northern and elvish legend.

Dalmar's Duel with Baphamont

In the days when the gods and demons warred freely against one another, there came a time when Baphamont led a great host through the kingdom of Glanfech, sacking Hlútrian strongholds throughout the banks of Lake Evrand. King Dalmar, the father of Rohiel, set out with a small outfit of his trusted companions to face Baphamont, while his army was a three-days march away. On the rolling hills of Glanfech, Dalmar met the ruinous host of Baphamont, a horde of savage men and Hlútrians, along with lesser demons each crueler than the last.

Dalmar alone rode out to a lone knoll on the hills, and challenged Baphamont to one on one combat. Even though Dalmar was renowned for his swordsmanship, it was a foolish thing for any mortal to face a demon in battle. Baphamont would have won that day had he not ordered his army to halt, for he chose to duel the Hlútrian king, buying time for Dalmar's army to arrive.

For three days and three nights, Dalmar matched blades with his demonic opponents. Both duelists were torn to shreds by the end of it, and had lost much blood on the field of battle. Dalmar was worse off than Baphamont, who had gashes on his side and his thigh. It was at this moment that Dalmar spotted his son, Rohiel, once but a child in his arms, regaled in full uniform, with a legion of ten thousand marching to his beck and call. His son had raised his army as soon as he heard of the duel, marching day and night to arrive in time. Dalmar knew his work was done, and so let his sword slip from his hand, and smiled as Baphamont sliced through him.

Rohiel, enraged by his father's death, took the field by himself, riding across the empty plain amount a black steed, named Tharion, meaning midnight. With his lance, he pierced Baphamont's leg, bringing the demon to his knee. With another charge, Rohiel sliced off Baphamont's head with a sword, sending the demon screaming back to his foul realm, his power faded once more from the land of Yennen. Thus, Rohiel came into his crown, the truest king of Glanfech.

The Tale of Prince Dothriel

In the ancient Hlútrian realm of Geladhithil, the kin of Duwel lived in harmony with both the natural and the urban. Their cities had great white walls, but were filled with greenery and forests dedicated to their god. These lands were filled with vineyards and large farms, where all who lived were satisfied and made merry. In these days, a brutal war chief, Mushag, of the Thyrs came east from the wasteland, bringing his whole host against these green lands, claiming it as the will of Trundor.

The prince of these lands, Dothriel, son of Dohri, set off alone to defend his land from the Thyrs at their doorstep. Most intelligent and cunning of the rangers, the prince took only his bow and blade, saying to his father king, "for these are all the things the truest of our folk need."

On the edge of the Suthon, the forest bordering Geladhithil, Dothriel set up camp and waited five days until he caught a glimpse of Mushag's roaming horde. They came numbering nearly three thousand, and the ground shook as they marched in unorganized ranks which swelled like a foaming sea. Dothriel, adorned in silver chainmail and blue cloak, met their host upon the edge of the forest realm. He cried out to the Thyrs. 'Come and see that there is but one elf who shall turn you from Geladhithil!'

With this taunt, the Thyrs became red with rage and threw themselves into a mad chase after the prince, who rushed through the forest like a swift jackrabbit. Dothriel hid amongst the trees and bushes, picking off Mushag's retinue one by one. For three days, Dothriel harassed this band of warriors, till the followers of Mushag rose in revolt, slicing off the head of their king and commander, and leaving it as appeasement for Dothriel as they returned home. With this, Dothriel became known as Sithrak, or Silent Hunter, in orc culture, forever a monstrous tale told to younglings of their great elven foes.

Regarding Glanfech, the Lost Country

In the hills of Glanfech, the elves thrived, building great halls adorned in golden trimming and became great rustic lords of the land. Their first king, Brenwi, established his capital city of Evrand, upon the lake of the same name. The three islands that spotted the lakes shimmering water, were connected by massive stone bridges, and significant buildings constructed, forging a city of the lake.

For hundreds of years, these folk ruled themselves freely, never submitting to the authority of the Erastrian pioneers nor the Nacian imperials. It was only by the power of Crassus Baal, and his servant Azrael that the kingdom's power weakened and collapsed. It was at the time of Azrael that the dark one came to spread a shadow across the sky, causing the people of Duwel to be separated from their supreme lord. In this time, the Hlútrians squabbled and engaged in civil war, they grew greedy and forgot their ways, and soon much of their kingdom was lost forever.

The king of Glanfech, Rohiel the Lightcrafter, son of Dalmar, scaled the highest point of the world, Mount Sveca so that he might pierce the shadowy blanket and commune with Duwel. Upon this mountain Rohiel cried to his lord, 'Duwel, your people are in peril, they cry out to you, but their prayers cannot pierce the thick darkness that corrupts them. Give me the strength to unite them.' And so Duwel gave Rohiel instruction to craft a lighthouse in Evrand, where the Hlútrians would survive.

For years, Rohiel worked alone on the tower, laying every stone himself, and all without written plans. When he had laid the final stone, a great bolt of flame descended from the sky and placed itself on the top of the tower, and the fire cleansed the air of darkness. With the sun once more shining bright, the Hlútrians were guided to Evrand, where they gathered and were protected from the shadow.

Though the Hlútrians were saved, their kingdom was forever lost, and today they maintain only a few holdings outside of Evrand, where they await Duwel's descending, where he shall bring his people up to his hall to feast and be satisfied.

Now Glanfech lays abandoned, their great roads and cities are but crumbling ruins, ancient reminders of a lost time. In the hills of Glanfech, the men of Lorine have expanded southward and claimed the golden fields as their own. The traces of Hlútrian culture have had their influence on the Northmen, who now bath in Hlútrian bathhouses.

The Dweor Halls

Welund, the god of the forge and fire, created his own kin, hardier version of men, who resided deep in mountain cities. They became known as the dwarves, and the first of their race worked side by side their master god, and together they forged legendary tools and weapons.

For many years, the Dweor resided in the Belfas and Lorinian mountains, where their people grew in song and strength. It was in Usham, the largest mountain hall, that the dwarves received their harshest blow to their venerated pride. The Dweor of Usham did not craft by hand their newest halls and shrines, rather, it was done by the labor of human slaves. Thousands of war prisoners were diverted to such work. They toiled in the deepening low halls of the Dweor, where no light could pierce the thick rock that became their tomb. One hundred years before Azrael's return, the slaves rebelled, and lit fire to the vast stores of Usham Fire, flammable when in open source, explosive when in compressed areas.

The lower halls were destroyed in an instant, taking whole centuries of amassed wealth and knowledge with them. The upper halls were consumed with flame in mere hours, and few had time to evacuate. It was Forrin, nephew to the King Angbar, who took leadership of the survivors. By wit and word, he led his people south, passing through the smaller kingdoms of the Eln as an honored guest, trading trinkets, and relics for bread and ale for his people. Years did pass, and the effects were true upon Forrin's body, for his younger flesh turned wrinkled, and his brown beard went white. The king never betrayed the needs of his people, for he thought himself their servant, and so he pressed on, ever southward.

After decades of harsh travel, the Dweor arrived at the Green Mountains, a ranging landscape of such teeming life, which lay snug between Berhungy and Sulita. At the sight of the Green Mountains, Forrin collapsed from his pony, and he wept for the beauty of the land. He composed a poem, dictated to his scribe, for his hands had long lost the accuracy to write. At the widest gap in the mountains, Forrin built a great hall, whose wall stretched from either side, henceforth known as Forrin's Gate.

Forrin's folk came to thrive in the Green Mountains, and they found themselves as often above ground as below, for the mountains were ripe for sowing and shepherding. Gone were the massive halls dedicated to ancestor and god, and in their place, snug hamlets of wattle and daub, where pastures lay filled with sheep.

Upon his deathbed, Forrin was surrounded by his many sons and daughters, and he found his life complete, welcoming death as an expected guest. In his final words Forrin blessed his sons, and gave them leave over divided sections of his kingdom, 'Rule not to lord over our people my children,' he said, 'Rule to serve our people.'

The Age of Erastrius

The Erastrian Conquest

In Erastrius, several powerful kingdoms came into being. The most powerful of these kingdoms was ruled by King Mathis, who fathered Baudoin. Mathis was vain and prideful, proclaiming that his line would last forever, and he laid the foundation of the capital, Avelem, which now stands as the largest city in the world. In his old age, he constructed the Golden Gardens at his, where he planted the most extravagant of plants from Yennen and Erastrius alike. His son, Baudoin, was enchanted by this botanical wonder, taking study of the plants from Yennen. This fueled his interest in Yennen, and soon, he had engrossed himself in maps and books regarding the land across the sea. When Mathis died, Baudoin ascended in glorious fashion, claiming the title, First-Born, ruler of Yennen and Erastrius, and he built a mighty fleet so that his armies could conquer the land.

Baudoin First-Born sailed across the Ecestial Sea and established many cities and sea fortresses along the eastern coast of Yennen, praising Matuar, the god of the sea who rises high above the waves in his castled flagship. Baudoin's journey ended nearly halfway up the eastern coast of Yennen, towards the realm of Geladhithil, where the silver Hlútrians reside. Baudoin died peacefully in his bed, crowing his son, Adémar, as the next ruler of his kingdom. Adémar sought to use his efforts and influence on growing his kingdom from within, focusing on shrewd diplomacy and expanding infrastructure. He also extended through the middle portions of Yennen, reaching the Sea of Stars on the western side of the continent. Adémar never sought to conquer the Tanari, for he could never tame that desert without losing his hold on his kingdom. The hordes of Tanaric cavalry bathed in steel would hold against Adémar in any battle, perhaps even overrun the Sea King. Adémar forged an alliance with the Tanari through marriage, his son, Pippin, to their queen, Athylan. From there the power and influence of Baudoin's heirs thrived for many generations, bring an age of prosperity to much of Yennen.

Athylan, the Jewel of Sulita, Queen to the Tanari, and wisest ruler in their people's history. She has no clear description, save that she preferred her hair draped down to her hips, and wore two rings on either hand. Educated by the finest tutors, she had been bred for court and command from her youth. Skilled in grand stratagem, she crushed the Arron Rebellion, and with diplomacy, ensured no noble would feel the need to rebel again. Her marriage to Pippin was her own scheme, and she is quoted as saying to her beloved upon the bedding, "I am queen to all, even you." Though proud and headstrong, she had compassion for her husband, and for her people who worshiped her as a champion to their lands. For centuries, this Tanari-Erastrian dynasty has ruled with absolute authority, bringing even the fiercest desert tribes into the fold. However, this happy union between Erastrius and Tanari was not to last long, not torn apart by war or plague, but by total doom.

The Great Collapse

The Great Collapse as it was known, the disintegration of the marine kingdom of Erastrius. In the last true generations of Baudoin, the kings grew fat and lazy, taking too much pleasure in hunting and festivals and not in the affairs of their kingdom. The king's debt increased to mountainous levels, till there was not a single copper for alms to spare. A severe cold period also left most cropland yielding nothing. Slowly power ebbed away, until Adémar III left his kingdom in a completely ruined state. His wild nights of debauchery and egotistical nature alienated him from his vassal lords, as well as the people who starved outside his palace walls. He was murdered in a coup, orchestrated by his closest advisors and friends. Bleeding out, the king rushed from his palace and onto the streets of his capital, proclaiming, "Erastrius dies with me!" His corpse was strung up on pikes, and carried through the streets in a crazed mob. That night, the mob became a revolt, destroying the palace, even burning down the Golden Gardens. With the capital in ruins, power quickly slipped away from the conspirators.

Adémar III's sons were entrusted to the same court that had murdered their father, and soon, almost all of them were dead, save his youngest, Hadrian. Hadrian had been snuck out of the city by his brave mother Dulia, a common concubine of the late king.

After this downfall, the Nacian Empire, an offshoot of Erastrian culture, came to dominate the middle regions of Yennen, lifting the Eln folk to the height of Erastrian learning and sophistication. Other areas did not fare as well. They were left to the devices of the king's criminal court. Soon, petty kings ruled every corner of the former empire, with no allegiance to the homeland.

The Age of New Kings

The People of Tanaria

After the Great Collapse, the distant descendants of Pippin and Athylan ruled a new realm, known as the Kingdom of Tanaria. It is a common misconception of the other folk of Yennen that this land is dry and barren, filled with fiends mounted upon humped horses. In reality, Tanaria is a lush land, teeming with rich and diverse life. Their religion is of the Stars, which hold the secrets of the universe in their constant shifting and brightening of the night. Their temples are the observatories which dot the land, harmonizing the lives of the people with the movements of the stars.

To the north of their Sancti Mountains, the Plains of Arron hold many grand estates and villas, and is the land most dominated by Erastrian culture. In those plains, Tanaric horse masters are as one with their steeds, and are the best-regarded cavalry in Yennen.

Along the western coastline, the Order of Telto resides. An elite order of warriors and scholars, who belong to the cult of Baudoin, whose duty is to always uphold the bloodline of Baudoin. Their castle, Telto, lies behind many layers of mountains and a long rushing river, ensuring natural defenses of their holdings from all directions. Telto itself is a massive citadel, accessible by a narrow stone bridge which climbs hundreds of feet in the air to reach the walls, which are situated on the top of a mountain.

Also in the west, the principality of Barila thrives. These folk carry heavy bronze shields, and build great works of amphitheaters and temples dedicated to the Stars. Men of science also work tirelessly, forming the finest essays on the natural world, such as medicine and engineering. The land of Barila is green along the coast, with fisheries and farms giving a great bounty. It becomes somewhat arid and mountainous further inland, where tribes of native Tanari live mostly unaffected by their Prince's doings.

To the southern coast, the Princes of Dardall rule as subjects to their liege lords. Sea lords like the Erastrians, their dormons, and oared warships crush any who would seek naval invasion of that land. Their flagship, The Leon, is a feared vessel. Rumored to be crewed by over a thousand rowers on each side, the ship is a behemoth of engineering, with stone towers upon the deck, which can hail bolts and rocks at any of those unfortunate to be at range.

It is to the east where the desert folk who ride upon humped horses get their reputation. That place is called, The Lands Where No Grass Grows, worthy of such a name. There, sand is the only profit of harvest, and water appears only as a miracle or mirage. The most autonomous region as well, the tribesmen do not dally in the affairs of the royal court, paying little tribute and abiding by no official laws. Many of these tribes have no recorded name, and have never been seen by outsiders; instead, they are just known as The Thousand Tribes Under the Sun. They have no unified government in the desert, often smaller tribes shall war against one another for water sources and land.

In current years, King Alcrius has fallen ill, infected wounds from his spectacle, The Grand Tourney of Roses, where his squire had pierced his side in a practice run. There is tension throughout the kingdom, for his heir, the Princess Edella is too young to rule, and the king's brother, Prince Ademon, has been filled with a burning flame of ambition. In the countryside, a rogue batch of bandits reave the poor folk, and pirates rule the coast. It will take more than a royal title to save this kingdom from anarchy.

The Holds of the Dradanians

North of the Erastrian colonies in Yennen, a proud and fierce people defied their expansion. The Dradanians, in their tongue, dragon sons, are a wild folk, civilized and enlightened by their neighbors of Erastrian and Ritter culture. To their north, the kingdom of Krivich stands with Boleslav as its trade capital, protected by the nearby sea citadel of Doros' Watch. To the southern border, the ancient castle known as Dragonscale Keep stands as a sentinel, forged from the flames of such creatures into hardened, solid rock. The line of Princes lasted for centuries, ruling the kingdom as vassals, to the Golden Horde, a roaming kingdom rumored to be one million strong in fighting force. For generations, the Princes of Krivich have been publicly humiliated and chastised by their overlords, and often the horsemen burn villages and fields if they so please, with the Princes powerless to stop them.

The Lowlands

In the southeast, known as the Lowlands, Clan Silverscale rules, the distant relatives of Dradanians. Less advanced in technology, though none the less in a flourishing and fiercely independent culture. In their great feasting halls and little villages scattered across riverbanks, lush forests teeming with game, and peaking mountains blanketed in soft snow. Here they wage war against Atruitas, the last kingdom of Yennen able to trace their heritage back of Baudoin. Locked in a stalemate for centuries, the war has devolved to little raids along the coast, for the Silverscale have not the political prowess to rally the whole of their people to war.

In their seaside cities, south of Silverscale, Atruitas still thrives, for with time came the building of defenses, and the Silverscale have not passed twenty miles into their kingdom for centuries. Weseso, the twin towers which bear the same name, watch over that northern border, garrisoned by thousands of chainmail and steel clad warriors. There are faint whispers in distant lands that the kings of Atruitas have seen fit to crown themselves lords of Yennen and rekindle the power that was lost so many years ago.

The Sea Fort of Ponar

In the Sea of Stars, along the western border of Yennen,

there is a kingdom of Elnish men who sail in ships as large as castles. The Ponari, worshippers of Matuar, god of the sea. They ruled the sea from the frigid north to the warmth of the southern deserts and received tribute from the smaller mainland kingdoms of their people. On the island of Ponar, they built the Sea Fort, a massive complex of jetties and docks that can house near five thousand ships at once.

The Sea Fort holds hundreds upon hundreds of halls, barracks, and towers, making it the largest castle in the world. Once the Ponari terrified the coastline of the Moonlands, waging war against the folk there. The glory has of the kingdom faded in recent years, as whole wings of the castle lay unoccupied since most of Ponar has sunken into the ocean, leaving tiny room for cropland to support a full garrison. Now the Ponari live as rustic fishermen, trading baubles of pearls and shellfish jewelry along the western coast of Yennen, their rich marine history kept alive by word of mouth story.

Hirdland, Home of Wandering Men

East of the mountains in the land of Sodeer, a vassal of Midland, there is a folk who know not of stone walls or thrones. The Hirdlanders move mostly in migrant populaces, resting in large tents sizable to that of a merchant's country home. Nestled between to mountain ranges, Hirdland is a grassy steppe, where rivers grow strong crops and cattle.

The pattern of these nomadic folk follows the weather, as they move north in the summer, and south in the winter. Though many of their folk cling tight to the old ways, a significant minority has settled in walled towns. The migrant tribes pass through these villages on their southern and northern routes, trading furs and raw materials for goods and minted coin.

It is often a mistake for their western counterparts to depict the Hirdlanders as nothing more than barbarians, as their only contact is with the mercenaries employed in wars amongst their petty lords. Even the bravest of the Hirdmen, still shiver in their beds at the mention of their neighbor, Falkland. In recent years, Falkland has grown fascinated with the politics of their southern counterpart, and some fear they are emboldened to strike with their superior arms and technology.

Falkland, the Black Dragon

Founded by traveling northerners, Falkland was once home to a now long dead race of dwarves, wise in technology, but deprived in all decency. It is a land of extremes in weather and appearance. To the south, the fields are as green as southern Elnish country and twice as rich in soil. The fields are also warmer than most land north, for the mountains shield them from sea's wind. The mountains the north still spew hot lava which seeps down the mountainsides, turning the soil black and rocky. The north faces of the mountains are also incredibly cold, for the sea winds of Vaal blow without mercy in their freezing howls. Upon the peninsula, which prods into the northern sea, the Black Forest, a name which breeds misconception. The Black Forest is as green in the summer as any, and orange as any in the fall. It is in the winter, when the leaves had died and withered, that the black bark of the colorful trees is revealed; hence the name was given.

Brosta, first king of Falkland, was the first to colonize the dwarven ruins. In their digging, the Falklanders discovered hidden rooms, buried deep underneath the stone. Here Brosta uncovered a massive library, filled with one million tomes of knowledge thought lost to history. When Brosta emerged from the room, his guardsmen reported that his hair had turned white, and his eyes were filled with tears at the spectacle of the library. Brosta continued the dwarven legacy, unearthing similar rooms in all the dwarven ruins, and continued their scientific practices. Soon, Brosta's people had gathered and translated many of the works, unlocking advanced technology never before seen. The Magi and shrines to the gods were cast out, with iron effigies of the Great Sciences, Urgar of Heavens, Zergar of Earths, and Algar of Waters, put up in their place.

Brosta founded two cities, in the likeness of dwarven architecture, Novce and Strovska, and rebuilt the dwarven halls of Belabis and Kovo. At the end of his rule, the whole of Falkland had been rebirthed in the power of the ancient dwarves. Their cities of iron and stone grew in magnificent splendor with each passing king, and their armies swelled with soldiers more akin to iron golems than men.

Ethics dwindled in the kingdom, not between Falklanders, but for the outside world. With such vast technology, it became apparent to the Falklanders they were the greatest civilization, brought into existence to destroy all lesser ones. Now they act as overlords to the southern-lying folk of Hirdland, and the isles to the north, where islanders fear the banners of the Black Dragon.

Now the king Zlava the Ever-Crowned rules with great ambition. His predecessors had grown fat and lazy, the foulest vices in Falkland culture. Brandishing an iron crown, Zlava ordered that it be molded to his head, forever sealing his authority as king. The call for knowledge and power drive the king onward, onto Hirdland, where he begins to exert his sublime authority over those he deems his lesser.

Emford and Verid, the Knight and the Sorceress

To the south of Lorine, there is a powerful kingdom of Elnish men, Emford. Snug in the mountains, it is a loose collection of local lordlings who swear fealty to the lord of Emford. Well versed in metallurgy and warfare, they are a deadly, though smaller force than most. The kings of Emford have often waged war against their neighbors, attempting to seize more cropland, for the dirt is arable in Emford.

Once a land bridge connected this kingdom to an island, Verid. Verid was a Ponari kingdom, not ruled by king or queen, but by a council of wizards. Separate from the order of magi familiar to the rest of Yennen, these wizards and sorceresses owe no allegiance to crown and do not abide by limitations on magic. Great feats of such power were demonstrated at this oligarchy. Whole mountains shifted, the sky and sea could be parted by the wave of a man's staff.

Argyle the Foolhardy, king of Emford, sought to bend these wizards to his will and invaded many hundreds of years ago. The war went well for him at first, baiting the forces of Verid into an ambush along the forested land which once connected them. It was all for nothing. Argyle marched his full host through this bridge, thinking he had crushed the Verid in total. The sorceress, Jelina, took vengeance for the death of many of her people. Throwing herself from those cliffs, she evoked the darkest magic in the world with human sacrifice.

When her body struck the jagged rocks, a storm which no other storm has since matched in utter destruction, came upon that bridge and plunged it into the sea. Argyle and his army were destroyed, swept below the raging water. A white peace was made between the two nations, now separated by an eternal storm which rages to this day, known as the Sea of Madness.

The Age of the Lion

The Taming of Nacia

In the southern lands between the Green Mountains and The Golden Court, Elnish men who allied and mixed with Erastrians built a great court in the city known as Nacia. Its founder, Hadrian, the Bold, born the youngest son of Adémar III, was spared the slaughter of his kin by the lesser nobles who grew greedy for kingship. His mother, Dulia, fled to the golden country of Eln, where the summer appears as every season. Dulia is the truest hero in Nacian culture, praised for her tact and shrewdness; the values held dearest by her people.

At Nacia, Hadrian's mother Dulia married the local king, a bedridden old man, with no male heir to his name. Hadrian was brought up at court, about thirteen now, learning diligently and ambitiously. From his tutors, the knowledge of the world and battle, and from his mother, the cunning, and pride that came with his ancestors.

Hadrian ascended to the throne of Nacia, which stood as a small community next to neighboring tribes of Elnish culture. Knowing that his legacy relied on conquest, Hadrian set out and tamed the lions of that land, assimilating his neighbors into his culture and territory. Hadrian had come to power with many Erastrian courtiers his age and decreed that they intermingle and wed the Elnish folk he had conquered. Their offspring became the new culture of Nacia, neither wholly Elnish nor Erastrian.

Hadrian's descendants were surrounded by enemies, for to the south, the kingdom of Ridiga was powerful and wealthy, ruled by the warlord Axterix. To counterbalance this, King Horace the Brilliant, great-grandson to Hadrian, wed himself to Axterix's daughter, Kyla, fair skinned with hair red as blood, with the temperament to match it. Horace was reportedly terrified as he traveled through the wild kingdom to claim his wife, for the men there were savage with painted bodies. When he had come to Becculi, the capital of the realm, he and his escort were thrown by a mob off their horses and dragged into the longhall. He was thrown upon a table, and he feared they would tear him limb from limb. Then Axterix appeared, bellowing a mighty laugh. This was no killing; it was a traditional wedding feast. Horace was placed next to his bride upon the table, and sacred ceremony bound the two. In Horace's personal memoirs, the late imperator takes much light humor to the event, "When I arrived, I feared myself doomed to die, only to find a fate worse than death, marriage."

With this new ally, the Nacians doubled the size of their legions. These Becculi levies were vital as heavy auxiliaries in campaigns against Nacia's greatest foe, the Lyrielians. Not painted savages as the Becculi had been, these were Elnish folk trained in the art of war and strategy, with iron swords and iron shields. They came from the isle off the western coast of that country, known now as Barbany, known for its many castles of white marble. For three generations, Nacia waged an indecisive campaign, until the fated Battle of the Cliffs at Cispam.

The Battle of the Cliffs at Cispam, the great triumph of the young King Aeolus, sealed his title as Aeolus the Gambler. The Lyrielians had come up from the beaches along the central shore of Nacia, and placed themselves on the cliffs of Cispam, in numbers two times that of Aeolus' force. When the two armies locked, Hadrian's right flank began to route, quickly giving ground to the Lyrielians. Aeolus himself saw this, dismounted his horse, pick up a shield, and joined his men in the right flank. The title gambler came from his next move, in which he called all the reserves and supply wagon guards up from the back, and into the right flank. If this failed, Aeolus would have lost his entire army.

This bold gamble would prove to be the saving move of the battle, and soon Hadrian's right flank folded over the center, and ultimately overwhelmed the Lyrielians. His center and right pushed the Lyrielians to the cliff's edge. The Nacian army sent their foe screaming to the rocks and water below. With this battle won, Aeolus secured the western border of Nacia, bringing numerous tribes and towns to his support, as well as the island of Lyriel, which he renamed Barbany.

By Aeolus' death, Nacia had near ten times its original landscape and came into a golden age of peace for the new Nacian Empire, ruled by the Lions of Erastrian and Elnish blood. Trade and culture flourished, and whole cities sprouted like new flowers in the springtime. Great monuments, both to man and to Nacia itself, were hewn from marble and iron, sealing an eternal legacy in stone.

The son of Aeolus, Cato the Magnanimous, was overburdened by his forefather's legacy and found himself and his council wading through extreme gluts of corrupt and inefficient bureaucracy. To remedy this, Cato established the Senate, to administrate his sprawling realm. Cato further renamed his title to Imperator, for as king implied he was equal to foreign rulers, an insult Cato refused to bear.

For many generations, this empire thrived, expanding through the north all the way to Lorine, where they established some smaller colonies such as Gessex, in the north of Glanfech, which still bears a few functioning bathhouses. It was in Glanfech that the Nacian people learned the culture, mathematics, and art of the Hlútrian, or Elves as known in the common language of man.

But with absolute powers comes the absolute of problems. The tower, meant to ease the role of government, had grown fat and lazy, ruling as petty kings in their provinces. No longer did the senate work for the people, but for their personal coffers.

Furthermore, years of bad harvest led to a sharp decline in trade and economic growth. Over the course of many decades, the Empire of Nacia began to fade, until the day barbarians sacked the sacred city.

The Imperators of Nacia soon found themselves employing whole armies of barbaric mercenaries from the north, who fought in exchange for fiefs and landholdings in the golden land of Nacia. The strongest of these factions, the people of Essaroth, united their settled tribes and overthrew the boy Imperator, Caligula. The Essaroth were not pleased with mere conquest, they also laid waste to Nacia and the countryside, destroying centuries of art and culture.

Now the Nacian have fallen, their imperators, now dubbed as common kings, rule only an isle to the east. From the city of Vindorium, the latest king, Lucan, rules as an odd character. Never actually intended to rule, Lucan is the younger brother to Vespasian, who had been physically impaired, meaning he was unfit to serve as the holy ruler of Nacia.

The young Lucan has many personal issues, which he must hope to resolve if he has a chance of ruling his kingdom properly.

The Age of Many Kings

The Modern Kingdoms of the North

After the collapse of Nacia, the old alliances and subjects of the lion faded, leaving power vacuums across Yennen. At this time, Lorine, Midland, and Belfas came into being. Lorine was claimed by the former governor of that Nacian province, a man by the name Adalfarus, ancient ancestor to King Oswine. Midland went to the Crawes, the power merchant family from Kruithia and the other Elnish kingdoms. Belfas however, remained wholly untouched by Nacian rule, and thus is governed by a Witan of lords who owe no allegiance to a specific king.

The Prophecy of the Black Elk

In Zelphi, the southern land closest to Erastrius, several fortresses and cities had been established. The king of these lands, Rogbert, had come to hunt in the Zelphine Forest, known for its gray trees which appeared as though they had been turned to ash in a burning flame. While on his hunt, Rogbert and his host were blinded and collapsed to their knees from a blazing light. From the forest, a huge elk, black in coat and with glowing eyes, had come before them.

The beast approached, and it spoke in a booming voice deep as cracking thunder. 'Pay homage to me, small lords, for I shall reward you greatly! Abandon Matuar, for he has divided your people and allowed your enemies to gather in strength! Only in my burning gaze can you restore the glory of your houses!'

The host of lords ran terrified from the forest, shouting words of worship for the Black Elk. In the capital of Zelphi, Esden, the shrines to Matuar were destroyed, and in their place, a bundle of black antlers, between which two flames burn in oiled lamps. When this had been done, the commoners of Zelphi grumbled and prepared to rebel, for they had considered themselves blessed by the sea god. It was in this time of dissent that Tanari to the west laid siege to many the Zelphine castles. Rogbert, adorned with a crown as golden and burning as a flame, led his host from Esden and set out to turn back the foreign invaders.

They came to the eastern edge of the Zelphine Forest, where the Tanari had rallied and made camp. Rogbert collapsed onto his knees and prayed facing the forest, crying out for the Black Elk to hear him. 'Lord hear us today, and deliver us from this foul foreign host! I shall order my men to paint your burning eyes on their shields, and if we are victorious I shall build you a temple where I slay their commander!'

And so, the Zelphi army painted their shields black, with red and yellows eyes at the center. The Elk worshippers charged forward, overwhelming the Tanari in the veil of the night. Rogbert slew the Tanari commander, raising his helmet to the cheer of the Zelphine army, who relished in their victory with drinking and feasting.

Rogbert made good on his promise, constructing a massive temple that rivaled the splendor of his palace. Now his descendants are bound to the forest, giving great bounties of sacrifices to their Elk God, and his line of kings has long held their kingdom together, by will or supernatural powers is known to none.

The Areni Isles

Off the southern coast of Yennen, where the sea is heated as a pool with summer sun, four large isles, known as the Areni, hold a proud and ancient people. The Areni themselves are of mixed descent, half of their blood hailing from their native isles, where the folk had a tanner skin, though by no mark as dark as the Tanari to the northern continent. Their other blood, from Eln, from the line of Bandabras. Bandabras was a famed Elnish explorer, with scores of ships in his large fleet. He was the first man to chart Yennen and the Areni Isles accurately, and his maps are coveted as priceless relics and invaluable tools.

With the full array of his fleet, Bandabras landed on the Summer Isle, the northernmost of Areni, and proclaimed himself as king. Taking the princess of that Isle, Helia of Fane, the ruling family of that land, Bandabras gained a legal right to rule. Though Helia first thought herself a prisoner in a foreign man's court, she came to respect the wisdom and ambition of her husband. Though they did not deeply love one another, they found it an opportunistic union, forming a strong bond with one another.

In a few years' time, the Summer Isle, Calto, the Comet, Melos, and the rest of the islands were under Bandabras' rule, the first time in history such a feat had been done. Though this was not to last. When Bandabras lay dying upon his bed, he had four sons, and only one was mothered by Helia, the prince Badabran. The others were his bastards, who carried his ambition and intellect, and each vied for their father's affection. At last Bandabras spoke his final word, the sealing word of Areni that would proclaim his heir. 'To the Strongest!' The king shouted the phrase from his bed and passed from the world.

It was not long after before his sons divided up his kingdom, and prepared to make good on their father's request. To the Summer Isle, Badabran retreated with his mother as regent, for he feared his brother would attempt to overthrow him, before going at each other's throats. Calto was taken by the oldest, and wisest of the bastards, Thyngen, born from a northern courtesan in his father's employ. To Melos, Arioto the Black, fairest and kindest of the bunch, decided to rule as poet and singer, rather than an iron-fisted lord. Though his people did not grow a mighty army, they relied instead on their wit and word, cunning diplomats and shrewd tacticians. To the Comet, Nasirian, the runt of the lot, and cruelest in nature. He was the weakest in physical strength, making up for it with a great mind, prone to all manner of evil-minded perversions of malice and passion. The smaller islands were likewise divided, and given to lords loyal to their respective princes.

The coming war, known as the War of Four Brothers, did

not last long, consisting of a few naval skirmishes and small scouting battles, for none of the brothers wished for an escalation, save for Nasirian. Nasirian, in the Winter Palace of the Comet, brewed away in his laboratories, forging disease and pestilence like Beelzus herself. He spawned from his dark dungeons, Wither-Eye, a disease which rots away the brain and eyes, leaving hollow husks of flesh. Nasirian's master plan began, and he sent rats infested with the disease on three trading ships, one traveling to each of his brothers' holds. But by luck or the gods, each ship sunk in a terrible storm, and even further, the disease spread through the Comet itself. Soon the whole population of the Comet was dead. The three remaining brothers declared two laws, white peace, and that none may enter the waters or land of the Comet, for fear of spreading the disease.

In the Isle of the Comet, nothing now grows, and the rock, once gray, now has turned black. It sits as a place told in the stories to keep children in order, from the Areni Isles, to even the northern tip of Yennen, for no child wishes to be shipped to the black island. There are rumors some still live there, for sailors who pass it swear by all the gods they see strange figures wallow on the shoreline. Such things are only rumors, for the disease took all life, and now, it seems, it may have brought it back.

For decades, an uneasy peace has remained amongst the heirs of the original brothers, kept away from war for fear of the impact on trade and their personal safety. It is a land ripe for the claiming, a son of Bandabras who could take up the name his ancestors once claimed, not as a principality, but as a whole kingdom.

Ritter, the Land of Strong Castles and Fair Maidens

To the east of Lorine, nestled in the heartland of Yennen, the noble knights of Ritter rule the land which teems with mild weather and abundant game. Founded years ago by the Knight King Frederick the Red, they rule as a rigid and immobile structure, the peasantry tied to land as the subjects to their local lords.

Upon their sixteenth birthday, each son is given an oath, the Oath of Sickle, or the Oath of Sword. The Oath of Sickle is reserved for the common folk, who vow upon their life to uphold and shepherd the property of their lord and to answer the call to war as levy if need be.

> Oath of the Sickle
> *I solemnly vow, humble son of Ritter*
> *Upon my life and blood and all those before and*
> *after me*
> *That my back shall bear the burden of my lord*
> *With all my strength and will, I shall defend him*
> *With healthy bellow or dying breath*
> *This I solemnly vow upon my life and blood*

The Oath of Sword is for the sons of a lord, upholding the values on which their nation was built. Here it is revealed that the oaths are less servitude and more contract, as both parties are obliged to the defense of others.

> Oath of the Sword
> *I solemnly vow, noble son of Ritter*

On my father's sword and name
To protect my folk, as they protect my holdings
My life is no longer my own to bear
It is in the will of my king that I live or die upon
the sword
This I solemnly vow upon my sword and name
As I rise a knighted man

The Warriors of Trundor

Trundor's Hunt

Before the time of man and elf, when all lay barren on the earth, Trundor, son of Domovoi, lord of the hearth, and Veria, of fertility, knelt before his great-grandfather, Loden, and requested to fill the empty lands with creatures worthy of hunting. He spoke saying, 'Father-God, your ancestors have created such an empty land, do Cinder and Kryn not see the agonizing waste of it all? Give me dominion over but the brainless things, so that I might fill this world with rich life, worthy of your praise!' Loden agreed, and Trundor filled the earth with great and powerful beasts, such as dragons, behemoths, and great sea monsters able to consumed entire oceans in a single drink. Trundor was fickle, and became bored with the solitude of his hunt, and, taking the heartiest of soil, he could find in the world, crafted a people to kill by his side.

Thus, the Thyrs people entered the world. A folk unlike man or elves, with brutish features and often slow wits. Green-skinned and savage eyes, they came into being at the Irgorian Wastes, a land harsh as the Thyrs themselves. The Thyrs became known as the pioneers, establishing the first settlements in the world, all the while hunting in the service and glory of their master.

When they had slain a vast number of beasts throughout the world, the Thyrs diminished, their lord once again had turned fickle and bored, now only occupying himself with eat and drink in his great hall, his people were neglected. The Thyrs turned to one another for sport, hoping to please their master through a sacrifice of blood upon the field of battle, and yet their master still ignored them like a child bored of a toy. Their numbers grew ever fewer as their wars escalated from small squabbles between warbands to full-scale battles pitting the whole of their race against each other. Their shamans and priests knew that their god had abandoned them, and so, the few of the Thyrs that remained from their brutal killings were called back to their ancestral land.

This land is now known as Brynbor, the last hold, in their tongue, where the few Thyrs that survived now wait in a wasteland for their master's return when the Thyrs shall once again hunt the great beasts of the world by the side of their master. In the present day, they exist as somewhere fewer than one thousand, and each young pup raised in the tribe is sent out into the green world, where they must hunt a great beast as their ancestors once did, as their rite of passage into adulthood.

The Folk of the Forest

The final creation of Trundor was to be the ones known as

the Unseen Ones or Awaerian in elvish. They were forged from union between the two visages of man and beast. The noblest of these races, the Centaurs, once ruled over the hills of Midland, traveling in great stampeding herds, hunting down Wisent that grazed freely in the land. To the same effect, Satyrs and their kin made fruitful farmsteads and thrived throughout the north save in the unforgiving cold of Belfas.

Once this rural folk held council with Azrael and even supported his claim in the north. The Awaerian helped the servant of Crassus Baal, to reclaim their territory lost to the kingdoms of men. Casting down the shrines to Trundor, Azrael brought the Herd of Trundor nearly into his master's clutches. Pine, lord of the east of Ithon, led a coalition of loyalists to Trundor, sacking the camps and huts of any conspiring with Azrael. At the end of the civil war, a quarter of Trundor's wild people remained, and they could not rouse strength to fight anymore. For centuries, the Awaerian have stayed in their forest, not even the cleverest rangers of Midland can catch sight of the elusive folk.

Trundor's Last Creation

Again, for the third time, Trundor grew bored with his creation, and so he said to himself, "Let me go where no man, elf, beast, or Thyrs, can survive, there I will make a truly mighty people." So Trundor went north of Yennen, to a continent named Vaal, where the summers were colder than the winters of the south.

Taking full oak trees, he molded giants, the Vaal. Rugged faces, and long beards which reached to their bellies, they were closest to the image of dwarves, save in height. They cultivated the cold fields of Vaal, and built many drinking halls and walled burgs. Their eyes were set on the south, to the place of green field and fatted cattle. The Vaal came in longships, sowing discord and sorrow in the hearts of men. From High Hold, an ancient citadel carved from the largest mountain in Vaal, the kings rule their sworn fiefdoms.

For hundreds of years, the Vaal have raided the coastline of Belfas, taking what they please when they please. Now their horns have stayed unused for near a decade, and all hold their breath in frightened anticipation of what is to come.

The Lands Where None Dare to Sail

The Expedition East

In Baudoin's final years as ruler of Erastrius and Yennen, he took a small vessel, crewed by one hundred souls, and sailed east of his home island. He named the waters there the Greendawn Sea, for the sun's rising appeared to turn the whole ocean a gorgeous shade of green. Not much was recorded, save that naming, for when Baudoin returned, he came back pale as a ghost, with only himself on board the expedition ship. All his crew had vanished, and he refused to give any word on the matter.

After Baudoin's death, however, his personal journals were discovered, where had a kept a log of his journey. They had come by a peninsula bearing a single gray tower, which stood proud and somewhat alien in the green shoreline. It appeared purely black as they saw it, for the sun was rising directly behind it; thus, Baudoin named it the Tower of the Void. Next, the crew passed along the southern coast of this strange land, where they saw a charred coastline, which they named the Scorched Shore. They were filled with an ominous dread at these portents, for they had yet to see a single inhabitant of this strange country.

The crews' hearts sank as they passed by a third warning, a set of statues set along the shore, fifty times the size of average men, crumbled and half standing, stoic faces still recognizable. Baudoin's final entry discusses his contact with the folk of this land, in a city known as Yosel. The people there dressed in loose garb of bright colors, and they wore stones in their beards as well as jewels in their ears. They called themselves the A'Rik, and many revealed teeth of black stone as they smiled at their guests.

Baudoin was given supplies, and his men set off deeper into the land, where the forests grew as thick canopies of vines and messes of living things. Baudoin describes how the vines seemed to lunge at his crew with claws and thorns, and how the birds' peaceful songs turned into eerie and sour notes as they passed. That is the final entry, with nothing else to help his court understand, Baudoin's legacy became the stuff of gossip. Many claimed he had killed his crew, and hoarded a great treasure for himself. Others, that he made a pact with an evil spirit of that land, bargaining his life, for the life of his crew. More still believe he was attacked by the A'Rik he described and was simply the soul survive. None of these claims have been verified, for none who have sailed east since have returned.

Thank You!

Thank you for reading our book and for supporting stories of fiction in the written form. Please consider leaving a reader review on Amazon and Goodreads, so that others can make an informed reading decision.

Find more exceptional stories, novels, collections, and anthologies on our website at: **digitalfictionpub.com**

Join the **Digital Fiction Pub** newsletter for infrequent updates, new release discounts, and more. Subscribe at: **digitalfictionpub.com/blog/newsletter/**

See all our exciting fantasy, horror, crime, romance and science fiction books, short stories and anthologies on our **Amazon Author Page** at: **amazon.com/author/digitalfiction**

Also from Digital Fiction

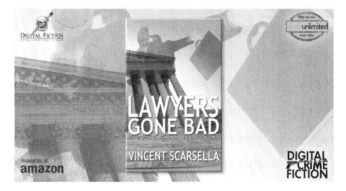

About the Author

Peter is a current student at the University of San Diego. *The Sword to Unite* was Peter's senior thesis, in which he researched the mythology from the cultures of the Anglo-Saxons and Celtic peoples, as well as the classic legend of King Arthur. Beginning with a simple map on white paper, Peter built the world of the novel over the course of nearly two years. More art and poems on the world of Yennen can be found on the book's official website, theswordtounite.com, where the author discusses elements of fantasy and the various cultures of his own fantasy world.

Copyright

The Sword to Unite
Written by **Peter J. Hopkins**
Executive Editor: Michael A. Wills

22417056R00263

Printed in Poland
by Amazon Fulfillment
Poland Sp. z o.o., Wrocław